A
TRUE
NOVEL

# A
# TRUE
# NOVEL

## VOLUME II

## Minae Mizumura

*Translated from the Japanese by*

### JULIET WINTERS CARPENTER

OTHER PRESS

*New York*

Original title: *Honkaku Shosetsu*, by Minae Mizumura
Copyright © Minae Mizumura, 2002
Photographs copyright © Toyota Horiguchi, 2002
Originally published in Japan by Shinchosha Co. Ltd., Tokyo
English translation copyright © Juliet Winters Carpenter, 2013

*This book has been selected by the Japanese Literature Publishing Project (JLPP),*
*an initiative of the Agency for Cultural Affairs of Japan.*

Production Editor: Yvonne E. Cárdenas
Text Designer: Chris Welch
This book was set in 12.75 pt Perpetua by
Alpha Design & Composition of Pittsfield, NH.

10 9 8 7 6 5 4 3 2 1

Library of Congress Cataloging-in-Publication Data
Mizumura, Minae, author.
[Honkaku Shosetsu. English]
A true novel / by Minae Mizumura ; translated from the Japanese by
Juliet Winters Carpenter.
pages cm
ISBN 978-1-59051-203-6 (pbk. original : acid-free paper) — ISBN (invalid)
978-1-59051-576-1 (ebook)  1. Japanese—United States—Fiction.  2. Rich
people—Fiction.  3. Karuizawa-machi (Japan)—Fiction.  4. Love
stories.  I. Carpenter, Juliet Winters, translator.  II. Title.
PL856.I948H6613 2013
895.6'35—dc23
2012046090

# CONTENTS

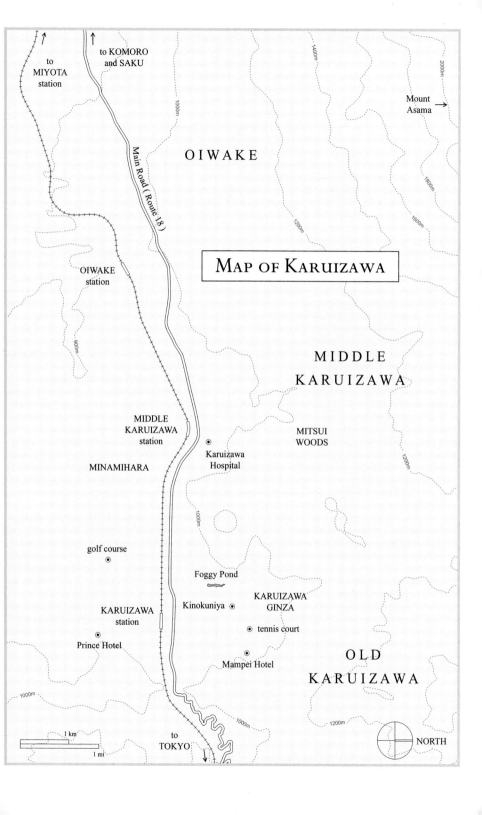

↑ to
MIYOTA
station

↑ to KOMORO
and SAKU

1400m

2000m

Mount
Asama →

1000m

Main Road ( Route 18 )

O I W A K E

1200m

1800m

1600m

MAP OF KARUIZAWA

OIWAKE
station

900m

M I D D L E
K A R U I Z A W A

MIDDLE
KARUIZAWA
station

MITSUI
WOODS

1200m

MINAMIHARA

⊙
Karuizawa
Hospital

1000m

golf course
⊙

Foggy Pond

KARUIZAWA
station

Kinokuniya ⊙

KARUIZAWA
GINZA

⊙ tennis court

⊙
Prince Hotel

⊙
Mampei Hotel

O L D
K A R U I Z A W A

1000m

1000m

1200m

1 km

1 mi

to
TOKYO ↓

NORTH

A
TRUE
NOVEL

5

# Lightbulbs

Y OKO WAS LONELY. This didn't really occur to us until her grandmother and I heard her chattering away with such animation that day. She couldn't go and play at a friend's house since that would mean leaving her grandmother alone, and bringing a friend home would probably have seemed doubly wrong—awkward for the friend and an imposition on her grandmother. At the local elementary school her classmates were a motley collection, the children of farmers, cooks, station-front shop owners, carpenters, and real estate agents—few of them the kind to become close enough for her to ask over in the first place. Her mother, who was gone all day, had drummed into her that she mustn't make friends with "vulgar" children. Yoko herself, although she was sickly, and shy around strangers, was the classic example of someone who at home turned into a little autocrat: she certainly lorded it over her grandmother and me. Making friends didn't come easily to her. Still, she must have been lonely with no one but an old lady and a housemaid for playmates. That day when old Mrs. Utagawa invited Taro into the house, I'm sure she did so on an impulse, just to give him a break from the usual grind; but to Yoko the invitation meant that here was a ready-made friend, one who had her grandmother's approval.

Then came the incident of the following day. If that hadn't happened, I doubt if Taro would ever have become such a fixture in the Utagawa household. And I doubt if Mrs. Utagawa would have taken it on herself to become his protector to the extent that she did.

The afternoon this occurred, after she came home from school we couldn't find Yoko anywhere in the house. She'd called out a cheery greeting, and her red leather backpack was right by her grandmother's low desk where it was supposed to be, but there was no sign of its owner. She wasn't upstairs or in the toilet. Mrs. Utagawa hastily opened the glass sliding doors that overlooked the front yard, then the front door facing the gate, calling "Yoko! Yoko!" in a loud voice, but there was no answer. Finally when she called from the back door, there was a response.

"Over here, Grandma!" Yoko's high-pitched voice came from the direction of the Azuma house. Mrs. Utagawa and I exchanged looks and thrust our feet into wooden clogs, wondering what on earth was going on. We hurried past the wooden fence to find the sliding doors on the veranda wide open and Yoko's little sandals lined up neatly on the stepping-stone beneath.

Mrs. Utagawa went and looked inside the small four-and-a-half-mat tatami room. For a second she seemed unable to take in what was going on—and then the blood drained from her face.

The day before, I had missed it—either O-Tsune had
blocked my view when she came toward me, or else I just
didn't try to look in—but at that moment I saw just how
unsavory that cluttered room was. In the center was a flesh-
colored mound, a heap of tiny arms and legs. Looking more
closely, I saw naked rubber dolls with blond hair, each one
about the length of my hand. They lay piled up by the dozen,
surrounded by fluffy nylon cloth, thread, and ribbons of
blue, orange, and pink. But that alone wouldn't have ac-
counted for Mrs. Utagawa's turning so pale. What was genuinely obscene, made worse by the mound of naked rubber
dolls, was a scattering of pages that had been torn from old
magazines—men's magazines—and crumpled into balls
for packing. Black-and-white photographs of women sus-
pended upside down in their underwear; garish woodblock
prints of naked young women, their hair piled high, being
assaulted with bamboo spears . . . Fragments of such scenes
were like poisonous thorns, stabbing at my eyes.

In the midst of this mess Yoko was sitting with her knees
bent inward and feet splayed, as usual, her skirt flaring
around her. To show off what she was doing, she grabbed
a doll by the legs, turned around, and held it out for her
grandmother to see.

As my shock wore off, it sank in that Yoko was just helping out, putting skirts on rubber dolls. When she went over
to ask if Taro could come out and play, they must have told
her that he had work to do and couldn't leave till the job
was done. So she pitched in, determined to do her bit so
that he could play sooner. Since she was only eight years old

and clumsy to begin with, she couldn't have been much use, but O-Tsune's character was so twisted I'm sure it tickled her to think of an Utagawa girl doing such work. Instead of stopping her, she probably egged her on. No one else from the Utagawa family had paid the Azumas a visit since they moved in, and I doubt very much that she expected Mrs. Utagawa to show up. Like most people, she knew only her own world and could never have imagined how appalled we might be to catch Yoko in these circumstances.

What would her parents say? That thought must have been uppermost in Mrs. Utagawa's mind. She was pale and speechless.

The air was so thick with dust from the cloth and paper, floating in shafts of afternoon sunlight, that my throat felt scratchy. I didn't know if it was because Roku lay sick in bed in the next room or because so many people lived together at close quarters without bathing frequently, but even with the sliding doors open the room stank of urine and sweat. Yoko had been sitting there a good half hour without so much as a cushion under her, but fortunately the day was warm, with lingering summer heat.

Realizing from Mrs. Utagawa's reaction that the situation was more serious than she had supposed, O-Tsune probably regretted taking this risk. Yet a certain condescension in her manner suggested that she had heard from Mr. Azuma (who used to do odd jobs for the senior Dr. Utagawa) that the old lady standing in front of her was once a geisha. Her usual insolence showed through the lame excuse she offered with an artificial smile: "She said she wanted to have a try too . . ."

Taro sat gripping a doll by its rubber leg, his face burning with rage and humiliation as he looked back and forth between the two women. He must have wanted from the start to chase Yoko out of the house but held back in case she never wanted to play with him again. Whatever else was churning inside him, I don't know. All I could suppose was that he'd been trying to finish up as quickly as possible. Yoko, for whom playing, helping, and working were much the same, must have chattered on, but I suspect he barely answered her.

Mrs. Utagawa was looking at O-Tsune in disgust.

Just then a sound came from the adjoining room, and the door slid open to reveal Roku, standing there in his night *yukata* like a ghost. His eyes were sunk deep in their sockets and the neck of his robe hung open, showing his bony ribcage. How much he understood of what was happening, I'm not sure, but in the toneless, frenzied way of the fainthearted, his voice froggy with phlegm, he gave O-Tsune hell. For her part Mrs. Utagawa was so startled by how much he had wasted away since the summer that she couldn't stop staring at this ghostly figure. Finally she said, "Roku, have you seen a doctor? You must have a proper checkup." Then she swung her attention back to Yoko. Pulling the little girl up by both hands, she set her on her feet, saw that she put her sandals on, and led her home firmly by the hand.

This little episode had two results. For one thing, it was obvious that Roku's remaining time was short. At Mrs. Utagawa's request I spoke to Dr. Matsumiya, the doctor across from the station who always came to examine Yoko, and arranged for him to come over the very next day. He did some tests and found that Roku had pulmonary edema and his lungs were already filled with fluid, a bad sign. In fact the poor man only lasted till January. It was as if he lived just long enough to help the Azuma family settle in as the Utagawas' tenants.

The other result was that Mrs. Utagawa made up her mind to take Taro under her wing. I believe she lay awake the whole night. For one thing, realizing how lonely Yoko had been all this time was acutely distressing to her. For another, seeing with her own eyes how badly the boy was treated must have come as a shock. Her late husband had lived a self-indulgent life, but he also did whatever he could for other people. After nearly thirty years at his side, she probably felt the same sense of responsibility that close contact with human misery had given him.

In the morning, everything was as usual until we had seen the others off. When I went into the sitting room, broom in hand to do the sweeping, I found Mrs. Utagawa leaning against the hibachi brazier she kept out all year round, smoking a thin *kiseru* pipe and looking preoccupied. Her sewing was nowhere in sight. Even when she saw me, her expression did not change.

That afternoon, when Dr. Matsumiya finished examining Roku, he came by to report to Mrs. Utagawa. Afterward she saw him out, and no sooner had the front door closed behind him than she turned to me with a severe look and said I was to bring O-Tsune to the service entrance. Before the doctor's arrival she had changed her kimono and put on a more formal sash. I had been surprised that she would bother to do this for someone who was always dropping by to see Yoko, but then I understood: the change of clothes was for O-Tsune's benefit.

When I ushered O-Tsune in, her eyes darted around as she took in her first sight of the Utagawa kitchen. Mr. Azuma was always the one who brought over the monthly rent. I announced her arrival, and Mrs. Utagawa emerged with slow dignity and stood looking down at her visitor in the concrete-floored entrance, not inviting her up into the house proper.

"I have just had word from Dr. Matsumiya," she said. "He doesn't yet know exactly what the trouble is, but apparently Roku is in a bad way."

"Yes, ma'am," answered O-Tsune, pretending to look humble and shrinking her shoulders.

Mrs. Utagawa kept her eyes trained on her as she continued: O-Tsune and her family owed their present circumstances to Roku and were to look after him with all due care until the end. From now on, she would be sending over her maid to check on Roku's condition from time to time, and if there was any change, O-Tsune was to let her know. She spoke in her usual low, raspy voice, but there was something new in the tone, an unaccustomed forcefulness.

"Yes, ma'am."

I could sense O-Tsune actually succumbing to this.

"And if the worst happens to Roku, and you and your family wish to go on living in that house, you may do so for the time being."

"Yes, ma'am."

"At the same rent, for the time being."

She said this with studied casualness, the effect being to impress upon her listener that the property was hers to dispose of, however and whenever she liked. Where she had been hiding this strength till then, I don't know. Maybe it was a quality that anyone who has ever been a geisha acquires, or maybe I was reading too much into it, but I thought I detected in her the toughness of someone who had seen a great deal in life. O-Tsune was by then so tense that her shoulders were hunched, making her even smaller. Looking down on her from a step higher, the old lady spoke with such blunt force that even to me she seemed completely different from the familiar Grandma who always sat bent over her sewing.

Was it calculation on her part, pausing at that moment as if she had finished speaking? O-Tsune bowed. As she was preparing to go, Mrs. Utagawa caught her eye and held it a moment before adding, "One other thing. This concerns your youngest boy. From now on, when he gets home from school, send him over here to me. He can help around the house instead of Roku." She paused again. "Besides that, I hear he is rather an unfortunate child, and for the time being I plan to oversee his schoolwork. All right?"

"Yes, ma'am, of course." O-Tsune's face was slightly flushed. She must have been aware that her abuse of her stepchild was common knowledge in the neighborhood, but since his father was Chinese, I suspect she thought the neighbors were on her side, sticking up for her. Realizing that she had just received an indirect rebuke seemed to leave her in a tangle of resentment and embarrassment.

Mrs. Utagawa let her eyes confirm the accusation, saying nothing to rub it in. Before letting O-Tsune go, she even offered a word of support. "Things aren't easy for you either, I know . . . Anyway, that will be all."

When she returned to her room, she sat there again for a long time, leaning against the hibachi and smoking her pipe. Acting tough went against her nature. The performance had clearly left her exhausted, and something in the slump of her shoulders made her look older than ever. She soon complained of a headache, and when Yoko came home she was lying down, her head on a folded cushion.

That was the first and last time I ever saw her take that tone with anyone.

O-Tsune could put two and two together as well as the next person. Once she calmed down and thought things over she must have realized it was owing entirely to old Mrs. Utagawa's goodwill that they were able to rent that place so cheaply. With two men in the household already earning wages, the extra income to be gained by forcing a schoolboy to do piecework was next to nothing, as she well knew. It was sheer spite that made her try to keep Taro from going out to play—a way of getting even for having had to take him in. But if the old lady objected to his doing this work at home, why should she insist? And if the old lady meant to take him under her wing, then there was nothing to be gained by knocking him around. In short, O-Tsune saw clearly that it was in her own interest to avoid any friction with Mrs. Utagawa.

Soon after that, when Taro got home from school he would call out "I'm back" (not bothering, as was proper, to slip off the rough cotton shoulder bag he wore slung around his neck as he said it) and then make a beeline for the Utagawa house. I'm sure he would rather have dispensed with the greeting altogether, but Mrs. Utagawa insisted that he keep up this custom, so, reluctantly, he did. He stayed with us until suppertime. Sometimes she even gave him supper, first sending me next door to let O-Tsune know.

One Sunday morning about ten days after she'd had words with O-Tsune, Mrs. Utagawa brought her stepson up to date. "The boy will only be bullied if he's left in that woman's care. I am having him come over to help out after school. That way, he and Yoko can do their homework together too."

She said it was "to help out" in case he was thought an unsuitable playmate for Yoko. In those days, there were plenty of household chores children could be expected to do, so this didn't sound unusual.

"Fine," said Takero. "Why not? Yoko can help him with his homework."

"Sure, I will!" said Yoko.

"See that he gets something to eat," Natsue told me. "That boy is as thin as a rail."

I assured her that I would. I already was feeding him, of course, but I pretended otherwise. Mrs. Utagawa and I had become accomplices.

"Oh, and have him get rid of that wasps' nest under the eaves, would you?" Natsue added. "If Roku got well I would ask him, but it looks as if that won't be happening."

Ever since Roku was laid up, heavy work that needed doing around the house had been neglected. Firewood for heating the bath needed chopping, and with the cold weather coming on, someone had to clean out the garden shed and make room for a load of coal. Just how useful the boy would make himself, I didn't know, but I agreed that there was plenty for him to do.

This turn of events must have raised Taro's spirits no end. But he wasn't the only one for whom it broke new ground. I'm sure she had never imagined or anticipated this, yet as Taro began to settle in at our house, Mrs. Utagawa found it gave her a pleasure she had never known before: the joy of raising a boy she could spoil and scold to her heart's content, knowing that she personally was indispensable to his happiness.

In the course of my years with the family, I came to realize that after Mrs. Utagawa married, she had raised the doctor's son Takero from infancy, not as her own but as someone left in her charge, to be treated with special care. She couldn't have done otherwise, for he truly was the family's only, precious hope. Congenital syphilis had carried off two other sons in a row, so everyone feared for this baby's life, though he eventually survived with nothing worse than a slight disability in one eye and one ear. When, soon after giving birth, his natural mother died of the Spanish flu, he was coddled by wet nurses and maids anxious to ensure that he would live to carry on the Utagawa name. At that juncture Mrs. Utagawa came into the picture, no longer a mistress but a wife. It was her job to raise Takero as the future head of the family. That responsibility would affect her to the end of her days. As far as I knew, she was always extremely respectful toward him, beyond what you'd expect just from not having a blood tie.

Late in life she was given Yoko to raise, but in the end Yoko was still Natsue's daughter—once again, not Mrs. Utagawa's own but a child entrusted to her keeping. Taro, who had come to her out of nowhere, was nobody's child, someone she could do with as she liked. And he was a male child too. Since she belonged to the older generation, you could see in her treatment of him as he grew older that this mattered to her. Added to this, I'd guess that, because he was an outsider not only in the world at large but even in his own family, she could identify with him, she herself being something of an outsider.

The closer she got to him, the more she took on the role of his protector. She was so retiring by nature that, had she known how heavily involved with him she was to become, I doubt whether she would have taken those first steps at all. But after six months, then a year, she had gone too far to turn back. At first she gave Natsue and Takero sketchy reports on the boy, thinking he was scarcely worth bothering them about, but before she knew it things had progressed to the point where she dared not do even that, fearful of revealing what a fixture he had become.

Of course, she would not have grown so involved if Taro had not proven to be such a surprise, demonstrating far greater potential than anyone could have suspected. That he could hardly read before was strange, given that brain of his. Perhaps it had been impossible for him to learn anything with his brothers always filching his pencils and notebooks, and with O-Tsune giving him endless chores to do. It could be that he wasn't even sent to school before they settled in Tokyo. Or, since he had been an outsider from the beginning, he may simply have thought the letters on the pages had nothing to do with him. Once he started to look at the textbooks with Yoko, he quickly learned to read, and before long he was at the head of the class.

Between school lunches and the snacks we gave him—and, believe me, we saw to it that he ate as much as possible—Taro's skinny frame soon filled out. He became scrupulously clean too, not wanting to disappoint the girl who on that first day had leaned in close and said, "Mm, you smell nice!" When I offered to run a bath for him, unlike most boys he never objected, but rather nodded, a bit bashfully. In the bathroom, he would fill the wooden basin partly with running cold water, then add hot water from the kettle and work the soap into a good lather before scrubbing himself from head to toe. Yoko used to make him mad by peering in and asking, "Aren't you done yet?" When his nose ran or he sniffled, she would make a face and point, so he took to using the tissues Mrs. Utagawa gave him. Over time, his way of speaking also became less rough.

The Azuma family let up on their abuse. O-Tsune knew it would do her no good to have old Mrs. Utagawa find Taro being mistreated, so she persuaded his brothers to lay off. "That's enough, you two," we would hear her snap, her voice purposely loud enough to carry. The occasional gift of sweets, soft drinks, or used clothing from Mrs. Utagawa also had an effect. Of course, his brothers were unimpressed and went on tormenting him behind their mother's back—but since O-Tsune was home most of the time and Taro spent long stretches at the Utagawa house, they had less opportunity to bully him, however much they may have wanted to. The usual uproar fell off considerably.

FOR TARO, THE next two years—the years from age ten to around twelve, when he first went off to Oiwake—were surely the happiest of his young life.

When he first started coming over it was autumn by the calendar, but the days were still summery. Mrs. Utagawa would sit near the veranda with her sewing while, close by, Taro and Yoko sat at her low desk with their small heads together, doing their homework. Her room, equipped with the old furniture from the Utagawa Clinic, also had a small family altar, a porcelain hibachi with a kettle on top, and, when it turned cold, a *kotatsu* heater with a quilt cover. In that one room, it seemed as if time stood still, fixed at a certain year in the Showa period. I would leave the sliding doors open and sit in the adjoining room, folding the laundry or ironing. At three our little quartet—Mrs. Utagawa, Yoko, Taro, and me, not one of us related to the others—would gather in a sunny spot for the customary snack. That was the most peaceful time of the day.

When her homework was done, Yoko used to sit quietly next to her grandmother in her usual splayed-legs position and play with her dolls or gather kimono scraps or color in a coloring book. After Taro came, she was much more active. When the weather was nice, they would go out into the front yard to play. This was hidden from the Azuma house and surrounded by fields and bamboo groves that had somehow remained untouched as new houses went up all over the neighborhood. Since the yard was private, they could play there undisturbed.

There was a swing in one corner, and they took turns on it, each child being allowed a certain number of swings. As I sat in my room reading, in the distance I'd hear Yoko chanting over and over again:

Swing, swing, here comes the train.
When you hear the whistle, then we change again.

Children have such short attention spans, and yet they will cheerfully go on repeating the same thing endlessly, beyond the endurance of any adult. One day that everlasting "Swing, swing" kept up for a good hour, until finally I shut my book and went to have a look. Yoko was standing on the wooden seat while Taro pushed her from behind, her hands clutching the ropes and her feet braced, her whole body quivering with joy as she pumped her little legs for all she was worth and laughter poured out of her. When it was Taro's turn, sometimes he got so carried away he'd swing right around, full circle.

They also bounced balls while chanting songs to the rhythm:

Tell me where you're from, sir.
I'm from Higo, sir.
Where in Higo, sir?
Kumamoto, sir.
Where in Kumamoto, sir?

And they tried high-jumping over a long chain of elastic bands attached to trees. It was never higher than Yoko could jump—so actually low-jumping—but Taro didn't seem to mind. They played jump-rope games too. One time Mrs. Utagawa and I were summoned to join in, everyone dancing in and out and changing places until, before I knew it, Yoko and Mrs. Utagawa were turning the rope and Taro and I were competing to see who could last the longest. I jumped so easily in my wooden clogs for such a long time that finally he said in amazement, "Fumiko, you're the best. You're an athlete!"

Besides the front yard, the children also played in vacant lots in the neighborhood. Their favorite one was diagonally across from our house, half hidden by what was left of an old hedge that you couldn't see through from the street. The lot had thick clusters of tall, silvery pampas grass, and toward the back there was a small abandoned house with an air raid shelter. They dragged me there, tugging me by the hands. The dirt-floored entrance was overgrown with weeds, the raised wooden floor was full of gaps, the posts blackened in places by fire. It was a spooky place, which was exactly what the children liked about it. "The people who used to live here didn't make it to the shelter in time and died in an air raid, so ghosts come out right in the day-time," Yoko would say in a scary voice, and then Taro, hiding somewhere, would make an ominous sound, trying to frighten me. A shrine only ten minutes from there had a little playground in one corner where they could have fun on the slide and teeter-totter. Many were the times Yoko came home with dirt stains on her skirt.

When the weather was bad, they romped around the house. Looking on, it wasn't always easy to say just what kind of game they were playing. Natsue was of the firm opinion that girls needed to sit on chairs, not on the floor, and sleep on proper beds at an early age or else they'd grow up "with those awful, bent Japanese legs"; so not long after Taro started coming to the house, two bedsteads showed up in the sisters' tatami room—and were promptly used for games. Unlike the beds in Karuizawa, which had only straw mattresses on iron frames, these had actual springs. Yoko loved them. She and Taro would perch side by side, one at the foot of each bed, and bounce up and down as if holding reins in their hands, pretending to be stagecoach drivers. Sometimes they put what looked like scrolls in their mouths, tied long cloths to their backs, and jumped down the stairs to land on a heap of cushions at the bottom—like ninja or Superman, I couldn't tell which. Other times they would line up the dining room chairs and teeter across, as if inching across a hanging bridge over a great ravine. For all I know they thought they were tiptoeing under towering cliffs wrapped in spring mist, with wild, thundering rapids below, but all I could see as I whipped around getting dinner on the table was the room in a shambles.

Now and then they would sneak into Takero's study and play "English," typing random letters on the typewriter there. They also played "poor family," imagining that the tiny playroom was their house. Where she had picked up such notions I have no idea, but Yoko would announce, "There's no more rice in the cupboard; I must go to the pawnshop," and begin tying up one of her grandmother's kimonos in a wrapping cloth. As Taro was genuinely poor, it always made me smile to see him play along with this, looking quite serious.

Before he came on the scene, Yoko used to enjoy typical girlish pastimes like making multicolored braids of silk yarn, flipping tiny *ohajiki* disks, or playing house. But Taro had never had any boys for playmates, let alone any toys of his own, so he knew nothing about marbles, cards, or tops. One day when I went out to do the marketing, I saw a boy his age by the hardware store playing cleverly with a *kendama* peg-in-the-hole, and I decided on the spur of the moment to stop at a toy store on the way home and pick one up for Taro. I handed it to him with instructions to keep it a secret from Mrs. Utagawa, who, I thought, would disapprove of a lowly little toy like this, but sharp-eyed Yoko spotted it right away. "Oo look, a peg-in-the-hole!" she shouted, and promptly showed it to her grandmother. After that they played with the toy openly in front of her, with instructions to keep it secret from Natsue instead. Yoko soon tired of the toy, but Taro, whose coordination was much better to begin with, would go on practicing for so long that she'd get bored and pout. Soon he could do tricks with the effortless skill of a circus performer. It made me think how much boys his age would have looked up to him if he had ever played with them. But Taro himself seemed to enjoy just being at Yoko's beck and call.

One day the elder girl, Yuko, found the toy hidden away in the back of a drawer in the playroom. "Hey, look what I found!" Fortunately, she didn't tell her mother. Her sister, Yoko, was a chatterbox, but she kept quiet about things that really mattered to her, and never told Yuko anything about Taro. Even so, perhaps because the girls were so close in age, Yuko seemed to know intuitively what was going on. She certainly had a better idea than Natsue of what was happening while the two of them were out.

At the first beat of the drum that announced the arrival of the *kamishibai* man, a picture-board storyteller, Taro and Yoko would rush through the front gate and watch enviously as neighborhood kids flocked to buy a variety of traditional sweets—candies made like paper cutouts, say, or drooping lollipops—which emerged like magic from the box on his bicycle. Unlike the other children, Yoko was not given any pocket money as a rule, and buying snacks was forbidden anyway. The two looked on from behind the crowd as the man told his tale.

The big drum for the autumn festival had a deeper, throbbing sound you could feel down in your belly. Festival day was a special enough occasion for the children to get some pocket money from Mrs. Utagawa. At one time I used to take Yoko myself, but after she had Taro as a companion, I could send them off to the local shrine after they'd had supper and tidy up the kitchen at leisure before setting out to keep an eye on them. Taro, I noticed, preferred games of skill like fishing for water balloons or scooping out goldfish, while Yoko concentrated on buying and eating goodies. By the time I arrived she'd have already made the rounds of the stalls selling cotton candy, peppermint pipes, and sauce-dipped crackers and be ready to go again. As soon as she caught sight of me she'd hold her hand out and wheedle. "I'll pay you back at New Year's, so don't tell Grandma, okay?" I would give her five yen—then ten yen—and another ten yen. If we happened to run into Taro's brother, the one with the pimply face, out with his pals from middle school, Yoko would panic; but with me there, all they could do was leer. Usually a play would be in progress on a stage thrown together in the middle of the compound. The part of the woman was taken by a young male actor in a wig and white makeup, dressed in a flimsy kimono, who shrieked and ran away when the man playing the warrior brandished his sword. The two children gaped at it all, peering between grown-up spectators.

I remember strings of lanterns hung between the pines, a shiny gold portable shrine, a mound of sake casks wrapped in rush matting, and the shrill piping of sacred *kagura* music in the background. The shrine itself, hidden away among trees so tall that sunlight never reached the ground, was normally cool and quiet, but on that day it was transformed, buzzing with color and activity, crowded with people in bright summer *yukata*. The children loved it.

"Grandma, I want to wear a *yukata*!" Yoko begged when she got home, draping herself around her grandmother's hunched back where she sat at her usual place, near the hibachi. The three Saegusa sisters were too modern to dress their children in old-fashioned cotton kimonos, even for festivals.

"Well, then," said Mrs. Utagawa, "one of these days I'll sew you one. Next summer we'll go and buy the fabric together, shall we?"

LATE IN THE autumn I took the children out to gather chestnuts and acorns. For chestnuts, we went as far as a stand of trees some distance away and knocked the branches with sticks to dislodge the nuts. When we got back, we peeled them and then I cooked them with rice. We picked up acorns at the shrine, where they covered the ground, and then we strung them together to make necklaces, just the way I used to do when I was a little girl.

Around the time the wind turned cold, we raked up the leaves in the yard and made a bonfire.

*Sasanquas, sasanquas,* blooming on the path.
A bonfire, a bonfire, a fire of fallen leaves.
Shall we stop now to warm our frozen hands?
Yes, let's stop and warm our hands.

Yoko warbled this for us proudly, having been chosen as one of twenty children in the entire school to sing in a radio program. Once she got started, she'd get carried away and sing one autumn song after another: "Rabbit, little rabbit, what makes you jump so high? It's the harvest moon, so big and round up in the sky . . ." "Listen to the cricket sing, *chinchiro chinchiro chinchiro-rin* . . ." "In the light of an autumn sunset, in the shining golden light, see how mountain maples glow . . ." Out they came, song after song that she'd learned at school. In the meantime, the sweet potatoes buried at the bottom of the burning leaves cooked through, and we ate them together, peeling off the burned black skin and blowing on them to cool them.

At that same time of year, we trooped out to clean up clutter in the garden shed. Taro helped chop firewood as well. Since I was still far stronger than he was, I would stand a block of firewood on a tree stump and split it in two. His job was to carry the pieces to the shed and stack them neatly, though he sometimes picked up the hatchet and had a go himself. Mrs. Utagawa would be off at one side with a cloth wrapped around her head, grilling some mackerel pike on a portable stove for dinner, fanning life into the coals. Doing it indoors would have filled the house with the smell; so as not to offend Natsue, she always did it in the back yard.

Yoko, the only one with nothing to do, just stood behind her grandmother watching the thin plumes of white smoke rise high in the air.

When it turned cold, the *kotatsu* heater would make its appearance in Mrs. Utagawa's room, and the two children would sit there with their feet tucked under the warm quilt cover, doing their homework. Once they were done, they went to play in the main room, so the stove that used to be lit there only in the evening was started earlier. Everything became a game, and they took turns throwing coal through the little slot in the stove. When they put in too much, the iron body would glow red, looking as if it might chug off like a locomotive.

AT SOME POINT every winter, Yoko would catch a cold and take to her bed with a fever and swollen lymph glands or tonsils. Much as Taro would have preferred staying there with her to going to school, he knew that Mrs. Utagawa would never approve, and so, reluctantly, he went. But as soon as school let out he was back. He'd draw up a chair to the head of her bed, and then it would start: "Need anything? Want me to put some more ice in the cold pack? Shall I change the water in your hot-water bottle?" Since Yoko was allowed to read manga only when she had a fever, he would head off to the book-rental shop by the station with some coins from Mrs. Utagawa and bring back several volumes of the sort that girls liked, then set off again to borrow new ones when she had finished them. Taro himself seemed to have a strong immune system: he never caught any of her colds.

Yoko's asthma scared him stiff. During a long spasm her face would turn red, while his turned white. When her spasms were especially bad, he would sometimes stand and knock his head against the wall. One day when the spasms had finally calmed down and she was asleep, he picked a time when he must have thought no one was watching and went up to her pillow. I saw him put his head next to hers and whisper in her ear, "Yoko, don't die. Please don't die, okay?" He kept his face pressed into her pillow for a while without moving, as if he were breathing in the smell of her neck. I had never seen anything so touching. Having found a friend for the first time in his life, his heart must have actually hurt from the pressure of such love.

Another time, I went into the bedroom and found Yoko crying, her face buried in her pillow.

"Just go away and leave me alone!"

Taro was standing blankly by her side, holding a comb. His endless offers to do this or that sometimes got on her nerves.

Actually, they quarreled frequently. Not wanting her grandmother to know, Yoko would go outside by the kitchen door and sob convulsively, red-faced, smothering the sound. Taro's affection for her was so intense it must have been a strain on her. When it made her cry, he would sulk, or apologize reluctantly, or cry like a girl himself. It varied.

ROKU'S FUNERAL TOOK place early in the new year. Toward the end, I was going over to the Azuma house nearly every day. By then he couldn't get anything down his throat, so there wasn't much I could do for him except to make sure he was warm and had clean underwear. After he died, it seemed that he'd managed to set aside a little money, much to the surprise of everyone in the Utagawa family.

With no need to support Roku anymore, Mrs. Utagawa herself had a little extra cash at her disposal every month. She had already been paying out of her own pocket for any expenses Taro's presence incurred, but soon she began spending money on him more freely. The amount wasn't much: she would buy him notebooks and pencils, and give him some money for school excursions. The Azuma family was no longer as badly off by then, yet O-Tsune was still happy to have the boy get whatever came his way. Natsue and Takero of course knew nothing about it.

Roku's death freed up a room for the boys where Taro could have slept with his brothers, but he kept to his cushions in the kitchen, insisting—understandably—that he preferred it that way. When she heard this, however, Mrs. Utagawa got out some of her husband's old kimonos, unstitched them, and sewed them into a narrow futon and coverlet, filled with layers of thick cotton, so that Taro could sleep a little more comfortably.

At some point he stopped wetting his bed.

IN THE FOURTH grade the two children were put in different classes, but the days went peacefully by. As the weather turned warm, once again they started to play outside. In the front yard of the Utagawa home was a concrete patio overhung with grapevines, and they would go there to draw pictures in white or colored chalk on the floor. In addition to the empty lot with its air raid shelter where they usually played, they found another close by that got more sun. They used to pick wild horsetails and bring them to Mrs.

Utagawa for her to cook with sugar and soy sauce. I sometimes took them to paddy fields a little farther out, where
we picked Chinese milk vetch, flowers of reddish-purple
and white that grew along the paths in between. As with
the acorns in the autumn, we wove them into necklaces—
again, just as I used to do when I was a little girl.

Weekends were dreadful for Taro. Saturday afternoons,
when Yoko went for her piano lesson in Seijo, were not so
bad. After she got back from school and had her lunch, she
would change into her good clothes and set off with her
piano books, Taro tagging along at least as far as Chitose
Funabashi station. I often went with them—it was a good
way for me to get my shopping done. Whenever we passed
somebody wearing glasses, they would say he was a monk
and howl with laughter—some bit of nonsense they'd
picked up reading a child's version of the old comic novel
Shank's Mare. They tossed the music bag back and forth,
playing as they went. Afterward Taro used to stand at the
railway crossing, watching till her train was out of sight.

It was strange how Yoko never minded being seen with a
ragamuffin like Taro back then. When other children from
school spotted the two of them together and jeered, she didn't
like it, but she had no qualms about walking alongside Taro in
his shabby clothes while she herself was dressed smartly in
a wool blazer, skirt, and felt beret. To a lucky girl who had
never once felt ashamed of her own clothes, his shabbiness
didn't seem to be a problem, though dirt was another matter.
Occasionally Mrs. Utagawa would buy him something new,
but clothes back then were expensive. Besides, if it attracted

too much attention his brothers might give him a harder time. So in a way it was unavoidable that Taro should go on dressing like the rest of his family. Yoko, on the other hand, had plenty of fine clothes, the sort that would have made her stand out in any ordinary elementary school. Seijo Academy, where her sister and her two cousins went to school, had no uniform. There was so much material left over from Primavera that the three of them had clothes in abundance, and of course Yoko, getting everybody's hand-me-downs, had the most of all. New outfits were continually arriving even before she had had a chance to outgrow or wear out the old ones, which were bundled up and sent to the Elizabeth Saunders Home, an orphanage for biracial children born during and after the Occupation. The injustice of it all used to bother me. Fortunately Taro, who helped send the clothes off, had no interest in clothes, being a boy, and was only intent on tying the string as tight as possible around the bundles.

For Taro, Sundays were the worst. After a leisurely breakfast, Yoko's father would usually set off for the university, but her mother was home nearly all day, so Taro had to stay away from the house. Even if I saw him hanging around the well, I had no choice but to ignore him. On weekdays after supper, Yoko poked at the piano for half an hour or so, but her sister Yuko took her music seriously, and on Sunday she would practice for hours at a time, the sound carrying through the surrounding space. At dusk Taro would sit with his arms around his knees on his favorite tree stump, looking as if he were listening intently. Sometimes the Utagawas spent the whole day out.

The Azuma family, for their part, had Sunday outings now and then, but usually they left Taro behind. Feeling sorry for him, Mrs. Utagawa had him carry her bags when she called on acquaintances in Kichijoji, visited her husband's grave in the area, or went shopping at Mitsukoshi department store in the Ginza; there she would buy him a pair of trousers or something as a reward. Every other Sunday I had the day off, and I also took him out with me once in a while— sometimes to the Variety Restaurant in Isetan department store, where he would have the children's lunch, sometimes to a Disney movie Yoko had seen with her family the week before. And I even took him to Korakuen Stadium to watch a Giants game.

One time we went together to visit my uncle Genji, who lived in Soto Kanda then. The husky-voiced woman was running a restaurant in Tamachi with his help; the restaurant was doing well, and they seemed to be leading a comfortable life in a small house they'd built. On hearing what a bright child Taro was, Uncle Genji told him solemnly, "Son, learn English. If you do, no matter what happens, you'll always have food on the table." Taro listened equally solemnly to this advice.

ONCE AGAIN THE Utagawas' annual summer pilgrimage to Karuizawa drew near.

One day Takero again aproached Mrs. Utagawa with the idea of building their own summer house. "For my sake, Mother, why not buy a small plot of land in Oiwake and build a cottage there?" he said. "Summer in Tokyo gets hotter by the year. You'd be far better off spending the entire summer in the highlands yourself, you know."

"I suppose I would." She said. "But, dear me, what a waste. And without Fumiko around to help out, do you really think I could manage there on my own?"

"I'm sure you could get someone local to drop in regularly."

"I suppose so . . ."

"If I had my own place I could go there any time I wanted, not just for the Bon festival."

"That's true. Why don't we think it over this summer?"

"If we're looking for land to buy, the easiest way to do it is while we're in Karuizawa anyway."

"I suppose so . . . Let's just think it over for one more year, shall we?"

As the family's departure drew closer, Taro's expression grew more despondent, and Yoko, unable to enjoy playing with someone so down in the mouth, grew exasperated and peevish. "Come on," she'd say, "you know perfectly well we're coming back soon!" Perhaps one reason children get so depressed is that they have no voice in what happens to them. The day before Yoko left, Taro was utterly miserable. Yoko seemed affected by it and was moody on the train, but once we arrived in Karuizawa and she was let loose in the front garden, she was red-faced with excitement in no time, chasing after the others and playing as usual. It was as if she'd forgotten all about life in Tokyo.

Even with Yoko gone, Mrs. Utagawa had Taro come over every day to do things around the house, to fill in for me. He was a great help to her that summer.

Then, of all things, his right arm got broken. It happened in August, during the ten days Mrs. Utagawa spent in Karuizawa as she always did, around the time of the Bon festival. I didn't find out about it until the end of summer, back in Tokyo. Taro himself told Mrs. Utagawa that he broke it falling out of a tree he'd been climbing, but she quickly guessed it was those brothers of his who were to blame. O-Tsune did take him to a doctor to have the bone set, and his arm was in a cast, supported by a sling, but Mrs. Utagawa didn't trust any doctor O-Tsune might choose, so she personally took him to a nearby hospital and had the fracture X-rayed again to make sure that all was well.

When I got back and saw Taro with his arm in a grimy sling, I was obviously surprised, and Yoko's eyes widened too. She accepted the story that he had broken it climbing a tree and touched the cast in a gingerly way, commenting that it was lucky he was left-handed. But if she looked sad at all, it was less out of sympathy for him than because school was starting the next day.

"I haven't done my arithmetic yet, have you?" she asked. Every summer in Karuizawa, Yoko would go on playing right up to the last minute and then, fretfully, cram all her summer homework into the final two days. That summer, though, she had apparently decided to cheat, hoping to be able to copy Taro's answers.

Her face broke into a smile when he nodded. "Goody," she said, holding out both hands without the least sense of shame. Taro was just as bad. "Be right back," he said, and dashed off with a look of dumb happiness on his face. That night I saw Yoko copying his answers on the sly so her mother wouldn't catch her.

One evening a few days later, I went out into the front yard to bring in the laundry. Mrs. Utagawa was watering the flowers, her figure outlined against the red sky. Yoko and Taro were squatting side by side on the concrete patio, he still with his right arm in a sling. Using his left hand, he was making mud pies with her, decorating them with the petals of bellflowers, cockscombs, and marvels-of-Peru from the garden. They produced a row of these colorful pies. Mrs. Utagawa, having emptied her watering can, went over to leave it on the patio. Instead, she held the can over his head and pretended to be watering him.

"Grow, grow, nice and big," she said playfully. "Oh, if only you were a little tree, Taro, I could water you like this and you'd grow big in no time. Then you could stand up to anybody!"

By then she may have already made up her mind to build a summer cottage in Oiwake and take him along as a houseboy.

I don't know when she told her stepson of her decision, but by the time the leaves started changing color, they were already deep in discussion about buying land up there. Natsue must have been feeling guilty that she spent over a month in Karuizawa every summer while old Mrs. Utagawa stayed only ten days or so; she had no objection to their building a separate summer house. Oiwake was a fair way from Karuizawa, nearly half an hour by car, but Natsue knew that her husband had always loved it there, and since she intended to continue spending her summers over in Karuizawa, she had no problem with the location, either. For my part, I arranged for my family in Saku to work with a local real estate agent to look for a suitable spot, somewhere close enough to the main road for Mrs. Utagawa to catch the bus to Karuizawa. She was keen on the idea. By the time my family found a likely piece of land, it was so cold that she needed gloves and a heavy shawl in addition to her winter coat, but she went with me willingly to take a look at it.

She was the one who settled on the rough layout of the house too, in consultation with Takero.

One day after the groundwork began, she took out a simple blueprint of the house, spread it out on the tatami floor, and asked Taro what he thought.

"What is it?" he said.

"A house we're going to build in the mountains. Right near the place where Yoko goes every summer."

He leaned forward, all ears.

"Here's the room where we'll have our meals, and this will be the study for Yoko's papa. These two adjoining rooms will have tatami. This one will be my sitting room, and when Yuko and Yoko come over to visit, they'll sleep here with me."

Taro stared at the layout, looking quite grown-up for his age.

"Tell you what," she said. "How about if next summer
you went there with me as my helper?" Just to do the shopping along the main road would mean a fifteen-minute walk
each way through the hills. Taro must have been in the picture from the beginning. "Where would you sleep, do you
think?"

He pointed silently to a square behind the main house,
off to the northeast.

"What a clever boy you are. Do you know what that is?"

He was quiet, with his head on one side, so she said, "It's
a shed." Then she told him that she would put in a bed for
him there, a straw mattress on top of wooden slats, with a
window above so that when he woke up the first thing he'd
see in the morning would be a burst of green leaves.

"Everything is green there, everywhere you look. It is
very, very pretty."

His eyes now lit up with childish excitement.

I think she decided to put Taro in the shed in case
Takero, when he came to visit, found the boy's presence
a nuisance.

Taro looked serious again as he studied the blueprint and
asked, "Where will Fumiko sleep?"

"Well, she won't be going there very often, so she won't
need a special room of her own." It wouldn't be often that
everybody was there at once, and since the main room for
meals had enough extra space, they could make do when
the time came.

"Hm." He stared at the blueprint awhile longer and then
asked, biting his lower lip, "Can I see Yoko there?"

"She'll be some distance away, but you'll be able to go and see her now and then, yes. And sometimes she'll come over and stay with us."

"Taro!" Yoko came in carrying a light-blue hula hoop in both hands. She'd been waiting for him in the playroom, but had grown impatient and come looking for him. Her grandmother asked her to come nearer, and she plopped down next to Taro. Together they peered at the blueprint. Since Natsue was always saying that the family "didn't have that kind of money" for various things, Yoko seemed to find it hard to believe that there was really going to be a new summer house.

"Have we got that kind of money?" she asked.

Mrs. Utagawa gave a vague answer.

"Can Taro come for sure?"

This time the answer was firm. "Yes, for sure."

Before long Takero too took it for granted that Taro would be going. Having grown up surrounded by nurses, maids, manservants, and live-in students acting as house-boys, he found nothing strange in the arrangement. He also knew what a help the boy had been to his stepmother while I was away in Karuizawa, going to the post office and so on. If Taro himself wanted to go, then there was no reason to object.

That day Taro hung around as long as he could, poring over the blueprint and making suggestions. For one thing, he proposed having people go in and out of the cottage through the porch, without an entrance hall, and using that space as a small maid's room instead. When Mrs. Utagawa

SUMMER IN OIWAKE

presented this idea to Takero that night he was impressed. "Seems practical, and since there'll be no guests to speak of anyway, why bother with an entryway?" In fact, I found it very helpful later to have a little room of my own. Taro also said that since summers up there would be cool and moist, maybe my north-facing room should have a wooden floor, with a raised platform for the futon. Putting bunk beds in the shed was his idea too. It might just have been a boyish wish to sleep high up, but the idea ended up increasing storage space, which came in handy.

Before midwinter, when the ground froze, the foundation work was done. My stepfather kept tabs on the workers' progress until the job was finished. Then Mrs. Utagawa began making bedding. She collected some old kimonos that she said had become "too flamboyant" for her—though they seemed plain enough to me—and started to unstitch them, getting Taro to help. When Natsue saw what they were doing, she also brought out some "too flamboyant" ones of her own, although she added generously that I was welcome to them if they looked like something I could wear. Of course, they were far too glamorous for me, and I'm sure I would never have had the courage to put them on, so they became bedding as well. Taro took to studying the layout of the Oiwake cottage almost daily. The seriousness with which he did this made it seem as if it were his own house that was being built.

One Sunday in late December 1958, I took Taro to the top of Tokyo Tower, which had just gone up. He stared out at the city spreading endlessly below under a gray sky and then pointed off into the distance. "Oiwake's that way," he said. I remember how stunned I was by the strength of his attachment to, or longing for, a piece of land he had yet to lay eyes on.

BY THE FOLLOWING April, just as the entire country was swept up in the excitement of the crown prince's wedding, the Oiwake cottage was nearly complete. Taro and Yoko entered the fifth grade. Yoko's sister and her cousin Mari started at Seijo Academy's middle school together, and Mari's sister became a sixth grader at its elementary school. Masayuki Shigemitsu, who was clever, was accepted at a prestigious national middle school attached to the University of Education.

"They say it's a school for kids who are so smart they're practically geniuses," Yoko reported to Taro in the admiring voice she always used when speaking of Masayuki. But Taro had no reason to be glum. "If you took the exam you'd get in too," she continued, her voice sounding perfectly sincere.

Yoko was convinced that she was Taro's superior in every respect except for athletic ability and intelligence, two areas where she conceded him the advantage. In fact Taro was regularly at the top of his class, and the bullying had stopped. Even so, his classmates gave him a wide berth, and boys still didn't invite him to play with them. His own reserve was no doubt partly to blame, along with the aura of poverty he had. But the main reason, it seemed to me, was the old rumor that he wasn't Japanese. O-Tsune took every opportunity to bring it up, telling anybody who cared to listen, so the rumor never had a chance to die a natural death. Meanwhile, the hard time his brothers gave him had left him with an instinctive dislike of other boys, so he had no interest in joining in their games anyway. He seemed to want nothing other than to be with Yoko.

I do wonder what was going on in Mrs. Utagawa's mind at the time. I doubt that she had gone so far as to consider the idea of Yoko and Taro marrying one day, but from around the time she set out to build the Oiwake cottage her attachment to Taro seemed to deepen. There is something mysterious about relations between people of the opposite sex. She considered herself his protector, yet somewhere inside she was leaning on him, relying on his ability—almost like a lover. He was still shorter than she was, but she used to say admiringly, as if he was bigger than her, "In times of trouble, a general—that's you."

He didn't know what exactly this meant, but he knew it was praise and so he beamed with pleasure.

TAKERO MADE A couple of trips to Oiwake to sort out various details, and by early summer the cottage was ready. I moved in first, in mid-July. My presence would be needed in Karuizawa once the holidays started, so I had to get the cleaning and unpacking done in Oiwake beforehand. Then, on the very first day of summer vacation, Mrs. Utagawa arrived with Taro in tow. The two of them were not the only ones to show up that day, either. After Taro had looked excitedly around the cottage, inside and out, he took off for the main road, exploring, and while he was gone we had a surprise visit from the three Saegusa sisters. On their way to Karuizawa by a later train with their parents and children, the three had decided to have a look at the new summer house and had traveled on to Oiwake station. From there they took a taxi and dropped in without a word of warning. Natsue had a quick look around the place and said in a loud voice to Mrs. Utagawa, "Mm, it's certainly well made for a house so small." To me she added in a hushed aside, "There's something rather lonely about it, isn't there?" Harue, the eldest, declared it "just perfect for Takero," and the youngest, Fuyue, said that it was "nice and rustic, nothing cheap about it." The taxi was waiting, so they descended on us like a typhoon and then were gone. By the time Taro came back, only a faint trace of perfume lingered in the air. "Gracious! What a whirl they do live in!" said Mrs. Utagawa. I stayed over that night, then took the bus to Karuizawa the next day.

Yoko was eager to visit the new cottage right away, but Natsue suggested she wait a little till everyone was settled in, and so two days went by, then three, until she stopped asking, perhaps because she'd got used again to the pleasures of life in Karuizawa. She may also have realized that sooner or later she would be going to Oiwake by herself for several nights, and decided that in the meantime she should make the most of being with the other children. Her visit kept getting put off for one reason or another, and as it happened, she first saw Taro in Karuizawa instead.

It was the first *Sunday lunch* in August. As usual, I was working alongside Chizu in the Shigemitsu kitchen, under the Demon's direction, when Yoko came in and tugged at the sleeve of my smock.

"Grandma's coming today, isn't she?"

"Yes, she'll be here."

This had been decided quite some time ago.

"If Grandma's coming, then will Taro come too?" She was whispering, standing on tiptoe to reach my ears.

"I wonder." I tilted my head doubtfully.

It seemed likely to me that she would bring the boy with her. If it were only a question of his helping her on the way, she would probably leave him at home, but given his longing to see Yoko, I just didn't think her capable of setting off without him. At the same time, I thought she must be feeling uneasy. I myself felt a vague anxiety—or, rather, a premonition of disaster—about his showing up in Karuizawa and had tried to avoid thinking about it. He wouldn't be able to play alone with Yoko. Neither could I imagine him playing with the other children. The Shigemitsu and Saegusa families would never approve.

I asked Yoko a question of my own. "If Taro comes, what will you do?"

"There's so many things to show him! There's lots here in Masayuki's house and over in ours too, and there's Foggy Pond, and the monster mushrooms that came up after the rain yesterday, and huge golden dragonflies and the mist when it's getting dark . . ."

She looked up at me as she eagerly ticked off the attractions on her fingers. I suppose she was getting bored because the older children often left her out of their games.

"They've got huge golden dragonflies in Oiwake too, you know." My tone may have been a bit harsh, for she closed her mouth and looked at me blankly. "Anyway," I went on, "when Taro comes he probably won't be eating with you and the others, but here with me in the kitchen."

"How come?"

"Because he's not a guest."

"Oh."

She seemed to sense something in this vaguely and repeated "Oh," as if trying to convince herself.

Blessed with good weather that day, we lined up garden tables on the large east-west porch and covered them with white tablecloths. The Saegusa sisters were in high spirits, chattering away as they flitted around. While the elderly members of the two families sat talking in rattan chairs in the garden, Yayoi's Masao went off alone to read in the shade of a birch tree and Harue's husband, Hiroshi, also alone, practiced his golf swing as usual.

Mrs. Utagawa and Taro came onto the scene like two clouds over a sunny landscape.

I was on the porch with the Demon, Yayoi Shigemitsu, and the three sisters, and we were so busy that I never even noticed when the taxi pulled up at the back. Suddenly there they were, walking toward us between the two houses. Despite the blazing afternoon sunshine, the atmosphere they brought with them was chilling, almost as if they were shades from the world below. I couldn't help a slight shudder myself, and I'm sure the others felt the same way. Only Masao kept on reading, oblivious. Hiroshi had raised his arms, on the point of taking a swing, but just let them drop.

Even Yoko, standing at a distance, seemed momentarily taken aback.

It was as if I was blushing inside, invisibly. I felt guilty, as though our life in Chitose Funabashi had been exposed, and something about it was shameful. With her drab kimono and her hair in a tight bun, Mrs. Utagawa had always seemed out of place in Karuizawa, but on that day, perhaps because she'd brought Taro with her, she looked like some old woman who had stumbled onto someone else's property with a street urchin in tow.

Why did poverty stand out so much more back then? Taro was wearing a discolored, patched, short-sleeved shirt and black trousers that had become too short for him, so that between the cuffs and his canvas shoes his skinny bare ankles stuck out. That's all there was to it, but he might as well have worn a sign around his neck marked POOR BOY.

What stood out more clearly still, however, was Taro's own sense of inferiority. The moment everyone's eyes turned his way, he seemed to read something in their gaze, and recognition that he was somewhere he didn't belong, that he had no right to be here, was wretchedly apparent on his face. His discomfort was transmitted to Mrs. Utagawa, who must immediately have regretted bringing him along. On her old, strained face, a similar apprehension was no less apparent.

Harue and Fuyue, who were setting the tables on the porch, inclined their heads doubtfully and turned to Natsue for an explanation. Though surprised by the extra visitor, Natsue saw no need to take Taro's inferiority personally and responded promptly, in a casual tone of voice.

"Oh, him? Well, you know about the old rickshaw man named Roku who lived behind our house? That's his nephew. Or, no, it's his nephew's nephew. Complicated!"

While she was explaining that Taro was there to help Mrs. Utagawa in Oiwake, I watched Yoko leave the cluster of children and run over to the newcomers on her own. Then the Demon, who had been standing near the porch steps, went up to the pair with deliberate slowness, took the bundle Taro was carrying, and said something. Mrs. Utagawa looked more dismayed than ever.

"Oh really? How old is he?" Harue squinted at Taro from afar, appraising him. Told he was in the same grade as Yoko but a year or two her elder, she just repeated, "Oh really?"

The Demon shooed Yoko back into the garden and led Taro around to the service entrance. The sight of the shabby boy heading for the back door seemed to reassure everyone, and they all resumed what they had been doing. I went back into the kitchen from the porch just as he came in through the back door, led by the Demon.

There was a glassy, vacant look in his eyes, a look that I hadn't seen for a long time. The poor child didn't so much as glance at me.

That day, Taro was first made to wash his hands in the kitchen. Then, after waiting for a while on a chair in the *servants' hall*, he had a Western-style meal with the rest of us staff. Apparently Mrs. Utagawa couldn't bring herself to tell him that he might be eating separately from Yoko, a development that seemed to take him completely by surprise. Dining Western-style seemed to be equally surprising to him. The heavy china plates embossed with a design in burgundy red were a set the Shigemitsus had brought back from London for everyday use, and for *Sunday lunch* even we maids used them. The Demon saw at once that Taro, accustomed only to chopsticks, didn't know how to handle a knife and fork. In a dry voice, not bothering to conceal her scorn, she gave him instructions: knife on the right, fork on the left, do as I do. Taro's earlobes turned scarlet, but he meekly managed the knife and fork as told. The presence of a boy with a strained expression, who never uttered a word, put a damper on the lunchtime conversation.

Sometimes the silver bell would tinkle, and then Chizu or I hurried out to the porch. Depending on what was wanted, we might all get up and sit down again. A peaceful meal was never ours to enjoy anyway.

I knew that Taro was fighting the urge to run away, but I also knew that he had far greater self-control than most adults. Besides, it was unlikely that a boy like him would simply have come over here in high spirits, focused only on the prospect of seeing Yoko again. Having heard so much about Karuizawa from her, he was bound to arrive with worries and misgivings, full of imagined scenarios, wondering what that world was like and how he would be treated in it. But how could he ever have imagined the existence of something like this? The quiet fir-lined road, the imposing gateposts of dark stone, the two Western-style villas casting shadows on the moss garden—a world he had never seen or dreamed of, unfolding magically in front of him. And yet for his constant playmate, Yoko, this was a perfectly ordinary scene, one that she had known all her life. On top of the indignity of being made to eat elsewhere, that recognition must have tormented him. But because Yoko belonged to this world, he knew he would have to do exactly as the grown-ups told him if he wasn't to be shut out altogether.

We ate in silence.

"Taro." Yoko cautiously opened the door from the hallway. She must have escaped by pretending to go to the toilet or something. The Demon's presence was intimidating, so she just stuck her head in the doorway without coming in. Her eyes were instantly drawn not to Taro's face but to the food on the table. Only then did she seem to realize that we didn't eat the same dishes as the family—that there was hardly any meat. The longer she stared, the redder she became.

"Come on out and play later, okay?" She shut the door behind her cautiously, as if she'd done something wrong.

Taro let nothing show on his face. The Demon had raised an eyebrow on hearing Yoko's invitation, but since Taro made no response, there was nothing more to say.

Out in the garden after lunch, it was customary for the family to have some tea. The Demon and Chizu got up to prepare it while Taro and I began to clear our table. Neither of us spoke. Despite what Yoko had said, I didn't feel comfortable about telling him to run along and play. I wondered what I should do with him as I stacked the dirty dishes.

Just then Harue came swooping in from the porch. "Hi! Mrs. Utagawa just told me I can borrow this boy of hers. He's very handy, she says, and I can certainly use him. So many things need doing next door!" She signaled briskly for him to follow her, and opened the door to the hallway. Before I could catch the expression on his face, the heavy oak door closed behind them.

Oddly enough, I felt relieved, free of the dilemma I'd been in. Until then it had never occurred to me that this might happen—that after eating in the *servants' hall* Taro would be used as the Saegusas' servant, unable to play with Yoko at all—but now that it had happened, I saw that nothing could have been more natural.

Just as I started washing the dishes, including the ones brought in from outside, Yoko opened the door again. "Taro!" When she saw that he was gone, she turned to me with a puzzled look. "Where'd he go?"

"I think he went over to the other house to help out."

"Help out?"

"That's right."

"Help out how?"

"I'm not sure."

Yoko left, her head tilted to one side in puzzlement.

It was only around three-thirty when I went out to the porch to clear away the folding tables and chairs; but the sky had darkened suddenly, and like a wet cloak over my shoulders, the air was chill and damp. Before long the famous Karuizawa mist would creep up from the valley.

Out in the garden, the adults were sitting here and there in clusters, having cups of tea. There among them was Mrs. Utagawa, balancing her cup with some unfamiliarity as she chatted with Yayoi, a gentle person who often kept the old lady company, even though they had little connection with each other. Behind the tea-sipping adults, the children were getting ready for a game of tennis. I squinted but could make out only Masayuki and the three girls. Yoko wasn't among them.

As I crossed the yard and went into the Saegusa house from the porch, an unexpected scene met my eyes. The big oval dining room table had been pushed aside, and under the hanging light fixture on the ceiling was the tallest stepladder I had ever seen. Standing on the very top of that ladder was Taro, with both arms stretched above him. Predictably, at the foot of the stepladder was Yoko, gaping up at him. Harue stood off at a little distance with her arms folded, also looking up. She spotted me.

"Lightbulbs," she said. "I'm having him change them for us."

"I see."

The ceilings were so high that for a long while they'd been putting off the business of replacing burned-out ones, and now Taro was doing them all, in order, from the attic down. After explaining this, Harue asked, "Is Mrs. Utagawa leaving?"

"No, ma'am, I just came to check on things."

"Oh, good. You know, I can't tell you what a help this boy of hers is! I am so glad she brought him." Seeing me look at the tall stepladder, wondering where it might have come from, she added, "We keep it at the back of the garden shed. It's so awkward, though, we hardly ever get it out."

At that moment Natsue came in. When she saw Taro changing the lightbulb, she smiled, showing her dimple. "Well, how about that! Good for you, Taro!" Then she turned to her elder sister. "The fog's come out and, *brr*, it's cold." She rubbed her arms. "I came for Yuko's cardigan. I told her to get it herself, but she's in the middle of a game of tennis. You two brought yours down together, didn't you?"

This last was addressed to Yoko. In Karuizawa, the temperature often drops so quickly in the evening that a woolen cardigan or pullover is a necessity. Sweaters belonging to various people were scattered around the house and garden. Natsue herself wore a red cardigan loosely over her shoulders.

"Uh-huh."

"Where are they?"

"On the sofa," said Yoko, without taking her eyes off Taro. She was following his every move.

"Yours too?"

"Uh-huh."

Her mother made a *tsk* sound and went into the parlor, coming back with a pair of matching white angora cardigans. She handed the smaller one to Yoko.

"I'll go and get the other girls' sweaters too, then," said Harue, and started to leave the dining room. But she

FOGGY POND

abruptly halted, as if struck by an idea, and turned to me. "You know, I'll bet the house next door has lots of dead bulbs too. Since we've gone to the trouble of bringing the ladder out, would you ask O-Kuni about it for me?"

Needless to say, Taro ended up replacing all the burned-out bulbs in the Shigemitsu house too, top to bottom, under the Demon's supervision. Perhaps out of fear of her, or because she'd grown tired of watching Taro at work, Yoko gave in to her mother's urging and went outside, rejoining the other children. I returned to the Shigemitsu kitchen. As Natsue had said, fog was moving in. While Chizu and I dried the rest of the dishes, we watched from the kitchen as heavy mist swirled like a white veil in the gathering dusk.

Eventually we heard Taro and the Demon coming downstairs with that huge stepladder. I went into the dining room to find it set up under the chandelier. Just then, Yayoi happened to come in from the porch with Mrs. Utagawa, whom she had apparently decided to bring indoors, since even with her shawl on the old lady was getting cold. Yayoi's eyes widened in surprise when she saw Taro climbing high up, on the Demon's orders.

Mrs. Utagawa looked startled too.

Yayoi was extraordinarily sensitive. Hearing all about Taro from Mrs. Utagawa earlier might have had something to do with it, but when she saw him perched so high in the air, she seemed immediately to grasp how difficult his day had been. I saw her settle Mrs. Utagawa in an armchair in the parlor and then slip quietly upstairs. By the time she came down again, Taro was no longer in the dining room.

She found us in the *servants' hall* just as the Demon was pressing a bit of money into Taro's unwilling hand, saying, "Here you go, a little something for your trouble." Yayoi, who by this time was wearing a fluffy beige cardigan herself, had two more sweaters over her arm. As Taro started leaving the room, she went up to him and knelt down so that her eyes were level with his.

"I checked upstairs, and you changed all the old bulbs, didn't you? I can't believe how brave you are, climbing up as high as that! Thank you so much. I don't know what we would have done without you." She stroked his hair, probably wanting to give him a hug. For once unable to resist, Taro stood in a daze. She went on: "This sweater belonged to my brother who died. I could never throw it away, but it just doesn't look right on my little boy. Would you wear it?" She chose one of the sweaters, moss green in color, and held it out to him in her small white hand. Taro stiffened. He gave her a good long look before breaking loose and fleeing.

Out in the garden was a boy his own age whose mother was this gentle, beautiful young woman; and the other sweater, the sky-blue one, was for that boy to wear. How much of this Taro grasped consciously at that moment, I don't know. But sometimes in a flash, without even realizing, people understand something beyond their scope, and I imagine this was one of those times. He must have felt a stab of envy and longing, mixed with an instinctive animosity toward the boy.

Yayoi knelt there, astonished, holding the two sweaters. Mrs. Utagawa, having followed her into the *servants' hall*, tried to apologize. Chizu had witnessed the whole episode with me, and her narrow eyes flashed in indignation: "Who does he think he is? The rude little scamp!" When I went to look for him, I found him leaning against the big stone gate, making lines in the gravel with the toe of his shoe—waiting, apparently, for Mrs. Utagawa to say it was time to leave.

White mist drifted around us.

Comfort from me would be no comfort at all, I knew. I went back, found Yoko watching a game of doubles, and whispered in her ear: "Taro is out by the gate, and he seems upset."

"What?" she yelped. "I told him to come here!" She tore off as fast as her legs would carry her. The white cardigan that matched her sister's looked even whiter in the fog.

I watched from a little distance as Yoko took him by the hand and tried to pull him back into the garden, but he shook her off. She slowly flushed red. Uh-oh, here come the tears, I thought, and sure enough, she started to sob like a little child, digging her fists in her eyes. Perhaps because he knew I was watching, Taro stared balefully into empty space and let her cry.

I had my time off then, from late afternoon till noon the next day, but I gave it up to go back with Mrs. Utagawa and Taro to Oiwake. Harue's husband, Hiroshi, drove us: he had just bought a new car called a Nissan Bluebird, which had only recently come on the market, and which he wanted to try out whenever possible. Even with Harue in the car there was still room for one more, and after what had happened that day, I couldn't bear to see the two of them return to Oiwake alone.

Hiroshi, in the driver's seat, had Harue next to him, with Mrs. Utagawa, me, and Taro in the back. We could have put him between us, but he had so few chances to ride in an automobile that I wanted to let him sit by the window—a gesture that backfired.

There was still daylight, but waves of thick fog kept rolling in. The ride felt strangely unreal, as if we were weaving in and out of clouds. When we got to Middle Karuizawa the fog started to thin out a bit, and the tension inside the car eased off as well.

Harue turned around and said to Mrs. Utagawa, "They tell me the boy was in Manchuria. Is that right?" She had apparently heard other things about Taro from Natsue as well. Her face was lively with curiosity. Only politeness kept her from asking about his being an orphan with Chinese blood in his veins. "He really is a wonderful helper," she said. "Clever too."

Something in her tone brought Mrs. Utagawa swiftly to his defense. "More than just clever. He does very well in school."

"You have simply got to bring him back again. The houses are so old, with so many things that need doing! Really, I would love to have him come and stay with us for a few days."

"Well . . ."

"You know what I think?" she said, turning to her husband at the wheel. "It would be nice if a boy like him could *caddy* at the golf course, don't you think? Dress him properly and he would be perfect."

"Absolutely," said Hiroshi. "There's nobody else around here but old farmers' wives, in those baggy work pants they wear—no good at all!" He craned his neck to look at Taro in the rearview mirror.

The three of us in the back seat didn't know what it might mean to "*caddy*," but the tone of the conversation made us squirm.

By the time we reached Oiwake, the fog had disappeared and we could see Mount Asama, stained purple in the last rays of sunset. The sight of the mountain was somehow re-assuring. Soon now it would be just the three of us again, I thought, feeling the strain of the day begin to ebb. But the final insult to Taro was yet to come.

When we pulled up in front of the house, Mrs. Utagawa, who was seated on my right, got out first, while I bent over to pick up the bundles at my feet. Taro on my left grabbed the handle for rolling down the window, pushing and pull-ing with both hands as he tried with all his might to open the door. I realized his mistake just as Harue turned around in the passenger seat to see what was happening.

"Goodness, the boy doesn't know how to open a car door!" Twisting her mouth to one side, she managed not to laugh, but the car seemed to ring with high, mocking laughter.

AFTER SUPPER TARO took two neatly wrapped packets of money out of his pocket and showed them to us. They were from the Shigemitsus and the Saegusas, and each one con-tained a fifty-yen bill. Back then, fifty yen for a bowl of hot noodles would have seemed steep, so this was no mean tip for a schoolboy. Mrs. Utagawa seemed in two minds about it, but she told him, "Why don't you set it aside so you can have some spending money when you want it?"

That was the first money Taro ever earned.

He stared at it on the table with a look of concentrated ferocity.

After he'd gone inside the shed, Mrs. Utagawa changed into her night *yukata* and began brushing her teeth with some old-fashioned tooth powder. She spoke half to me, half to herself. "I had to take him along. I couldn't see leaving him alone here to fend for himself."

What had she expected to happen when she took Taro with her? Perhaps she thought that if he was going to come to Oiwake every year, he would have to visit Karuizawa sooner or later anyway, so he might as well get it over with right at the start. That reasoning probably led her to take him with her.

As I went around the house closing the rain shutters for the night, I looked in on the shed, where the lights were off. I knew that didn't mean Taro was asleep. I could see him in my mind's eye, a scowl on his face as he stared up into the darkness. The next day, I went back to Karuizawa by myself only to find Yoko running around playing with the others, the events of the previous day apparently forgotten.

MRS. UTAGAWA'S NEXT visit to Karuizawa was for *Sunday lunch* in the week of the Bon festival. She didn't bring Taro: although Takero was in Oiwake by then, he had some sort of pressing deadline for a manuscript, so he stayed at the cottage too. She arrived alone.

As soon as Harue caught sight of her, she asked, "Where is the rickshaw-puller's boy? Has he gone back to Tokyo already?"

"No, he's still here."

"Oh, good. Make sure you bring him with you next time, will you?"

Natsue chimed in. "Yes, do! Remember how high he climbed, without getting scared? We've been saying we'd like him to come back and wash all the windows."

Mrs. Utagawa tightened her lips. Evidently she had left him behind on purpose, and he had not objected. That afternoon Yoko was scheduled to come back to Oiwake with her grandmother and stay ten days; knowing this must have made a difference.

It was decided in advance that I too was to go to Oiwake with Yoko that day. I would spend the night there, and after making sure that everything was all right, go back to Saku for a three-day visit to my family. Plans then escalated. As long as the three of us were being driven over, why not take two cars, with the Shigemitsus in one and the Saegusas in the other, so all the children could see the Oiwake cottage too? The decision was made on the spur of the moment and led to some arguing among the adults about who should go and who should stay. We were supposed to get an early start and arrive in Oiwake around four-thirty, but by the time we piled in and set off, it was already later than that.

I rode in the Shigemitsu car, with Masao driving. We arrived first and parked on the side of the road. Masayuki jumped out and ran down to the gate. Taro, who had been counting the minutes until Yoko's arrival, had never imagined that any other child would jump out of the car—much less the very one who had been so much on his mind. In a flash, he moved in front of the gate and stood with his arms spread wide, barring the way.

Dumbfounded, Masayuki blurted out, "Hey! This isn't your house!"

He said this in an authoritative, grown-up way, being now in his first year of middle school. He could not have had any idea what profound significance his words would later take on. It was probably the first time he had ever spoken to Taro, but he'd seen him in Karuizawa and knew from the Saegusa sisters' conversation what sort of child he was. In his surprise, the words must have popped out of his mouth.

Taro was livid. If Masayuki had tried to push his way in, I could see from Taro's eyes that he would have a go at him.

I caught up with them then and gave Taro such a fierce look that the minute he saw it he turned on his heels and ran off to the shed. Masayuki was still recovering. But then the other car arrived and soon everyone trooped in, inspecting the house inside and out. Unlike the girls, Masayuki spent most of his time exploring the outdoors, but he seemed leery of Taro and went nowhere near the shed.

"Masayuki!" Yoko called in a flirty sort of voice.

I was outside chatting with Fuyue, and turned toward the sound to see Yoko standing on the porch in a crisp new *yukata* with a design of scattered crimson koi, her face flushed. The other girls were clustered around her. Mrs. Utagawa had finished sewing the *yukata* in time for her to wear it for the Bon festival dancing that night. Yoko had been so eager to show it off that she must have begged to put it on as soon as she arrived. Neither her sister Yuko nor her cousins Mari and Eri had ever worn one, so they stood there fingering the long sleeves and the dangling ends of the sash with mixed curiosity and envy. When Masayuki came out where he could see her, he said "Wow!" and headed straight for the porch, all thought of Taro clearly gone. "You look terrific, Yoko." She flushed even more and, catching hold of her long sleeves in both hands, swung them back and forth, trying her best to look fetching, like a little dancer.

Taro was hypersensitive to Yoko's voice. When she called out "Masayuki!" in that coquettish way, the shed door opened and he came out. He went and balefully watched the children on the porch, his face still pale.

Shortly afterward, when the two cars had gone, Yoko finally began to explore the summer house properly. Although Mrs. Utagawa promised to help her put the *yukata* on again when it was time for the Bon dancing, she wouldn't take it off, happily waving her sleeves as she wandered through the rooms and outside and even into the shed, flitting about where Taro would be sure to see her. Taro, meanwhile, was out in the yard, pointlessly picking up twigs and ignoring her. Without him there to explain things, it was no fun for her to look around. Above all, she was disappointed that he'd made no comment about her new outfit.

"Taro!"

She called his name several times and even went up to him, but he wouldn't respond.

The two children had an early supper of a local specialty, steamed buns with vegetables inside, eating by themselves at a small Formica table in the kitchen. While Takero was here in Oiwake, Mrs. Utagawa had ensured that Taro kept a low profile by feeding him there first alone, and, with Yoko staying, she apparently planned to go on that way, feeding the children together ahead of the adults. Taro sat diagonally across the table from Yoko and reached silently for a bun, looking sullen. Yoko picked up her red plastic bowlful of miso soup with both hands. She had no idea why Taro was so angry with her, but she was cross with him for being angry, and sulked. Mrs. Utagawa seemed to think this was a holdover from the recent trouble in Karuizawa, so she kept quiet.

After the dishes were done, Taro went back to the shed. Since he hadn't asked her along, Yoko stayed in the main house with nothing to do. She stood in front of the glass doors with a round festival fan in her hand, admiring her reflection from various angles, but soon got bored and settled in a rattan chair with an illustrated book. I kept an eye on her while I prepared supper for the adults and set the table. Off in the distance came the sound of singing and the beating of a drum.

Yoko perked up her ears like a small animal and started up, then sank back into her chair, waiting for Taro to summon her to go. But Taro did not appear.

Too impatient to wait, she flew outside. Soon I could hear her calling his name over and over by the shed. "Taro! Taro! Taro!" The cries grew more insistent: "Taro-Taro-Taro! T-A-A-R-O-O!" The last was a screech.

The shed was close to her father's study, so I grew concerned. Mrs. Utagawa poked her head out of the kitchen and looked at me as if to say, "What's all the noise about?" I was forced to step outside into the dark and do something about it. The door to the shed was open, but the lights were out, the interior pitch dark. Just inside the doorway stood Yoko. I went closer and saw that she was clutching her fan in her tiny fist, her frizzy hair flaring out as she glared furiously at Taro, who lay on the upper bunk staring at the ceiling.

Pale moonlight filtered in at a low angle behind her.

"All right, never mind, I'll go by myself! Don't blame me if I get lost." With that she turned, whirling her long sleeves, and went outside. To think that the worst threat she could come up with was that she might get lost made me smile in spite of myself.

Taro sat up and stared morosely through the open door for a second, then bounded down, grabbed a flashlight hanging from a peg, and went off in pursuit.

I noticed then that there was a full moon that night.

I stopped to close the shed door, so by the time I reached the gate Taro had just caught up with Yoko some way up the slope. I watched them with a wary eye, wondering what would happen next. Yoko kept right on walking, paying him no attention. He must have grabbed her by the arm, for I heard her cry out with exaggerated pain, "Ow, that hurts!"

Immediately afterward, I saw her start sobbing like a little child again, and then, between convulsive sobs I caught the faint sound of her shrill command: "Say you're sorry! Say you're sorry!" As she saw it, she had sacrificed the pleasure of spending time with the others in Karuizawa in order to be with Taro in Oiwake, and it made no sense that he should be so grumpy. Anyway, in the end, as he alone knew—and knew only too well—she held absolute sway over him.

"You apologize!" The demand rang out more insistently.

In the white light of the full moon I saw Taro drop down on his knees and, supporting himself with both hands, lay his forehead flat on the ground in an attitude of abject apology. The flashlight he'd laid down shone on the pebbles. I gasped as Yoko slipped off one wooden clog and put her bare foot on his head to press it down farther. There was no need for me to intrude, however. As soon as her toes touched his head, she lost her balance and toppled over, landing on the ground beside him. Now she began bawling even harder, fists in her eyes, elbows sticking out in the air. Taro jumped up, grabbed her by the hands, and pulled her up off the ground. Then he was on his knees again. He took her bare foot in his hands and slipped the wooden clog back on, then brushed the dirt off the hem of her *yukata*. His slim figure was radiant in the light of the moon.

I watched in bemusement as the two children disappeared hand in hand up the dark mountain path to the strains of the "Tokyo Ballad."

Yoko stayed for ten days in Oiwake, as planned. As for myself, I went the next morning to stay with my family in Saku for a two-night visit and then directly back to Karuizawa. How the children spent the rest of their time in Oiwake, I don't know. But over and over again I saw in my mind's eye those two small figures climbing the mountain path, like a vision from another world.

THAT SUMMER, TARO showed up in Karuizawa again. First he came with Mrs. Utagawa, bringing Yoko back from Oiwake. One look at his face told me he was braced for whatever might come. I suspect that Mrs. Utagawa had hesitated to bring him after what had happened the time before, but he must have insisted on coming.

Since it wasn't Sunday, instead of a full meal at the Shigemitsu villa we had a simple lunch at the Saegusas', where there was no separate *servants' hall* but a spacious kitchen with plenty of room for the help to eat. Taro ate alongside Chizu and me without batting an eye. After the meal, Harue came in and said to Taro, "Thanks so much for coming! You are *such* a help." Then she handed him a pile of wet old newspapers—"This is how they clean windows in England"—and set him to washing all the windows in the house, from the attic to the first floor. He took this in his stride. He seemed to have told Yoko in advance what things would be like for him in Karuizawa, because when she came darting up to him while he was straddling a windowsill and polishing a pane, he couldn't conceal his pleasure, but only spoke to her for a few minutes before sending her back to the other children. Since they were playing doubles on the tennis court, she would plainly rather have watched or even helped him work for as long as the tennis game lasted. She left dragging her feet.

The window-washing wasn't even half done when night began to fall and it was time for him to leave, so the next day he got up early and took the bus to Karuizawa by himself. It took him all day to finish. As usual, Yoko scampered back and forth, but with Mrs. Utagawa absent, there was no one to be concerned about her comings and goings, and I doubt if anyone noticed but me.

There in the highlands, by the end of August, autumn winds begin to blow, and from that year on, that became our cue to close up the summer houses in both Karuizawa and Oiwake. Once we were back in Tokyo, the daily routines of life got under way again.

# 6

# A Stolen Day

WIND AND FOG, pine and birch, horned beetles and stag beetles, slowly rotting windowsills and dirty stucco walls, stairs that creaked with every step, the smell of wood burning in the fireplace, the clink of delicate china teacups on saucers, the laughter of a bevy of lovely women—to Yoko, Karuizawa was a place where these were familiar, established things. But for Taro, Karuizawa could only symbolize a closed world into which she might one day disappear, removed from him before he knew it; a world that he would never belong to or make his own. For as long as he could remember he had lived in darkness, and then Yoko had suddenly come and lit up his life, like a fairy. The fear that she might as suddenly vanish must always have been there. But from the time he set foot in Karuizawa that summer, what had been a vague dread turned to clear alarm.

When summer ended and he went back to the city, Taro naturally began to look on Seijo as Tokyo's version of Karuizawa. Just as in Karuizawa, there was in Seijo a pair of neighboring houses inhabited in the same way by the same people, among them the boy Masayuki. And so naturally enough, on Saturdays when Yoko went there for her piano lesson he could no longer see her off with an easy mind. One time he came up with the idea of using the money he'd earned in Karuizawa to board the train and see her all the way to Seijo, but Yoko had a fit. "No, don't! I don't want you to!" He sneaked on board a different car anyway, which was fine, except that when he stepped off the train at Seijo station, she caught sight of him and was so mad that she took the next train back.

What kept him from feeling too wretched was that Yoko was less drawn to that other world than he feared; she seemed surprisingly content with her life in Chitose Funabashi.

Proof of this was not long in coming. A Keio University student who lived nearby began coming over to tutor Yoko, and in due course she was safely accepted into Seijo Academy's middle school and began commuting there by train— but only for the first few days did she take the trouble to stop by the Saegusas on her way back, out of sheer novelty. After that she generally came straight home to Chitose Funabashi after school, and so life went on largely as before. She must have come back in part to keep her grandmother from feeling lonely. As for Taro, who can say whether she acted out of consideration for his feelings or because rather than be ignored in Seijo she preferred to come home and be pampered by him? Ever since that summer in Karuizawa, she seemed to understand in her own fashion that the time she spent with Taro was somehow unallowable, and yet she seemed happy to let it continue. "Today Grammy's baking

a cake," she might say when she set out, to explain that
she'd be dropping by the Saegusas later on, or she would
telephone—by then there was finally a telephone line in
Chitose Funabashi—to say she was there and would be staying till nighttime. "Sorry. I'll come back with Mama and
Yuko." About Masayuki, whom she saw now and then, she
talked in the same awed tone as ever. Yet she never seemed
to feel any more at home in Seijo than before. Taro was a
determined boy, and so I'm sure he thought a good deal
about all of this at the time, but he found no cause for further distress or jealousy.

In any case, considering what happened later, it seems a
miracle that those peaceful, humdrum days lasted right up
to the day that Mrs. Utagawa died. As the two children grew
up, they stopped romping around the house. Even in fine
weather they would sit on the sofa and talk—though Yoko
did most of the talking. At other times, they would sit reading something from the *Girls' Library of World Literature* or the
World Literature Series, or play records from her father's
collection. Any vocal music, whether in Italian, German, or
French, Yoko followed by reading the lyrics included inside
the cardboard sleeve, singing along heartily as Taro listened
in some embarrassment. The Utagawas had resolutely resisted television, but after they went and bought a set once
Yoko was in middle school, she and Taro would sometimes
watch a show as well. A television set was one thing the
Azumas had bought early on, so for Taro it was nothing special. He couldn't wait to turn it off, in fact, but during the
first couple of months, Yoko would sit mesmerized, mouth

open and eyes glued to the screen. She used to mimic the
hit song "Tokyo Dodonpa Girl," flouncing around the room;
every time the line "Dodonpa!" came up, she would take
a big step forward, then one to the right, then one to the
left, just like the singer onscreen, with Taro rolling about
on the floor laughing. Now and again one of the young Primavera staff taught her some proper dance steps too, and
she would try to teach Taro what she had learned. It used to
drive her to weepy hysterics when he just stood there like a
sack of potatoes. Also, at some point, the two of them took
over the responsibility of looking after the garden from the
aging Mrs. Utagawa. When they went outdoors together,
they tried to avoid any local middle school boys who were
sure to tease them—one more reason why they continued
to visit the vacant lot across the street, with the abandoned
house and air-raid shelter surrounded by clumps of pampas
grass. Sites like this were fast disappearing from the neighborhood, so it was a special place.

Things continued, therefore, much as usual. Takero went
on staying late at the university and Natsue went on spending most of her time in Seijo. As for Yuko, the older girl, she
took after her father as she matured, becoming increasingly
serious. Even after she came home from Seijo she would
practice the piano until as late as she could without disturbing the neighbors. When Eri and Mari went on to Seijo
Academy's high school, Yuko auditioned for the high school
attached to the prestigious Toho School of Music, met their
demanding standards for technique and ability, and was accepted. That, however, did not change her routine. After

class she took the bus to Seijo and stayed at the Saegusa house as she used to do, coming home with her mother in the evening. The Saegusas had another grand piano besides the one Fuyue used for teaching, and practicing on that was supposedly Yuko's reason for visiting there every day. But Yuko knew that if she ever did come home early, she would feel out of place, and that it was more natural, all things considered, for her to spend time with her cousins. She and her sister, Yoko, lived in different worlds; while they never quarreled, neither did they ever seem to have very much to talk about.

O-Tsune kept a low profile in the house out back, ingratiating as could be, since the rent never rose and Mrs. Utagawa supplied her with a steady stream of handouts. Taro's brothers had moved on to adult life, the younger of the two also finding a job straight out of middle school, which was probably why they lost interest in tormenting Taro. Mr. Azuma worked till late at night, so we hardly ever saw him.

Every summer Taro routinely accompanied Mrs. Utagawa to Oiwake, where there were always chores for him to do: going down to the main road to shop, doing the washing and hanging it up to dry, burning paper trash, burying kitchen garbage in a hole in the ground, raking leaves. Besides all that, he willingly sought other ways of making himself useful, and as the years went by, the old lady grew increasingly dependent on him. Yoko would spend the first two-thirds of her vacation in Karuizawa and the last in Oiwake: after losing her to Karuizawa for that period, Taro was always keen to have her all to himself in Oiwake. I was usually off

in Karuizawa, so I don't really know how the two of them
passed the time, but apparently they went walking quite a
bit. North of the main road was a trail marked as the Writ-
ers' Path, and in front of Mount Asama was a smaller mountain, Mount Sekison, with a cemetery at its base. Here and
there among the personal graves were stones in memory of
*meshimori onna*, "food-serving women"—women who had
ministered to travelers in the old post town inns. South of
the main road was virgin forest stretching from beyond the
irrigation canal all the way to the Miyota rice paddies, with
groves to explore on foot. The remains of sparklers were
always scattered in the garden, so they probably enjoyed
watching them blossom like small chrysanthemums in the
night air. Small birdhouses hung from branches too.

It became routine for Taro to be summoned to Karuizawa
to do the work of a handyman. In no time he was spending
the night two or three times a summer, sleeping on a futon
spread on the Saegusa kitchen floor. The grounds were
spacious and the house old, in need of all sorts of attention beyond the responsibility of a gardener, electrician, or
plumber. Taro was well aware that if he made a bad impression on any one of the three Saegusa sisters, his access to the
Utagawa home in Chitose Funabashi could be affected, and
so he always swallowed his feelings and got the job done.
The money they paid him no doubt helped him to bear it.
He must have found it reassuring too that spending time
in Karuizawa let him learn more about this other world of
Yoko's from which normally he was excluded. And although
the Saegusa sisters were taskmasters, as they grew used to

CANAL IN OIWAKE

seeing him summer after summer they became fond of him in their way. If they baked a nice meat pie, someone would say, "Oh, that boy Taro is coming tomorrow, we must give him some!" Old fountain pens or men's wristwatches that had been replaced by new ones were set aside for him— "That boy Taro could use this, don't you think?" To make it easier for him to come to Karuizawa, they even bought him a bicycle.

I don't know how aware Natsue may have been that Taro was in and out of the Chitose Funabashi house on a daily basis, but she made the exaggerated claim that "his family has been in the Utagawas' service for generations." It pleased her that the family she had married into was able to provide her own family with someone so useful to them.

In the Shigemitsu household, Yayoi seemed to feel it wasn't right to use a boy the same age as Masayuki as a handyman, and so, although the Demon made occasional demands of him, she herself never did. Ever since the sweater incident she kept her distance, as though she had done something wrong, and if she happened to pass him she would greet him with the sudden shyness of a girl. Taro in turn would respond with a bashfulness that is not unusual in adolescent boys but that was rare with him.

Time's pace was so slow and ambling that it scarcely seemed to move, but one thing did change quickly, and that was Taro's physique. He was rather late in developing, but from around his second year in middle school he shot up, and his voice deepened. Yoko entered puberty around the same time, but girls' physical changes are not as dramatic as boys' to begin with, and although her asthma had retreated, she was still delicate in health and childish in appearance. Taro, by contrast, though he had once been as sweet-looking as a girl, became decidedly masculine. Sometimes I would sit and marvel at his cheekbones and jaw. When he worked up a sweat, his armpits gave off a strong sweet-sour smell like that of some animal at night. I think he knew that once he became a full-grown man he could not go on being with Yoko the way he had all these years, so he did what he could to minimize this transformation, talking to her in a high voice and acting childish around her. Mrs. Utagawa had grown so used to seeing him every day, and he was so much like a grandson to her, that she may not have noticed the changes particularly. But others did.

Harue teased him outright. "Well, look at you! You've turned into quite a charmer, haven't you!"

She was right too. As he matured, the appeal of his rather unconventional looks gradually attracted attention. Now that I think of it, Yoko might have been the one most immune to his charms. Taro hung so eagerly on all she did, from morning to night, and Yoko took their rather peculiar relationship so much for granted, that she never seemed to realize how others might see him.

Harue even made the same uncalled-for comment to her sister Natsue: "You know something? That boy Taro is turning into a real charmer."

"Is he?"

"Yes, indeed. If he gets any more grown-up, you'd better not let him hang around Yoko too much."

That conversation took place in Karuizawa, and it must have stuck in Natsue's mind. Some six months later, one balmy Sunday morning, she and I were in the kitchen of the Chitose Funabashi house, making breakfast with the windows open, in an atmosphere fragrant with the smell of coffee. From out back we could plainly hear O-Tsune yelling angrily: "The way you pigs stuff yourselves, you eat up every yen we earn!"

Natsue and I exchanged wide-eyed looks. Then, as if remembering what Harue had said that time, she turned with a frown to Yoko, who was setting the table with her sister, and asked, "Does Taro still come over every day?"

"Not *every* day," Yoko lied, her face bent toward the table as she laid out the knives and forks.

"It's one thing to help him with his schoolwork, but you mustn't spend all your time with a boy like that."

Yoko was silent. By then she couldn't possibly have helped Taro with his schoolwork, but there was no point in her saying so.

"He will only have a bad influence on you."

When Yoko didn't answer this but just kept on with her work, head down, Natsue raised her eyebrows. Takero, who had been drinking his morning coffee and reading the paper, spoke up. "Look, there's no need to worry about Taro. He may have grown up with those people back there, but he's no lout. I've seen him at Oiwake. The boy knows how to behave."

"You may think so, but Yoko will be starting high school next year, and I don't think it's right for her to be spending so much time with him."

"Maybe so, but once she's in high school, things will change anyway."

Yoko had just turned fourteen, but she was so small and childish for her age that she looked barely twelve, standing there beside her more mature sister. Looking at her, her mother evidently thought pressing the matter any further would be pointless and let it drop. Probably she ought to have had the girl spend her afternoons at the Saegusas' after school, but because of old Mrs. Utagawa, she wanted to avoid that.

A FEW MONTHS after that exchange, in the summer of 1963, after a long lull, time was jolted forward. It started in Oiwake when Taro noticed that the whites of old Mrs. Utagawa's eyes had turned yellow. When she went to Karuizawa Hospital to be examined, the diagnosis was senile jaundice, a sign that she didn't have long to live. Frail though she seemed, the old lady had a strong constitution, and had never been infected by her husband's syphilis. I always assumed she would live on for years, and the news left me dazed. It was decided that she should stay in Oiwake, since she would only suffer in the heat if she returned to Tokyo. Yoko came over from Karuizawa, and she and Taro looked after her together. Yoko's father spent more time there than usual that summer, and her mother came visiting several times, driven by Fuyue, who had just passed her driving test.

I too went over as often as I could to check on her condition.

AGED TREE

Taro and Yoko gave up trekking around the countryside so that she wouldn't be alone. But even though they learned how to cope, and could cook things she enjoyed, not having any adults in charge must have been tough for them on their own. When she saw me arrive, Yoko would jump up and down, clapping the tips of her fingers, and Taro looked relieved too. With the four of us together again, much the way it had been from the time Taro first began having after-school snacks with us, we felt like a family.

One day when I was staying there in Oiwake, I sat at the small dining table mending Mrs. Utagawa's night *yukata* while Yoko used some garden shears to snip green soybean pods off the stem before they were steamed. Mrs. Utagawa was in the tatami room next to us, dozing, and Taro was out on the porch with his schoolbooks spread on the folding table. Earlier when he tried to help Yoko, she had chased him away, insisting that he study. Some time ago Mrs. Utagawa had offered to pay his school fees and train fare, and he planned to take the exam for Shinjuku Municipal High School, his school of choice. Watching him write intently with his left hand, his face twisted in a scowl, I asked Yoko, "After Shinjuku High School, what will he do?"

"Go to the University of Tokyo."

"And then?"

"Be a doctor like Papa."

In her innocence, she seemed to think that everyone should end up like her father.

"When he's a doctor, what then?"

She paused in her snipping and cocked her head, considering.

"Spend all day every day in his lab, is that it?" I asked, teasing.

This seemed to catch her off guard, her round, childish face showing that a life like her father's wouldn't be much fun for those left at home. For a while she was stumped—but then her eyes lit up.

"He'll be somebody like Dr. Schweitzer, and work for the good of mankind."

Somehow she made it sound as if her father wasn't lifting a finger for "mankind." "Oh, really," I said, wanting to laugh. "Dr. Albert Azuma, is it?"

"That's right," she said, and slowly intoned in English: "*Doctor . . . Taro . . . Azuma.*" She clicked her shears triumphantly in the air.

"What about you?"

"Me?" The question seemed to surprise her. "I guess I'll work for the good of mankind too." Spoken with considerably less confidence.

While we carried on like this, Taro alternately looked up moodily at the sky or sighed and laid his cheek on his book. A swirl of unsettling thoughts—his guardian might soon die, he might never come to Oiwake again, might not go on being a frequent visitor in the Utagawa house or even be able to attend high school at all—must have fed a deepening anxiety that made studying impossible.

Nothing will ever be the same again: that thought surely preyed on him, and caused his usual caution and restraint to break down. Soon after this a scene took place that set Harue firmly against him. It was a little thing, but I doubt whether she ever forgave him for it.

IT HAPPENED TOWARD the end of summer, when I was in Karuizawa. The curtains in the dining room and parlor had been sent to the cleaner's for the first time in years, and when they came back the Saegusa sisters decided to have Taro rehang them. I phoned Oiwake, and the next afternoon he came over on his bicycle. The day was sweltering in a way that was unusual for Karuizawa, the atmosphere heavy with an oppressive languor. Taro had pedaled all the way under a burning sky, and his tanned arms and neck glistened in a most discomfiting way.

He had left Mrs. Utagawa asleep in the Oiwake house, and with Yoko there too he went straight to work, clearly eager to finish up and get back as soon as possible. The three sisters, on the other hand, were in a lazy, self-indulgent mood brought on by the heat and humidity. They sat sprawled on the chaise longue and armchairs in the parlor, fanning themselves and sipping glass after glass of iced tea while they chatted idly about nothing at all, watching without really seeing as Taro went back and forth between the dining room and the parlor, dripping with sweat. A crack of thunder and a rainstorm would have cleared the air, but as evening drew nearer the heat continued to simmer. In that setting, the presence of a new maid called Mie proved especially provocative.

That Mie was a problem. She was the third maid to enter the Saegusa household after Chizu: fresh out of middle school, a precocious little thing with a high bosom and rounded hips, the sort of girl whose whole body shouts her need to fall in love. I heard that back at the Seijo house, when she carried a tray in Masayuki's presence, her hands shook so much that everyone noticed and smiled. She fell hard for Taro the first time he came over in early summer to weed the garden, and ever since then had made herself the target of the sisters' teasing by dropping things, getting her orders mixed up, and giving little shrieks whenever he was around. Hearing the story of his origins one day put a damper on her ardor, but even so, once he was in front of her she seemed to lose control. That day too, she let out a series of funny little squeaks that might have been laughter or excitement, and for no good reason went in and out of rooms where he was. When he was hanging the curtains in the dining room, she went into the dining room, and when he was hanging them in the parlor, she went into the parlor.

He had finished putting up the lace curtains in both rooms and the heavy brocade drapes in the dining room. All that remained were the parlor drapes. Just then Mari, Eri, and Yuko came trooping in from a game of tennis, declaring it was just too hot out there, sheer torture! They tossed their rackets down carelessly, toweled themselves dry, and dabbed some ointment on their mosquito bites before taking the iced drinks I'd prepared. Then, each with a glass in hand, they sank wearily into chairs, just like their mothers.

At that point Taro reentered the parlor with the stepladder. When Harue caught sight of him, she looked around at everyone and whispered, "Watch now. Mie will come wandering in."

Sure enough, not long after he had set up the stepladder by the windows and started to hang the drapes, the door opened cautiously and Mie peered furtively in. She took one step inside the room before realizing that everyone's eyes were on her and fleeing in consternation.

"Now *that* is what's called a sex bomb," said Harue in a low voice as soon as the door was shut, eliciting a chorus of shrill protests from Mari, Eri, and Yuko. "I can't help it, there it is."

"A pity she's so short," said Natsue.

"No, shorter is better!" This from Fuyue. "A pocket pinup, they call it. Made in Japan to suit Japanese taste."

"The common man's taste," supplemented Harue.

After a languid silence, fanning the neck of her cotton dress with an ivory-handled fan, Harue turned and looked up at Taro, who was perched on top of the stepladder. "Taro," she said, "Mie's been popping in and out for no reason— had you noticed?" Her tone was teasing. She was addressing him directly by name nowadays. Instead of a reply, he only showed a trace of a wry smile and went on working in silence.

"Seems to me she has a bit of a crush on you."

Taro's smile disappeared as he stood facing the window, showing only a boyishly slender, stiff neck.

"Something wrong?" His failure to respond to her baiting made her perverse. She fluttered her fan as she continued to address the back of his neck. "Not your type?"

Still with his back to her, Taro said nothing. He kept working steadily, hands on the curtain rod.

"Girls like her are called pocket pinups, did you know that?" Still no response. Harue exchanged looks of roguish humor with her sisters and the three girls sitting in front of her before turning back to Taro and increasing the pressure. "Well? What do you say?"

He kept his back to her.

Harue drew up her shoulders and, with a certain hauteur, turned to face the front again. Then, in a deliberately flippant tone, she said, "Well, who could blame you? You've been spoiled, after all."

She looked around the room with satisfaction. Two sets of beautiful women from two generations were draped in various careless, almost seductive poses—the Saegusa sisters and three of their daughters, all but Yoko. The elder women were still lovely to look at, but Mari, Eri, and Yuko were like flower buds on the point of opening, mirror images of the beauty of their mothers in their youth.

From the top of the stepladder, Taro turned and looked down at the room. He was holding the brocade drapes in his arms, puzzled. Harue's remark made no sense to him. But then, seeing her satisfied gaze sweep the room, he understood, and a smile came to his lips—the sort of smile people wear when confronted by human folly—a detached, dismissive smile. Not boyish in the least, either, but completely mature.

As Harue turned to look back at him again, she unfortunately caught sight of that smile. Worse yet, when they saw her frown the others followed her line of sight, and so everyone in the room saw it.

That was all there ever was to it, but I do believe that that single incident turned Harue permanently against him. Afterward Yoko's sister Yuko came into the kitchen and murmured in my ear, "Doesn't Aunt Harue know he's in love with Yoko?"

Afraid that if I said something amiss it would get back to Natsue, I gave Yuko a noncommittal look. Her face was very like her mother's, but its expression could not have been more different. When had she become so grown-up, I wondered.

Later, Taro rode his bicycle back to Oiwake through the evening gloom. Many years were to pass before he set foot on that Karuizawa property again.

SUMMER ENDED, AND Mrs. Utagawa went back to Tokyo stretched out on the back seat of a car driven by Harue's husband, Hiroshi. Dr. Matsumiya examined her and found there were already signs of dropsy of the belly. Counting back, I realized she had been able to use the Oiwake cottage for only five summers.

The old lady knew that her disease was mortal and, before it was too late, shortly after returning to Tokyo she gave her will verbally to Takero and Natsue. In part, it referred to me. She asked them to let me have things of hers that I might want at such time as I married: her low writing desk; her full-length mirror, its frame carved in the Kamakura style; her paulownia dresser. Takero of course had no objection, and Natsue, too, readily agreed. She was sentimental by nature, and there were tears in her eyes as she knelt by her mother-in-law's futon, nodding.

Mrs. Utagawa's other request referred to Taro. He had a good head on his shoulders, she said, and had done many things for her. Over the years she'd grown fond of him, and although of course she shouldn't have gone ahead and done this without first consulting them, she had promised to help him financially so that he could go on with his schooling. He was applying to a municipal high school not far away, one that would cost very little in the way of either transportation or fees, and she asked that her funeral be kept simple and her savings used to help him go there. Even after that, she wanted Takero and Natsue as far as possible to go on helping him to get an education. She avoided using the word "university," perhaps afraid that Takero would balk at the extent of the commitment involved and say no. When she was finished, he was silent for a moment before saying quietly, "All right, Mother." Natsue chimed in, "We can easily come up with the money, don't worry," her eyes filling again with tears.

But as it happened, Mrs. Utagawa had not finished making her final wishes known. One afternoon around the beginning of November, I had been busy unstitching some of her old night *yukata* and sewing them into diapers. As I sat beside her, folding the diapers, she suddenly said, out of nowhere:

"Don't breathe a word of this to Takero or Natsue."

She had been staring up at the ceiling, but then turned her head toward me and looked at me. "If Yoko wants to marry him . . . if she says she's willing, then I want you to do all in your power to make it happen."

She had been thinking about Taro the whole time.

"It's a great deal to ask, I know." She turned her face up again and closed her eyes. Tears rolled down her cheeks. "But otherwise, it's just too cruel."

When I had finished folding the diapers I went and sat alone on the sofa, stunned and at a loss. Once Mrs. Utagawa passed on, what excuse would Taro have for coming over every day? What could I do for him on my own? I had no idea. In the lingering afternoon sun, the Formica table and vinyl-covered chairs stood out with strange clarity, along with the clock, vase, sugar bowl, and other objects on the built-in shelves. For a moment I felt as if I were seeing them with Mrs. Utagawa's dying eyes.

MY FEARS PROVED unnecessary. At the end of the year, well before the old lady died, the Utagawa family was swept by a sudden breaking wave that changed everything. Though I had never dreamed such a thing could happen, I myself had no choice but to leave the family's service. It all began with Takero's promotion. He was an associate professor at the University of Tokyo, specializing in immunology, and early in December he learned that he had been offered a professorship at Hokkaido University in Sapporo. For a long time he had not been on good terms with the senior professors in his department, and he was eager to leave. Talks with Hokkaido had been ongoing since spring. He kept this to himself, however, until the professorship could be signed, sealed, and delivered.

Knowing her, he assumed Natsue—who would object even to a move to nearby Yokohama—would bitterly oppose moving to the northernmost island, and at that point he doubted his chances of getting the offer position anyway. When and if it became official, he would try to persuade her, and if she resisted he would simply go alone. Sure enough, when the time came, she refused to accompany him.

"Why should someone like me, born and bred in Tokyo, have to go all the way to a godforsaken place like Sapporo? Isn't your stubbornness the whole problem to begin with? You know very well I've got my work here with Primavera. A woman's career means nothing at all, is that what you men think?" She was furious, as expected, and I worried about old Mrs. Utagawa, listening to their raised voices as she lay on her futon in the back room.

But in a week or so, word came of a different promotion, this time for Harue's husband, Hiroshi. He was being transferred to the New York branch of Mitsubishi Corporation for several years, with his family. The arrangement was still informal, but definite nevertheless.

The evening she came home after hearing this news, Natsue sat with me and cried like a baby. "Why does Harue get to go to New York while I have to go to Sapporo? It's not fair." But already she seemed resigned. Whereas before, Harue had been deeply sympathetic ("How awful! Sapporo, really!"), as soon as talk of her own impending move came up, she changed her tune and began urging her sister to accompany her husband to Sapporo. Since she and her family too would be away from Tokyo, the timing was right, and nothing was so important for a man as knowing that things at home were under control so that he could focus on his work. Besides, if she let him have his way now, someday later on she would be better placed to have her own way, Harue argued seriously. She even offered to let Yuko, soon a third-year high school student, stay with them in New York. This was a great comfort to Natsue. Yuko and her cousins Mari and Eri had always done everything together, and if one of them had to stay behind, it would be terrible. What was more important, Harue's offer meant that Yuko could start studying the piano abroad, and at little cost to the Utagawas. Since Yuko was so serious about her music, Natsue had long been thinking of sending her abroad but had no idea how to come up with that kind of money. Should she ask Grampy Saegusa for help? Would that even be enough? Then this suggestion came along. Though the thought of her favorite daughter going overseas made Natsue feel desolate, this arrangement solved the problem neatly.

This was a time when the very word "America" had a glamor that is simply impossible to imagine today. Once before, Hiroshi had been posted overseas, to Hong Kong for two years, but when that happened Harue had used Primavera to beg off going with him. When talk of Takero's going to Sapporo first came up, she joined Natsue in asking indignantly, "What about Primavera?" But no sooner did she get wind of the move to New York than she made up her mind to quit the business, leaving it in the hands of her best pupil, the young woman who sat at the children's table when I first met the Saegusas and who occasionally visited them in Karuizawa.

One Sunday morning near Christmas, matters resolved themselves, as Natsue told her husband she would go with him. Takero beamed with pleasure.

"Primavera has fulfilled its *historical mission*, " he said, using the English phrase.

"What does that mean?" she asked, so he repeated it in Japanese.

This was just when Japan was entering a period of rapid economic growth, and department store racks were lined with stylish clothes produced in bulk at affordable prices. The next day Natsue repeated her husband's remark to me. "It's true," she said, "Primavera has fulfilled its *historical mission*." It amused me that she found saying it in English more persuasive. To me the words seemed to apply to my own life as well.

"So he's going to be a full professor." Mrs. Utagawa expressed pleasure at the news before adding wistfully, "I would have liked to go to Sapporo too."

At the start of the new year, 1964, Dr. Matsumiya predicted that her end would be quick, but she held on over a month longer. Her death came in early February. When they interred her cremated remains in Kichijoji, Taro was allowed to go along.

No one was thinking about Yoko. Everyone just took it for granted that she would simply accompany her parents north. Only when another professor who had made the same switch of universities—and had pushed hard for Takero's promotion—mentioned that Fuji Girls' High School would be a good choice did they take the younger child into consideration. "That's right! Something must be done about a high school for Yoko." Takero went with her for the entrance exam, using it as an opportunity to scout for a house to rent. The ferry between Aomori and Hakodate alone took four hours, and that was after a twenty-one-hour train ride from Tokyo. When Yoko got back, she was limp and gray with exhaustion.

Only she and I know how devastated Taro was by the news. As the day of departure drew near, even she was increasingly somber, and when her mother wasn't watching she would slip out to the back yard to exchange a few words with him, even at night. Unlike most boys, once he started crying Taro had a hard time stopping, a trait she usually found exasperating—but now that they faced separation, for once she was patient and consoling.

The Utagawas left for Sapporo in time for the start of the school year in April. Taro secretly tagged along as far as Ueno station. I saw his face peering out from behind a distant column, looking like death. Yoko seemed not to notice. She was an ungovernable child, and if she had spotted him there's no telling what she might have done amid the crowd of people there to see the family off, so I pretended not to see him.

Taro successfully entered Shinjuku Municipal High School. This must have irked his brothers no end, as both had joined the workforce straight out of middle school. But Takero, as head of the Utagawa family, had handed their father a full year's school fees in a lump sum, including the cost of commuting, and he also had authority as their landlord, so Mr. Azuma made them simmer down.

I GOT MARRIED. Starting with the fish seller, I had had my share of proposals, including one from an office worker in a business suit, but I turned them all down until, before I knew it, I was all of twenty-seven, well past the usual marrying age in those days. I had been with the Utagawas going on eleven years, ever since I was seventeen. The family did show some concern, but I was good at making myself useful, and besides, I always made a face when the subject of marriage came up, which was how I had managed to stay single so long. Now, however, postponing matrimony any longer would have obliged the Utagawas to take me with them to Sapporo, since they were unwilling to leave me on my own in Tokyo and I would not hear of going back to Saku. Taking me along would probably have meant looking after me for the rest of my life, a considerable financial burden—not to mention the additional burden of knowing that being in their employ had made me miss my chance at marriage. Times had changed after the war, and neither responsibility was one that any family would have been comfortable taking on. Once it was settled that they were all going to Sapporo, they began to ask around on my behalf.

"Fumiko would make any man a superb wife!"

Left to myself, I would rather not have married at all. After over a decade with the same family, I was not the same Fumiko who had first come here from the country. The sort of man I would have liked to marry—the sort whose company I might have enjoyed—would not have given me a second glance. Even if a likely mate did exist somewhere out there, what chance did I have of meeting him? I was never one to paint a rosy picture of marriage to begin with, but the older I became and the more I understood of life, the less romantic I was. Rather than marry, I would have preferred to make a go of it alone in Tokyo, even if that meant just scraping by. But my refusing to marry at that late date would only have caused a problem for the Utagawas, and that I couldn't allow. Whether marriage offers are generally available for the asking, or whether this one came along purely by chance, I don't know, but a suitable offer did come along quite quickly.

He was a company employee three years older than me. Dr. Matsumiya down by the station had seen the way I looked after old Mrs. Utagawa, and he recommended me to a frequent visitor to his clinic as soon as he heard from Natsue that they were on the lookout for a husband for me. The man in question had graduated from high school in Chiba and was working for a fairly large pharmaceutical company. Just his being an office worker was enough to make him good husband material by the standards of the day, and for someone without a college education he had a very promising future, having caught the boss's eye, apparently. Moreover, his people ran a futon store in Kashiwa, and his elder

brother and sister-in-law were living with his parents and
would eventually take over the business, so there would be
few if any in-law problems for me to worry about. On top
of it all, he was good-looking, not slow-witted, and well-
spoken. I suppose because he was involved in sales, he had
a smooth, persuasive way of talking. Anybody could see he
was too good a match for someone like me. The only problem was that I myself wasn't particularly drawn to him, nor
was there any apparent reason why he should find me to his
liking. Thinking about it later, I could see that not knowing
why in the world he would choose me did secretly bother
me from the start. I decided to go ahead with the marriage
anyway, partly because I felt obliged to marry quickly and
partly because he seemed like someone I could introduce to
the Saegusa sisters without embarrassment. I must admit I
had my share of vanity. However strongly I felt I owed it to
the Utagawas to marry, I entered the marriage with shallow
motives.

Things moved along at quite a clip. The matter was settled while Mrs. Utagawa was still alive, so I had my hands
full. By then she was as willful as a child, and some days
her mind was unclear, but when I reported to her that I
was now engaged, she sounded like her old self. "I see," she
said. "Congratulations." Then, in a phlegmy voice, staring
up at the ceiling, she asked, "Do you have enough money
saved up?"

"Yes, ma'am," I said. "I have a long-term savings account."
I thought she was worried about the money I would need
for the wedding, but I was wrong.

"Fumiko, this may sound like meddling, but it's a good idea to set aside some money for yourself that no one else knows about. There are two kinds of people in this world, those who have something to fall back on and those who don't, and which one you are makes all the difference."

That, I think, was the last coherent exchange I ever had with her. It might not have been the sort of advice that would occur to a woman who had had an arranged marriage and raised a family in the usual way, and I felt as if she had dashed cold water on my prospects, but from that moment on, any intention I might have had of proudly showing my future husband the savings I had accumulated over the past decade began to fade.

"Getting married? You, Fumiko?" Taro looked incredulous. He may have thought that I existed solely for him and Yoko.

Our formal marriage interview came at the end of the year. For us to make our final vows by the end of March, before the Utagawas left for Sapporo, seemed like rushing things. My fiancé had no objection, though, so I hastily got ready and we had a simple wedding ceremony in mid-March. The guests on my side included Harue and Fuyue from the Saegusas, the entire Utagawa family, my parents, and my siblings and their spouses, who came down for the occasion. Uncle Genji, by then in his mid-sixties, with a head of white hair, came accompanied by his husky-voiced partner. Before the wedding, we visited his house in Soto Kanda to pay our respects. All my uncle did was laugh and say he'd figured I was never planning on marrying at all.

Perhaps no longer as sharp as he'd been in his younger days, he was pleased that I seemed content with my choice. My parents insisted on doing something for me after all this time, and so they paid for our honeymoon. I wore a rented bridal kimono and, for the reception afterward, a Primavera cocktail dress. After a four-day trip to the seaside resort of Atami, the first thing I did was go back to the Utagawa house to help with the move. I saw the family off to Sapporo, then moved my own things into the apartment my husband had rented for us in Iogi. As part of my dowry, the Utagawas bought me a fine chest of drawers—Western-style—at a luxury department store that had recently opened. They also told me to help myself to any of the furniture they weren't sending along to Sapporo, but our apartment was so small—just two tatami rooms, one six-mat and the other four-and-a-half-mat, and a tiny kitchen—that all I took were the things that Mrs. Utagawa had bequeathed to me. Even so, those items added to all the stylish clothes in my trousseau amounted to quite a pile. My husband was bug-eyed when he saw what a person of property his new bride was.

That husband of mine turned out to have problems after all. Ordinarily he was pleasant enough, but it took less than a month for me to discover that when he was drunk and alone with me a change came over him. He became mean and spiteful. Certainly I tried the best I knew to be a good wife. I took in mending from the neighbors to help out, picking up the basics from a pile of how-to-sew manuals that Natsue had given me when she didn't need them any-more. On my own, I made do with simple meals of hot tea over cold rice so that I could give him an extra side dish for his evening meal. He seemed happy enough, but for some reason, whenever he had too much to drink, all trace of contentment would evaporate and complaints would come pouring out instead. As the sake took effect he would pick away at what he saw as my faults: I was only a middle school graduate; I talked in a fancy, "stuck-up" way; I somehow looked down on him. This last point had never crossed my mind, but as soon as he said it I realized he might be right, though how on earth had he figured it out? I'm ashamed to say that when he accused me of this I felt myself smiling—which of course only made him madder.

Once he started drinking, he couldn't stop. One night, past two in the morning, I decided I had listened to enough. I laid out my futon and pretended to go to sleep, but shock-ingly, he threw a cup of cold water in my face and just went on with his badgering. Luckily he never resorted to actual violence, but it was plain from the first that he had no inter-est in making our marriage a genuine partnership. In the daytime I used to wonder what prompted him to marry me in the first place.

It was six months before I found out the truth. He had a long-standing relationship, going back six or seven years, with his boss's wife. When he learned that rumors about the two of them were circulating, he rushed into marriage to cover up the affair, taking it for granted that someone like me would have no choice but to stay quiet even if I found out about the other woman.

WHILE ALL THIS was going on, around the start of the rainy season in early summer I received a bulky envelope from Yoko: a short two-page letter for me and, enclosed with it, a long letter addressed to Taro. According to her, they had been corresponding ever since she went to live in Sapporo, and even though she heard from him barely once or twice a month and the letters he wrote were innocent, nothing she couldn't show her parents, her mother complained that this was still too much to be getting from "a boy like that." Anyway she had a favor to ask. Would I please hand the enclosed letter directly to Taro within the next few days? It contained some money that he needed, and she knew from him that his stepmother was opening his mail without permission. There wasn't a word about how things were going in Sapporo or any proper reference to my marriage, just a line tacked on at the end: "How are you two lovebirds getting along?" Very silly indeed.

Considering all that I owed her parents, I ought to have ignored this request. Yet I also had in mind the request that old Mrs. Utagawa had made toward the end. I wavered, but two or three days later I went over to the house in Chitose Funabashi around dinnertime, when I thought Taro would be home, and caught him just as he was coming out through the gate. Although it was only three months since I'd last seen him, his shoulders had broadened and his cheeks looked sharper, as if because he no longer needed to hide how grown-up he was getting to be. He seemed altogether a different person. I expected him to pocket the letter, but he opened it on the spot, giving me a glimpse of sheets of stationery and thousand-yen bills. He was quick-witted, and probably opened the letter in front of me in case he needed my help with something. But as he read, his face stiffened. I dared not ask him what the money was for. We boarded the train together. He said he had to work part-time two nights a week, three hours at a stretch, at the factory along the Koshu Highway where Mr. Azuma worked.

"It's to pay my board." The ironic lift of his eyebrow showed his annoyance.

About my married life he made no inquiry, but neither did he make any silly comment about it as Yoko had done. He got off the train at Gotokuji and walked away from me, a person somewhere between a boy and a young man.

Soon summer was upon us, with the Bon festival holidays just ahead. My husband, who apparently didn't get on with his elder brother and sister-in-law, said there was no point in our going to visit his parents in Kashiwa, and offered to go with me if I wanted to visit my family in Saku. I instantly lost all desire to go there after hearing this. If I went at all, it would be to steep myself in the atmosphere of the old, familiar villa in Karuizawa, but I doubted whether I could take off on my own and leave my husband with my parents. The thought that he might insist on going along to Karuizawa to pay his respects gave me the shivers, and so I abandoned all thought of going back. For the first time in a decade I spent my summer in Tokyo. Oppressed by the heat, the humidity, and the lack of space, I kept the fan going as I sat nose to nose with my husband in our tiny apartment. With the 1964 Olympic Games scheduled for the fall, Tokyo was full of construction projects, and the constant noise and dust made the summer feel that much more sticky and gritty.

THIS EXPLAINS WHY it was well into the fall before I learned about Yoko and Taro's first "misconduct."

A postcard came from Fuyue saying that the Utagawa family had decided to sell the property in Chitose Funabashi, land and all, and would I please come over to help her decide which furnishings to discard and which to send to Sapporo? And so one fine autumn day I met her at the station.

I knew that the Utagawas had been living in a rented house in Sapporo, but now, it seemed, they were planning to build a place of their own. Since professors at Hokkaido University were considered prominent figures locally, it wouldn't do to get a cheap sort of place like the Chitose Funabashi house; but they didn't have enough savings to build something suitable, so Natsue had immediately suggested putting their Tokyo property up for sale, since it had no sentimental value for her anyway. Next year Yuko would be graduating from high school in New York; in order to send her to an American conservatory, even with Grampy's promise to help out, they would still have to scrape together their share of the dollar-based tuition. That also contributed to the decision to sell.

It was daytime when we arrived, too early for Taro to be there next door. I went out behind the house and called to

O-Tsune from the veranda to let her know we'd come to clear the place out. All her old insolence was back in the thin, sneering smile on her face when she emerged. Her behavior, which gave me a jolt, had something to do with the "misconduct" I heard about on returning to the main house.

"I wonder if the Azumas will leave without giving any trouble," I said when Fuyue and I sat down side by side on the sofa in the chilly main room, still wearing our coats. One of the two rental houses was already empty.

"Oh, they will, all right," said Fuyue. "They signed a pledge to leave whenever asked to do so. They're not actually entitled to a single yen, but after Taro's misconduct, now they've even come into some money."

"Misconduct?" I looked at her in surprise and confusion. "Money?"

"That's right. Takero has already given it to them."

"To the Azumas?"

"Yes, didn't Natsue say anything about it to you?"

"No, ma'am, she didn't." I shook my head with a vague sense that the inevitable had finally happened. I looked around the room. I felt that the ghosts of Yoko and Taro when they were little were still there, loath to leave this place where every nick in the posts and walls was familiar. I heard Yoko's excited chatter in the distance, followed by the sound of footsteps running down the corridor.

The alleged misconduct had taken place that summer in Karuizawa. With her sister and cousins all off in New York, and Masayuki studying at a cram school in Tokyo for the summer, young Yoko had the place to herself. She passed the time lounging about reading novels, working in the garden, going for long walks, and, after starting singing lessons in Sapporo, accompanying herself on the piano. Then one day she left for a walk and didn't come back, even after dark. Natsue's natural instincts must have come to the fore, for it suddenly dawned on her where her daughter was. She had Fuyue drive her over to Oiwake, and the moment they got out of the car, Yoko came flying barefoot onto the porch. Natsue charged straight at her, sending her staggering, with Taro standing stock-still just inside the house.

"Shame on you—acting like a bitch in heat!" Those were ugly words, coming from this well-mannered woman. Hysterical, she started to beat the girl until Taro rushed out and grabbed her by the arm.

Yoko was hysterical too. "It's not his fault," she cried out in tears. "I invited him here in a letter."

When I heard about the letter, I realized that the one I'd brought to Chitose Funabashi that day must have specified when the two should meet up in Oiwake, and had contained Taro's train fare. Yoko had apparently kept quiet to her mother about the role I played—less to protect me, I'm sure, than to keep me in reserve for possible use in the future.

Later, after removing her husband's dictionaries, the good dishes, and the relatively new bedding, Natsue had the telephone, water, gas, and electricity cut off at the Oiwake cottage and shut it up. With old Mrs. Utagawa dead, there was no point in keeping it going anymore; until Harue and her family returned to Japan, even if Takero joined them, the house in Karuizawa was large enough for everyone.

"That child never did know how to behave," Yoko's mother would grumble about her.

Judging from their appearance when they were found, Yoko and Taro had not been intimate, but it was clear that if they were left on their own, it was only a matter of time.

This "misconduct" also provided the Utagawas with a ready excuse to sever all ties with the Azuma family. They had been on the point of disposing of their property in Chitose Funabashi anyway. In line with the original agreement, there was no need to offer any compensation for forced removal, but to honor his mother's dying wish, Takero handed over a sizable sum of money for Taro's further education, at the same time instructing the family to vacate the house and make sure that Taro had no further contact with Yoko.

Fuyue laughed and said, "Takero is so conscientious, they ended up throwing good money after bad."

When her father told her that she mustn't have anything more to do with Taro, Yoko apparently had a fit. "Papa, you're the one who said people aren't born higher or lower than each other!" To which he replied that that was not the problem; the problem was that any young man who would arrange to meet a fifteen-year-old girl behind her parents' back could not be trusted. This was a perfectly reasonable answer, but how could she possibly see someone like Taro except behind her parents' back? Anyway, once they had discovered how big a role he played in their daughter's life, Natsue and Takero must have been relieved to be able to cut their ties with the Azuma family, even if it did mean "throwing good money after bad," since there was no telling how Yoko would have acted later when Taro went on to high school and university. Takero was a fair-minded person, with a strong sense of responsibility too, so I'm sure he wondered whether the steps he was taking were unfair to Taro, but as a father he naturally had to give his own daughter's interests priority.

Natsue blamed Takero's mother, saying it was her fault for letting Taro practically live in their house the way he had. The point could also be made that Natsue herself was no less at fault for turning Yoko over to old Mrs. Utagawa and practically living in Seijo. But as someone who knew both women, I can say that without a doubt, the arrangement contributed greatly to each one's happiness during all those years. In addition, the way Natsue gravitated to Seijo wasn't only due to the general decline in the family fortunes but also to Takero's being so wrapped up in his work and so seldom at home. All in all, it was hard to know where to lay the blame.

"The ties have been cut," Fuyue said to me, "but if the Azumas do make any claims, I hate to ask, but could you step in and handle it, Fumiko?" She also made another request: when it was time to turn the family's unwanted belongings over to the secondhand dealer, she, Fuyue, would be there, but she hoped I would be around when the Azumas left their place.

They moved out on a Sunday toward the end of the year. When I arrived, the Azumas had just begun loading their things into a vehicle borrowed from the subcontractor. It was not even a regular truck but a battered Daihatsu

Midget—a three-wheeled minivan, so popular that at one point it was everywhere on the city streets and even I knew its name.

When O-Tsune saw me she smirked and said, "That girl of theirs is mental, isn't she?" She said it straight out, without any pretended deference. She must have felt she'd had all she was ever going to get from the Utagawas.

"She's a nympho, that's what." This comment from the eldest boy caused some jeering laughter.

The other brother got into the act. "Taro's got a big one, like a horse."

Silently Taro helped load the van. Next to his brothers I could see that tall though he was, his build was still slim and boyish. If those two brutes took him on together, he wouldn't stand a chance. The memory of him years ago with his arm in a sling came back to mind.

He saw me but kept his lips pressed tight, avoiding my eye. He was trying to load a big carton onto the bed of the van by himself.

I went over to him and told him, "If anything happens, come to me," and for the first time he looked me in the face with a strained expression.

Mr. Azuma alone said a proper sort of farewell, and handed me the address in Kamata where they were going.

AFTER NEW YEAR'S, when the plum buds were tinged with color and spring was in the air, I got a divorce. I had found out about the other woman not long before. When I was alone I often used to open the drawer in the paulownia dresser old Mrs. Utagawa bequeathed to me, take out the bankbook I kept secret from my husband, and look at it. He had married me trusting me to keep quiet if I ever discovered what was going on, but once he realized I was bent on divorce, he seemed afraid I might make a fuss and call attention to the situation, so everything was settled swiftly. Our marriage lasted less than a year and was childless.

Once divorced, I felt that I'd paid my dues to society. Rather than pain, there was only a sense of liberation. Now, finally, I could live my life as I chose. I took with me only the things that were mine to begin with and rented a small flat—one four-and-a-half-mat room and a cramped kitchen—in a humble, two-story wooden building in the Sangenjaya area of Tokyo: Evergreen Apartments No. 2. Even after being stung for key money and the security deposit, I had enough left to live on for a few months, but in any case I soon found an opening at a company that manufactured measuring instruments, with an office in Shibuya. The company was small, and I was already twenty-eight. Assuming they were unlikely to check up on what I wrote about my background, I fiddled my educational record on my résumé, putting down that I had graduated from Saku High School. For my work experience too, I exaggerated the size of Uncle Genji's restaurant and said that I had worked there in the office. My handwriting is good, if I may say so, and that got me noticed. Also the interview went well, and I was hired more or less on the spot. With my smooth telephone manner and a decent wardrobe from the Saegusa sisters, no one had any reason to doubt me. I couldn't help feeling a bit amazed that I had actually pulled off this deceit, being a cautious sort of person, but honesty would only have led to tedious, physically tiring jobs, and I chose the lesser of two evils. Earlier, I had worked up enough courage to tell my uncle about the divorce. Seeing me in tears, he blamed himself for not seeing through someone who turned out to be such a rat, and promised to do all he could to help. He approved of my falsifying my work record and agreed to be my reference.

THAT SUMMER, I went back home for the Bon festival holidays and visited Karuizawa for the first time in two years. Fuyue came out on the porch in an apron and rubber gloves and cried out, "Fumiko!" before ushering me through the dining room into the kitchen, where she brought me up-to-date. She and her parents were the only ones staying there that summer. Harue and her family were still in New York, and Natsue and her family had decided not to come: the new house in Sapporo was under construction, and with Takero absorbed in his research as usual, even during the summer, Natsue needed to be around for consultation with the workmen on a myriad of little things. Yoko wasn't allowed to travel by herself, after the previous summer's "misconduct," so none of the Utagawas would be putting in an appearance. But though their house was relatively quiet, the one next door was lively for a change. Masayuki was now a student at the University of Tokyo and looked even more like his late uncle Noriyuki than before. He cut such a striking figure that he turned heads, and girls from neighboring summer houses came by on various pretexts. The Demon was undoubtedly hard at work sorting out which of them were from "good families." As for my news, I had sent a postcard informing everyone of the fact of my divorce and nothing more, so Fuyue only heard the details on this visit and seemed angrier at my ex-husband than I was.

Knowing my way around the Saegusa kitchen, I joined in and helped while we chatted. So many people had migrated from the countryside to Tokyo that farming villages no longer had any hands to spare, and maids were becoming scarce in Japan. With Harue and the others off in New York, fewer people lived in the Seijo house in Tokyo, and after Mie, the "pocket pinup" girl, quit her job, they had switched to a housekeeper who had a family and commuted from home. She came with them to Karuizawa only for the first few days; the rest of the summer they had to fend for themselves. "It's all the harder because Grammy still wants to sit back and live a life of leisure," Fuyue said, adding, "It's such a help, Fumiko, to have you come and pitch in!" As I was leaving she invited me to come back again the next day if possible, which I decided to do. At home I had to tiptoe around my mother, who in turn tiptoed around my stepfather, and being a woman, I had to do kitchen work wherever I was anyway. I felt more at ease in Karuizawa; I enjoyed myself more. Moreover, since I was no longer a maid but someone who was "kindly helping out," I was also treated differently. In part it was because Fuyue was lonely, I'm sure, that I was invited to have meals and tea with the three of them, her and her parents. Before I took my leave at the end of the day, she slipped me an envelope of money. But, Fuyue being Fuyue, she wasn't like her sisters: as we worked around the house together, even though I knew my services were hers to command, I began to feel that we were half friends. From that summer on, my relationship with her shifted to another level.

IN TOKYO, LIFE settled back into its monotonous routine. My emotions were steadier than when I was married, but six days a week I was shut away inside an office. My only luxuries were paperback books and the occasional movie. With the image still fresh in my mind of my parents and grandparents toiling in the fields at home, hardly able to straighten up and stretch, I couldn't complain. Yet once the excitement of living alone in Tokyo wore off, there was nothing glamorous about ill-fitting rain shutters, stained ceilings, and tatami mats turned brown by the sun. At night, lying on my futon feeling the vibrations of trucks going by on the street outside, I couldn't help being depressed at the thought of living that way for the rest of my life. The smell of urine from the shared toilet at the end of the hallway, which no amount of scrubbing could reduce, was another constant irritant.

THE FOLLOWING SUMMER, I talked to Fuyue on the telephone and arranged to go to Karuizawa for two nights. While there I saw Natsue and Yoko for the first time in a long while. It had been well over two years, I realized, since I had seen them off for Sapporo. As soon as she laid

eyes on me, Natsue dimpled and exclaimed with pleasure:
"It's been so long! How nice to see you again! The housekeeper we have in Miyanomori is the slowest old thing. I'm
always saying how much I wish we could have someone like
you, Fumiko, but I've simply given up hope." This didn't
seem like empty flattery. Yoko greeted me with a quick,
rather shy smile. She was in her last year of high school,
all of seventeen, but she seemed neither to have matured
as a person nor to have become the least bit more feminine or pretty. Cast as a delinquent ever since the "misconduct" of two years ago, she may have made a habit of
sulking for days on end. She looked untidy, as if she never
so much as splashed water on her face or combed her hair
in the morning. The Shigemitsus, who would otherwise
have been next door, were spending their summer vacation
in New York; with the other young people all in America,
Masayuki included, it probably wasn't much fun for her to
be left on her own. Her mother had wanted to take her to
New York, but the Saegusas had asked them to postpone
the visit, since they didn't have room for that many at one
time, so she had given up the plan.

The cicadas kept up a loud droning all day long, and just
as they fell silent, white mist rose from the valley, marking
the onset of evening. I joined the rest of the family around
the oval dining table for dinner, and afterward did the
dishes. Even when Yoko was alone with me in the kitchen,
the name "Taro" never crossed her lips. The evening wore
on, and still she didn't mention him. As I bustled around
the house, going upstairs, downstairs, and back again, her

silence began to weigh on my mind. I realized for the first time that one of my main reasons for coming to Karuizawa had been my concern for those two. After the tongue-lashing her parents had given her a couple of years ago, perhaps she was trying to give him up, or may even have done so already—I remembered Taro's strained face at our last meeting. Thoughts like these flitted through my mind.

That night, just after I had crawled under the quilts in the attic room and settled down to read, I heard a soft knock on the door. At this, I felt a wave of relief. For Taro's sake, I inwardly said a prayer of thanks.

"Fumiko?" Yoko had come tiptoeing down the corridor from the bedroom at the other end. She had on a pair of woolen socks and was wearing a cardigan over her pajamas. As soon as she came in she plopped down on the tatami by my pillow, looking despondent.

"Fumiko . . . ," she said again, and pulled an envelope folded in two from the breast pocket of her pajamas. "Here."

"Another letter?"

I sat up on the futon. I didn't let my relief show in my face. At some point I had decided, without even consciously realizing it, to do what I could to help the two of them, even though I had scruples about conspiring against my former employers, who had been so good to me.

"Yes, another letter," she said awkwardly, and turned it over. "This is the address of the post office in the town next to Miyanomori. I thought I could write to Taro by general delivery." She looked at me pleadingly. "We're not going to do anything naughty."

She'd wanted to write to me sooner to ask for my help, she said, but was afraid that after what had happened last time I might refuse to act as a go-between. If she could stay in regular contact with Taro, she would feel a lot easier, and she wouldn't try to see him without her parents' knowing. She just wanted me to give him this address.

When I didn't reach out for the letter, she sagged, and seemed on the verge of tears. After a few moments she began to speak again in a muffled voice.

"You know where he's living, don't you?"

"Yes," I said, "I do. Yoko, dear, you'll catch cold. Sit on a cushion." I drew a cardigan around my own shoulders. "I do know where he lives, but even if I deliver your letter, there's no telling whether it will reach him. Your father left strict orders with Mr. Azuma to keep an eye on Taro, you know."

"An eye on him, ha!" Yoko straightened her back. "That nasty old hag of a stepmother and her sons will just gang up on him, that's all!" Sitting on a cushion, she tossed her frizzy mop and rocked her small, thin body in agitation. Then she slumped back and spoke in a pleading tone of voice.

"I know it won't do any good to send it through the mail. That's why I want you to find a way to hand it to him in person. Have him come to you, or you go to him."

Without really knowing why, I sighed.

"I promise I won't cause you any more trouble, ever again." Her face was full of entreaty. Not knowing about her grandmother's dying request to me, she seemed to have only modest expectations of help.

I took the envelope, promising only that I would do what I could to get it into his hands. I warned her, though, that when I sent him my new address after becoming single again, there had been no response, and I couldn't be certain that he was still living in the same place.

Yoko nodded, then launched into a long lament. Ever since the incident two summers ago, her mother had cracked down on her, keeping a sharp eye on her every move and opening all her letters. Her private life was an open book. She wanted to go to college in Tokyo, but that was no longer an option. Instead she would have to attend Fuji Women's University, which she could get into straight from her school without even taking an entrance exam. And so on.

"Anyway, trust me, it's not fun having a mother with time on her hands. After letting me do as I pleased for so long, now all of a sudden she starts interfering."

The sarcastic tone had an adult ring to it, but the sallow face in front of me remained that of a child, with lingering traces of her features as a baby. No doubt Taro was to be pitied, but this childish girl who had a future far brighter than mine yet was haunted already by a ghost from the past, aroused my pity in her own way, and this replaced the feeling I'd had a moment ago when I heard her soft rap on the door.

"Are you unhappy in Sapporo?"

"I wouldn't say that . . ." Her eyes were on her lap.

"Have you made any friends?"

"Yes, some."

I was silent. She looked up and began ticking off the pleasures in her life.

"The new house is nice, and I like singing in the church choir, and I love Hokkaido crab." She looked down again. "But the thought of how unhappy Taro must be in Tokyo makes me feel such pain, all the time; I can't bear it."

She was quiet for a moment, still looking down, then raised her head and looked into my eyes. "Fumiko, did you know our old house in Chitose Funabashi is gone?"

"Gone?"

"Whoever bought the property decided to tear it down and rebuild."

"Is that right?"

"Yes. Not even the gate is there anymore."

"Oh dear."

"The whole neighborhood's changed. Including the vacant lot where the air-raid shelter used to be. It's gone too."

"That's awful."

"I know."

The skin around her eyes slowly reddened, but perhaps because she had matured a little, she did not cry.

WHEN I RETURNED to Tokyo I sent Taro a postcard inviting him to drop by for a visit sometime, but by the time the cold winds of autumn set in he still had yet to come. My brother's wife had a baby, and in return for the present I sent, they mailed me some soba. I wrote to Taro again: "Soba noodles from home—come and have some with me." He never showed up, but neither were my postcards returned in the mail. One day I made up my mind to go and see him. After work I took the train to Kamata and asked the way at the police box by the station. The place turned out to be one of a number of little factories all jumbled together.

In the center of the room, on a floor of packed dirt covered with iron filings, the first thing that met my eyes was a huge lathe. Mr. Azuma was busy turning something on it. When I told him that I happened to be in the neighborhood and thought I should stop by, he paused in his work, but only to say with more than his usual gruffness that Taro wasn't back from school. He avoided my eyes and seemed so anxious to get back to work that I told him I would come back another time, and started to leave. Then O-Tsune came in from a room at the rear with a fussy baby on her back that she was trying to soothe. She barely nodded at me in greeting. There was a look of obvious annoyance in her eyes. I was shocked to think that she'd had another baby at her age, until she explained it was the eldest boy's child. Later I heard from Taro that his brother had managed to get a seventeen-year-old girl pregnant, a live-in waitress at the corner eatery, and after considerable wrangling had been forced to marry her.

It was already pitch dark outside. On my way back to the station, the whine of motors and the heavy thud of punch presses echoed in my ears, while sparks from welding torches briefly dazzled me. Men with deep creases in their dark-brown faces, and bodies showing the accumulated weariness of years, were at work loading and unloading trucks. It occurred to me later that there in the noise and commotion was the very sound of Japan's new economic growth, the "economic miracle" of the late 1960s.

IT WAS JUST before New Year's when Taro finally came to see me.

The company where I worked had closed for the holidays. I spent the day doing a major cleaning before packing without enthusiasm to go back to my parents the following day; and I had just made myself a pot of tea, settled down at the *kotatsu* heater, and was looking at a picture postcard from Fuyue. On it was a brightly colored photo of a gigantic Christmas tree. She had gone to New York with her parents, Grampy and Grammy Saegusa. It was cold, she wrote, but they'd wanted to see Christmas in New York, so they were taking advantage of the music school's winter vacation and were going to an opera or a concert every night. Calculated in yen, even the cheapest seats were so expensive that they had almost bankrupted themselves. The lines were dashed off in an energetic hand. An enviable way to go broke, I was thinking, sipping hot *bancha* tea, when someone knocked at my flimsy door. I turned, and the door swung open without a sound. I'd been going in and out for some time, carrying out the trash and whatnot, and left it unlocked. I watched as a young man in a beige jacket and black trousers came in, ducking to keep from bumping his head on the lintel. It took a few seconds for me to realize it was Taro.

It was two years since I had seen him. Back then he'd still made a boyish impression, but now he was definitely a young man. He hadn't merely grown up; something about him was different. It wasn't only the unfamiliar work clothes he was wearing. Whether just his face looked different or his entire body, I couldn't tell, but it seemed as if somewhere on the inside he had been reshaped, and that the inner change had seeped out, making him look like someone I hardly knew. I felt a surge of disappointment—or perhaps fear: fear of what the future might hold for him. His youth was no longer fresh and vigorous, but had settled like a thick sediment, with a stale smell to it. He had become like those young men you see lounging on street corners, men with no pleasure in life aside from throwing their wages away on *pachinko* pinball; young men who have run out of hope.

He stood there white-faced and silent. I remained where I was, unwilling to get up from the floor cushion by the *kotatsu* heater, the quilt cover pulled up to my chest. I told him to come in and shut the door, that it was cold outside, and that as long as he was up, he should fetch a cup from the counter by the sink. He removed his shoes and meekly got a teacup, brought it over, and sat down across from me to get warm. He may have felt that nothing had changed between us, but for my part I found his sudden presence so disturbing that instinctively I leaned back slightly. Without so much as looking around the room he stared down at the *kotatsu* tabletop.

"Do you want a cushion?" I asked, pouring him a cup of tea, but he shook his head, giving me only a quick glance. "What took you so long?"

Without answering my question, he finally spoke. His voice was husky. "How's Yoko?"

"Alive and well."

"You saw her in Karuizawa?"

"I did. She was worried about you."

Hearing this brought a spark to his eyes for the first time. I pulled myself away from the warmth of the *kotatsu* long enough to take out the letter I'd kept in the bottom dresser drawer, hold it out so he could see her handwriting, and put it in front of him. He stared at the general delivery address, written in her clumsy handwriting. Then he said in an abrupt, offhand way, "I dropped out of school."

"You did? Why?"

"Had to."

"Did you do something wrong?"

"You know I wouldn't. No, it's just that now, with the Utagawas out of their life, they've no reason to keep their promise."

He kept his feelings in check, but his shoulders were shaking with repressed anger. Of course, I thought, remembering how Mr. Azuma and O-Tsune had behaved when I saw them. Now that I heard what had happened, it seemed as if it had been inevitable all along, that no other outcome was ever possible.

From years back, the Azumas had wanted to go into business for themselves. Even with three breadwinners in the family, they had continued to scrimp and save to build up the necessary capital. Being evicted from the Utagawas' rental house was the perfect chance for them to turn their hopes into reality. They set up a sub-subcontracting plant in Kamata manufacturing household appliance parts, in the process using up the money from the Utagawas and leaving Taro with no choice but to quit school after a single year. Since the family—O-Tsune and the boys in particular—had never taken kindly to the idea that Taro alone should be able to continue his education, when their ties with the Utagawas were severed, it was obvious that they would feel free to ignore their promise.

Still, Mr. Azuma apparently wanted to avoid giving the impression that his treatment of Taro was unfair. On the condition that Taro work at the plant in the daytime and attend a night school afterward, he went on paying his tuition and train fare. But the situation at home was difficult. When Taro opened a book, one or the other of his brothers would interfere, and if it came to a fight, they ganged up on him. The baby howled morning and night, and the lights went off early. He could get no studying done at home. And although Mr. Azuma allowed him to leave for school as soon as he got a fixed amount of work done, O-Tsune and the boys kept a spiteful eye on how much he did, increasing his quota little by little on the grounds that he was finishing too soon. Mr. Azuma stayed out of it, finding it too much trouble to interfere as often as was required, which was constantly.

Before long, Taro was coming to class late on a regular basis, and then he was increasingly absent. He barely managed to chalk up the minimum number of days required during his sophomore year, and this year he didn't know if he would have enough. A night school diploma involved at least four years of study, instead of three, but at this rate he might not be able to last that long. Even if he did, how on earth was he supposed to attain the academic level he needed to apply to the faculty of medicine at the University of Tokyo? It was an open question. For the time being, he not only had to work the lathe but do the accounts, as well as drive around to make deliveries and collect payments. Also, since the plant was a household industry, his salary existed only on paper; in fact he received nothing in the way of spare cash. At most he was given an occasional handout with which to get some trousers to replace those he'd outgrown.

And yet the Azumas' business was by no means limping along. Orders increased steadily, month by month. Mr. Azuma built a small warehouse out back and bought a pickup truck, and the moment Taro turned eighteen he gave him the money to attend a driving school, which wasn't cheap. Success, though, only made them eager for more business. Even the eldest son, who at one time had shown signs of delinquency, settled down after marrying and applied himself to the family business. Now all of them, his bride included, were working like mules.

Taro wanted to get away from them as soon as he could and live alone, work somewhere in the daytime and, to save precious time, drop the drawn-out night-school classes to study on his own for a certifying exam that would qualify him to apply to a university. Lately this was all he could think of, waking and sleeping. But at his age, and without a high school diploma, he couldn't hope to earn enough to be on his own. Even if he did run away from the Azumas, he would still need to find a live-in position somewhere, which meant being a soba delivery boy or a grocer's order boy, or else working again at some household industry or other. Under these conditions, there wasn't much chance of getting enough time and space to study. Sleeping arrangements were bound to be crowded—three to a three-mat room, six to a six-mat room—and, while winter might be bearable, in summer there would be all the insects to put up with. Whichever way he looked at it, he kept coming back to the conclusion that he had no choice but to stick it out where he was. In the meantime, life went pointlessly on while he wore out his nerves and his body, and his mind grew emptier by the day. Living, he said, was simply torture.

Moving only his shoulders, he spoke at first in a strangely impassive way, but as he went on his thoughts seemed to grow darker, until before long his face was flushed with desperation.

I listened quietly, shaken by it all. It wasn't only the wretchedness of what he said. I was appalled by him himself, sitting there in front of me. What had happened to the little boy who was so sparkling, as if he wore a bright star on his forehead?

There was a short silence. Then perhaps I sighed too loudly, for he raised his head and looked at me.

"I'm sorry," I said.

"What for?"

"I used up my savings after the divorce, so I can't help you. All I can offer you is a little spending money."

"I didn't come here looking for a handout." He looked away and drew a deep breath. "Sometimes I think I'll help myself to some of their money and run for it."

"No, don't."

"All I'd have to do is take the cash I collect from other factories. It'd be so easy."

"Don't do it—that's robbery. If you were caught, your life would be ruined. You mustn't ever steal."

"My life's ruined already."

Then it came to me. "Why not stay here?" I said. "You could work somewhere nearby in the daytime and study at night for the high school equivalency test or the college entrance exam or whatever."

He stared at me for a moment, then slowly looked around the little room as if he were seeing it for the first time. I am a fairly well-organized person, so everything was tidy. The table was new, but the room contained a variety of other things that brought the Utagawa family vividly to mind: their wedding gift of the Western-style chest; the low writing desk, the dresser, and the full-length mirror Mrs. Utagawa had left me; and some familiar objects from their main room—a clock, a vase, a painting Grampy had done in oils of Mount Asama.

"Live here with you, you mean?"

"That's right. If it's too cramped, you can always sleep in the kitchen." I laughed.

The first time I ever saw Taro, he was nine and I was nineteen. Now, ten years later, we were nineteen and twenty-nine. But he was like a younger brother to me, one far closer than my real brothers, so there was no awkwardness between us.

"All you would have to pay is your board."

"Really?"

"Yes."

His face slowly lit up, showing some of his old animation. It was the first time he hadn't looked dismal since he'd come in.

"And when you've saved up enough money, you can find a boardinghouse or rent an apartment on your own."

After that we walked over to the stores in front of the station and I did some shopping, taking advantage of Taro's presence to pick up a few heavy items. Finally, I stopped at the fish shop and splurged on some tuna sashimi. Standing next to him to make supper in the kitchen, I saw that despite his size he was as deft as in the old days and not at all in the way.

When we had eaten dinner I saw him off at the station. "Explain things properly to Mr. Azuma," I told him. "Don't just run off without a word. He did bring you up after a fashion; you owe him that much."

"He might not like it."

"Yes, but he took your money. He can't complain."

"I'm leaving even if he does."

When I returned to my apartment, I felt so happy that I found it surprising.

Floor cushions I had two of, but there was just one full set of futon and quilts. I could let him use one slim mattress and a quilt, but I only had a single rice bowl and set of chopsticks. After New Year's, when I got back to Tokyo I could stop off somewhere after work and pick up this sort of thing, bit by bit. As I made plans my heart sang, far more so than when I was about to get married. Before I knew it, my mind spun with ideas, looking even further ahead. Yes, if I took in some sewing he might not have to go out to work at all, or at least would not have to work much. If he could focus on his studies, next spring might be too soon, but surely the year after that he could pass the equivalency test and, beyond that, start college. This way he'd be able to get on with his education with minimal loss of time. Even as a college student, he could take a part-time job and commute. Plans for the future rose in my mind one after the other. Tuition at the national universities was low at the time, even by my standards, so none of this seemed far-fetched.

Back in Saku for New Year's I must have been preoccupied with what would happen after I returned to Tokyo, since my little sister, home with her two children, gave me a sidelong look and said archly, "What's going on, Fumiko? You've got something up your sleeve, don't you?"

Then one Sunday a week or so after the holidays, Taro dropped by my apartment again. Though not quite cheerful, he was much more composed than on his last visit, and since he had brought no luggage I could tell immediately that the situation had changed.

The news that he was leaving had evidently dumbfounded the Azuma household. They were under the illusion that, since they'd brought him up out of obligation, Taro himself was obliged to do as they wished, and the idea that he might not go on living under their roof had never occurred to them. His brothers, both furious, would have beaten him up again if their parents, after the initial surprise and anger had subsided, hadn't sized up the situation for once in a more grown-up way. After all, as Mrs. Utagawa had well known, Taro had already made himself useful at the age of nine; he now got more done than their other two sons combined. The adults calmed the older boys down, and O-Tsune, though privately mad as a wet hen, pulled herself together. That evening they sat and talked with Taro, and the conclusion they arrived at was that they would pay him almost as much as a live-in worker; that he would only work during designated hours, from eight in the morning to six in the evening; that he would have Sundays and holidays off; and that he would no longer be stuck at the end of the hallway but would have a corner of the warehouse for himself, a place where he could sleep and study as he pleased. Point by point, they yielded to all his demands. Fortunately for him, O-Tsune had a good head for figures. For the first time, it sank in that he was old enough to go out and work somewhere else. She must also have realized that it was impossible to keep someone of his caliber with them unless he was given the pay and treatment he deserved.

Taro quit night school after New Year's and began studying on his own. His new routine was to go to the public bath around 6:00 P.M., eat supper as soon as he got back, and go to sleep around seven. He then got up at one or two in the morning and studied. His brother's wife brought him meals on a tray, covered with a cloth. The food might be cold or skimpy, but he was able to eat three meals a day away from the family. His brothers, once they began to think of him as outside the family circle, seemed to be resigned to the new arrangement and so far were causing no trouble. By the time he was ready for college, he would have set aside some savings, and there were also scholarships to be had, so if he left the Azumas and worked part-time as a tutor, or at worst if he took a leave of absence for a year or two and concentrated on making money, he should be able to graduate from the faculty of medicine within a reasonable time, even though it was a six-year program.

Perhaps for the first time in his life, Taro realized he was fully capable of standing on his own two feet.

"I see."

Rather than be happy for him, I felt thrown off course by this unforeseen development.

"Anyway, I'll try it for a while, and this time if they don't keep their promise I'll leave there and move in here."

"I see . . ."

It must have been the disappointment. I could think of nothing to say, and only fiddled idly with the teacup in my hands.

"What's wrong?"

Taro seemed unable to understand why I should be downcast. I'm sure he saw it in simple terms, and was glad he wouldn't have to impose on me when I was only just able to make ends meet. I myself wasn't really sure why I was so bitterly disappointed, but it felt as if a gaping hole had opened in my chest, where the wind moaned through.

"I've been thinking." I looked up as I said this. Maybe it had become second nature for me to hide my feelings. My voice sounded strangely dry to my ears. "I thought you could come here to my place and then just devote yourself to studying. I thought you could even go to college from here, get a part-time job."

He looked at me in surprise. I went on.

"It would be so much easier."

"But . . ."

"And then, even if it was a six-year program, you could finish it almost without any delay."

His mouth hung open, but no words came. I forced myself to sound cheery.

"Someday when you're rich and famous, you can pay me back."

"But Fumiko . . ." He closed his mouth for a moment. Then he said in a low voice, "If you did that, you'd have no future. You'd be unable to marry again."

"I have no kind of future anyway." After I said this, a different thought struck me. He might be put off by the prospect of having to shoulder responsibility for me. "Besides, I've had enough of marriage. I'd rather go on as I am than remarry." Forcing myself to sound cheerful again, I added, "You could marry Yoko."

Taro had been staring at me, but now he looked down at the tabletop. For some time we were quiet.

"Did you write to her?" I asked finally.

"Just the other day. Sent it general delivery." He was still looking down.

"So she knows?"

"Yeah, pretty much everything."

"And did she write back?"

"Yes."

"What did she say?"

He turned his gloomy gaze out beyond the window, into the distance. I had done the laundry that morning, so my washcloths, stockings, aprons, and so on hung on the line, and framed beyond them was a patch of pale cold wintry sky.

"That she'll wait for you?"

Without answering this, he said, "Before she starts college she's going to New York with her mother on spring vacation."

Then he was silent. Neither of us said anything until, as if on cue, we both laughed in a rueful way. "Going to New York on spring vacation" was such a far cry from our own lives that it sounded faintly ridiculous.

"If she doesn't marry you, that's all right too," I said. "Someone far better suited to be your wife will come along, Taro, someone who will appreciate you more than she does."

He looked down again. After a while he raised his eyes and said that as long as the Azumas kept their promise, he would stay where he was. So maybe he did dislike the idea of living with me indefinitely and being tied down. Or maybe he just didn't want to be in my debt, period. Ever since he was a little boy, he had never allowed himself to take advantage of people's kindness. He had never even taken old Mrs. Utagawa's kindness for granted.

The monotonous ticking of the old clock from the Utagawa house echoed in the silence. To me it had never seemed a disconsolate sound, but that day it did.

As Taro was about to leave, I handed him a small envelope.

"What's this?"

"A spare key."

"You had one made for me?"

"Yes," I said, and smiled. "When things get to be too much for you, when life piles up on you, come back anytime."

THE SECOND "MISCONDUCT" had far more serious consequences.

The cold eased up and the next thing I knew, it was spring. One Saturday around the end of March, as the season was building toward its peak, I received a phone call at work from Yoko. The second incident followed from that contact. After the two weeks of spring vacation in New York, she had come back to Japan ahead of her mother to attend the entrance ceremony for Fuji Women's University. She was staying in Seijo with her aunt Fuyue and grandparents and would be leaving for Sapporo in two days' time, she said, but Grampy had given her some spending money and the following day, Sunday, she wanted to take me out for lunch if I had time. Yoko had no sense of direction, but she insisted that if she just followed the signs she would be all right, and so we arranged to meet in Shibuya, by the statue of the faithful dog Hachiko.

She was dressed head to toe in an outfit straight from
New York, waiting in the crowd looking rather full of herself. Exactly what made her stand out I could not have said,
but the overall effect was quite sophisticated. From a distance you might have taken her for a film actress or someone of that sort. She was attracting glances. This was just
when the miniskirt had begun to be popular overseas, and
in her moss-green sheath with its high collar and high hem,
big gold hoop earrings, and matching bracelets, she looked
definitely stylish. Her curly hair too had been tamed and
waved, and looked quite unlike her usual mop. I supposed
her appearance was a mark of her pride in having been to
New York, together with an effort to look her best for her
first trip to Tokyo in quite some time. The previous summer in Karuizawa she'd been so determinedly scruffy that I
never dreamed she could look so attractive. But I reminded
myself that she was now eighteen, an age when it's almost a
sin for a girl not to look pretty.

It felt strange having Yoko treat me. A bowl of noodles
would be fine, I said, but she insisted that, now she was here
in Tokyo, she needed to satisfy a craving for genuine Edo-
style sushi, without spending a fortune. She wouldn't hear
of doing otherwise, so we went into a place I often passed
on my way to and from work.

After ordering, Yoko brought out two little boxes
wrapped with crimson ribbons, small enough to hold in the
palm of her hand, and declared, "Here, Fumiko, these are
for you! An Elizabeth Arden compact and lipstick. This one
is from everybody, and this one is from me."

She then plunged into all the news from New York. Her uncle Hiroshi had managed through a travel agent to hire a shiny black limousine with a Japanese chauffeur for her and her mother. They had gone out in style every day to see the sights of Manhattan—everything from the Empire State Building and the Metropolitan Museum of Art to Chinatown. Her aunt Harue was taking lessons in oil painting from a Japanese artist in Greenwich Village and must have inherited Grampy's talent, as she was really pretty good. Mari and Eri were students at Manhattanville College, which would allow them to transfer directly to Tokyo's Sacred Heart, the present empress's alma mater, when they returned to Japan. Her sister had been accepted into Juilliard and, although their mother wasn't to know, already had an American boyfriend, a cellist. In any case Yuko was much freer now that she was out from under her mother's thumb. On and on she went, the words tumbling out.

Thin as she was, Yoko had always had a good appetite, and she polished off the sushi in less than fifteen minutes. It was when we were brought some fresh tea that the topic of Taro came up.

Her animation abruptly faded and a quite different, much graver mood took its place. There was a short silence. Here it comes, I thought, and I was right.

"Fumiko," she said and looked straight at me, leaving her mouth open. She seemed almost angry with me. "What the Azumas did is just terrible."

"Well, that's life."

"It's awful."

"Yes, but it happens."

She kept looking fiercely at me, but finally said more hesitantly, "Actually, I thought I'd go and see him after this. I brought along his address in Kamata."

Now at last I understood why she was so dressed up. At the same time, I knew I would have to go with her. It was worrying enough to think of this pretty, doll-like creature wandering in the hubbub of that factory town with a lost, no-sense-of-direction look written all over her. Worse yet, the thought of her coming under the prying eyes of the Azuma family, people who had called her a "nympho," made me shudder—less for her sake than for Taro's.

"I'll take you."

"Would you really? That would be wonderful."

Apparently she'd been expecting me to say this. She smiled brightly, looking relieved.

She had told her aunt Fuyue that she was going to go shopping after lunch, so before we left she would need to pick something up, she said. Then she asked casually, "Has he changed?"

"He's grown up."

"Hm." She thought this over before asking, "What about me, have I grown up too?"

"Well, you are eighteen now," I answered a bit curtly, thinking that she was fishing for compliments. Perhaps I was wrong. She put down the teacup she'd been holding in both hands and looked straight at me.

"Taro is really grateful to you. More than you know."

"Is he?"

"Of course he is. Thanks to what you said he's now able to go on with his studies, even if he did decide to stay with that hag. Why wouldn't he be grateful?"

I avoided her eyes and looked at the tabletop. She went on, oblivious.

"And anyway, after Grandma died, you were the only one who was kind to him. I know it meant a lot to him."

Her voice caught, choked with sentiment. Looking back, later on that day, how very sweet and innocent that sentiment came to seem.

"HOW COULD I ever marry someone like that? He looks so rough, and his speech is rough too, he's so . . . oh, I don't know, he's just a total stranger. I couldn't do it! How could I upset Mama and Papa to marry him? What would Aunt Harue and everyone say? Or Uncle Masao and Aunt Yayoi? They might not say anything, they're so nice, but what would they think? And Masayuki—just the idea of what he'd think is so embarrassing I could die. What happened is . . . I saw it in a flash. Our future. I saw it, all of it, way into the future. There'd be . . . nothing. Everything would be so small . . . and narrow . . . and limited, I couldn't breathe!" From the moment we got on the Yamanote Line, tears welled in her eyes. The other passengers looked on in surprise as she got out tissues and blew her nose, big tears rolling down her cheeks.

"I don't want to be rich," she said. "I'm happy just the way I am."

"What do you mean, just the way you are?"

"The way our family is, I mean."

"Yoko, dear, your family is rich."

"No, we're not."

"Compared to most people, you are."

"Then I don't care, I could be poorer than this. And though maybe it's better to have a college degree than not, it doesn't really matter to me in the end." She shook her head petulantly. "But *that* I couldn't bear."

The hair that had been so prettily waved earlier in the day was back to its usual frizz, and in the course of all the walking and crying she'd done, her makeup was gone. To top it off, her nose was red from being blown.

She shook her head again forcefully, setting the gold hoop earrings swaying, and repeated, "I just couldn't."

"Couldn't bear what?"

"Oh . . . I don't know how to explain it." She went on, half to herself. "It's the look on his face as he kept droning on about the same old things. It was unbearable! When the equivalency test is going to be, how many subjects the University of Tokyo needs for its entrance exam, how tough it is to get into the science and physics department or whatever you call it. Also, how much the tuition costs and how much he'll need for living expenses and on and on and on about stupid things that I just couldn't care less about! All of it!"

"Money isn't something you can just ignore."

"I know, but going on about it the way he does is so petty. So narrow. So . . . small-minded. He's become so common inside. It shows in his face."

That day, the moment I brought Taro into the coffee shop where Yoko was waiting and she at last set eyes on him, her face drained of color. I think probably it was partly a young girl's shock at suddenly being confronted by her childhood friend's virility. But she also saw in him the same thing I had seen the other day, and felt a keen disappointment—and consternation. Taro for his part couldn't take his eyes off this new and prettier version of Yoko. He stared at her, embarrassed but wide-eyed; he looked to me like a hopeless idiot. I occupied myself for a little while in the station bookstore so they could have some time alone together, and then I went back to the coffee shop and took a seat some distance from their table. I pulled a paperback out of my purse and looked up from time to time to watch them. Whatever they'd been talking about, their conversation was now sluggish. They would exchange a few sullen words, eyes fixed on the table in front of them. Taro seemed to be resisting the urge to look at her. After an hour or so I went over and said maybe we'd better be going, as we'd come a long way and Aunt Fuyue would worry. Still looking glum, they stood up without protest. As usual, Taro wanted to go with her to Seijo, hoping to extend their time together as long as possible, and as usual she swung her hair and stamped her foot. "No! Don't! Not today. I mean it!" By way of a compromise, he got off at Shinagawa. And so they parted.

Since Yoko was going all the way to Shinjuku, I would be getting off before her, at Shibuya. Just before leaving, I said reproachfully, "I can't help feeling sorry for Taro, the way things ended."

"It's all right," she said. "We're going to meet again."

Swept along by the throng of departing passengers, I was ejected onto the platform with her words still ringing in my ears. She was traveling to Sapporo the next day, so they had precious little time. I wondered how they were going to manage it, but even if it was only for a short while, he can't have felt so downhearted after all, and Yoko herself couldn't be nearly as fed up with him as she had made me believe. For Taro's sake, I felt relieved. I saw no reason to warn Fuyue. The possibility that the two of them might go off to Oiwake together simply never occurred to me.

EARLY WEDNESDAY AFTERNOON, three days after that, Fuyue rang me at work. "Have your parents gotten a telephone?" She was always the calm one in the family, but that day I heard panic in her voice.

"Yes," I said, "they put in a line last year."

"I'll explain later, but I need you to call home immediately and have someone go to Oiwake to see if Yoko is there. If she is, they need to take her home with them, by force if need be, and if she's not, then I want them to go look for her in Karuizawa." She took a breath before going on. "It's possible that she and Taro may have eloped."

With my boss's permission, I called home. My brother happened to be in that day, and just over an hour later he called back.

"She was there all right."

"With him?"

"Nope, alone."

"Alone?"

"She's lying by the heater right now. Got a bad fever. I'm about to take her to the hospital."

"You are?"

"Yup."

"It's that serious?"

"She'll be okay, I think, but she's got herself one hell of a fever."

I left work early, met Fuyue at Ueno station, and together we took the Asama super-express bound for Nagano. On the way she filled me in. On Monday, the day after I saw Yoko, the Saegusa housekeeper had taken her to Ueno station, where she was due to board the afternoon sleeper express to Sapporo. They had arrived in plenty of time, and the housekeeper went on home, assured by Yoko that there was no need for her to hang around. Fuyue had taken it for granted that Yoko boarded the train. Tuesday passed without incident, and then Wednesday noon, that very day, Yoko's father had phoned from Sapporo to say that she hadn't arrived on the morning train as expected. Fuyue told him that Yoko had left on Monday, so she should have arrived the previous day. No, she was coming in time for Thursday's entrance ceremony, Takero asserted, so she'd been scheduled to leave Tuesday and arrive Wednesday. They went back and forth until finally it dawned on them that Yoko had contrived the whole thing. She had told her aunt that she was leaving Monday and her father that it was Tuesday, setting it up so that she would be on her own for an entire day without anybody being the wiser. Quite cunning, if true, but all anyone knew for certain was that here it was Wednesday and there was no sign of her in Sapporo. When Fuyue had urged her to fly home, Yoko claimed she was sick of airplanes and insisted on taking the train. In retrospect it all fitted together. Her father was ready to file a missing persons report with the police when Fuyue, remembering the previous "misconduct," proposed that she contact my family first and have them look for her in Oiwake or Karuizawa.

"You saw her on Sunday, Fumiko, didn't you?" Fuyue asked.

"Yes."

She looked at me. Leaving out the role I'd played in their correspondence, I decided to tell her everything that had happened that day. I finished my account with a humble apology, which she brushed aside. "No need for you to apologize," she said. "If you hadn't gone with her to Kamata, she would just have gone by herself. But we had better keep this from Natsue." How to deal with her sister was uppermost in her mind. "Just the thought of her finding out has me worried sick," she said. No one had yet sent word to New York.

It was cold in Nagano, with patches of snow on the ground.

We got off the train at Komoro and went by taxi to Saku Hospital. In the hallway outside the sickroom, under a fluorescent light, my sister-in-law was sitting on a vinyl-upholstered bench, wrapped in a padded jacket, waiting.

When my brother found Yoko she was lying curled under a quilt, naked and delirious. On the tatami at the head of the futon were two cups and two small, empty clay pots, a popular packed lunch sold on the Asama super-express.

Scattered at the other end were her clothes, lying where she'd thrown them off. From her condition it seemed likely that she had lain shivering on the futon for a day or two. Details came out later, but obviously this outcome was the last thing she had expected. Her plan had been to ride back to Tokyo first thing in the morning and set off innocently for Sapporo on the Tuesday afternoon train. Evidently, she and Taro had quarreled, he stormed out, and she stayed in bed, sulking, and the result was pneumonia. Had she managed to dress herself and make it to the main road before her fever shot up, it wouldn't have come to this; but no doubt she had stayed there counting the minutes, waiting for Taro to feel remorseful and come back. With no external injuries and so no role for the police, she had been admitted to the hospital without any awkward questions. The following day, Thursday, her father flew down from Sapporo, transferred to a train, and arrived in town. I had taken the day off work and went back to Tokyo as soon as he came.

When I left, Yoko's fever was still high and she was panting for breath, but according to the doctor the antibiotics were doing their job and she was out of danger.

WORN OUT, I dragged my way home to find the light on in my room at Evergreen Apartments No. 2, with a glimmer showing under the window curtains. For a moment I thought I must be looking at the wrong apartment, but no, that was definitely my room, and those were the curtains I had hung. I soon guessed who was there.

I opened the door and was assailed by a stale, yeasty smell, a mixture of alcohol and sweat. My eyes took in the sight of Taro sitting cross-legged on the floor in his jacket, which he apparently hadn't taken off since getting back from Oiwake. He stared up at me with bloodshot eyes like a crazed animal. In front of him was a big bottle of cheap *shochu* and a cup; looking around I saw another big bottle lying on its side, empty.

In a corner was an overnight bag I'd never seen before, which told me that he had left the Azuma house.

"Where's Yoko?" he asked.

"I'm tired," was all I said.

I removed my shoes with deliberate slowness before entering the room. When he had arrived I didn't know, but since I'd been away from the day before, he must have started worrying that something had happened to Yoko and was trying to muffle the anxiety in drink.

"Where is she? Seijo? Sapporo?" He rolled his head toward where I stood and asked again. His reddened eyes were fixed on me, his speech slurred. I wanted to look away.

"She's in the hospital."

"Hospital?"

"Yes, Saku Hospital, the biggest one in that area."

"What's wrong?"

I didn't answer immediately, but went to the kitchen sink and washed my hands thoroughly while he looked on in suspense. Then I poured a cupful of water and drank it down.

"She has pneumonia."

"Pneumonia? . . ."

"Yes, she stayed under the quilt the way she was and got pneumonia." Naked, I wanted to say, but I held the word back.

"'The way she was' . . . ?" He seemed to have difficulty understanding. "Stayed the way she was, under the quilt?" he repeated, the words slurring, then got unsteadily to his feet and staggered toward the wall, laid both hands on it, and began banging his head against it with great force. He seemed in danger of cracking that prize skull of his in two.

To make sure he heard me, I raised my voice. "You'll smash the wall! If you've got to bash your head against something, use the pillar, for heaven's sake!"

"Is she going to die? Is she?" He stopped and, hands still on the wall, turned beseeching eyes toward me, desperate to know. Even at that awful moment, I couldn't help noticing how graceful the ten long fingers bearing his weight looked.

"No, she's going to make it."

"She is?"

"Yes."

"Really?"

"Yes."

He breathed raggedly, shaking, then gradually slumped against the wall. He lowered one arm, bent the other one, and rested his forehead on the back of his hand. In a voice so low I could barely hear it he said, "Better she should die."

Then he was silent. I kept quiet too. After a while he went on in the same barely audible voice, but faster now. "She said she didn't want to marry me. Said she couldn't marry anybody so low-class and vulgar. Said marrying me would be so humiliating she'd die. With someone like me, there'd be nothing to expect from life, not in a million years. Not in a million trillion years—that's what she said."

"She went all the way to Oiwake just to tell you that?"

Taro lifted his forehead from the back of his hand and looked at me with a chilly smile. "Not only that."

"I didn't think so."

I said this scathingly, and he dropped that disturbingly mature, chilly smile of his to fix me with a probing look. I levelly returned his gaze. Pictures of the scene at the Oiwake cottage as my brother had described it—small, empty clay pots, Yoko's scattered clothes—passed through my mind like frames on a movie reel. Little Taro, whom I'd always thought of as a boy, seemed to change before my eyes into a man unknown to me, someone I had never seen before. The eeriness of the transformation brought sour bile rising from my stomach.

His face turned sad, with a lingering trace of the old Taro.

"She should've died," he muttered. "I should've killed her, then myself. I'd be better off dead."

He staggered and fell heavily, spread-eagled on the floor. Ever since coming he must have been alternately swilling rotgut *shochu* and passing out on the floor like this. The thought of this young, active person drinking himself into a stupor overlapped in my mind with memories of my ex-husband and the way he used to work himself into a rage, his hot breath stinking of liquor. Taro must have resorted to this cheap spirit, the commonest and nastiest of all alcoholic drinks, in an attempt not only to drown his sorrows but to deliberately degrade himself. Again the bitter taste of bile rose in my throat.

"You're right. Dead right. You'd both have been far better off dying than causing so much trouble for all the adults . . ."

I couldn't tell if he heard me or not. He just stared blankly up at the ceiling.

"Even Mr. Azuma, whom you sneer at, and your brothers, and O-Tsune, whom you call an old hag—they all work hard at their jobs. What about the two of you? What in heaven's name are you doing?"

Perhaps ten seconds ticked by. Taro kept on staring hollow-eyed at the ceiling; then all at once he got up and went to get his overnight bag.

"Now what?"

Bag in hand, he moved toward the door. I stood in front of him to bar the way. The reek of liquor, mixed with the sweet-sour smell of his unwashed body, choked my nostrils. As he tried to push his way forward, I resisted with all my strength. We grappled like that for a while before tumbling in a heap on the floor and rolling over. Taro, his forehead pressed into the tatami, started to sob like a small boy.

From that day until he left for New York six months later, he worked the day shift at a factory nearby and stayed with me in my apartment.

# 7

# Nothing But Romantic Memories

T HE SIX MONTHS from that day to the day Taro left for America, and the six months following, are a blur: Yoko's slow recovery, her father's concern, her mother's hysteria on returning from New York; above all Taro's nerve-racking silence as he soaked up *shochu*, then our endless fighting and finally the dazed numbness when he was gone. After getting so involved in other people's lives and being harrowed by it, body and soul, I felt drained when I was alone again. I'd never had something worth calling "a life of my own," but now my life seemed more thoroughly and bitterly empty than ever.

With Yoko in the hospital I couldn't sit still, partly because my own family had been involved in finding her at the Oiwake cottage. Though my sister-in-law visited her daily, parking the baby with my mother, the Saturday after the "elopement" I left work around noon and headed back to Nagano myself. Fuyue, after coming down to Tokyo to rearrange her schedule at the music school, drove back to Karuizawa, where she slept at the summer house at night and visited the hospital every day. Takero had gone back north to Sapporo, but he came down on weekends by plane and train.

"I did a terrible thing to Papa. I never thought he'd be so worried. I thought he only cared about Yuko."

After her father left the room, Yoko told me this in a frail, reedy voice, her neck as thin as a child's. I too hadn't expected Takero to be so affected. He seemed to have aged twenty years overnight.

Nearly three weeks after the incident, just days before Natsue was due back from New York, Fuyue finally decided to tell her everything. Yoko, who by then had been transferred to a hospital near Seijo, was dreading her mother's return. Knowing Natsue, Fuyue must have thought that unless Yoko was on the verge of death, having her rush home early would only create more problems. She persuaded Takero to have Yoko transferred to a hospital nearby rather than somewhere in Sapporo, not just because that took less time, I think, but because she felt responsible for what had happened and didn't want to dump everything in Natsue's lap. She knew Natsue lacked the inner resources to cope alone up in Sapporo, without her support.

When I saw Natsue at the hospital she gave full vent to her distress, repeating lines that she must have already wailed to Fuyue over and over again. Listening patiently and giving comfort was not easy. She had grown up when the ideal of sexual purity was something shared by Japanese women generally—a direct result of Western moral influence after the Meiji Restoration, I understand. Yoko's "elopement" occurred during the last period when that ideal held true.

"The child is ruined. She never did know how to behave, and now she's lost all hope of ever marrying into a
good family. How that boy Taro could do this to us I will
never know. I just don't understand. After all we did for
him . . . When I told Harue, she even said we should report
him to the police."

It was one thing for her to carry on like this around Fuyue
and me, but when she went into her daughter's sickroom
and said the same thing, things grew more complicated.

"Police?"

Yoko had been lying down in bed, but that brought her
bolt upright with a look so fierce that her mother, intimidated, fell silent.

"Aunt Harue said that?"

"Yes, she did."

Looking her mother straight in the eye, Yoko said quietly,
"I was the one who said we should do it."

Natsue gave a little shriek. "Is that how you treat your
father and me?"

"I'm just saying it wasn't Taro's fault."

"What if you got pregnant?"

A low, breathy hiss escaped from Yoko before she too
raised her voice. "That is totally impossible!" The pair were
alike; neither mother nor daughter could keep their emotions in check.

"How can you say that?"

"Because it's true!"

Again that sharp, breathy sound. Every time the incident
with Taro came up in conversation, Yoko made that voiceless

hiss and then went into a fit of dry, convulsive hiccuping that made her temperature rise. A fever would do her no good, so I signaled to Natsue, whose face had gone as pouty as a child's, and together we left the room.

About two weeks later I visited the hospital again, on a Sunday shortly before Yoko was scheduled to go home. Rain had been falling all day. Still wearing a thin raincoat, I stepped into the sickroom and shut the door behind me. Yoko saw at a glance that I was alone.

"Fumiko." She spoke my name like a command, sitting propped up in bed against a pair of feather pillows they had taken the trouble to bring from Seijo. "There's something I need to say in Taro's defense. He didn't do anything, even though I asked him to."

I stood silent in the doorway.

"End . . . of . . . story." She spoke the words slowly and deliberately, then shifted her gaze to stare at the wall in front of her. On the wall, white with a grayish tinge, hung a nondescript calendar. A window on the adjacent wall offered a rain-soaked view of a concrete wing of the hospital. For the first time, I spoke up.

"Why tell me this? Shouldn't you be telling your mother?"

I took off my raincoat carefully to avoid scattering drops of rain and moved farther into the room. Yoko turned her head toward me again.

"They'd never understand. They never can understand Taro. They can't conceive of there being someone like him." She answered in the plural, so evidently she was not referring only to her mother.

She looked straight ahead at the wall again, with a faint smile that was perhaps disparaging or embarrassed. "Of course I went to Oiwake with that in mind. I told him we should go ahead and do it and be done with it." Her mouth tightened. "He said if I wasn't going to marry him, he wouldn't."

She shot me another look.

"How could I marry him, the way he is? So I said again, 'Look, there's no way I can ever marry you, but let's do it anyway.'"

A vision came to me of Yoko casting off her clothes and flinging them at the foot of the quilts, exposing a body that was barely starting to show some curves, and shrieking wildly: "Let's do it! Let's just do it!"

She looked to the front and, after regaining control of her breathing, plunged on. "He shouted at me. He said, 'If you don't want to marry me, then the hell with it.' He was furious. He made me so mad, I said it again. 'There is no way I could ever marry you'—and he turned and left me."

I stood a short distance off with my raincoat over one arm and looked at Yoko with her hair matted on the pillow, staring at the wall. The day we went to Kamata, when she'd looked so pretty and grown-up—I couldn't help wondering if I had only imagined it. A memory came back to me of the time I first went to the Utagawa house and saw a savage-eyed little girl lying small and flat on her futon.

"He left me." She repeated the words hollowly, drained and dejected. She stopped looking at the wall and let her eyes wander in empty space. "He left me there at night all alone." Her flat chest, covered in a thin flannel nightgown, rose and fell. "I waited and waited, but he never came back." Abruptly she closed her mouth, shut her eyes, and slid down in the bed, pulling the covers up over her head. After a while her face emerged, the cheeks wet with tears. "I waited but he never came back to get me." She was staring wide-eyed at the ceiling. More tears. "I'll never forgive him." She pursed her lips. "No matter how he apologizes, I'll never forgive him as long as I live."

Taro never said anything to me. I only formed a hazy idea of what had gone on between them by piecing together the snippets that Yoko let out. She went to Kamata because meeting me had allowed her to get away from the Saegusas, and once she had the chance, she wanted to surprise and please Taro. Kamata wasn't part of her original plan, but the trip to Oiwake was something she had worked out before leaving for New York, making advance arrangements with Taro by mail. Apparently at that stage she had meant them to spend the night there, have sexual relations, and exchange promises to marry someday. Once they had been intimate, even if they were far apart, they could feel at ease. Not only that, with intimacy an established fact, when they broached the subject of marriage somewhere down the line, her parents would be more inclined to listen. But just before all this was to happen, when she saw him in Kamata, she realized that the image she had built up in her mind during the three-year interval was nothing like the actual, grown-up Taro confronting her. Her disappointment turned to anger, with him and with herself, and she no longer knew what to do. When she tossed her head at him and shrieked, "There's no way I could ever marry you!" I believe she meant every word of it.

But her refusal was that of somebody who could afford to entertain the idea of going back on her word if things changed. Her despair was not that of someone who'd been absolutely bent on marrying him; it was more that she pictured herself frequently quarreling with him and making up—and if along the way he regained his old spark, why, then yes, she might consider marrying him; but if not, he wasn't the only man in the world, and surely somewhere out there she could find a husband who would be less of an embarrassment, to her and to others. That, I think, was her frame of mind. Otherwise, how could she have shouted, "There's no way I can ever marry you!" to his face and still, after he'd turned and fled, expect him to come back—indeed bitterly resent it when he failed to do so? It was impossible for someone in that frame of mind to understand how shattered Taro must have been.

"Where is he now?" she asked.

"I don't know. Isn't he at the Azumas?"

"Does he ever come to see you?"

"No."

"Well if he does, you tell him that I'll never forgive him, no matter how much he apologizes. Tell him I'll never forgive him as long as I live."

I let this slide.

Although the two of them never had any intention of "eloping," somehow that was the way everyone came to refer to it.

UNTIL HE COULD feel easier about Yoko's condition, Taro remained almost completely silent. Night and day he holed up in my apartment, a cup full of *shochu* in one hand, saying nothing. He obviously had no intention of returning to the Azumas. As a courtesy to me he busied himself with household tasks, dipping into the cash in the candy jar under the sink to do some basic shopping and getting simple meals ready when I came home from work. He scarcely touched his own food and just sat drinking—something he must have started doing in broad daylight—with a harrowed look on his face. While I read on my futon before going to sleep, he kept right on gloomily drinking, and when I left in the morning he was still asleep. Or rather, he lay there sodden with drink and, to cover his shame, hid himself under the quilt, head and all. Only when he heard that Yoko had recovered enough to go home did he ease up on the *shochu*. A bit later, he began working at a neighborhood factory. He still drank steadily from the time he got off work until he went to bed, but that was only for a few hours, and he didn't get falling-down drunk. He began to talk to me; and sometimes I even thought I caught him smiling.

A month or so after Yoko had gone back to Sapporo, Taro and I began having daily quarrels. It turned out that while he was staring into space with bloodshot eyes, drink in hand, the wheels had been turning. One day he said out of the blue that he wanted to go to America—either there or Brazil, somewhere a Japanese could find work; in any case, he wanted to leave Japan. By spending so much time at the Utagawas, he felt he'd come too much under their influence, and this had led to the ludicrous notion of going to college like a good middle-class boy and studying to be a doctor. But he now realized how silly—and almost impossible—the whole idea had been. In Japan, for someone of his background to lead a respectable life meant making it his goal to become respectable—but a life focused on a goal like that wasn't what he wanted.

This provoked me. If he went overseas, there was no knowing how things would turn out, whereas if he stayed put, at least things could get no worse. I repeated my earlier proposal. He could stay on in my apartment and quit the factory job, either going back to high school in the normal way or studying for an equivalency test. He could commute to college from my apartment too and decide later what to do next. I tried to get him to listen to reason. I'd been waiting for him to pull himself together and give me just such an opening, so words poured out of me as if a dam had burst. Being male, as long as he finished high school he could certainly look forward to a better life than I'd had. If he graduated from university, he could have what seemed to me a pretty damn good life. I offered to do anything I could to make that happen. But he wouldn't listen. While I was unburdening myself, he bore it with a frown, but when he talked he simply repeated the same things as before. From the start of the rainy season, around and around we went, arguing in circles.

I realized something then for the first time. It made me feel small, and sad. Like old Mrs. Utagawa, I too had become dependent on Taro. What's more, I lived alone. If he disappeared from my life, I would have to endure the same old loneliness and dreariness; the thought was dismal, even horrifying. Taro must have guessed how I felt, and only brought up his plan to go abroad quite a while after he'd already made up his mind. Once his decision was out in the open, though, he was adamant. While I argued with increasing vehemence as he sat beside me with his cup of *shochu* in front of him, he would pull out a textbook for learning English that was among his few belongings and make a show of studying, turning away from me. The blatant rejection in this gesture was absurdly irritating, and in a harsh voice I sometimes said things I should not have. In the end I even wept and pleaded with him. It seems obvious to me now that part of his wanting to leave Japan was to avoid having me around his neck in the future, so the more I begged, the more difficult it must have been for him to endure.

Toward the end of the rainy season, I gave in, and decided to do my best to help him carry out his plan. I got in touch with Uncle Genji, whom I hadn't seen since my divorce, in the hope that he might have connections that would help Taro get started overseas. Together we went to his house in Soto Kanda. He seemed surprised at the sight of Taro, as if wondering whether this really was the same boy I'd brought to meet him before. He also seemed to get the wrong idea about us and embarrassed me by saying out loud, "Well, Fumiko, I see you've gone off the deep end this time." My uncle frowned at my request, claiming that his experience of foreign countries was a thing of the past. I plowed on, playing up Taro's merits. This young man, I said, has ten times the ability of any ordinary person, so he would never disgrace you, you can be sure of that; anyone who took him on would be grateful to you; please ask around on his behalf. Recent history forgotten, I pleaded his case as well as I could. Uncle Genji said that he would see what he could do but advised us not to expect much, adding as he looked from one of us to the other that if Taro spoke no English there was little point in even considering the matter.

After that Taro took to opening up his English-language textbook every evening after supper while listening to the Far Eastern Network, the all-English radio station run by the U.S. military. Soon it was summer, time for the Bon festival holidays. I didn't feel like going home or to Karuizawa, so I begged off with the excuse that things were too busy at work for me to get away that year. We stayed in Tokyo and sweltered. Taro's preferred destination was the United States, but on looking into it, he realized how hard it would be to obtain a visa that would let him get a job. He had just started talking about Brazil as an alternative when Uncle Genji called me at work. He sounded upbeat. He'd spoken to the cook at the Imperial Hotel, a former associate of his at the base, with the result that an American who came regularly to Japan had offered to take Taro on if he had a mind to work as a private chauffeur.

Since all he wanted was a way to get to America, Taro jumped at the chance, however unexpected the type of work, and by early October he was gone. To save money he took a freighter sailing by way of Panama, but he barely owned even a change of clothes, and getting him fitted out for the coming winter had exhausted my meager savings. By a quirk of fate he was heading for New York, where Harue and the others were.

I told Fuyue by telephone, thinking that everyone should at least be notified that Taro had left the country. As I learned afterward from her, she told Natsue, Natsue told Yoko, and the following morning Yoko stayed in bed for so long that her mother went upstairs to check, only to find her unresponsive and feverish, having spent the night curled on the rug at the foot of her bed. In a few days the fever was gone, but the lethargy remained. At the time, she was taking her first year of college off to recuperate from the pneumonia that had dragged on, and, apart from resuming her voice lessons, she spent her days hanging around the house doing nothing. Her parents were worried enough to take her to a mental health specialist. Privately, I felt that living in that privileged environment, where her emotions ran unchecked, had made her oversensitive and unstable.

At the end of the year a Christmas card, sent airmail— something I had never received before—came from Taro. He had apparently decided that his address, written in small English lettering on the envelope, would be hard for me to make out, so he'd written it out again in big capital letters in the middle of the card. He added that I should let him know if my address changed. That was all. Uncle Genji received a note of thanks from him, but he never wrote me a proper letter. As I studied those large roman letters in Taro's handwriting underneath the words *"Merry Christmas,"* which were printed in silver, I felt a wave of emotion. In reply I sent him the customary New Year's postcard with a message equally short.

The following spring, having heard that the Saegusas were finally back from New York, I used one of my days off to call on them at Seijo. Mari and Eri had grown from pretty little girls into beautiful young women, and their father, Hiroshi, had matched their growth, becoming stouter than ever. Harue, by contrast, gave the impression of having been rejuvenated. I'd heard from Yoko that she was studying painting with a Japanese artist over there, and much later I learned from Fuyue that she'd had an affair with the man, one that lasted for almost the entire duration of their stay. She had been at great pains to keep this secret from the local Japanese community. Since she paid her lover's expenses out of her own pocket, a source of funding he wasn't eager to have dry up, he himself had evidently been equally intent on keeping the affair quiet. Somehow this news came as a relief to me. It may sound presumptuous, but I had always thought it a pity that a woman like her should waste her youth and beauty as she'd had to do.

"They say that boy Taro is chauffeur to an American," Harue said, smiling scornfully. So she knows, I thought in surprise. She had already heard from Fuyue about Taro's eventual emigration after the "elopement," and when gossip about someone fitting his description began circulating among Japanese expatriates in New York, she had apparently put two and two together.

As I got up to leave, Harue looked me up and down, rather as if she were looking at some zoo animal, before saying, "Fumi, I must say, your figure has certainly filled out, hasn't it? You look more like a real woman." I was past thirty by then, so if it had, that was only natural.

"Yes," I said, "I suppose so."

Then she studied my face. "But you seem a bit tired."

Indeed, I was extremely tired at the time.

Again, I didn't go to Karuizawa that summer. "Things are too busy at work" was again my excuse for staying away from Karuizawa for the second year in a row. Having put Taro up for six months without the Saegusa sisters' knowing made me hesitate to go. Also, even though it was already nearly a year since he'd gone, I still felt run-down. Just getting through each day wore me out, and I was hardly in the mood to be around those high-spirited people. In December I received a second Christmas card from Taro, saying that he'd quit being a chauffeur after a year of it and had been working for the New York branch of a Japanese company ever since, as a camera repairman. His new address was again written in oddly distinct lettering in the middle of the card. As before, I sent a blunt New Year's postcard in reply.

I REMARRIED THE following spring.

As I mentioned at the very beginning, I have an Aunt O-Hatsu, a woman now in her nineties and still going strong. Her husband, my mother's elder brother, died at the end of the year, and I first met the man who was to become my new husband when I went back with Uncle Genji for the funeral. The man was the third son of a Saku farming family. I was thirty-two and he was forty-five, thirteen years my senior. After finishing his education at around the age of fourteen, he had taken various jobs before starting to work in the town hall. His wife had died years before, and his mother, who lived nearby, had looked after the children until her recent death. Of his three boys, the younger two were still in junior high and elementary school, so he was in the market for a wife. He came up and spoke to me several times as I was serving tea at the wake or helping out the day of the funeral. Apparently someone had told him that I'd been married but was now single again. When the mourning period was over, he stopped by my aunt's house with a proposal of marriage.

"The lady in Western-style clothes . . ."

Those were evidently the first words out of his mouth. Back then it was customary for women to wear a black kimono at funerals, and my style of dress must have struck him as unusual: a black suit handed down from Natsue and a brooch of black pearls which was a gift from Fuyue.

To ask me to leave Tokyo and marry him when he was not only poor but had three boys who needed looking after was asking a great deal, he'd be the first to admit, but he hoped she would at least convey the offer. He didn't think he stood a chance, but if by some miracle I accepted, he guaranteed that they would all be good to me. Being

SMALL SHÍNTO SHRINE

unaccustomed to writing, my aunt must have found the prospect of a letter daunting, for she placed a long-distance call to my company instead—which must also have required some resolution—and conveyed the message.

"I know she's too good for us, but if someone as ladylike as her would say yes, nothing could make me happier." He had kept saying this, her voice informed me on the phone. I tried to remember him, but all that came to mind was a man unremarkable in height, looks, and way of speaking. When I hung up I was inclined to say no. As a single woman living on my own in Tokyo, I'd had my offers, but none of them interested me, and so I had stayed single. Still, the phrase "too good for us" stuck in my mind, that day and the next. A month later there was another phone call from Aunt O-Hatsu. The man had some business in Tokyo, and if I was willing he would at least like to meet me. I met him and thought he was nice enough, but still couldn't make up my mind. Then in short order he came back to Tokyo, this time expressly to see me.

We met in a coffee shop in Shibuya, and no sooner had he sat down across from me than he bowed so low that his forehead grazed the tabletop and said, "We'll take good care of you." Nobody had ever said this to me before, and never did I dream anyone would. At the time, I let the words go by, but that night when I got back home I sat down without turning on the lights, put my elbows on the table, and cried. All the pent-up loneliness and frustration of the five years I'd spent working alone in Tokyo after leaving the Utagawas spilled over.

It was the second marriage for us both, so after my name was officially entered in his family register, we just had a simple ceremony at the house, attended only by the immediate family. Other than that, all I did was send out postcards announcing my marriage and change of address. I didn't send one to Taro: I had no intention of seeing him ever again. Since I was his one remaining tie to Japan, I felt sorry for him, and I also felt guilty; but I had made up my mind not to become entangled in other people's lives anymore.

The Shigemitsus, Saegusas, and Utagawas all sent unnecessarily generous gifts of money, but it seemed to me best at that point to end relations with them too and make a fresh start, so I sent only short thank-you notes. What was funny was that my husband's family name was Tsuchiya, the same as mine, so that even after I remarried I could go right on being Fumiko Tsuchiya.

And so, after having spent the greater part of my life in Tokyo, I found myself back unexpectedly in the place where I grew up. The mulberry fields were gone, replaced by acres of lettuce—a vegetable that was in high demand after everyone in Japan began eating salads. Only Mount Asama was the same as in my childhood, shifting in appearance moment by moment. After setting out for Tokyo at Uncle Genji's urging when I was a girl of fifteen, I found myself leading the same sort of life as if I had never gone anywhere. True to his word, my husband took good care of me. Where his first wife had been "Ma," I was promoted to "Mother." "Go ask Mother," he would tell his sons whenever anything came up. On evenings when I'd concentrated too hard on my sewing,

LOOKOUT POINT IN SAKU

after the boys went to sleep he would rub my shoulders as I lay on the futon. Somehow he even thought I was pretty. Having got myself such a kind husband, I felt grateful, and yet in the morning light and the last glimmer of dusk, when I caught sight of Mount Asama, the knowledge that, after all that had happened, I had ended up back in my hometown tugged at my heartstrings. It felt as if all my years in Tokyo were for nothing. After a few months, those years started to seem not just wasted but unreal.

Soon it was summer, and a postcard came from Fuyue. Since I was only a stone's throw from Karuizawa, she hoped very much I would drop by after they arrived. But I had already resolved to cut my ties with them. Telling myself it would be enough just to phone them to say hello when the time came, I filed the postcard away in the back of my desk.

As it happened, they were the ones who phoned me. "Fumiko, we just got in!" Fuyue sang out in that party voice that all three Saegusa sisters had, and the next thing I knew Natsue had grabbed the receiver and was saying with even greater gaiety, "Fumiko, are you very busy? You live so close by now, you must find time and come on over just as soon as you can." I mumbled something, and then it was Harue on the line. "Fumi, what are you up to this minute? Nothing so very important, I'll bet. I'm right, aren't I? In that case why not come over right now for a short visit? We'll pay the taxi fare." Mixed in with the gaiety was that domineering note so characteristic of her. The bright chatter and even the impetuosity and self-absorption were strangely comforting, bringing back a vivid memory of the time when I first called at their home in Seijo with my uncle Genji and the sight of those women looking so beautiful in the warm spring sunshine made my heart swell with emotion.

An hour later I was standing in front of the lava stone gateposts, looking at the two Western-style houses.

My husband and the boys were understanding, and our family's shaky finances were a factor too. The next day and the next, I took the train to Karuizawa, and ended up helping out all season long, for the basic reason that the money in the envelopes I brought home came in very handy. The eldest boy, though good at schoolwork, had given up on going to college, but I wanted him to go, and since his father had discouraged him only to keep from burdening me, we had decided recently to do all we could to help him continue his education.

THE KARUIZAWA THAT I came back to with a fresh approach was special to all the summer inhabitants of the two villas. Harue's family, having returned to Japan the previous spring, had summered in Karuizawa the year before, but this year Yuko was also back for a visit after graduating from Juilliard, and so for the first time in six years everyone from the two families was together again. That might have been one reason I was so keenly aware of the passage of time. The oldest members of the group, the senior Shigemitsus, had grown quite feeble, and members of the younger generation were needed at the afternoon bridge sessions to make up the numbers. The Demon was in her mid-seventies and she too had lost a lot of her pep, so the traditional English-style

*Sunday lunch* which had always been held at the Shigemitsus' place was now held at the Saegusa house instead. Not
only that, but though Harue had once pooh-poohed everything to do with America, her stay in New York had made
her a convert, and she switched to something called *Sunday
brunch*, a light meal in the American style. In Harue's absence Fuyue had taken charge, so I wasn't treated the same
way as before. "Fumi, you eat with us today," Harue would
also say, and I had my lunch or tea right at the table with
them. Her generation was getting on, but the young ones
were in the full flower of youth.

The happiest of those young people was Yoko's sister
Yuko, whose engagement was celebrated that summer
in Karuizawa. Her father made a point of coming down
for the occasion, even though for many years running he
had taken to remaining behind in Sapporo, where he said
the summers were just as pleasant. Yuko's fiancé was the
American she had fallen for soon after entering Juilliard.
He was a cellist but also wanted to compose, and, while
I don't pretend to understand such things, he was interested in Asian music—Indian and Indonesian, but Japanese music as well. When he arrived in Japan slightly after
Yuko, he was surprised to find that the Saegusa house in
Karuizawa contained recordings of nothing but Western
classical music. Harue and Fuyue grumbled about having
to speak to him in English but agreed approvingly that
he looked a little like the French actor Gérard Philipe, a
heartthrob of their generation. Natsue wasn't wholly content, since the daughter on whom she had lavished such

affection and money would now be living permanently in the United States, but Yuko was so radiant with joy that she could hardly complain.

Yoko was the exact opposite, spreading an air of gloom.

"Fumiko?"

One afternoon she came to see me, choosing a time when I was off alone in the kitchen, having brought out the silver to polish. Most of it consisted of things the Shigemitsu family had kept hidden during the war, not donating them to the army, and had passed on to the Saegusa family.

"Have you heard from Taro?"

"No," I lied. The moment I said it I felt a twinge of guilt as it crossed my mind that when I married and changed my address I had deliberately refrained from sending him a postcard. If he sent me a Christmas card this year, it would go back to him stamped "Address Unknown."

"Oh . . ." She bit her lower lip. "I wonder if he's still alive."

"I'm sure he is," I said, polishing the sugar bowl with a cloth. "He's young, and young people don't die all that easily."

Not listening, Yoko went on half to herself: "It's been nearly two years now since he went to New York. How many times do you suppose I've been to the post office since I got well?"

She was looking at me, but she didn't seem to expect an answer.

"Every single time, I ask if there's anything for me by general delivery. They all know me by sight—it's so embarrassing." She sighed and then said, again half to herself, "Why

't he write?" Her eyes were on the row of gleaming
sil.rware, unseeing.

"I wonder."

"Why doesn't he?" she repeated. She was so lackluster
that I couldn't help being reminded she'd been taken to see
a psychiatrist.

"I feel as if *I've* disappeared, myself." She sounded even
more remote. It was as if while she was standing there her
spirit had gone off to wander some far corner of the earth. I
was concerned, but the moment I opened my mouth to say
something, she came to and took up the petulant tone she
used with Taro.

"I will never, ever forgive him," she said in a low, firm
voice, and bit her lip again. "Never. Not as long as I live." She
put up a good front, but she may finally have begun to understand what it meant to be loved that much by someone like
Taro—in a life she was given only one chance to live.

AGAINST A BURST of green leaves under the summer sun,
with fine linen and dishes on the table, and bright laughter everywhere—amid all this, Yoko looked sullen and ab-
stracted, her mind elsewhere. Yet something unexpected
was happening to her even then. Masayuki, the heir to the
Shigemitsu family, had fallen in love with her. That was what
I first saw in Karuizawa that summer, an undreamed-of development that became reality.

Harue miscalculated badly.

Before our eyes Masayuki's attitude toward Yoko was
undergoing a change. As far as I could remember he had

never paid her much attention, but one day I realized that he would seek her out wherever she was on the grounds, go up to her, and engage in long talks. At *Sunday brunch* he sat where he could see her face. When the others ignored her, he would casually start up a conversation. Around Taro, Yoko was a little tyrant, but in front of Masayuki she was meek, and even when he addressed her she often thought it must be someone else he was talking to, and remained absent in manner. Then, when she realized the remark was aimed at her, she would break into a smile. Thinking back, that was the first summer the two of them had been together in Karuizawa in five long years. The first time after the Utagawas moved to Sapporo—the summer of her first "misconduct"—Masayuki was going to cram school and didn't come to Karuizawa. The year after that, the Utagawas were building a house in Miyanomori, and Natsue didn't send Yoko to Karuizawa. The third summer, Masayuki and his parents were away in New York, and the fourth, Yoko had been at a low ebb after the "elopement" and stayed in Sapporo. And so, that summer, a girl who had been fourteen the last time Masayuki had seen her was all at once nineteen. She compared unfavorably with other young women in appearance, but since he had never known her very well before, she undoubtedly came as a refreshing surprise.

Harue's miscalculation came ironically into play.

When had Harue become so fixated on it? When did she make up her mind that Masayuki belonged to her girls? Back when the war had just ended and all three women—herself, her sister Natsue, and Yayoi—had babies in Karuizawa at around the same time, was she already dreaming of such a thing? Or did the notion arise after she watched Masa-yuki grow into the spitting image of Noriyuki, his uncle who'd died in the war? Or was it that Masayuki himself had turned into the sort of young man every mother wanted for her daughter? There's no telling how far back it went, but Harue definitely wanted him to marry one of her girls—if not Mari, then Eri—and in fact based everything on the firm expectation that he would do just that. Everyone around her, me included, was vaguely aware that she lived with this assumption. Of course, Natsue hoped the same thing for her daughter Yuko, so there was always a certain undercur-rent of competition between the sisters. But Yuko quickly found a boyfriend on her own, forcing Natsue to abandon the dream. With Yuko out of the way, Harue must have been convinced that Masayuki was destined for one of her girls.

Had he gone on living next door after he graduated from university, Harue probably would have let things slide. But this was just when the political strife at universities was at its peak. The previous summer Masayuki had given up on the idea of doing graduate work in Japan and decided to pursue his studies in America instead, thus exiting the stage just when her daughters were at their most marriageable. She was determined to see him engaged to one of them before he left, or if not formally engaged, at least openly committed, and so she swung into action. But the more she tried to push him into the arms of either Mari or Eri the less interest he showed, possibly a natural response for any young man. He began to avoid the sisters and seek out

Yoko's company. This irritated Harue so much that, in addition to promoting her daughters, she began to pick on Yoko
in a roundabout way. That was her downfall. By midsummer
there was Harue on one side, being mean to Yoko at every
turn, and Masayuki on the other, being nice as pie.

If they were getting up a game of doubles at tennis and
Yuko was away with her fiancé, Harue would send for a
girl from one of the neighboring villas, on the grounds that
Yoko played badly. At *Sunday brunch* she talked of nothing
but New York, so that Yoko would be ignored and her own
daughters stand out. She even brought up Taro's name when
people came over for tea, and repeated her pet line: "The
rickshaw-puller's boy, a chauffeur! Isn't that rich?" Yoko was
used to being ignored or left out of things, but when her
aunt started up this sort of talk she would flush bright red,
and Masayuki's clean-cut features would turn pale in response. Now and then Yuko would accompany Yoko on the
piano while she sang, and compliment her: "Your singing's
really improved, you know. With a bit more coaching you
could easily have made it to Juilliard." But Harue, a great
Maria Callas fan, would wear a look of undisguised bore-
dom the whole time Yoko sang, wandering in and out of
the room for no reason and starting a random conversation
with whoever was around.

One moonlit evening at *high tea* when Yuko asked Yoko
to sing something and she started to perform, all but Harue
among those there listened attentively. The second the ap-
plause died down she looked around and said with a sweet
smile, "Now, everybody, how about a little Callas to cleanse

the palate?" She may have found Yoko's singing genuinely unappealing, but her spiteful remark propelled Masayuki out of his chair and over to Yoko's side to comfort her publicly. Fortunately, Yoko seemed not to have heard what Harue said and just stood motionless in the pale moonlight, as though spellbound.

Masayuki felt defiant, I'm sure. And his defiance was fueled by his natural gentleness. No one as clever as Harue could have failed to realize along the way that the meaner she was to Yoko, the more someone like Masayuki would sympathize and be drawn to her. I think seeing her long-cherished dream disintegrate before her eyes made it impossible for Harue to avoid the impulse to be mean. Why Yoko, of all people? That thought surely added to her frustration. Had it been anyone else, she might have been able to bear it—so why did it have to be Yoko? Not only did Yoko have less to offer than her own daughters in every respect but, as was common knowledge, she had caused that "elopement" scandal.

Damaged goods.

No one said the words out loud, but two years after the scandal, that was what everyone thought when they looked at Yoko that summer in Karuizawa. Perhaps out of girlish prudishness, Mari and Eri avoided her company. Also, now that the storm had blown over, her mother was going around saying that she'd gone through what no mother should ever have to endure. Even though Yoko was her own daughter, she acted as if she were some incomprehensible burden suddenly thrust upon her.

From Masayuki's perspective, however, Yoko's involvement in the scandal only increased her appeal. No matter how friendly he was with her, neither her mother nor she herself suspected him of any underlying interest; the idea that he might love her was something Yoko couldn't imagine and didn't want. To a young man as eligible—far too eligible—as Masayuki, this must have felt like a breath of fresh air. And to think that she'd caused such a fuss because of Taro, of all people; that she was miserable, haunted by memories of someone like him; and that romance with anyone, even someone of Masayuki's caliber, was the farthest thing from her mind . . . Surrounded by girls keen on marrying well, how different, how special she must have seemed! Harue's inability to forgive Yoko would soon extend toward Masayuki as well, showing just how frustrated she was with reality's continual disrespect—its utter unwillingness to conform to her wishes.

That summer, the only ones who saw their marriage coming and were afraid of it were Harue and me. I felt as if I were standing in for Taro, and that the qualms he would have had were mine as well.

It was the summer of 1969.

FROM THAT TIME on, for years I made it a habit to spend an entire month helping out at the Saegusas' house in the summertime. And that also became the one time of the year I always looked forward to. To enjoy helping with someone else's chores made me feel slightly guilty toward my own family; it looked a bit odd even to me. Yet that was the truth. At the time, for me Karuizawa was a place where I could breathe deeply, on my own in a crowd. Being able to head off there with a fairly clear conscience, since it helped the family budget, was a great boon to me. And the financial advantages did not end with the money in the envelope marked "A Token of Thanks" I received at the end of summer either. Since my marriage, I had started doing clothing alterations for the neighbors to supplement the family income, but Harue gave me a little push: "You can't make good money doing alterations, Fumi. You should design your own clothes and sell them. With your sophistication, all you'd have to do is model them and they'd sell." Well, it wasn't long before I was getting more orders for dressmaking than I was for alterations. Primavera might have finished its *historical mission* in Tokyo, but out in the country fashionable clothes were still hard to come by. The sisters let me borrow old Primavera patterns and copy dress patterns that Harue had bought in New York department stores. So in summer I helped out in Karuizawa, and the rest of the year I took in sewing. That became the framework of my life.

The daughters of the Saegusa sisters all married and had children. Of the four girls—Mari, Eri, Yuko, and Yoko— the first to marry and become a mother was Yuko. When her husband found work with the San Francisco Symphony, they moved to California, and she proceeded to raise a girl and a boy while keeping on with her music, winning international competitions in ensembles with her husband, going on tour in Europe, and making records. She was the most successful of the four, and while her father was of

NEAR MIYOTA

course proud, Natsue was thrilled to death. Harue might
have been a bit miffed, but Natsue's having a daughter with
an active life overseas and exotic grandchildren reflected
well on all three sisters, so when company came over she
would join Natsue in talking proudly about her niece's ac-
complishments. Yuko had a strong independent streak, and
like her father, wanted to follow her own path in life. As she
grew up she would probably have liked to distance herself
from her mother; but Natsue, as she got older, relied more
and more on her, which may go a long way toward explaining why Yuko chose to marry an American and settle in the
United States. But she was a sweet-natured girl at heart, and
she came back to Karuizawa for the summer as often as she
could, both to keep her mother company and to see that her
children learned Japanese.

Natsue for her part didn't retire quietly to Sapporo.
After moving there she somehow became a Christian, as
if to compensate for the absence of her favorite daughter,
and was energetically involved in Christmas and Easter
services, as well as other church affairs. In Karuizawa she
would suddenly let out some phrase like "the kingdom of
God," giving everyone a jolt. But as the price of airline tickets came down, she became less devout and began traveling
to San Francisco once a year for a good long stay. While
Harue settled permanently in this country after returning
from New York—and Hiroshi's career got on the fast track
here—Natsue, by contrast, would travel overseas. Behind
her ability to come and go freely, of course, lay her husband's acquiescence. He had originally intended to return

to Tokyo at the earliest opportunity, but in time he came to like it at Hokkaido University and decided to stay on there till retirement. Both before and after her annual San Francisco visit, Natsue spent a good deal of time in the Saegusa house in Seijo, and soon, counting summers in Karuizawa, she was spending easily a third of the year away from Sapporo. They had a housekeeper, but ever since her "elopement" Yoko felt responsible for her father's well-being and made herself useful taking care of him.

Between two and three years later, Mari and Eri each married someone they met at work. Fortunately, neither one of them had really shared Harue's plans for them, so the sight of Masayuki growing fond of Yoko right under their noses caused no great pain. Born after the war, the two girls were not in the same orbit as the preceding generation. The imposing Shigemitsu residence in Seijo, which the three sisters used to admire until their hearts ached, was, to the daughters, nothing more than a house they'd known all their lives, and which in due course was demolished. They had neither listened with rapture to the sound of the clarinet coming over the hedge from the other side, nor turned red with embarrassment when put down by the Demon. They had no reason to idolize Masayuki. Above all, they did not have strong enough characters to be obsessed by anything. I believe that a girl begins life as a doll her mother can dress up as she pleases, a mirror where her mother's fancies are reflected; but as she grows older, her own nature begins to show. In the same way that over the years Yuko became more and more serious like her father, Mari and Eri became more like Hiroshi, less resourceful than their mother but less poisonous. Harue knew both how high the mind could fly and how low it could sink; her daughters had more equable temperaments, whether for better or for worse.

Mari married a banker she met fresh out of college through a short-term job at Mitsubishi Bank, while Eri, after serving as an English-speaking guide at the 1970 World Expo in Osaka, brushed aside Harue's rude objections ("You'll be an airborne kitchen maid!") to become an air stewardess, working for a couple of years before marrying a Japan Airlines employee. The educational background of Mari's husband left much to be desired, in Harue's eyes, since he'd graduated from "a private university no one's ever heard of," but she was pleased that, like the Shigemitsus, his family had once held a baronetcy. Eri's husband had gone to high school in the United States before attending Keio University and spoke fluent English. For a while the two couples each lived in an apartment along the Odakyu Line, but as a matter of course the Saegusas soon built them a two-family place, divided right and left, on the Seijo property. From then on they were constant visitors in their parents' house. Their husbands hit it off, and, when they'd had a few beers at a Karuizawa barbecue, happily traded stories about their days as "sympathizers" in the student movement.

YOKO AND MASAYUKI's marriage came last of all.

Masayuki studied abroad at Yale's School of Architecture on a scholarship, coming back to Japan in the summer and staying in Karuizawa, where he patiently cultivated Yoko's affections. For an intellectual, he was an ardent lover; for someone so ardent, he was mild-mannered. He and Yoko often went on walks to Foggy Pond or drove to a teahouse on the ridge. I would also see them out in the yard, deep in conversation. Once, at dusk, when they were sitting side by side on a bench, I saw Masayuki gently lay a fingertip on her forehead and knew immediately that he must be touching the scar he'd caused long ago when he made her trip and fall. Yoko sat still with her eyes closed. As wisps of white mist drifted through the yard, it seemed as if the air around them stayed motionless.

He seldom talked to other people about his experiences studying abroad, but he often did to Yoko. And it seemed she told him things about Taro that she let no one else know. I saw him comforting her as she wept. One summer when her father had a heart attack from overwork and needed bypass surgery, Yoko couldn't come to Karuizawa. Masayuki went all the way to Sapporo to see her. With the "elopement" a matter of common knowledge, I'm sure his mother couldn't have been entirely happy, but it wasn't in her nature to put up any strong opposition. His father, Masao, did oppose the match, and for once this even-tempered man and his son clashed. But since in every other respect Masayuki was a perfect son—someone, I should say, Masao seemed rather in awe of—in the end he had his way. "Fortunately" might be the wrong word, but the senior Shigemitsus had died one after another some time earlier, so their attitude did not come into play. After a three-year stay in the United States, Masayuki got his master's, came back to Japan, and joined an architectural firm. That same year Yoko graduated from the English department of her university and started work as a private secretary in the faculty of economics at Hokkaido University. That winter, a group of radicals calling themselves the United Red Army staged a shootout at the Asama Mountain Lodge in Karuizawa, and the three Saegusa sisters and indeed all Japan were mesmerized by the events unfolding on television. Another two years passed before Masayuki and Yoko were married.

One day as I was ironing in the Karuizawa kitchen, Yoko came in and made an announcement. "I'm going to marry Masayuki," she said.

"Go right ahead," I said, not looking up as I sprayed starch on a napkin.

She walked over to the sink and looked out the window, her back to me. "There's been no word from Taro."

I said nothing.

"Seven years." She twisted her head around and looked back at me. "Seven years, and not a word."

I wasn't sure from her expression whether she was angry or weepy.

"So I'm going to marry Masayuki."

"No one's stopping you."

I folded the napkin and ran the iron over its surface one final time, then reached out and picked up another one, spraying and then pressing down with the iron. She watched me for a while before going on in a different tone of voice.

"Masayuki says that if Taro ever comes back, I can run away with him that same day if I want to. He's said it more than once." Her voice was no more than a murmur. "I never thought there could be anyone who would say something like that. Only he would. No one else in the whole world would think of saying it."

I kept on ironing as she talked. Her whispery voice filled the kitchen.

"I was so miserable back then, I never dreamed I'd ever be this happy."

They had a simple ceremony in Karuizawa, since that was where they'd found each other. Her father was there, wary about his heart yet also sincerely happy, as if he'd finally put down a heavy load. Natsue could hardly be disappointed that her daughter was marrying Masayuki, but the whole thing had been such an extraordinary turn of events from the start that even when confronted with the final outcome, she seemed unable to take it in. Harue was resigned, since the ceremony came well after both of her girls were married off. Still, she said some spiteful things behind the scenes.

"So Masayuki is more eccentric than we thought."

At the time I felt this was a mean thing to say, but looking back, the comment does not seem too far off target.

The young couple avoided Seijo. With help from both sets of parents they made a down payment, took out a loan, and moved into a small condominium in Nogizaka, in the center of Tokyo. Concerned about Yoko's frail health, Masayuki apparently did not want children, but Yoko felt that she ought to give the family an heir and, although in that sense a boy would have been better, she gave birth to a girl, her only child. The baby was born on a snowy day, so they named her Miyuki, with the characters for "deep snow." Since she had fair skin like her father the name suited her, even with Yoko for a mother—though everyone ended up calling her Miki, which is what she called herself when she was little. Masayuki began teaching architectural history at his alma mater and eventually opened his own small architectural firm. After she married, Yoko gave up her singing and actually went to a vocational school so that she could help out in her husband's company as an interior designer. But her mother was away from home so much that Yoko, who was concerned about her father's heart condition, used to leave Miki with someone— the housekeeper, or a part-time office worker, or even Natsue herself, if she was there in Seijo kicking up her heels—and go back to Sapporo as often as she could.

Gradually it became apparent that Masayuki and Yoko were an unusually close couple—that he took exceptionally good care of her, not minding how it might look. In Karuizawa, when the fog rolled in, I often saw him running upstairs to fetch her sweater. If she so much as sneezed, he would give her a sharp, worried look, wherever they were. She was still highly excitable and had trouble falling asleep, so he made a habit of sitting at her bedside reading aloud to her until she dozed off, then doing more work before going to bed himself. His mother, Yayoi, learned about this only from living with them in Karuizawa, and, discreet though she usually was, when she found out she was so amazed that she couldn't help telling the three sisters, and so everyone knew. Even Harue had to join in the laughter.

AS MORE TIME went by, both the Demon and Grammy Saegusa died, leaving only Grampy (who was in his eighties but looked no older than sixty-five) from that generation. But the sisters' grandchildren went on increasing in number, so the Saegusa villa was if anything livelier than before. Since the house needed repairs each year and grew more cramped as the number of inhabitants increased, extensions were added at the back and on top, and a separate wing was built in front, slightly off to one side. The two elder sisters were at this point approaching sixty, and their looks inevitably had faded. Their energy was steadily flagging too, and efforts to re-create "the good old days" seemed to be too much for them. Eri and Mari left their husbands in Tokyo during the summer and came to Karuizawa on vacation with their children, but they were less fussy than the Saegusa sisters were. *Sunday brunch* became still more abbreviated, often consisting merely of ready-to-eat dishes from the Kinokuniya supermarket. Yoko, as the young mistress of the Shigemitsu family, was of course no longer looked on as a cut below the rest. In the daytime she shared her time between the two houses, but slept at night in the Shigemitsu house. She was sensitive in all her dealings with her in-laws. In fact, perhaps from Masayuki's influence, she was in fact such an exemplary young wife that as time went by it began to seem that all the events at Chitose Funabashi and Oiwake were just figments of my imagination.

Changes happened in my life as well. As the area prospered, and one by one our boys went out to work, my husband and I weren't so hard-pressed for money anymore. Ready-made clothes became more popular, so fewer dressmaking orders came in, but we were comfortable enough by that time for me to reduce the amount of work I took in anyway. Instead of riding the train to Karuizawa I began driving there in a minicar. Our eldest boy was a godsend to us. After graduating from Shinshu University, he went to work at the local Ueda Credit Bank, helping out with the family budget as long as his two brothers still needed our support. He married young, bringing into the family circle a sensible, hardworking girl whose people made and sold pickles. Her first child was Ami, who later helped out in Karuizawa. Strictly speaking, Ami was my grandchild, but since I was still in my thirties when she was born, she didn't feel that way to me. Partly because our daughter-in-law helped out in her parents' business until her second baby came along, I really was a second mother to Ami when she was small. She was the same age as Yoko's Miki. I used to take her to Karuizawa with me piggyback, and in no time she fit right in as a playmate for the Saegusa sisters' grandchildren. My husband had thought I might want a baby of my own, and was relieved to find out I didn't want one in the least.

Eventually Uncle Genji died. After his health declined, I went to visit him several times in Tokyo, and toward the end I stayed in his house in Soto Kanda for nearly a month, nursing him while that husky-voiced woman of his added a hairpiece to her thinning hair, pinning it up in back, and went out bravely to attend to her small restaurant. His ashes were interred in a Tokyo cemetery.

Once Yoko married, no one mentioned Taro's name in her presence. Even Harue stopped referring to the "rickshaw man's descendant" in front of her. The Oiwake cottage might never have existed. I stayed away from it for a long time, but the thought of it rotting away gave me pangs, so once I got my little car and could drive over, I started dropping in twice a year to air the place in secret, not telling either Natsue or Yoko. I just opened the windows and closet doors to let in some fresh air. I couldn't imagine anyone ever living there again and assumed that in the end the building would be torn down and the property sold, yet when I stepped inside, the past seemed to swirl around me along with the dust, making me nostalgic.

It was all over between Taro and us. And yet we weren't left completely in the dark about his doings. He did so spectacularly well for himself in New York that whenever Harue's husband traveled there on business he would hear rumors about him, rumors that passed from Harue to her sisters and so to me. First we heard that after quitting his job as a chauffeur and becoming some kind of a repairman at a Japanese company he had gone right into sales, making such giant strides that he was soon riding around in a Mercedes. Then, although I'm not sure whether it's true or not, the word was that he'd done something dishonest and left the company. We were shaking our heads over this when we next heard that he'd gone into business with an American. The latest news was that he had become extremely rich.

In the fall of 1981, Takero died in Sapporo from a second heart attack. He was due to retire that year and had suggested to Natsue that they go back to Tokyo once he gave up his teaching post—only to end up dying on the eve of retirement. I heard the turnout at his funeral was huge.

Shortly after that, toward the end of the year, my brother, now the head of the family in Saku, was contacted by a local real estate agent whose records showed that some twenty years earlier the Utagawa family had bought a property in Oiwake through the Tsuchiyas. No one seemed to be using the cottage currently, and would somebody please contact the Utagawas and inquire whether they had any interest in selling? My brother passed the message on to me. Apparently some company wanted to build a vacation house for its employees and was negotiating with various local landowners. Whether out of ignorance or sheer determination, they were offering 30 percent more than the going rate. Since Oiwake was full of untouched woods, why anyone should go to so much trouble to buy land where other people's houses already stood I had no idea, but I didn't give it much thought. Rather, the knowledge that the Oiwake cottage would soon disappear left me mourning for the past and all the memories of old Mrs. Utagawa the place contained. There was nothing I could do about it, however, but pick up the telephone and call Natsue. Just as I thought she would, she treated the proposal as a godsend. Ever since Takero's funeral she'd been living with her sisters in Seijo, and as soon as she could sell the house in Sapporo she planned to buy two small condominiums in Seijo near the station, one to live in and one to rent out. Any cash she could come by was very welcome. Of the place where her daughter had caused such a scandal she had nothing but bad memories.

Yoko heard the news and called me from Nogizaka. "We're losing the Oiwake cottage . . . ," she said, her voice trailing off, and then, probably thinking about the house in Chitose Funabashi, she corrected herself. "We're losing the Oiwake cottage *too*." I realized then that she hadn't spoken the word "Oiwake" in years. She never mentioned Taro.

Around the end of January I had a phone call from Natsue. The papers had been drawn up and the deal would be concluded by the end of February, when the property would be handed over. The purchaser would probably tear the cottage down eventually, so there was no need to tidy it up inside, but the real estate agent had told her to remove anything she wanted before then. She had no intention of going all the way to Oiwake in the middle of winter. She had already taken out the things she wanted, things of any value, and as she was about to move from a house into an apartment that was significantly smaller, she certainly didn't want anything else. If the snow wasn't too deep, would I mind going in for a last look around? I was welcome to keep anything that looked useful. Big pieces of furniture could be left, but any small, personal items—the sort of thing it would be awkward to let strangers see—she would like me to dispose of. She had no idea I had been going there twice a year to give the place an airing.

LESS THAN A week after Natsue's call, the phone rang at about ten-thirty in the morning in my house in Miyota. My daughter-in-law handed me the receiver with a puzzled look, and a voice in my ear said, "It's me, Taro."

"Taro . . . ?" I said, half in doubt.

"Yeah, it's me."

I hadn't heard that voice in fifteen years, but it had the same diffident tone to it as when he was a child.

"Where are you?"

"Karuizawa."

Shocked that he was so close by, I felt the blood drain from my head. The hand holding the receiver started to tremble, but with my daughter-in-law watching I controlled myself, though hardly knowing what I was doing.

He was staying at the Prince Hotel, he said.

Afraid of my voice sounding too shaken, I said nothing. He asked if I could join him there for lunch, or if I wasn't free then perhaps dinner that evening or lunch the next day. At any rate he hoped I would come out to see him at least once. His Japanese sounded a little awkward.

"I'll come now," I managed to reply.

"Is noon all right? Or shall we make it a little later, around one?"

"One o'clock would be fine."

I hung up and turned to stare hollow-eyed at my daughter-in-law, standing there with her head cocked innocently to one side. I told her I was going to the Prince Hotel to meet an old friend, someone from the family I'd served during my Tokyo days. I kept my voice as expressionless as possible. Since the birth of her second child, she'd become a full-time mother, thus freeing me from the responsibility of babysitting and letting me go out whenever I pleased. I felt wobbly. My knees were weak, my head muddled. I couldn't think straight. I forced my uncooperative body into gear and got ready to leave, but putting on makeup, doing my hair, and choosing what to wear took twice as long as usual. I'd lived so long in the country, with so few opportunities to go anywhere, that my sense of fashion was not what it used to be. Harue's words rang in my ears as I dithered: "Common people hardly ever dress up, so when they do, they go overboard and end up looking like bar girls, all dolled up with ringlets and a ton of accessories." The last time I'd seen Taro, I'd been thirty; I was now forty-five. Go for a quiet, understated look, I told myself, surprised by my own intensity as I peered into old Mrs. Utagawa's full-length mirror for a final inspection. Memories of the nonstop quarreling Taro and I used to do came back to me as if it had been yesterday or a phantom scene from another life. Such an urge to see him filled every corner of me that I could hardly believe I had sworn never to set eyes on him again.

It was just one o'clock when I drove up to the hotel. A man in a smart dark suit—Taro—was seated on a sofa in the lobby. He seemed to recognize me instantly too, getting swiftly to his feet. It wasn't only female vanity that made me pray that he wouldn't be disappointed or feel awkward around me, that I wouldn't look painfully old. As to what feelings he may have had on his return to Japan, I had no idea, but I did not want to ruin whatever memories connected him to his past. He'd made a reservation, he said. When we entered the hotel restaurant he held the door for me, ushering me through in a manner I'd never seen anywhere but in foreign movies. Although I seemed to make him a bit nervous, he was completely at ease with the headwaiter, who bowed politely and led us to a corner table marked "Reserved." His way of walking across the plush carpet, sitting in the chair, and taking the menu was flowing and natural. That alone showed how far he had come in the world.

When he sat down across from me, I had my first good look at him. He gave an impression of intense vitality. It seemed incredible that he had once been a boy whose snotty nose I used to wipe. Never in all my life had I imagined dining in such a place, face-to-face with a man who looked like this.

"Is this your first trip back?" I said, to start the conversation.

"Second." As if embarrassed, he opened the menu and studied it.

"When was the first?"

"I came in November."

"Last year?"

"Mm-hm."

"On business?"

"No."

He looked up. Then for the first time he in turn looked me full in the face, his eyes roaming from my hairline to my throat as if to assess how much I had aged. I didn't know whether to be relieved that I was wearing a gray suit that was on the sedate side or to wish I'd chosen something a bit more daring.

"I went to Mrs. Utagawa's grave first thing," he told me. "Maybe the one person who'd have been pleased to see me back."

He said this with a wry smile, and I couldn't help joining in. It was true: the old lady was the one person he might have counted on to welcome him wholeheartedly after an absence of fifteen years.

"I thought her grave at least would be the same, but it was all different . . ."

"Her son died." When Takero died, the ancestral graves and that of old Mrs. Utagawa had finally been combined into one family grave.

"I know," he said, glancing at me.

"You knew that?"

Yes, he said: he'd read his obituary in a Japanese newspaper.

The waiter came to ask if we'd like something to drink before lunch, and Taro waved his left hand at me, urging me to order. Since it wouldn't really do for a wife to go home with the smell of alcohol on her breath, I asked for water, and so did he.

"Aren't you going to have a drink?" I asked, memories of the days when he used to drain bottles of *shochu* vivid in my mind.

Again he looked down at the menu before saying, "I'm on the wagon."

"Since when?"

"Since sailing across the Pacific."

"Fifteen years ago?"

"Yes, ma'am."

"You haven't had a drink in all that time?"

He shook his head, eyes still on the menu.

"Really?"

"Not a drop."

"Well, you certainly drank enough for a lifetime in those six months."

For a while we were silent. When I spoke again, my tone was surprisingly caustic.

"So you reformed."

Taro said nothing, his eyes still cast down.

"Good for you."

If he'd done it out of shame over those months of hard drinking in my apartment, then was that whole period something he wanted to forget completely, to pretend never happened? As if my cynical tone had made him stiffen, he turned a page of the menu and answered in a cheerless voice, "When I find out there's no point in life, that's when I'll start up again."

"Oh, I see." Impulsively, I added, "Life has no point to it anyway, and you know it."

He looked up in mild surprise and studied me with an expression that was hard to read. Here I'd rushed over after hearing he was back, intending to give him a warm welcome . . . Under his scrutiny, I felt ashamed of failing to be pleasant.

There was a long pause during which the waiter came to take our orders. After he left, it was Taro's turn to ask a question.

"How's marriage?"

"Mine, you mean?"

He looked ruffled for a moment, then nodded.

"Fine, thank you."

"A good husband this time?"

"Yes, a good husband."

I looked away. Not because I was lying but because his probing eyes made me uncomfortable.

"I got rich," he said after a pause.

"I know." I laughed. "You're a big name now."

"Hardly." The old, gloomy look I'd seen so many times before came faintly back into his eyes. "I was such a money-grubber, I'm still an uneducated boor." Another searching look. "Fumiko, is there anything you want?" He said this with his eyes slightly upturned. "Anything money can buy, I mean."

"No . . ."

Most of the time I lived from day to day thinking, "If only we had a bit more cash . . . ," but that feeling had vanished. When he put the question to me like that, I knew at once that the only things people ever really want are the things money can't buy.

"Nothing?"

"Not a thing," I said, then added: "The moon. That's what I want. The moon." I spoke the cliché for the fun of it, but even to my ears it didn't sound funny.

Taro looked straight at me before looking down at the tabletop. Then he said, "I'm the one who bought the Oiwake place."

How can I describe my reaction? I thought I knew how dogged he was, how annoyingly obstinate, but perhaps in the fifteen years since I'd seen him last, my knowledge of him had dimmed. I felt my face turn pale.

"That was you, Taro?"

"Yeah, it was me."

He answered with a casualness that was perhaps deliberate, then looked up and added an explanation. "I used a Japanese company as a broker so Natsue wouldn't know. It would've attracted too much attention if a foreign company had gone after a place like that."

On reading in a Japanese paper that Takero Utagawa was dead, he'd had a sudden impulse to buy the Oiwake cottage, he said. The purpose of his trip to Japan the previous November had been to look up the real estate agency and have them contact my family in Saku. That's how he found out I was married and living in Miyota.

"Did Natsue say anything?" He asked this nonchalantly, as if to cool off my reaction.

"About what?"

"About the cottage."

"She did call last week, as a matter of fact."

As I gave him the gist of the phone call, a faint smile came to his face. The reason he'd tried to push through the sale so the transfer would take place in midwinter was that he figured that Natsue, always the laziest of the three sisters, would be unlikely to come to freezing Nagano at that time of year and would instead contact me with instructions over what still remained inside the house. He'd worked it all out ahead of time. His ability to see several moves ahead was now combined with an adult's ability to take action. There was something unnerving about it.

"Actually, I have a favor to ask of you, Fumiko," he said rather formally. I felt my face stiffen.

"I want you to leave the place just the way it is."

I looked at him, deflated. His strong, masculine face was completely serious.

"Don't throw anything away, just leave everything the way it used to be for when I take over."

His determination to keep everything the same had also led him to negotiate the purchase of the lots behind, on either side, in front, and diagonally across from the cottage. It seemed crazy to me.

"What are you going to do with it?"

"Thought I'd come back for a couple of weeks in the summertime and use it."

"Every year?"

"Maybe."

"Use it for what?" I asked, knowing there was no point in asking.

"I've never had a real vacation . . ."

"Yes, but that place is in no condition to use. I air it out once in a while, but the futons and the quilts were too much bother, so I never touched them once in fifteen years. I never swept the floors, either." Other emotions swelled in me, but these details were all that came out. "It's just not usable," I said firmly, though I knew it was a waste of breath.

"It'll be fine. I'll fix it up as I go along."

He stared into space. A vision rose in my mind of this man, who handled more money daily than I would see in my lifetime, hanging out damp, moldy bedding to air and sweeping frayed tatami mats in the little highland cottage. He was always good at working with his hands; he probably would look after the place himself well enough, however ridiculous the whole undertaking was.

After a moment I said, "When will you be back this summer?"

"Don't know yet."

"I'll fix it up so you can use it by summertime."

His eyes widened. "That's not why I got in touch, Fumiko. I just wanted you to leave it as it is."

"It's all right. I'll clean it up for you."

After a short pause he said uncertainly, "You will? . . ."

"I'll do my best to see everything is just the way it used to be."

Even as a child he had never been able to say thank you at the right moment, nor did he now. He merely said in a slightly more relaxed voice, "When I came back to Japan before, I went to Chitose Funabashi."

I said nothing.

"Now there are three little houses crowded together on the old plot, and close by is a big highway, Ring Road 8 I think it's called. It's all changed. I tell you, Japan is one scary place, the way things change."

Noticing my distracted expression, he fell silent. He might be feeling relieved, thinking we were reconciled, but I was filled with conflicting emotions. I already regretted having

offered to do his cleaning, as if he and I were accomplices—
though in what crime, I couldn't have said.

The meal had ended and coffee was served when Taro
reached inside the breast pocket of his suit jacket and produced a bulky envelope. It was a horizontal, Western-style
envelope; he mustn't have had any Japanese-style ones on
hand.

"Here."

He held it out, looking almost angry. Thinking it was a
letter to Yoko, I hesitated, and he thrust it at me again till
it almost touched my chest. Though I had known it would
come to this in the end, now that it had happened I felt too
weary to react.

"Here," he repeated, still thrusting the envelope at me.

I waited a full beat before taking it with an audible sigh.
It was strangely hefty, almost as if he had handed me a bar
of lead. I turned it over, immediately seeing through the
unsealed flap that it contained a wad of crisp new ten-
thousand-yen bills.

"What's this?"

"Well, you know . . ."

"What is this for?"

"Look, I don't know what I'm supposed to say, all right?"
He slowly reddened.

"How can you be so rude!"

I might have turned red too. I felt a rush of anger. After
all I had done for him out of pity, my heart going out to
him, now that he was rich he wanted to repay my sympathy
with money? I thought of the time I'd scrubbed his grimy

little body in the Utagawa bathroom; the time he'd shown up on the doorstep of my apartment looking desperate, in work clothes; the time I'd sat and bowed my head down to the tatami before a grudging Uncle Genji, begging him to help Taro go abroad. Scene after scene from the past flickered through my mind. The next thing I knew, I had flung the envelope back at him. For once I'd given vent physically to my anger—not only anger at Taro, but also an unfocused resentment that I had kept pent up inside me all those years.

"What am I supposed to do?"

He sounded pained. The envelope had landed on the table, upsetting a small espresso cup that fortunately was empty.

There was a brief silence. Then he said in a low, choked voice, staring distractedly at the overturned cup, "How can I thank you in a way that wouldn't be rude?"

"You can't!" I retorted. "You can't ever thank me in a way that wouldn't be rude. Not ever in your whole life. That's your comeuppance."

He stared at me, his shoulders heaving slightly. Under the surface of the sterling young man he'd become I saw the face of a much younger Taro, eyes tightened as if he might start crying. After fifteen years of hard work crowned with brilliant success, he had returned to Japan without a tickertape parade in his hometown or a family to rejoice with him. Once he had visited old Mrs. Utagawa's grave, the best he could hope for was to come and see me. And here I didn't even treat him properly, but just heaped sarcasm on him.

I reached out, picked up the envelope, and removed two bills from the wad bound in white tape.

"My housecleaning fee."

"Thank you."

He took the envelope I handed him and pulled out another bill, then another and another and another until he'd counted out eight in all and was holding them out to me. "Please take this," he said with a look of such entreaty that I gave in. He thanked me again; and that's how Taro and I entered into our strange and ambiguous employer–employee relationship.

That day of our reunion, we went the whole time without once mentioning Yoko's name.

FUMIKO'S EYES WANDERED several times to the old-fashioned wall clock before she announced, "Time's up." She bent her head back slightly as if easing something off. "I'm almost done, but the rest will have to wait for another time."

In less than an hour she was supposed to pick up Taro Azuma at Middle Karuizawa Station, where he was arriving on the last train from Ueno.

She bent her head back again, then straightened up and let out a long sigh as she looked at the dinner table.

Lit by a dim yellow bulb, the tabletop looked suddenly messy to Yusuke too, crowded with the remains of their makeshift meal: coffee cups, teacups, and small plates; serving dishes that held corncobs and empty steamed soybean pods; plates with bits of smoked salmon, cheese, and pickles scattered on them; slices of lemon and crusts of bread. While it was still light outside they'd sat out on the porch where the insistent sound of the cicadas echoed in his ears as he listened to her talk. When daylight faded and the cicadas quieted down, the mosquitoes then became unbearable and so they had moved indoors, where he kept on listening. The two of them had eaten and drunk whatever she found in the refrigerator, making do.

They quickly cleared the table and went outside to another bright moonlit night.

When Yusuke brought his bicycle around to the gate with its two wooden posts driven into the ground, Fumiko came out that far to see him off. Her purse was in her left hand and car keys dangled from the other.

In the moonlight he saw she had put on some lipstick.

"According to tradition, today's the day you light a farewell fire to see the spirits off again," she said. "But Taro's suddenly become superstitious and told me not to do it."

With the toe of her shoe she poked at the foot of the posts, where just the other day she had lit the *ogara* straw in welcome.

"Anyway, he wants to be haunted, like you, apparently. He's been sleeping in the shed ever since that night. Waiting for her ghost. Just crazy." She laughed, before gazing up the narrow gravel track with a faraway look in her eyes, as if searching for the ghost.

"What about your friend?" she asked as Yusuke straddled his bicycle. "Will he be there for tomorrow's *high tea?*" She seemed to take for granted that Yusuke would come.

"I somehow doubt it."

The memory of Kubo's face as he'd said, "Think I'll bow outta that one," brought a smile to his face. Watching, Fumiko understood, and gave a small smile of her own.

"All right. I won't expect him then."

Keys dangling from her hand, she returned to her car, which was parked inside, while Yusuke began pedaling up the rising gravel path. Soon the headlights of her car drew near, briefly lighting up his figure as he stood pressed into the shrubbery on his bicycle, before finally overtaking him and moving past.

WHEN HE GOT back to the summer house in Middle Karuizawa, there was no sign of his friend yet. Kubo didn't get back till past midnight. Yusuke heard the front door open, then the refrigerator door open and close, the toilet flush and so on, but getting up to talk seemed too much trouble, so he just lay in bed. Soon he heard Kubo coming upstairs and moving around in the room next door. At some point, while Yusuke lay unable to sleep, he heard snoring. Was Kubo drunk? He'd never snored like that in high school. Yusuke tossed and turned, watching through cracks on either side of the shades as the sky grew lighter. That was the last thing he remembered before waking up at ten in the morning.

"So how come you slept later than me?"

When he went downstairs, Kubo was sitting on the sofa in front of the television with the sound turned off, his wet hair gleaming blackly as he turned to greet him. For someone just out of the shower, his face was puffy and slack. At last night's party in Minamihara, just as predicted, there had been bottles of Dom Pérignon everywhere, bobbing in ice water, all you could drink. He got greedy, drank more than he should have, and so woke up with a splitting headache.

"Still, it's up and at 'em again today." Sitting on the sofa, he hit the back of his neck with the edge of his hand like a middle-aged man.

"How so?" asked Yusuke from the kitchen, putting the kettle on to boil.

"I'm scheduled to take the ladies out for a drive." At the party he'd been making light conversation and before he knew it had agreed to drive to Onioshidashi Volcanic Park with his sister-in-law and her sister and mother. "While in the meantime my brother and his father-in-law will be playing a round of golf. Not fair!"

"Coffee or tea?"

"Coffee."

Kubo turned off the TV, came over to the breakfast bar, and sat down facing the kitchen. He waited until Yusuke had poured two mugs of coffee to ask, "So, what were you doing yesterday?"

Yusuke sat down before answering: "Spent the whole day in Oiwake."

"The whole day?" Kubo reached for the cream pitcher. "What, in the cottage where that maid lives?"

"Yeah."

"You were there till nighttime?"

"Yeah."

Kubo cocked his head dubiously.

"Listening to her tell her story."

Kubo looked even more dubious. Yusuke put some cream in his mug and stirred the coffee with a soup spoon—he'd been unable to find any teaspoons—while he explained that it was a long story, that he hadn't yet heard how it ended, and that someday when he'd heard it all he'd tell Kubo. Kubo seemed on the point of making a joke, but seeing the look on his friend's face, he clamped his mouth shut as if he'd thought better of it. After sipping his coffee in silence he asked seriously, "So are you going to Karuizawa today for *high tea* or whatever with her?"

"Yeah, I think I will."

"If you came on the drive with us, I'd make sure we got you back in time."

"That's okay."

"Hmm." Mug in hand, Kubo looked intently at Yusuke, then said without so much as a smile, "Whatever, man. Suit yourself."

Kubo left before noon with the others. The plan was to stop somewhere along the way to the volcanic park and pick up some grilled char for lunch.

"What a perfect day for a drive!" The younger sister, a size slimmer than her sibling, made this comment to no one in particular as she drew her pink-sandaled feet inside the car. Yusuke, who had come out to see them off, glanced up at the sky. Directly overhead was the summer sun, baking the car roof. Where yesterday there had been a scattering of white clouds, today the sky was a deep, clear blue.

He went back inside and had another cup of coffee. Then
he ran a tubful of hot water in the spacious bathroom where
red crepe myrtle showed through the window, climbed in,
and took a bath, carefully shaving his none-too-heavy beard
afterward. Next he stir-fried the chicken he and Kubo had
bought together at the supermarket the other day, first driz-
zling the chunks with olive oil and soy sauce, and ate this
with bread from Asanoya for brunch. Even when he had
finished washing the dishes it was still just a little past one.
For once, time hung heavy on his hands. He was short of
sleep, so a nap was in order, but he was in no mood to lie
down again. He soon decided that he would spend the rest
of the time until five, the hour designated by Harue, stroll-
ing around Old Karuizawa. Since the idea of working up a
sweat on his bicycle was unappealing, and seeing that for the
first time in his life he was going to a *high tea*, whatever that
might be, he took advantage of the number on the wall next
to the telephone, labeled "Matsuba Taxi," to call for a cab.

The driver, at pains to point out that he was not a summer employee but a local, avoided the main road and took
a shortcut that landed Yusuke at Kinokuniya supermarket
in under fifteen minutes. Yusuke headed away from the
crowds, off to the quieter, more distant areas. For over
two hours he walked around from one summer house to
another. He found himself searching for old Western-style
buildings. There must be some somewhere, he thought, but
managed to find only a few. When he did stumble on one,
it was generally apparent that it had sat unused for years,
the windows shut up and the yard choked with weeds. In

WESTERN-STYLE SUMMER VILLA WITH BAY WINDOWS

his wanderings he covered quite a distance, as he eventually realized in dismay. He hurriedly retraced his steps, but by the time he found himself in front of the familiar lava stone gateposts, it was well past the appointed hour. The two Western-style villas stood side by side in the special, limpid twilight of a clear day.

On a day like this the famous Karuizawa mist would probably not invade.

When he went into the garden, he found a dozen people sitting outside in two groups on white wicker or plastic chairs. The trio of ladies from the other day made little squeals of welcome when they spotted him. Harue, the eldest, raised a hand in greeting and then lowered it straight to an empty chair beside her, pointing. Seated on her left was Natsue, the middle sister, wearing a broad-brimmed red hat. The youngest of the three, Fuyue, was in the other group, and waved when she recognized him, her bespectacled face all smiles.

Yusuke went up to Harue, who looked him up and down as she said, "Welcome! How lovely to have a young person join us. From the moment you came in, I could sense a difference in the air."

Beside her, Natsue echoed the greeting: "Lovely to see you!" She stretched forward, dimpling beneath the red hat. Around her neck was a red silk scarf.

Yusuke looked down at his jeans. "Sorry I didn't have anything better to wear."

Without comment, Harue said, "We were just talking about you. Fumi said you were coming, but when you

WESTERN-STYLE SUMMER VILLA WITH TIMBER FRAME

didn't make an appearance, we thought you must have run away after all."

The average age of those present was indeed quite advanced, and most were old women. The only men in attendance besides Yusuke were an elderly gentleman and someone who looked middle-aged. A young girl among them of high school age was evidently someone's granddaughter.

"This is Mr. Kato." Harue introduced him to people who she said were longtime neighbors. Yusuke was surprised she remembered his name. "He is an editor," she said, and named his publishing house. "I happened to make his acquaintance the other day and insisted that he come today so we could have at least one young man among us. I quite forced him to say yes. He is staying over at Mitsui Woods in the house of a friend of his." After introducing him smoothly like this, she tilted her head toward the porch.

"Now go and help yourself to a drink, young man."

The girl they'd called Ami the other day was standing behind a deck table loaded with drinks. The other, younger girl was deep in conversation with her, leaning on the table with both hands. She might have been discussing future plans, for he heard something about the department of environmental design at such-and-such a university, but when she noticed him approaching she stopped talking, then backed away.

Ami's blunt-cut black hair swung along her jawline when she returned his little bow.

"What can I get you?"

WESTERN-STYLE SUMMER VILLA WITH ENCLOSED VERANDA

A variety of bottles, along with cups and wineglasses of every description, were lined up in the sunlight. Before answering the question, Yusuke asked one of his own.

"Do you help out here often?"

"Yes, but usually only in the daytime."

In the evenings she worked from five on in a restaurant on the Karuizawa Ginza, but today, as she was staying overnight here, she had asked a girl from the day shift to take her place.

"You're staying overnight?"

"Yes. For *baito* like this I usually do. It's just once or twice a summer, though."

The familiar word *baito*, from the German word for "work," *Arbeit*, had become student slang for "part-time job." Without realizing it, he was scrutinizing her face. She was neither a country girl nor a city girl. She just had the intelligent face of someone who must always have done well in school. He wondered what this thoroughly modern girl who did *baito* here and saw those old ladies almost daily thought about it all.

Ami seemed amused, laughing as she asked again, "So what can I get you?"

"What do you recommend?" he countered, eyeing the bottles.

"How about some sherry?"

"All right then, a sherry, please."

She picked up an old-fashioned piece of cut glass shaped like a miniature wineglass, then extended her arm and held it up to the setting sun. The laughter of a moment ago continued to play faintly around her mouth as she held the glass in her fingertips, watching it gather the sun's last rays of light and scatter them in its facets.

Yusuke took the glass, filled now with amber liquid, and went back into the garden. When he sat down as directed next to Harue, she craned her neck and called in a loud voice, "Mr. Shirakawa!" The elderly gentleman in the other group turned his head. The golden retriever crouched at his feet turned its head too.

"Over here! You must come and sit next to this young man. He is from Kyoto."

"Coming, coming," said the gentleman in a comical way and got to his feet. "*Wolfgang, komme,*" he said to the dog in what sounded like German, and walked over, remarking loudly enough to be overheard, "Can't disobey the royal summons," before taking the empty chair on Yusuke's right. "*Sitz,*" he said, patting the dog's collar, and it crouched again at his feet.

Whatever line of work he may once have been in, he was clearly well trained in the social graces, smoothly introducing himself in a voice that retained the soft cadences of the Kyoto dialect. The name was Shirakawa, he repeated. Before the war he had become friends with someone called Ando at Kyoto University and had enjoyed an association with the Saegusa family ever since, one that now spanned half a century.

"Ando was always a bit of a hermit, living quietly away from the hurly-burly, while I was more of a hooligan, living right in the heart of Gion, with all those *maiko* and geishas around."

Unsure who Ando might be, Yusuke made polite sounds as he listened, but soon figured out that it must be Yayoi's husband Masao, who had taken the Shigemitsu name on marrying into the family. Shirakawa began to speak about his friend's late son Masayuki, lamenting that while a useless old fart like himself lived on and on, someone as gifted as Masayuki had died before he turned fifty; the one blessing was that Ando himself had died first, sparing himself the sadness of outliving his only child. The conversation continued in this vein for some time.

Shirakawa spoke as if he imagined Yusuke to be on closer terms with the three sisters than he actually was.

"What shall we have next?" Harue suddenly leaned forward and addressed Shirakawa across Yusuke.

"Beg pardon?"

"Music, I mean."

"Ah, right."

Only then did Yusuke realize that the piano music had ended.

"Who was that playing the Liszt just now?" Shirakawa asked.

"An American, Russell Sherman."

Natsue, seated next to her, craned forward and said with obvious satisfaction, turning her white-powdered face to Shirakawa, "You know my elder daughter is in San Francisco."

"Yuko, isn't it?"

"Yes, that's right. This Russell Sherman is someone she particularly recommends. Someone admired by those in the know."

"Aha."

"His teacher studied with Schoenberg, they say."

"Well, then. No wonder it was so good."

Harue interrupted to ask if perhaps he would care to listen to one of his beloved Mozart concertos.

"No, enough Mozart for today. Rather than that, since it's getting late, I'd say it's time for your Callas, Harue."

"Really?" She smiled slightly with pleasure. "It's so noisy— you really don't mind?"

"Of course not."

"Then shall we listen to one Callas recording and then retire inside?"

"Great."

"Something from *La Sonnambula*?"

"That would be great."

"Or maybe 'Una voce poco fa'?"

"That would be great too."

"Mr. Shirakawa!" she said in mock exasperation. "Is that all you can say—'that would be great'?"

"Not at all," he responded. "The screams of the *Turandot* princess are actually more grating than great!"

She laughed appreciatively. "Then shall we listen to *Lucia* for a change?"

"Nothing would please me more."

While Harue called Ami over and gave her instructions about the next CD, Natsue spoke to Shirakawa. "People nowadays have become such avid operagoers, haven't they?"

Harue picked up on this. "Absolutely! Even people you look at and think, that's an opera lover? They are mad, mad, mad about opera, opera, opera."

"And pay absurdly high prices for tickets to the 'Three Tenors.'"

"Yes, so when you do go to a performance, all you see around you are the sort of people you want to tap on the shoulder and ask, 'Excuse me, might you be looking for Koma Stadium?' You know the variety hall, the one where country people ride in by the hundreds on chartered buses?"

Natsue tittered.

"And the way they dress up is so awful, it lowers the tone of the theater."

"I know!"

"I tell you, it is so off-putting, lately I would just as soon stay at home and listen to a CD."

"Yes, much better."

"That way you're spared some ghastly sights!"

Shirakawa, who had been following the two sisters' remarks with an indulgent smile, turned to Yusuke. "At this house and the one next door there was always live music, you see. Quite a luxury."

Before the war it was chamber music; after the war there had been two top-level pianists among them, from two different generations, and along the way another young woman had taken up singing. That was Yoko, the one who later became Masayuki's wife. That reminded him: it was over twenty years ago, but one evening Yoko had sung Lucia and it had been wonderful.

"She sang in moonlight, wearing a lovely white dress . . . ," he reminisced, the eyes behind his glasses staring back into the past. His voice too was nostalgic. "There's an old saying

in these parts that a girl who stands alone in the moonlight too long falls under a spell. I must say, that's how she
sounded when she sang that night."

As he talked on, caught up in his memories, moment by
moment the darkness deepened.

"I am sorry you had that inflicted on you," Harue said,
remembering too. "She should have chosen an easier, more
Japanese piece, a ballad like 'The white citrus flowers are in
full blo-o-o-o-m.' But she picked that instead. Lucia has to
be a coloratura."

"Yes, it is a coloratura role."

"Well, she managed the easy bits well enough. She was
sickly as a child and never had any lung capacity to speak of."

"But her Lucia was marvelous."

Natsue got a word in. "I did a bit of singing myself, you
know, back when I was in school. I could hit a high A perfectly. I think it must be hereditary."

Presently a soprano voice of richness and depth floated
from the open windows of the parlor, resonating over the
darkening greenery. All at once it was as if the entire scene
before them was awakened by that voice, infused with
unexpected life: the western sky, streaked with bands of
pale gold and purple; the two houses, standing gray and
disconsolate against that sky; the clusters of trees casting
deep black shadows here and there across the ground. The
same voice that brought everything suddenly to life also
drew them into another, much deeper world—a world
that was normally hidden, a world that stretched out into
eternity. Yusuke, who had at first looked on with a sense

of distance as everyone else sat listening, their faces intent on the music, found himself being gradually drawn in as well, forgetting the moment and the place, lending his ear during that unworldly stretch of time as if entranced. No one spoke. The singing could not have lasted ten minutes, but when it ended he found the darkness all at once grew deeper.

WHEN THEY TROOPED into the dining room, the oval table he remembered from before had been extended to half again its original length and was covered with a lustrous white tablecloth. A pair of lit candlesticks was in the center, one on either side of a small floral arrangement, and in front of each person's chair were two matching plates of edged chinaware, one on top of the other. Harue seated herself at the head of the table and said, while spreading in her lap a napkin that matched the tablecloth, "Instead of the usual *high tea*, I had the table set formally for once. Our young ones are all gone this year, and there are so few of us left." At this, Fumiko began to serve, looking like a consummate maid. Ami, whose role at mealtimes was evidently behind the scenes, did not make an appearance.

The conversation began at first with discussion of the Thai beach resort where the others in the family had all gone; how absurd it was that in this heat anyone should have a wedding in Thailand; how they wouldn't have wanted to go even if Masayuki hadn't suddenly died. From there the topic moved on to Masayuki himself. People's voices grew hushed. The forty-nine days of mourning were not yet over.

How young he'd been, how brilliant, what a doting husband. Yes, someone said, but he doted on his wife too much, that was behind the tragedy. Someone else suggested that since both his parents had died of cancer the disease must run in the family. In a voice that signaled imminent tears, Natsue remarked that at least Masayuki never lived to see the Karuizawa property pass into strangers' hands; in that sense he was lucky, like Yoko.

"This might be the last *high tea* here, for all we know!" she said, not for the first time, her eyes now actually glistening; then she looked at Yusuke. "Oh yes, this young guest of ours!" she suddenly remembered. She opened her eyes wide, as if to banish tears, and smiled winningly. "We invited him so we could tell him about Peter Jansen."

"Oh, that's right. Peter Jansen." Harue too looked at Yusuke as if just remembering. "Everyone else knows the story." She looked around the table before turning back to Yusuke and saying proudly, "It's a very romantic story."

Fuyue added in a slightly flustered tone, "But one we concocted ourselves, mind you."

"And what's wrong with that?" retorted Harue. "Oh, put on the Clarinet Quintet again someone, would you please?"

"Yes," agreed Natsue. "It's practically the theme music for it."

"Fuyue, do put it on."

"Yes, do! This may be the last time, after all."

"All right, all right."

As Fuyue got up, Harue began to relate the succession of misfortunes that had befallen them.

CANDLELIT TABLE

The sisters' father had lived to the age of ninety-seven before dying in 1990, when the economy was at the peak of what came to be known as the bubble. That was the first misfortune. The second was that the land they possessed in their father's name was in Seijo and Old Karuizawa, two areas where land prices had lately gone through the roof. They had been forced to sell one home or the other to pay the inheritance tax, and since Seijo was right at the heart of their lives and Karuizawa a summer luxury, they had decided very reluctantly to let go of the latter. Just by coincidence, in that same year of 1990, Yayoi, who had inherited the Shigemitsu property next door, passed away, leaving the Shigemitsus in much the same circumstances. In 1991 the Saegusas and Shigemitsus spent a last summer in Karuizawa for old time's sake before putting their respective properties on the market.

"It was exactly like something from Chekhov's *The Three Sisters*," said Harue.

"You mean *The Cherry Orchard*," Fuyue corrected.

"Not *The Three Sisters*?"

"No. *The Cherry Orchard*."

Natsue cut in. "But then a savior came along." Her wide eyes blinked.

A mysterious buyer had turned up, working through a Tokyo lawyer. This was a foreign company with its main office in The Hague, in the Netherlands. The deal was that until it decided at some point to use the land for its own purposes, the Shigemitsus and Saegusas could go on living there, as long as they paid the local property tax between them. All communication with the company was to take place through the lawyer. When they heard about it, the sisters decided that the purchaser might actually be the Dutchman Peter Jansen—a young tycoon who used to come to Karuizawa regularly before the war to escape the heat of Indonesia, and had become a friend of both families. That Peter Jansen.

"He was a wonderful violinist," Natsue commented. "He and the Shigemitsu heir next door and a few others often played this piece together." She turned toward the parlor, from which music could be heard.

It was not entirely unreasonable that the three Saegusa sisters should have assumed the mysterious buyer was Peter Jansen. Back in the summer of 1991, when they were getting ready to bid Karuizawa a sad farewell, Jansen's son had come sightseeing to Japan with his wife and made a special trip to visit them, having been encouraged to do so by his father. It was a good thing he had come then, as they were just on the point of having to leave this place, they told him, and he had responded sympathetically: "My father will be so sad to hear that. Because of the war, a lot of Dutch people have a grudge against Japan, but thanks to Karuizawa my father has nothing but romantic memories of it."

"'*Nothing but romantic memories,*' he said, in such beautiful English," sighed Natsue.

"Naturally there's no proof whatever that Peter heard about it and bought the property on our behalf, but there are some pretty eccentric people in the world, so you never know. We think it's possible."

Wondering what sort of company it was, they had had one of Harue's sons-in-law, a banker, do some investigating using the bank's internal network. He found out that it was a joint-stock company, but the director listed was someone no one had ever heard of, and since the company wasn't on the stock exchange, its business dealings were not disclosed.

Fuyue, who alone had a rather skeptical look, spoke up. "But a company's main motive is profit making, isn't it? It doesn't make any sense, as far as I can see."

"It's precisely because it makes no sense that we think it possible," said Harue.

Natsue chimed in. "You were so young at the time, Fuyue. You can't imagine what it was like when there was still some Taisho romanticism in the air, before the country became so militaristic."

"Taisho romanticism would mean nothing to a Westerner. They wouldn't even know what the Taisho period is!"

"Oh, you just don't know. Westerners too were much more romantic back then."

That winter they had written to Peter Jansen for the first time in decades, sending him a Christmas card at the address his son provided, with a few lines that could be read as an expression of their gratitude, only to hear some months later from the son that Peter had died. Even then there was no word from the lawyer about the Karuizawa property— to their great relief—and they had gone on as they were throughout 1992, 1993, and 1994. Now this summer, just when things were rather hectic because of Masayuki's death, word had finally come from the lawyer that the Dutch company needed to sell off the property. He would fix it so they could stay on through the summer and, depending on who the new owner was, they might or might not have to leave soon after that. In any case the company wanted to move quickly, and so even though it was the middle of the Bon festival holidays, the lawyer would be arriving in Karuizawa from Tokyo tomorrow evening.

Having explained this much, Harue looked around as if she were only just facing up to the reality of their situation.

"To see all of you when we knew for certain that it was the last time would be altogether too sad. That's why I asked you to come now, before we know exactly what is going to happen."

BY THE TIME *high tea* was over, it was past ten.

Fumiko, who had promised to drive Yusuke back to Mitsui Woods, disappeared shortly before they were to leave and emerged from the house next door carrying a department store shopping bag. Yusuke offered to carry it for her but she said that it wasn't heavy, so she could manage. When they reached the car she raised the paper bag slightly and, after catching Yusuke's eye, said, "The urns—with their remains. They were on the mantelpiece at the sisters' villa, remember? These are the small ones for the separate burials. That's why the bag's so light."

She opened the back door of the car and put the bag casually on the back seat, as if it contained groceries.

Masayuki's will had stipulated that he wanted his bones and those of his wife ground together and scattered on their property in Karuizawa, but the three old ladies found the idea gruesome and had asked Fumiko to do the honors, if she didn't mind.

"I think it's pretty gruesome too, actually," she said, although to Yusuke she didn't sound particularly bothered. Her car, bearing two people in ashes and two people still alive, rolled out of the dark woods and onto the main road. Yusuke felt prompted to ask a question. The shadow of something that had flitted through his mind the other day was taking clearer shape.

"Who really bought the Karuizawa land?"

Fumiko answered in a heartbeat. "Of course it was Taro." She was looking straight ahead, her eyes squinting slightly as if the lights of the oncoming cars were too bright. "I'm glad there's no fog. When the fog rolls in you can barely see the car right in front of you."

Yusuke said nothing, waiting for more. Fumiko drove along in silence for a while and then, without turning her head, explained.

"Oiwake he bought for himself . . . for the sake of the memories he and Yoko shared there. As for Karuizawa, when the inheritance tax problem came up, he decided to buy it for Masayuki and Yoko. I didn't know it at first either, but when I heard that a company based in The Hague had made the purchase, it all fitted together. I knew Taro had set up a holding company there to save on corporate taxes."

After glancing in the rearview mirror, she looked at Yusuke for the first time. Her face was expressionless. "He probably intended to keep it indefinitely, but then Masayuki died. That must be when he made up his mind to sell."

That was all. After a brief pause Yusuke said, "A pity about the old ladies." He quickly corrected himself. "A bit of a pity, I mean."

"A huge pity," she told him, eyes forward. "I wish he could just have let things go on the way they are until they got too old for it." She then gave a mocking sort of laugh. "But I suppose Taro doesn't owe them anything to that extent."

They rode along in silence.

"You know, I'll miss it. Ever since I was just a girl . . . it's hard to believe, but starting when I was seventeen I've been going there nearly every summer of my life. Even Ami. She's been going there since she was a baby, so I know she'll miss it too. I suppose both houses will be torn down . . ." As if she had suddenly come to herself she added, "Well, in any case . . . it's all over."

The highway that had been so crowded earlier in the day was clear. The car's headlights swept smoothly over the road, and in no time they had arrived in Middle Karuizawa.

"Would it be all right if I go over to Oiwake again tomorrow?" he asked.

"Yes. Come in the afternoon. He'll be gone overnight tomorrow."

When Taro reserved a room in the Prince Hotel for the Tokyo lawyer, he had made a reservation for himself as well. The two of them would dine together that evening, and in the morning Taro would play a solo round of golf before coming back to Oiwake, she said.

"Does he often stay in a hotel?"

Fumiko shook her head. "Heavens, no. This is a first." Her lips curved in a smile. "Maybe he's afraid that when the three sisters find out the truth from that lawyer, they'll come flying down on Oiwake like the Furies," she said, and laughed.

THE FIRST-FLOOR LIGHTS were on in Kubo's parents' place. Lined up in the entryway was a pair of pink sandals with heels. Making a clatter without being too obvious about it, he entered the living room and found the little sister stretched full-length on the sofa, winding her fingers in Kubo's hair as he sat by her on the floor. In front of them the television was on with the sound turned down.

# 8

# Career Woman

AFTER TARO'S RETURN for the first time in fifteen
years, the long winter stretched on. It was April by
the time the snow melted, the black ground thawed out,
and spring arrived. Soon even the snow on top of Mount
Asama sparkled and began to run down in rivulets. From
that late Nagano springtime into the summer, I took time
to ensure that the Oiwake cottage was brought from the
brink of ruin to something like its original condition. I
knew from the start what might lie ahead. I felt alarmed,
and wished I could make time stand still. All the same, it
was not without a certain satisfaction that, as tree buds
swelled and the woods turned lush all around, I watched
the little house, whose life had all but ended, begin to
revive again.

"How I'm going to use the place I don't exactly know, but
would you at least see to it that it's livable?" That was Taro's
request. Once I inspected it with this in mind, I realized that
any house neglected for so long naturally needs more than
a thorough cleaning, and indeed problem after problem
with the roof, doors, windows, and plumbing turned out

to require the attentions of skilled workmen. My husband
and I could have paid the cost of labor in advance and asked
for reimbursement, but since I didn't want to get ahead of
myself, I copied out Taro's address on an envelope, strug-
gling with the unfamiliar alphabet, and sent him a note
asking for instructions. I almost immediately received
a phone call from a capable-sounding Japanese woman
who lost no time in transferring the large sum of five
million yen to my account at Ueda Credit Bank. That was
when I first learned that Nakada Associates in Tokyo's
Akasaka district was the law firm representing Taro in
Japan. I opened an account in his name so that I could pay
for the cost of restoration work out of it. I also arranged
for telephone and other utility bills, including propane,
to be paid from there. My family hadn't heard anything
about Taro after I had lunch with him at the Prince Hotel
back in January, so I told them he was a distant relation
of the family I used to work for in Tokyo, someone who
had made his fortune in America, and left it at that. Since
I already worked summers at a villa in Karuizawa, no one
thought anything of it if this Taro Azuma person asked
me to be the caretaker of his place in Oiwake. I complied
with his wish to leave the cottage looking as close as possible to the way it used to be, and all I personally did
inside was dust and scrub. Of the futon covers that still
seemed salvageable, I had the original materials washed
before stuffing them with fresh cotton. When old Mrs.
Utagawa's tea chest turned up in a closet, I checked the
contents, saw there was nothing particularly worthwhile

inside, and left it all there. The house key that I sent Taro
by airmail was an old one—purposely so.

THAT SUMMER, SOON after I went to work in Karuizawa,
Natsue asked me out of the blue one day, "Whatever hap-
pened to that Oiwake property?" I felt a pang of guilt and tried to cover it up. "The cottage
is still there . . . ," I said.

She smiled ingenuously, her dimple showing. "My, after
all that rush to buy, they certainly are taking their time
about rebuilding!"

I thanked heaven that she didn't have a mind inquiring
enough to suggest that we go over and have a look. Whether
Taro would ever actually use the place, I was still not entirely certain, and there was no point in my upsetting her
with information she had no need to know.

Taro's next visit came a few days after Natsue brought
up the subject of Oiwake. The telephone rang while my
daughter-in-law and I were clearing the supper dishes. She
answered it and handed me the receiver, murmuring "Mr.
Azuma" in a voice that showed she now knew who he was.
He was calling from the Hotel New Otani in Tokyo and
would arrive in Oiwake the following afternoon to stay a
week. I had already explained that I worked for the Saegusas
in the summer so my time was limited, but before hanging
up I agreed to see him at the cottage on my way home the
following evening. In the morning I took advantage of the
fine weather to go to Oiwake and lay out Takero's recondi-
tioned striped futon in the front tatami room, where the

sun would reach it and fluff it up, before going on to Karuizawa. A slight alteration of my customary route was all it took. I did my morning work as usual, but by afternoon, around the time when Taro had said he would be arriving, I found myself getting nervous. Perhaps he was already in Karuizawa and was driving around and around this block. I kept leaving off whatever I was doing to crane my neck, trying to see beyond the hedge. Surely he knew that Yoko was married to Masayuki. My eyes also strayed toward the Shigemitsu garden, where Yoko was puttering about with a trowel.

I had intended to slip off early, but on that day of all days, just as I was leaving I was asked to do one thing and another, so that by the time I arrived in Oiwake it was past six. What looked like a rental car was parked inside the gate, and the yellow porch light was on as if waiting for me. The sound of my car brought Taro out onto the porch, and when he saw it was me his face lit up with pleasure. He said he would make us a pot of tea. My son got home at all hours from the bank where he worked. But my husband, who had retired from the town hall and was now helping in our daughter-in-law's family pickle business, was always home by six, waiting for me to get back and join the rest of the family for supper. I really had no time, but stayed with Taro just to keep him company. I was braced for the inevitable question, but he didn't say a word about Yoko. You might almost have thought he had traveled all the way from America just to escape the heat in this small, run-down cottage in the mountains.

The next day I was able to leave Karuizawa early and stopped in on my way home, half expecting him to be out, but the car was still parked there and the porch light was switched on. Once again he stepped out to greet me, showing no sign of restlessness. When I sat down at the table with a cup of hot green tea in front of me, he told me matter-of-factly that after years of living overseas, sitting and sleeping on the tatami floor had become a bit much for him and so he'd decided to use Takero's old study, which had a built-in wooden bed in one corner. He had laid out the futon there the night before, he said. I got up to have a look, curious to see how he had set things up. Sure enough, there on top of the wooden frame was Takero's striped futon, and on the desk opposite were some papers in English, with shirts from the cleaner's stacked in their clear plastic wrapping on the bookshelf overhead. For a second I felt as if Yoko's father was there in the cottage, before realizing afresh that Taro had finally come back.

I was anxious to settle money matters first, so as soon as I was back at the table I showed him a notebook where I'd kept a neat record of how the five million yen from Nakada Associates had been used to open an account in his name, with withdrawals in such-and-such amounts. He gave the figures only a brief glance before talking about something else. On a daytime walk, he said, he had found that within a two-kilometer radius, twenty-one new cottages had been built in fifteen years, which worked out to an average of 1.4 per year; at that rate the area would soon be more crowded than an American suburb, although plenty of the houses were empty. Again, he didn't once mention Yoko's name.

When I stopped by the next day, he was out on the porch repainting the rattan furniture white. He seemed so plainly to be killing time that I couldn't help asking, "What do you do for dinner?"

"Go out to eat."

Yes, but when was he going to get in touch with Yoko? I was on tenterhooks. As if to put me off, he again brought up an unrelated topic. Lunch he fixed himself, but the compressor in that old refrigerator wasn't working. Nothing got cold.

Time went by in this fashion until there were only two nights left. Yoko and Masayuki usually went out together, whether for walks or to do the shopping, but there was nothing to stop her from going out alone. If Taro would just get word to her, he could see her in some way. He wanted me to make the initial contact, I supposed, and I was waiting for him to bring the subject up—or rather I was even trying in roundabout ways to draw it out of him, but he said nothing.

That night, knowing he only had two nights left, I took the plunge myself as I toyed with my teacup.

"Taro, you're leaving the day after tomorrow, aren't you?" It would be too awful if he went back to America like this. "Just what are you planning to do?" I looked him straight in the eye, trying to pin him down. Even without hearing Yoko's name, he knew what I meant and looked away.

"Why are you being such a damn coward?"

He still looked away.

"Why?" I said again.

As I watched, his cheeks went rigid. The skin under his eyes twitched. If this were the old Taro, he would soon be in tears, I thought, but in the course of fifteen years—fifteen difficult years—the poor man had probably forgotten how to cry. All he could do was sit tight-lipped under the light. As the silence dragged on for one minute, then two, then three, I felt something shift inside me, as if he had made some unspoken appeal.

Before I knew what I was doing, I went around to the other side of the table, crouched down beside his chair, and gently laid my left hand on the small of his back. My other hand I put on his knee. Then slowly, soothingly, I began to stroke him. It was like holding a crying child in my arms, yet somehow I was the one crying, unable to keep back the tears. Taro didn't resist, but held strangely still. For a while I kept on silently stroking him, and as the warmth of my hands conveyed itself to him, little by little he eased up and began to talk in low snatches. I heard for the first time that he had been trying various approaches on his own.

Twice he had telephoned. Both times she had picked up the phone, but when he heard her say, "The Shigemitsu residence," in a slightly affected voice, he had hung up, unable to speak. Every day he drove quietly around the two villas, hoping she would come outside, but she never did. Time and again he had started to write to her, but it was fifteen years since he had written anything in Japanese, so it wasn't easy, and anyway, he had no idea what to say.

Besides, sending a signed letter might cause her trouble, something he wished to avoid at all costs. The idea of sending an anonymous letter was so pitiful that the urge to write had died away.

For some reason he felt he couldn't ask me to act as a go-between—that itself weighed heavily on me and made me sadder still. Not that I wanted to do it. There were Yoko's husband Masayuki and their daughter, Miki, to consider, not to mention what others might think if they ever found out. But just imagining how Taro would feel if he went back to the United States without ever contacting Yoko nearly drove me to distraction. In Karuizawa the next day I did my work mechanically, following Yoko's movements out of the corner of my eye. Finally, at dusk I made up my mind.

I had seen Yoko in an apron in our house a little while earlier. I asked Natsue, who was curled on the sofa in the parlor reading an old novel, where she was. "She's in the attic making up the beds for Yuko and her children. Taking her time about it too, I must say." Yuko would be getting in from San Francisco in a couple of days' time with her girl and boy, Naomi and Ken, and Yoko was busy getting things ready for them. The Saegusa villa had been enlarged and had wings added on as the family grew, but Yuko and her family came only once every two or three years and stayed for no more than a couple of weeks, so they slept in the attic, in the former maids' rooms.

I climbed the steep attic stairs and found all three white doors on the corridor standing ajar. One by one I checked the rooms, and in the last one, at the east end, I found Yoko sitting on the bed holding a pillow half stuffed into a pillow-case, looking absently out the window at the sky.

"Oh, hello, Fumiko. Are you going home now?"

By then in her early thirties, she had filled out and was finally losing her girlish looks, becoming more matronly, but perhaps because she was sitting in her old room she looked quite childlike to me and I couldn't help talking to her as if she were still a little girl.

"What were you doing, sweetie?"

"Remembering when I was small."

"Any time special?" I asked, wondering if she'd been remembering the days she spent with Taro.

"Back when I was really small. The first time you ever came here. That's about my first real memory, you know."

I too had vivid memories of the first summer I had ever spent in this villa. As I kept coming back summer after summer, over the years it grew increasingly difficult to sort out what had happened when. Events overlapped in my mind, memories were tangled. But that first summer was special. I could remember exactly what Yoko had looked like, lying in bed in this room with a white bandage around her head and a sullen look on her face.

She turned back to the window. "The morning sun shines in here through cracks in the blinds, but it's completely different from the way it came through the rain shutters in the old house in Chitose Funabashi. Whenever I woke up here it always used to amaze me."

She gave the pillow a smart pat and stood up, then walked over to the southern window and looked down at the garden below with a little smile. I moved next to her, and side by side we watched the three little girls at play.

"I was younger then than Miki is now."

Her daughter, Miki, was in the second grade. To make up for her being an only child, they had decided to send her to Seijo Academy, where she'd become fast friends with the two little girls who were Harue's granddaughters and her own second cousins. Harue had five grandchildren in all, Mari's two boys and a girl and Eri's boy and girl. Adding Miki to the mix meant there were three girls, so the "three sisters" tradition continued in the third generation, at least in some form. In Karuizawa Yoko spent a good deal of time at the Saegusa villa during the daytime, partly because her mother was always asking her help with every little thing, but also because Miki was always playing with her cousins. By coincidence, all three were the same age.

Miki's laughter sounded especially shrill. Seen from above, the girls were hard to tell apart at first since they were all the same size, but Miki was the most active of the three and soon stood out. Yoko followed her around with her eyes, delight on her face.

That little girl was fortunate in every possible respect. To begin with, she was the Shigemitsu heir, which naturally gave her a certain prestige in everyone's eyes. Yayoi and Masao of course doted on her as their only grandchild. And Natsue, being Natsue, fussed endlessly over the girl, her one grandchild in Japan. Not only that, Miki luckily took after her father but also for some reason closely resembled her maternal grandmother, Natsue. This meant she had the

"Hirano face," a synonym for beauty, and was the prettiest of the three little girls. Even Harue, with all her prejudices, seemed partial to Miki, favoring her over the offspring of her two sons-in-law, neither of whom she had ever cared for much. With every advantage on her side, it only stood to reason that Miki should be growing up in a manner quite different from what her mother had experienced as a child, always looked down on and left out of things.

"Time for her to put on a sweater," murmured Yoko.

For once there were boys playing down there too. The three of them were older, so they ignored their little sisters and were yelling themselves hoarse, taking turns as pitcher, batter, and catcher. They had staked out the lion's share of the area. I was a bit surprised to find myself annoyed that the Karuizawa garden we all cherished was being treated like an ordinary schoolyard.

"Did you want something?" Yoko turned and looked at me standing next to her, as if suddenly remembering I was there.

I shook my head. "Not really. The attic door was open so I just came up for a look around."

No need for me to go out of my way to bring the two of them together, I thought. She obviously couldn't have forgotten Taro, but her life without him was peaceful. Why muddy the waters? If Taro intended to invade her life, I decided, he would just have to do it on his own.

THAT RESOLUTION WAS shaken by my visit to Oiwake later that day. Hearing me come in, Taro emerged from the study.

One look at his face and I felt myself go pale. My bringing up the subject the night before must have unleashed emotions he had been holding in check. He looked as if he had been through hell.

"Oh, Taro!" I said, in shock.

Overnight his face had become hollower, with dark circles under the eyes. Half in tears, I had to ask: "What are you going to do? Go back to America without seeing her?"

"Yeah, there's nothing else I can do . . ."

"What will you do with the cottage?"

"Leave it. I might come back again someday."

"Someday? What in the world is wrong with you?"

"Yeah, well . . ."

He looked away, breathing heavily, his chest moving. Even after doing so well in America, he must have wavered for ages before seeing Takero's obituary and deciding to come back to Japan. That much I had guessed, but never did I imagine that when he had finally made the journey back he would be so scared of meeting Yoko again. His dread that their past together was truly over and done with outweighed his need to see her.

Abruptly I said, "I'll call her for you."

He showed a sudden eagerness, but only for a moment. Holding his breath, he stared at me. He kept on staring agog as I walked over to the telephone and punched the number.

"The Shigemitsu residence."

"Yoko? Is that you? It's Fumiko."

"Oh, hello, Fumiko. What is it? Did you forget something?"

"No," I said, shaking my head. Just then my eyes met Taro's. After holding my gaze a moment he turned and disappeared down the dimly lit corridor. I heard the study door close. I looked back at the porch, training my eyes on the gathering dusk beyond the screen door as I spoke. "I have a surprise for you."

"A surprise? What is it?" she asked, her voice alert. As I hesitated, she repeated, "What kind of a surprise?"

"Taro is at the Oiwake cottage right now."

For a moment she was speechless.

"Our Oiwake cottage?" She seemed confused.

"Yes."

"Alone?"

Strange question. "Yes," I said, then added, "I'm here with him for the moment."

Her reply was unexpectedly composed. "I'll be right there. I'll leave now. I'll just tell Masayuki and be right over."

"What about dinner?"

"He'll cover for me. Anyway, I'm on my way."

I knocked on the study door and opened it. The back of Taro's white shirt floated up in the gloom. He was sitting at the desk, looking outside. The atmosphere in the room was perfectly still.

"Yoko is coming over."

He didn't move

"I'm off, then," I said to his white back.

Just as I turned to leave, the swivel chair spun around and he called out, "Fumiko. Stay here till she comes. Stay . . . or I can't cope." He looked frantic.

As I stood there, he said again, "Please stay . . ."

His face was ashen, there's no other word for it. It must have taken nerve for him to get where he was at work, yet here he hadn't the courage to see Yoko alone. He had never been one to lean on other people for anything, so the request was all the more pathetic. I remained motionless in the doorway, dismayed by the sight of him. Still, whether it was pity or compassion, that all-too-familiar feeling came over me again—the same feeling I'd had when I used to imagine what was going through the mind of the small boy he'd been.

"Has she changed?" he asked in a low voice, still white-faced.

I didn't know what to say. I didn't think she had changed so much that she no longer cared for him, and yet changed she certainly had. But I did not want to be the one to tell him so.

"Has marriage changed her?" The look in his upturned eyes was insistent.

"Marriage can't help changing a person."

"It didn't change you."

Unconnected to the present moment, the words echoed loudly inside me. I was silent, lost in my own emotions, and he seemed to misunderstand. With a painful groan he said, "So she has changed." His face twisted. "Yoko's not the same."

"She'll be here any minute, so judge for yourself," I said flatly, then went back down the corridor, turned on the porch light, and sat down again at the table. Taro didn't come out of the study. I couldn't hear him stir. No doubt he had swiveled back to stare out the window at the gathering darkness.

About half an hour later I saw car lights approaching down the lane. As I got up and went to the screen door, a car door slammed shut. The movement of headlight beams showed what looked like a taxi backing up, turning, and driving off. Yoko came up the steps, kicked off her shoes impatiently, and opened the screen door.

"You came by taxi?" I asked.

"Yes, Masayuki said it wasn't safe to drive over alone at night when I'm this worked up." Flushed with agitation, she answered absently, scanning the room. If Taro's inability to face Yoko alone was absurd, Masayuki's cautious insistence that his wife take a taxi to see a former lover was no less so. Just then Taro appeared silently from the hallway.

"Taro!" Yoko's voice rang out sharply. The night air swayed, and her hair, which lately she'd worn nicely smoothed down, seemed to fly out in all directions. "You got married, didn't you!"

She was glaring at him with the fury of a she-demon. Her breathing was rough and she stood with her hands pressed against her heart, as if she might keel over. Taro looked at her in astonishment. Apparently, her words made no sense to him.

"You did get married, I know it!"

He came to his senses and answered quietly: "No."

"You didn't?"

"No, I didn't."

"Not ever?"

"Never."

"Liar!"

"I'm not lying."

She tilted her head to one side and narrowed her eyes suspiciously before asking in a slightly calmer voice, "But you had a girlfriend?"

"No."

"You're telling me you never had a girl?"

"I never did."

"Not even one?" Her eyes slowly widened.

"Not even one."

"You liar! I know that's a lie!" She was shouting again, but Taro seemed in raptures. "You mean it?"

"I mean it."

He answered her calmly, an unmistakable smile on his lips. His smile seemed not to register on Yoko, who kept staring at him in deadly earnest.

"So you were miserable the whole time?"

"The whole time."

"Oh, yes? How miserable were you? Enough to die?"

"Yes. I was heartbroken." He said this glowing with delight.

"Ah, but you didn't die, did you! You came whimpering back, alive as ever!"

"To see you again . . ." His face clouded for a moment. "I wanted to see you, Yoko, and find out if there really was nothing worth living for."

"I see." Perhaps she was satisfied, for her breathing gradually got quieter. She stared at him. I thought she was calming down at last, when all of a sudden she blazed up again: "Even so, I'll never forgive you!"

"What for? . . ."

As she took a step back, he moved forward. She retreated further, stopping when her bare heel came up against the threshold.

"For going off that night and leaving me, and never coming back . . ."

Fifteen years had gone by, but the pain of that night seemed to revive in her as if it had been only days ago. It was as if she had spent every night of those intervening years reliving it, staring out into the darkness.

"I waited and waited for you." Slowly she was giving way to tears. "Even afterward. I waited, and waited, and waited . . ." Her face scrunched up, making her look even more like the little girl she had once been. "For *years* I waited for you."

With a wail, she turned and ran barefoot out onto the porch and down the steps. Taro quickly started after her, but the low table was in his way, and by the time he reached the porch she must have already gone out through the gate. I had been standing transfixed, watching the two of them, but after a minute I too slipped on my sandals and went out.

Looking up the road from beside the gate, I saw them together in the moonlight.

Taro had fallen to his knees. I thought perhaps he was going to lay his forehead flat on the ground and apologize, the way he had when they were small, but instead he reached out with both arms, wrapped them around her knees, and abruptly lifted her off the ground and swung her over his shoulder. When he came through the wooden posts I could see her bent double over his shoulder, her arms and head dangling limply down his back. Before, she'd been excited and shrill; now she was like a dead woman.

He bent down and laid her gently in a rattan chair. She slumped back and watched vacantly as he wiped the dirt from the soles of her feet. A trace of resentment flickered in her eyes. After a while she brushed his hand away impatiently. Then she slid off the chair and sat flat on the floor, knees together and legs splayed as she once used to do, her eyes still vacant as she took his hand and began to speak almost in a trance.

"Is it really true that you're not married?"

She ticked off the fingers of one hand, then the other, as if addressing the question to them. She might have been playing a game of "he loves me, he loves me not," with fingers instead of petals. Starting with the little finger, she would work her way to the thumb of one hand, then do the same with the other before starting all over again. Repeating this seemed to help her regain possession of herself.

"Don't work with your hands much anymore, do you?" She sounded a bit shy, her voice now normal. "And you really never had a girlfriend?" She slid her hands up and touched his arm through the sleeve of his shirt, pressing it with all ten fingers as if she could scarcely believe she was doing it.

"No, I never did."

"Truly?"

"Really and truly."

She sighed with contentment and then, moving her legs to one side, lay her head in Taro's lap and quietly began to cry. Taro, sitting cross-legged, looked down at her, not moving a muscle. After a minute he closed his eyes and leaned forward slightly, inhaling deeply—perhaps checking that the smell of her neck was the same as in years past.

The ceiling lamp surrounded the two of them in a circle of light.

I had always known that Yoko still cared for Taro even after she married Masayuki, but until I saw her with him that night, I never realized how much. Or realized, I should say, how her feelings for him had steadily deepened after he left her that time. But until I saw what happened next, I never knew, either, how deeply she had come to love Masayuki as well.

Thinking that my presence couldn't possibly be wanted anymore, I had just laid a hand on the screen door to leave when I saw headlights approach and stop in front of the cottage. It was Masayuki.

"There's a car out front," I said. My voice caught in my throat. I realized that I hadn't spoken for quite a while.

Yoko quickly raised her head from Taro's lap and said to herself, "Maybe it's him." She scrambled to her feet and came to stand beside me, looking outside. The car was parked in front of the gate with its headlights on. She opened the screen door without hesitation, put on her shoes properly this time, and ran down the steps, disappearing into the darkness. Left behind, with the object of all this happiness suddenly gone, Taro sat alone in the circle of light with a stupid look on his face.

From some distance away came a steady murmur of talking or crying. She did not come back. I sighed and sat down at the table again. Taro uncrossed his legs and stood up, then sat down on the rattan chair, as if he didn't know what to do with himself. He was silent, and so was I. Finally, knowing that if I stayed out any later my family would worry, I told him I should be on my way, took my car keys out of my purse, and stood up. For the first time he looked me squarely in the face, but still said nothing. Outside, the car's headlights were now turned off, but the car was visible in the light from the porch and the moon. Two figures were illuminated as well. Masayuki was leaning against the car with his forehead pillowed on both arms, crying. Wisps of his hair, which had never lost its brownish tint, had a bright golden sheen in the moonlight. Yoko had her arms wrapped tightly around him, clinging like a cicada to a tree, and she too was in tears. "I'll never leave you . . . That could never happen . . . You know we'll be together all our lives . . ." Through her sobbing came these broken snatches.

WHEN I WENT to Karuizawa the next day, Yoko wasn't there, having gone out in the morning. Miki was playing with her cousins while Masayuki strolled restlessly around the yard. Yoko came back just before noon. Masayuki went out to meet her, greeting her warmly on the spot, and together they went for a walk, brushing shoulders and murmuring.

That evening, without a word to me, Taro flew back to New York from Tokyo's Narita Airport.

OVER THE NEXT twelve months Taro visited Oiwake twice more, once in October and again in May. Both times, Yoko left her daughter, Miki, in Masayuki's care and made the trip up from Tokyo. Whether they slept together, I have no idea. All I could tell was that Taro seemed unwilling to have me see the two of them there. I had no desire to see them together anyway. When I went into the cottage after they left, I found innocent traces of their activities: they must have been to the antique shops in Komoro or somewhere, because the kitchen cupboards were full of bowls and plates that, to my eyes, looked less antique than just plain old; they had amused themselves with sparklers for old times' sake, littering the ground with black threadlike cinders; and birdhouses hung from the branches again. I aired the rooms and while I was at it swept up the leaves and pulled weeds.

I told Taro to let me know if anything needed attention, but as he made no demands, I went ahead and arranged to make the cottage more habitable, getting the refrigerator fixed, for instance—although it turned out to be too old to salvage, so I bought a smallish new one instead. Toward the end of the year, to my surprise, I received notice that a payment of 600,000 yen had been deposited in my account for a year's "cottage maintenance"—amounting to 50,000 yen per month. Once the cottage was set up, there had been precious little work for me to do. I considered sending back the money untouched but changed my mind, thinking it would probably only be an annoyance for Taro to have me make a fuss about a sum of money that meant nothing to him. I decided to save it for a rainy day.

THE NEXT SUMMER when I went to work in Karuizawa, I told the three sisters that Taro, the boy who had made a fortune in America, was actually behind the purchase of the Oiwake cottage. When he first returned to Japan, I explained, he had phoned me out of the blue from the Prince Hotel in Karuizawa, and that was the first I knew anything about it. Which wasn't entirely untrue. But Taro's call had come eighteen months earlier, and I personally had made the cottage ready for him, so it wasn't the whole truth, either. I would have preferred to get by without telling the sisters anything, but if they happened to find out later, I did not want to have to pretend to be in the dark, so I'd decided to break the news.

They looked at first as if their hearts had stopped. Natsue's shock was the most apparent, since she was the one who had been so quick to dispose of the property.

"No!" she shrieked, making a circle of her shapely, lip-sticked mouth. "What could he possibly want with that old place!"

"I know what," said Harue spitefully. "I'll bet he just wanted to own something of the Utagawas'. Honestly, the thought of that boy's vindictiveness gives me the chills."

"Or he wanted to own something that brought back childhood memories," said Fuyue thoughtfully. But then she added, "Either way, that property is no great prize, if you ask me," so you couldn't tell if she was defending him or running him down. Her sisters chimed in.

"That's certainly true. It's in the middle of nowhere even for Oiwake."

"So even if he did buy it, the price wasn't all that much."

"It's a dinky plot of land."

I don't know why I did it—perhaps I was indignant at their stubborn failure to acknowledge just how rich and successful Taro really was—but I said something I probably had no business telling them.

"As a matter of fact," I said, "he bought up quite a large parcel of land, including all the surrounding property. The lot behind, the ones on either side, and the ones facing it too."

All three widened their big, round eyes and looked at each other.

"Is he that rich?" This honestly inquiring remark came from Fuyue.

"I don't exactly know."

"I said he was vindictive and that proves it," Harue spat out. "Going to such ridiculous lengths. That just takes the cake."

Natsue, as Yoko's mother, seemed to realize that they couldn't go on cutting up Taro forever. After a little pause, she bit her lip and looked up at me. "What about . . . does Yoko know?"

I wondered if she had any idea how much she looked like Yoko at such times. It was really quite funny.

"Yes, apparently."

"She does? What if Masayuki finds out? What's she going to do then?"

"Actually he seems to be aware of the situation too. I think she probably told him herself."

"Wha-a-t!" Natsue gave another little shriek. "Heaven help us! This is *exactly* why I never took to that child. I can never fathom what she's thinking."

"But I don't think her in-laws know," I said quickly. "I believe Masayuki doesn't want to cause them any unnecessary concern, so he probably won't tell them."

This last was pure conjecture on my part, but I said it to stop the Saegusa sisters from saying anything inappropriate to Yayoi, or at least to delay the blow. I don't know how much they did tell her in the end. Harue, I suspect, would have dropped hints at every chance, but Yayoi never spoke about it directly to me.

A few days later, the three of them went all the way to Oiwake to have a look for themselves, Fuyue driving. After they came back, Harue said to me with an inquisitive look, "Judging from the outside, he means to use the cottage without rebuilding it, wouldn't you say? But it does look as if perhaps it has been repaired." She was flanked by her younger sisters, all three of them wearing the same inquisitive expression. They seemed to suspect me of involvement, but I pretended to know nothing about it. Periodically they would ask me leading questions about Taro, but I never took the bait. Their three faces would look back at me with dissatisfaction, though they refrained from probing further.

FROM THEN ON, Taro came regularly to Oiwake two or three times a year, staying a week or two each time. He avoided the summers, when everyone was in Karuizawa, mostly coming in late spring or in the fall. Yoko would go to meet him on the pretext of buying antiques as an interior designer. Her frequent absences in the past to look after her ailing father in Sapporo meant that fortunately Miki was used to having her mother disappear from time to time. Since the girl was allowed to go to the Shigemitsus in Seijo after school and spend a few nights next door to her cousins, she actually looked forward to those occasions. More often Taro went to Tokyo on business and met up with Yoko there. On rare occasions she took a flight abroad to see him. What was extraordinary was Masayuki's reaction. Since I myself had played the role of go-between in reuniting Taro and Yoko, for a while I didn't dare look him in the face. At some point, however, that reservation disappeared. Whether others noticed it or not, to me it was clear that he and Yoko were even more loving than before. It was as if, with Taro's sudden reappearance, the three of them had taken off hand in hand, out of the fog and into a realm of blinding light.

AS FOR ME, every time Taro came to Oiwake it became customary for him to give me some sort of treat. He seemed to think it would be wrong to spend time only with Yoko,

BAMBOO GROVE

and since he was embarrassed to have me around when the two of them were together, he made a point of taking me out to dinner before she turned up in Oiwake or after she went back to Tokyo. The first place we went to was an Italian restaurant called Scorpione at the foot of Mount Hanare. I passed it on the road between Karuizawa and Miyota, so it was a familiar sight, but the small parking lot was always crammed with foreign cars that even I could tell were expensive makes, and the restaurant gave an impression of being out of the reach of us locals—which was why when Taro asked me if there was somewhere I would like to go, it immediately came to mind. That first night I felt intimidated and parked my minicar with its Nagano license plate on a back street, walking down the dark road to the restaurant. But people change with astonishing speed: after two or three visits, I felt thoroughly at ease there and began to think of branching out. We ate not only at the restaurants in the historic Mampei Hotel and the Kajimanomori Hotel, but also at the Chinese restaurant Eirin near Karuizawa station and the Japanese place, Daimasu, in Middle Karuizawa—in other words, at all the smartest, most desirable spots in town. We even ventured down to Komoro to eat slices of koi washed in cold water, a local delicacy. I tried to eat out with Taro in the daytime for my husband's sake, but sometimes we went out at night. My husband was generous, though, and understood that I had connections with a world that wasn't his; and when I put on a little makeup and went out the door dressed up, he saw me off without a word of complaint.

With Taro I would talk about my family—my husband, our eldest son and his wife, our granddaughter Ami. He listened, managing to look as if he cared. I talked about the families in Karuizawa too. Yoko must have chattered about them as well, for he surprised me by knowing the names not just of Yuko's children, Naomi and Ken, but also of Mari and Eri's five. He told me about America in bits and pieces. At first when he worked as a chauffeur he had been amazed at the size of his employer's house, but years later he was hobnobbing with investors from all over the country and no longer batted an eye at even the biggest mansions. His work consisted of finding investors in order to set up companies to manufacture new medical instruments, then selling them at a profit. He explained without expecting me to understand, so I only half listened. I was just impressed by the scale of his operations; he mentioned place-names from around the world. If it had been anybody but Taro, I would have dismissed half the talk as hot air.

"It's a good thing you went to America, isn't it?" I said to him one day when I was feeling ashamed of my vehement opposition at the time.

"Yes, it is."

"What was the best part?"

He thought for a moment and then answered with a mean-looking smile. "Losing my hatred of Japan and the Japanese. Now I'm actually grateful."

Back in the old days he had definitely felt deeply resentful, and even after crossing the Pacific he hadn't been able to shake off certain grudges for quite a while. But over time he came to feel that, compared with other immigrants who'd arrived in America equally without resources, he was one of the lucky ones. Whatever hardships he might have endured as a child, he had still grown up in postwar Japan, free of famine or war. Not only that, once he was in America, his nationality had allowed him to ride the wave of Japanese economic growth by working for a Japanese company. So, in the end, he'd come to think he ought to feel grateful to the country.

That smile was still on his lips, but he sounded serious enough.

"So you're glad to be Japanese?"

He didn't answer the question.

A YEAR PASSED in the blink of an eye, then another and another. Maybe it was the change of life, but the stiffness in my shoulders got worse until finally I gave up my sewing, which caused no inconvenience to anyone. Untroubled by any financial or emotional strains, my days passed peacefully from one season to the next. The town of Miyota became more and more developed, and the sight of butterflies in spring grew rarer, along with the trilling of insects in the autumn grasses. Only the sight of Mount Asama, peering out from between the surrounding hills, was unchanged. My life flowed on uneventfully, punctuated by Taro's visits. I would happily have gone on living like this, except his generosity toward me made for unexpected changes.

It began with my husband's sudden death.

It happened five years after Taro's return, in January 1986, when we had been married seventeen years. One night he felt unwell on the toilet and called for me. As I was helping him back to the futon he felt faint, and then he was gone. He was only sixty-two. His blood pressure had been high, but after his sixtieth birthday he had stopped helping our daughter-in-law's family in their pickle business and spent his time in a leisurely way tending a vegetable patch the size of a postage stamp. I never dreamed he would have a stroke.

His death completely changed my status in the family. To put it bluntly, I had no real place in it any longer. Even in retirement, my husband had remained head of the household. When the eldest boy took his place, he and his wife naturally made all the decisions. They both addressed me as "Mother" and treated me with respect, but he was already an adolescent when I married into the family, and I had never been a mother to him in any real way. His wife was able to devote all her time to their three small children, and showed no sign of needing a helping hand. Still, I couldn't simply lounge around the sitting room all day reading, which I'd been too discreet to do after marrying. A woman's lot is never easy.

I began to think that, once the forty-ninth-day memorial service was over, I would be more comfortable moving out to a small place close by where I could live on my own. It didn't take me long to come up with the idea of staying in the Oiwake cottage as a caretaker. I had been involved with that cottage from the start, doing everything from helping with the purchase of the land to going over alone to give it an airing; it was the one place on earth in which I felt I had a small stake. During the cold winter months from

CEMETERY

December to March, as well as the times when Taro and
Yoko came, I could stay in my husband's house. And thanks
to the long years he'd put in at the town hall, I had a small
monthly widow's pension, plus savings that I could use as I
pleased. Several years back, after my husband received his
retirement bonus, when it came time to rebuild the house
our eldest son had applied for a generous loan, so part of
that bonus had remained unspent—and with my husband
gone, that money now belonged to me. There were also the
yearly payments of 600,000 yen for "cottage maintenance"
that I had let accumulate. As long as I didn't have to pay any
rent, I could live comfortably on what I had.

As soon as this occurred to me, I sat right down and
wrote a letter to Taro. He had told me to call him collect if
anything came up, but in those days I found making overseas
calls rather intimidating. I soon got a call from Taro.

"Fumiko, how about working as my *assistant?*" he proposed. He said the word *assistant* in English, which sounded
to me like "sistan," leaving me baffled for a moment. He was
proposing that I rent an apartment in some convenient part
of Tokyo and work for him. Thanks to the booming economy, he was traveling to Tokyo in search of investors more
frequently these days, and because staying in hotels all the
time was becoming a nuisance, recently he'd been considering renting a condominium. Ideally, I would move into my
own place and keep the condominium shipshape so that he
could live there whenever he was in town. It would be nice
if I did some office work for him too, he added. The legal
assistant who used to handle his affairs at Nakada Associates

had quit to take care of her elderly parents. Though a succession of temporary workers had taken her place, they changed so often that it was hard to get anything done that required continuity, and he had been thinking about hiring someone as his personal assistant anyway.

Taro was doing all the talking, unlike his usual self, and I just listened. "Some office work too," he had said. But I knew this was only to make me feel less beholden to him. He wasn't expecting anything more from me than what a maid does, and even then there wouldn't actually be much work. He just needed reasons to give me enough of a monthly stipend so that I could live in the big city by myself.

He seemed to be waiting for me to say something, but I had no idea how to react. Dinner was over and I could see the grandchildren on the tatami floor squabbling over what television program to watch, but I felt entirely detached from the scene, as if I weren't really there. Eventually my common sense told me that I shouldn't take advantage of Taro's goodwill to that extent.

"If you want a place to live in Tokyo, Taro," I said, "I could come down from Oiwake from time to time to keep it up for you."

"Come on, Fumiko." He sounded exasperated. "Why not go to live in Tokyo yourself? Have a place of your own there, and go back to Oiwake whenever you feel like it."

I fell silent again. For the past few years, I had been content just to have him take me to a stylish restaurant two or three times a year. Tokyo was far away, and for the past seventeen years I had never thought of living there again. Yet something deep inside me stirred as I heard him say this.

My daughter-in-law, kneeling on the tatami, finished stacking dirty dishes on a large tray; she stood up, hoisting the heavy load, carried it past me, and disappeared into the kitchen.

"You always wanted to live in Tokyo alone and in style, remember? You could even take classes."

"What do you mean, classes?"

"I don't know exactly, but you know, culture centers or hobby courses or whatever—schools for ladies of a certain age with time on their hands."

I smiled despite myself.

"How much would you be paying me?"

"As much as you want."

"A million yen a month," I joked.

"Done."

After a pause, I answered. "All right, let's do this. Fix it so that after taxes, health insurance, and the rest, my take-home pay is a hundred fifty thousand yen a month. I don't want to live in poverty in Tokyo, after all."

"A hundred fifty thousand yen?" Irritation was obvious in his voice. "Look here, Fumiko. That would be what people call living in poverty. At Tokyo prices it would barely cover the rent!"

"I have my husband's monthly pension of a hundred thousand yen. I'll put that toward the rent."

"Don't be dumb!" I could imagine his angry face on the other end of the line. "It's stupid! Please. There's no reason to pinch pennies like that when that kind of money means nothing to me."

"But there wouldn't be any actual work for me to do."

"There's a lawyer here I see only a couple of days a month, and him I pay the equivalent of several hundred thousand yen."

When I didn't answer, Taro spoke in the particular, slightly nasal voice he always used when pleading for something. At such times he was deadly serious, but the softness of his voice invariably caught me off guard and distracted me from what he was saying.

"Fumiko, for once in my life I want you to let me do something to make you a bit happier."

I was quiet. At the other end of the line, Taro too said nothing. The fleeting thought came to me that, at international rates, this mutual silence was a terrible waste of money, but I didn't know how to answer him. After a pause I said in a voice slightly husky with emotion, "All right, then two hundred thousand yen a month. Any more than that I cannot accept. It's just not proper to take that kind of money from someone who's not family—who's after all only an acquaintance."

I could picture him gritting his teeth.

"Promise you won't pay me more than two hundred thousand yen a month."

"What about inflation?"

"We'll worry about that when the time comes."

Before hanging up I got him to agree that I would go on working summers in Karuizawa as always.

At first my family tried to dissuade me, but I gently stressed that this was not the sort of job that involved either daily commuting or hard physical work, and that I wanted another try at life in the city while I was still healthy and not yet even fifty. They were well aware that it would be easier on everybody if I did move out, so they eventually gave in. And since in small towns people talk, I took the trouble to spread the word among relatives and neighbors that, though my son and his wife had actually tried to prevent me from going, I was leaving of my own free will.

Since the Miyota family house and land were too small to divide, I had renounced any rights to them. My late husband's younger two sons did likewise, as was customary in the countryside. But I left my name on the family register in the town's public records. When my health declined or there was any change in my working relationship with Taro Azuma, I would of course be back, everyone assumed, and the arrangement would only be for the interim, probably less than ten years. I knew that my husband would have wanted me to see how his children and grandchildren were getting on, and I intended to come back for the Bon festival and New Year's, to do what I could to maintain family ties.

TARO MUST HAVE told Yoko about the deal, for she telephoned me soon afterward.

"Leave the hunt for a Tokyo apartment to me," she said, so I reminded her that the rent had to be no more than a hundred thousand yen a month. In no time she came up with a place in Gotokuji, which she picked because it was convenient for the Odakyu and Tokyu Setagaya Lines and would be familiar to me. It was a two-bedroom apartment with a main room that included living and dining areas and a kitchen workspace, over a total area of sixty-two square meters, located on the southeast corner, on the fourth floor of a five-story building a five-minute walk from the station. She sounded like a real estate agent as she rattled off all this information. Moreover, it was not a standard rental apartment but a personal property that the owner was renting out, so it was solidly built, and a hundred thousand per month was a real bargain. Because it was undergoing renovation, it would not be available for another couple of months. Still, it was an unbeatable deal. Her enthusiasm left me little choice. I had no sense of the Tokyo market anymore and no idea if the rent was high or low, but I decided to take it. "Now let me pick out the furniture," Yoko said in that same bossy tone. She was a professional interior designer, after all. "Not too expensive, now," I warned her. Which did I prefer, sleeping in a bed or on the floor, she wanted to know, as one of the bedrooms had a tatami floor. I immediately said I would prefer a bed. She laughed. "What a modern girl you are, Fumiko."

"I've slept on futons all my life," I commented. "Time for a change."

The only items of furniture I took with me were the ones that old Mrs. Utagawa had given me, less because I needed them than because I couldn't bear to part with them. Beyond that, all I really needed were my clothes and some personal things, so I only packed a few cardboard boxes and sent them ahead. My daughter-in-law offered to leave the children with their father and help me move in. She shouldn't have bothered when I had so few belongings, I thought, but rejecting her offer would have been rude, so one weekend we went up to Tokyo together. Yoko was there in the apartment wearing an apron, all ready to help, having likewise left her daughter in her husband's hands.

The apartment was astonishing. The only way I can describe it is to say—however silly it sounds—that it looked like something straight out of the glossy photographs in a magazine spread. Everything was brand-new—not just the walls and floors but the fitted kitchen and bathroom, all white and modern and stylish. As for the living-dining-kitchen area, which was easily larger than ten mats in size, one entire wall was taken up by built-in cabinets. Though I was hardly qualified to judge, the materials and workmanship seemed to be of a high quality. Standing in the middle of the room, my daughter-in-law declared it was "just like New York." I was none too sure about that, but it still made me gasp in amazement. Unable to believe my eyes, I went around opening and closing the cabinets over and over again.

An explanation came later when I saw Yoko off at the station, leaving behind my daughter-in-law, who was going to stay the night. "Let's talk about it another time," Yoko said. "After you're settled in." She kept trying to change the subject, but I squared my jaw and kept pressing for an answer. Finally I got her to reveal that the apartment had actually been bought by Taro's company and completely renovated at considerable expense. A place like that would normally cost at least two hundred thousand yen a month, since there were maintenance fees as well, but because this was company-owned housing, all I needed to pay was a hundred thousand yen each month to Nakada Associates—utilities included. I also learned that Taro had deliberately chosen a smallish place, thinking that otherwise I might back out of it.

I wasn't sure whether it made me happy or sad to have him do so much for me. I had pressed Yoko relentlessly until she told me everything, but once she did, I had no more to say. I walked unseeing along the busy thoroughfare near the station, until we were at the crossing.

"Fumiko, you're like a big sister to him." Yoko stood beside me and turned to look me in the eye. In time with the jingle of the warning bell, the light of a red crossing signal blinking on and off was reflected on her face. As the train roared past us, she shouted, "I know he's always wanted to look after you. But you were married, so he held back, out of consideration for your husband. You've got to let him do at least this much for you."

The next evening, after my daughter-in-law had gone home to Miyota, I leaned against the balcony railing and looked out absently at the scenery. The wind was blowing. Sometimes it carried the sound of a train on the Odakyu Line. What a difference from twenty years before, when, after my divorce, I had rented that tiny four-and-a-half-mat walkup in Evergreen Apartments No. 2! There in winter I would sit huddled in the *kotatsu* trying to get warm, and in summer I would head off to the public bath, dripping with sweat, to freshen up. True, Japan itself had become wealthier, but my good luck was out of proportion to the country's prosperity. And yet, there was this loneliness. It felt like there were suddenly a gaping hole in my chest. There was nothing more I could ever do for Taro and Yoko—nothing. From that point on, they would be the ones doing things for me. I never dreamed that this turnaround would make me feel so lonely.

FOR TARO, YOKO found a luxury apartment for expatriates in Yoyogi Uehara. It was only available as a rental, which meant he could use it as a tax write-off. As my first job, I handled the paperwork involved. Yoyogi Uehara station was on the Odakyu Line as well, but it also linked up with the subway line that led directly to Nogizaka, where Yoko lived. The neatness of this location showed an astuteness that struck me as uncharacteristic for Yoko, and I rather suspected that Masayuki's brains had played a part in it.

I SOON ORDERED postcards printed with my new address to announce the move. On the card I mailed to the Saegusas I added a note saying that one of these days I would drop by to say hello. Almost immediately I got a call from Fuyue. "What's this all about, Fumiko?" she wanted to know. Before I could say anything, Harue came on the line, shoving Natsue out of the way, as it were: "Fumi, you could have knocked us over with a feather! Moving here to Tokyo out of the blue—what on earth is going on?" She seemed unlikely to let me go unless I told her the whole story, so I explained that just as I was starting to feel awkward about living with my stepson's family after my husband's death, Taro happened to offer me a job in Tokyo as his assistant, to do various chores for him. She listened quietly, with occasional grunts. I had no idea what she might be thinking. Then abruptly she said, "Well, do come and see us sometime," and hung up.

A little while later, I visited them in Seijo. The three sisters, by this time in their sixties, gathered noisily in the parlor. Three pairs of eyes lined up, alive with interest. Ever since Taro had bought the Oiwake cottage, they had suspected me of being involved, and now they must have thought they had proof.

"How very *convenient* that this offer should have come along just after your poor husband died." The sarcasm in Harue's voice was ill concealed as she said this, looking me full in the face. "But what kind of 'chores' do you actually do?"

"Oh, just a little more than what a maid usually does."

"That boy Taro mostly isn't even in Japan, is he?"

His business contacts here were increasing all the time, I replied, so he had plenty to do in this country. She then pressed me for particulars about the nature of his work, but I had only recently arrived in Tokyo and couldn't give a satisfactory answer. Besides, I wanted to avoid talking about him with these women if I could help it.

Harue kept up her interrogation a while longer but finally gave up, throwing herself back in her armchair with exaggerated force. "Oh dear!" she sighed. "He's taken Oiwake, he's taken Fumi . . . if we aren't careful, he'll make off with every last thing we own . . ." Then she asked me quickly and casually, "So what about this summer?"

Outside, the hydrangeas were at their peak. One month more and it would be time to go to Karuizawa.

She no doubt thought she was being offhand, but her eyes were all too earnest. All of a sudden I saw that Natsue and Fuyue had the same look in their eyes. For perhaps the first time in the thirty years I had known them, I felt a vague pity for the three sisters, and at the same time I was glad that in their self-seeking way, they needed me. I sensed that I was needed not only as a source of labor but as a kind of emotional ballast.

THE NEXT TIME Taro was in Tokyo, he came over just once, to check out my apartment. He planted himself in front of the window, legs spread wide, and looked out over the jumbled cityscape with buildings of every color, shape, and size.

"It's so ugly," he said.

"You think so?"

"Ugly and sordid."

I always appreciated the fact that there were no high-rise buildings around, so I had an unobstructed view of the sky.

"At least the inside is nice," I said.

He went on, ignoring this. "They say Japan is rich, but it's just not true."

He wasn't asking my opinion, so I said nothing but kept my eyes on his tense profile.

"Materially rich but spiritually poor, everyone says, but whenever I hear that I think, 'Oh yeah?' If Japan were really

materially rich, that would be one thing, but all its surplus money has done is fill the country to overflowing with
ugliness."

He spun around with a grin. "Then again, surplus money
is what keeps me in business."

I OWED MY own good fortune to that surplus money. My
move to Tokyo came in the spring of 1986. Luckily for me,
during the next three years Taro continued rounding up investors in Japan, where there was an abundance of money.
He ended up coming back to Tokyo far more frequently
than he had first anticipated, which meant a corresponding increase in work for me. I started heading into the office of Nakada Associates a couple of days a week. Most of
my work involved communicating with clients, so although
back in Miyota I had never so much as touched an answering machine, soon every day I was using not just that but a
fax machine and copier too. I actually went to a language
school and learned to read basic English with the help of
a dictionary. Soon I knew my way around a computer too.
In no time my bedroom became a bedroom-cum-office,
lined with an array of office machines. I'd expected to be
given nothing but housemaid's work, but now I was working really and truly as an assistant. I suppose I had certain
abilities that I myself had never suspected in all my fifty
years, including that time I worked for a manufacturer of
measuring instruments. The more I was given to do, the
more I showed the makings of a first-rate office worker. It
got so that when anything connected with Taro came up,

the people at Nakada Associates would say, "Let's ask Mrs. Tsuchiya." Taro was impressed, and wanted to raise my salary. When I declined the offer, he scowled and accused me of being "a tough nut to crack." But besides my net monthly income, I was also getting paid for my nominal caretaking of the Oiwake cottage, so my actual monthly income was 250,000 yen a month, a princely amount. As for the rent for the apartment, which was set low for me on purpose, my husband's monthly pension covered it perfectly. No reasonable person would feel entitled to more.

The days passed by in a whirl with plenty of work for me to do, and that was my salvation. Because I was busy, when I did have time to myself I didn't waste it. I read whenever I could, and attended lectures on literature, history, and economics at Setagaya Citizens College. In the summer I showed up in Karuizawa as usual, but I couldn't very well let Taro's affairs slide all summer long, so little by little I put a limit on my time there, going only for the week the three sisters arrived, for example, the week they had guests, or the week they went back to Tokyo. Still, helping in Karuizawa was an important, not-to-be-missed annual event for me. During those intervals, since I stayed in the Oiwake cottage, I also used to visit my eldest son and his family in Miyota and go to Saku to see my mother, who was now a widow and still living with my brother's family. This gave me a chance to take her out to see Aunt O-Hatsu too, and to be greeted by the old familiar voice saying, "Well, if it isn't Fumiko." With Ami, my granddaughter, I retained a close tie though we were no relation by blood, and when she got old enough to ride the train by herself, she would come down to Tokyo for the weekend sometimes and sleep in my tatami guest room. I had my health, I had people I could call family, and I had work that was more than domestic service. I also had money of my own. I even had time to myself. Though my life was nothing out of the ordinary, I had achieved a degree of happiness beyond anything I ever expected.

One day when Yoko met me at a coffee shop, she looked me over with amusement and said, "Fumiko, look at you— you're a real *career woman!*" using the English expression that was becoming popular among working women. That morning I had felt a special surge of excitement. As I put on my lipstick before leaving for work, I peered at myself in the bathroom mirror and said gaily, feeling quite youthful, "Look who's got herself a career!" Yoko must have picked up on the mood I was in.

Sometimes I thought how pleased Uncle Genji would have been about this new life of mine. I remembered my first day off from my job with the Utagawas back in Chitose Funabashi, when I went to Ueno Park and sat weeping alone on a park bench, convinced that I had nothing to look forward to. Had I known then that all this lay ahead of me, I wouldn't have cried that way—or so I thought. But sometimes on weekend evenings as I leaned against the balcony railing, looking out vaguely at the scenery, I would feel so desolate that I didn't know what to do. When the wind

brought the distant sound of the Odakyu Line to my ears, I
even had a fleeting impulse to hurl myself under the wheels
of the train. At times like these, rather than try to distract
myself, I found the best thing was to go on leaning against
the railing, looking up at the slowly darkening sky as car
after car went by on the railway line.

# 9

# Windrush

TIME MARCHED ON. Two of the Saegusa sisters, Harue and Natsue, were now in their late sixties. They went on dyeing their hair, using bright-red lipstick, and dressing stylishly, but they took to referring to themselves mockingly as the Three Witches. Yoko was now in middle age, and she had her share of the usual problems. As her daughter grew, she became harder to deal with, and Yoko's mother, with Yuko abroad so much of the time, became more and more dependent. But all of this was nothing compared to the burden of looking after sick members of the older generation.

First, her mother-in-law, Yayoi, developed uterine cancer. Surgery was fortunately successful, but the treatments dragged on until Yayoi's husband was so worn out and worried that he fell ill himself. Yoko had to look after both of them, often sleeping at their house in Seijo. Around the time they both finally recovered, the Saegusas' Grampy lost the use of his legs and started to need care of the sort the three sisters couldn't provide around the clock. Mari and Eri, who lived next door, announced that they'd had enough of nursing him, and so Yoko had to continue commuting to

Seijo. The Saegusas hired another housekeeper to help, but unlike the way it was in the old days, there were limits to what they could ask her to do, and I'm sure Yoko was also involved in helping Grampy relieve himself.

What was strange was that none of this left any mark on her. Even as she grew older, her life left no sediment behind. It was as if she had a protective membrane, making her seem to be living in another world, separate from the one at hand. Inside that separate life was a radiance that, wherever she was, made everything around her somehow brighter. Her happiness certainly seemed to bring both Taro and Masayuki under its spell. How the three of them could keep up that three-cornered relationship was beyond me. Looking at them, I used to feel a sense of wonder and disbelief.

DURING SUMMERS IN Karuizawa I constantly saw Yoko and Masayuki together. In contrast, I had few opportunities to see Yoko with Taro. When I first moved to Tokyo, Yoko would telephone once in a while when he was in town and invite me out to dinner with them, but Taro was always so self-conscious and awkward during the meal that I took to excusing myself as often as I could, and so the invitations tapered off. There was nothing more I could do for the two of them, and I had no wish to interfere in their time together. Seeing them individually was of course another matter. I saw Taro as his assistant, and when he was out of the country, Yoko, perhaps feeling sorry for me living alone, would call up. "Fumiko, let's go out and get something good to eat," she'd say, so I saw her too. But as time went on, meeting as a threesome became rarer and rarer. Still, there was one evening I recall when the three of us did have dinner together, in Taro's luxury apartment in Yoyogi Uehara. Taro had just flown in that afternoon. The day before, I had laid out on his desk all the documents he needed, but one more arrived from the law firm and I decided to stop by his apartment. Since this was several hours after his plane had landed, I slipped the document into his mailbox thinking he and Yoko might already be inside, and turned to leave. At that same moment the two of them stepped out of a taxi and came in at the front entrance.

They were arm in arm.

"It's our Fumiko!" Yoko said to Taro, stating the obvious, her voice echoing in the high-ceilinged space of the granite entranceway. She withdrew her arm and tugged hard on the sleeve of his coat. I remembered her doing exactly the same thing to her grandmother when she was a little girl, yanking on the sleeve of the old lady's kimono when she wanted something.

"I know what! Let's eat together tonight, the three of us. There's plenty of food here." She glanced at the shopping bag Taro was carrying in his other hand.

Automatically, I looked at Taro's face. Just as I thought, he seemed uncomfortable. Before I could open my mouth to say no, Yoko looked up at him and said, "You know, come to think of it, we three never have had dinner together at home. It's funny, isn't it? Let's eat here tonight, just us. It'll be nice, we can take our time and relax . . . I left word with Masayuki that I'd be out late anyway. All right?"

Her words were a bit girlish, but she spoke straightfor-
wardly, without any coyness. Taro gave in. His face cleared
and he said, "Sure, if Fumiko is willing."

I hesitated momentarily, but for a woman who lived
alone to turn down the offer might have seemed needlessly
disobliging. "All right, then," I said. "I gratefully accept your
kind invitation."

"Goody!" Yoko clapped the tips of her fingers together,
just the way she used to do.

I never expected the evening to be so delicious in every
way.

"You're tired, so just sit and rest," Yoko told Taro, but he
joined us in the large kitchen. Though she looked impressively domestic in an apron, all she actually did was transfer a variety of store-bought foods from plastic containers
onto serving plates. "Taro's practically a vegetarian, which
is a real bother," she said, so I thought she would at least
boil or stir-fry some fresh vegetables for him, but no; she
just reached into the bottom of the shopping bag and kept
pulling out side dishes such as spinach with sesame and sea-
soned *kyona* leaves, all with the label of Nadaman, an old,
exclusive Kyoto restaurant. According to her, at home she
cooked almost every night, so when she was out with Taro
she never went to the trouble. He didn't seem to mind.
"Today we're having Japanese food, so let's go back to 'life
on the floor,'" she said, laughing. Instead of using the dinner
table, she spread everything out on a low coffee table in
the spacious sitting room—all the side dishes, some sushi
wrapped in bamboo leaves, and pickles from Kyoto. The

plates and chopstick rests she laid out looked quite elegant. Her good taste was obviously inherited, a family thing. The three of us went back and forth between kitchen and sitting room, trading little jokes along the way. Neither the surroundings nor the food was remotely like the old days in Chitose Funabashi, and yet it felt like an extension of those happy times.

Yoko was in especially good spirits. No sooner were we seated than she jumped up—"Oh, I forgot something!"— and brought back a bottle of red wine and a pair of wineglasses. "This is the only bottle left," she said, "but it should be just enough for you and me, Fumiko." She handed it to Taro to uncork and pour, then raised her glass to mine in a toast. "Tonight I'm going to see you get blotto for once, Fumiko!" After just one sip, though, the area around her own eyes flushed red. By the time the flush had spread from her throat to her fingertips, she was chattering away even more than usual. Her mood was catching. As the wine took effect I found myself babbling too, and even Taro, who didn't drink, let down his usual defenses. The content of our conversation was forgettable, but it wasn't what we were saying so much as the fact that the three of us were together, having a good time, that made us so happy, each in his or her own way. By the end Yoko was doing imitations of the Three Witches, her red face all scrunched, rolling on the floor and laughing till the tears came. Taro and I were rolling about too.

After the meal, we felt washed out—it was like the mood after a festival. In a completely different voice Yoko said, "Taro, you're tired." This wasn't a question. She said it in the gently scolding tone a mother uses to a child.

"No, I'm not."

"Oh, yes you are."

In fact, instead of his usual direct flight from New York he had come on a long, roundabout route, stopping on business in Tel Aviv, The Hague, and London before arriving in Tokyo. He had bags under his eyes.

"While we do the dishes, you take a little nap."

"I'm not sleepy."

"Now, now. When we're finished I'll bring you some nice cherries for dessert, so go ahead and lie down, close your eyes and get some rest." She twisted around and patted the sofa they were leaning against. They were sitting on the carpet with their backs against the sofa and I was across from them, also on the carpet, my back to an armchair.

"I'm okay."

"Be a good boy."

"I'm okay, really."

"Come on. Be good."

Tipsy as I was, I listened to this conversation with my ears pricked up. Yoko spoke to him in a way I had never heard her do before, a gentle, soothing way. Did she speak to him this sweetly as a child when the two of them were alone? I wondered. Or had she picked it up only after they met again as adults? Taro looked embarrassed. He shot me a glance and told her a little gruffly, "I said I'm okay."

Yoko wasn't bothered by this and simply said, "What am I going to do with you?" She got up and knelt down on the sofa, placing herself directly behind Taro, then reached up and flicked the switches on the wall to turn off the lights. The soft recessed light that was trained on the coffee table went dark, as did what looked like some antique Chinese lamps on the end tables. The big room was lit only by one dim lamp, made in a modern style with handmade Japanese paper.

"What are you doing?"

"If you won't sleep, I'll 'grandma' you."

What she said made no sense to me. I thought I must have heard it wrong, but she said the same thing again.

"Okay? I'll 'grandma' you."

Taro seemed to know what this meant, since he tried to sit up and get away, but she was already holding him down by the shoulders. While she tapped them lightly and rhythmically with her fingertips, she leaned forward and whispered, "Good boy, sweet boy," breathing the words in his ear. Whether it was the effect of her fingertips or her whispering, Taro soon lost the power to resist, his whole body unable to move. The moment this happened, she slipped her hands around in front of his face, fingers together, and blindfolded him.

For a bit there was silence.

Then—how on earth was she able to produce a voice so haunting? The sound of an old woman whose lilting voice was a memory; the voice of a woman twice her age, low and broken. She sang a lullaby, a song full of sadness, the kind of song a woman who never bore a child might sing to a child who never had a mother.

*Nennen korori yo okororiyo*
*Boya wa yoi ko da nenne shina.*

(Hushabye hushabye
Good little boy, go to sleep.)

She sang it slowly, very slowly, with her eyes closed, rocking slightly forward and back. When she had sung it three times, she gently lifted her hands from his face. For a time no one spoke. Taro's eyes were still closed. I was sitting with my arms around my knees, staring into the darkness. I felt transported into the past—a past beyond their childhood and deep into my own—a time before I could remember, though one in which a vague sadness had already taken root.

SEEING YOKO AND Taro as children, I never imagined that one day the kind of serenity I saw that night would ever come to them. Adulthood alone could not have done it. I believe the delicate balance they achieved was thanks largely to Masayuki. An outsider like myself was unable to see this till the very end, and yet even so I must have begun to sense something as the years went by. That would explain why an exchange between Yoko and me that took place not long after their curious three-sided relationship had begun often came back to me later.

"What Taro does is actually helping humanity," Yoko declared one day, out of the blue. "That's what Masayuki says."

She said this expecting me to approve. But at the time I was still unused to their relationship, and my first reaction was the usual mixture of skepticism and dismay: just what was going on with these people?

It could have been her father's influence. Yoko always did like to go on about what would or would not be of service to mankind—the prerogative, or possibly the sheer nerve, of someone who has enjoyed a privileged upbringing. The amount of money involved was never very much, but she joined a program called the Foster Parents Plan that helped educate poor children around the world; she also responded to the year-end appeals for donations to charity by NHK, the national broadcasting service; and she regularly contributed to Doctors Without Borders. I'm sure she didn't think for a minute that any of this alone qualified her as a benefactress herself—but benefiting mankind was a principle she believed in. The richer Taro became, the uneasier she undoubtedly felt about his wasting his life making money when by rights he might have been doing something more humanitarian. But Masayuki made her see how wrong she was. Raising capital to mass-produce newly developed medical devices allowed them to become widely available at affordable prices, thereby directly benefiting humanity; so, ironically enough, Taro was useful to a far greater number of people than he could ever have been by merely becoming a good doctor. Her husband's comment helped soothe Yoko's conscience, and Taro's too.

"That's what Masayuki says," she repeated, in the same reverent tone she had always used in childhood. She made it sound as if whatever he said was the pure and simple truth. "He says Taro's work is in a completely different category from a useless field like architecture."

Hearing this overstatement attributed to Masayuki, I felt obliged to protest. "Architecture is a form of art, so why should it be useful?"

"Yes, but he doesn't mean 'useless' that way, he means it really has no value."

Back when he was studying in America, Masayuki had still believed that architecture could be used to beautify the world. But as time passed he increasingly felt that the more architects went on designing buildings in their own styles, to suit their own tastes, the uglier the world became. He had come to think that in a country like Japan, where history and tradition got thrown out the window and architectural principles were lost, the architect was a blight on society.

As I listened to Yoko prattle on enthusiastically about his way of thinking, it slowly dawned on me how unconventional, despite his mild exterior, her husband really was. He was someone willing to go to extremes. In his effort to be fair to his wife's lover, he was willing to be unfair to himself. A faint sense that this idealism of his was what held the three of them together occurred to me then for the first time.

Whether it was because Masayuki was like that or because Yoko trusted him so completely I don't know, but over time, as the threesome continued, I could clearly see Taro beginning to change. The intense gloom that used to come over him sometimes began to dissipate. The clearest indication of this shift in character was a different attitude toward money.

"I was such a money-grubber, I'm still an uneducated boor." The first time I saw Taro after he came back from America, he said this with a dour look on his face, mocking himself. In his eyes the funds he'd gone to such trouble to accumulate weren't something to be proud of but actually had a certain taint to them. Yet gradually he found a way to "sanitize" them, at least in his own mind. It's apparently an article of faith among rich Americans that charitable donations are a way of returning a portion of their wealth to society. Perhaps because of something Yoko may have said, at some point he started donating money to charities left and right. When I heard about this, I thought of the old Buddhist term for pious donations: *jozai*, "purifying money." Taro's wealth also gave Yoko's family a good deal of financial leeway, and from little remarks she let drop I got the impression that money was freely available to her. Taro's money was his, but it also belonged to Yoko and Masayuki and, even more so, to society in general. I think this generous attitude benefited Taro most of all.

Under these circumstances, what happened in fall 1986, a few months after that evening when Yoko sang the lullaby, was hardly a surprise. Taro bought an old mansion in America, and plans for its reconstruction and landscaping were naturally entrusted to Masayuki's architectural firm. The mansion was situated on an inlet on the north shore of Long Island, near Manhattan. It was a grand but dilapidated Romanesque-style residence known as Windrush, built early in the twentieth century by a millionaire—American nouveau riche, Taro said—who hired artisans from Italy for the task, even importing Italian marble. When Taro heard that Windrush was available, he talked it over with Yoko, and she talked it over with Masayuki, and Masayuki flew all the way to New York to have a look at the place, and Taro decided to buy it. I gather that Windrush was a place well and truly shut off from the world, situated so that you could get a full view of it only from the sea at the end of the inlet. The mansion itself was of course sprawling, and the sadly neglected grounds, with cypress trees from Italy that had withered and died, were large enough to get lost in.

"Even if we three live there, it's so big that Masayuki and Taro will never have to meet, so we can live there in our old age," Yoko said. It would be like retiring to a monastery, she told me, half joking and half serious, after she heard Masayuki's description. "You could come and spend your old age there too, Fumiko."

"What would I do in a place like that?"

Yoko grinned. "Why, praise the beauty of God's kingdom," she said—a mocking reference to her mother's one-time flirtation with religion. Then, serious again, she stared off at something distant. "Our Karuizawa house is like a gatekeeper's lodge, he says."

One reason for picking out an old mansion like Windrush was that Masayuki had always said he would rather tinker with the design of an old place than come up with a new design of his own.

Once the purchase was concluded, their planning picked up speed. Yoko knew nothing about the tea ceremony, but she declared, "I want a Japanese teahouse where I can invite Americans. Then I can get Grandma's hanging scrolls and incense burners out of storage and use them." So they decided to uproot a teahouse in Japan and reconstruct it there. Then, in order to include a building of Masayuki's own design, they also decided to put up a small outbuilding on a promontory on the inlet.

The scale of the project was unimaginably lavish, not just to me but to the three of them as well. Once the decision to buy was made, things moved quickly, but the project, including landscaping, took a full three years and was not finished until just before Yoko died, done in collaboration with an architectural design firm in New York that specialized in the restoration of historic buildings. Masayuki went several times to oversee it in person. He and Taro, who never saw each other after they grew up, exchanged a stream of faxes. They were all swept up in a carnival mood: every possible idea was tossed around, with Masayuki making sketches and architectural models, and Yoko, supposedly as interior designer, sticking in her comments. Looking back, I think that might have been when the three were at their happiest.

WHEN DID IT all start to come apart? That is something I do not know, but I suppose it comes down to our inability, our human inability to make time stand still. As someone who bears direct responsibility for Yoko's death, I know I have no right to entertain such thoughts. Yet I cannot get

over the feeling that time itself was unwilling to allow the
happiness of those three to go on.

THE FIRST SIGN might have come when the Saegusa sisters caught on to their three-sided relationship. Because she
had her daughter, Miki, to consider, even Yoko actually ex-
ercised some caution, which may be one reason why the
relationship stayed hidden for so long. Not that the sisters
weren't suspicious. Probably when they learned that Taro
had bought the Oiwake cottage, the idea that he and Yoko
might be together again had already cropped up in their
minds. After I moved to Tokyo their suspicions must have
deepened, without going beyond the realm of suspicion.
Then, early in 1990, just at the start of the new year, twice
in a row the sisters happened to catch Taro and Yoko together. Both times it happened in Shibuya's Tokyu complex
of buildings.

Fuyue told me about it later. The first time, the three
sisters had gone to Bunkamura Orchard Hall to see a ballet
or something. After the show they went to the basement
for a late supper at Les Deux Magots cafe, paid the bill, and
were just going through the glass doors when, lo and be-
hold, there they were, the two of them, Yoko and Taro, riding down the escalator. The Bunkamura basement is a stylish
place with a distinctive interior. There is a large open space
with a big long escalator, twice as long as most, so you can't
help seeing who is on it. Yoko and Taro spotted the three
sisters at the same moment that they themselves were seen,
but they couldn't very well jump off midway. They simply

rode on down to the bottom and nodded in greeting before disappearing somewhere, away from prying eyes.

Even greater than the sisters' surprise at catching the two of them together had been their shock at how impressive Taro looked, dressed in a classic black suit. They gaped, unable to take their eyes off him. To put it in Fuyue's words, he looked like "a prince from another planet" who had just arrived on earth. All the way home in the taxicab, Harue was out of sorts, and the reason was plain. Even earlier, she must have considered my working for Taro as showing a want of respect for the Utagawas, and now she had plain evidence that Yoko was involved with him again—and this when she was married to Masayuki. At the same time, I wouldn't be at all surprised if in her heart of hearts Harue found it hard to forgive Taro for turning into such a fine-looking man.

The next day, Natsue waited till Masayuki had gone to work and then, apparently put up to it by Harue the night before, telephoned Yoko and started making the usual fuss: "What did you think you were doing? Just who do you think you are, young lady?"

Yoko quickly cut her off. "Mother, it's our business."

"What if Masayuki finds out? Then what will you do?"

"When I say 'our' business, that includes Masayuki. He knows all about last night."

Natsue didn't know what to say. Yoko repeated, "Honestly, it's our business," then added, "'Bye, Mother," and hung up. When Harue heard about this conversation, she turned pale and never referred to it again. But less than a week later, the three of them ran into Taro and Yoko in Shibuya again.

This time it happened at the Salvatore Ferragamo shop in the Tokyu department store itself. When the three sisters went inside, they caught sight of Yoko and Taro looking at neckties, and they immediately turned around and left. The next day when Yoko came to Seijo to look after Grampy, Harue glared at her but said nothing. Since she herself had had a lover—her art teacher in New York—she was in no position to criticize anyone on moral grounds, even privately. Only when Yoko came to say goodbye did she let her know that they knew: "Last night you were out with that boy Taro again, weren't you? We went to Ferragamo too."

Whether or not it was an act, Yoko answered in the most ordinary way imaginable: "Yes, we were looking for a birthday present for Masayuki. It's almost his birthday, you know." Afterward Harue was apparently fit to be tied, ready to explode with anger. This all happened while Yoko's mother-in-law, Yayoi, was in the hospital after being hit by a bicycle at New Year's—which was just as well, actually, or Harue might have said something indiscreet. Even then, Yayoi was the sort of person to mull things over in the privacy of her own thoughts and would never have said anything to Masayuki, of that I'm certain.

From then on, it was just one thing after another. A few months later, in May 1990, Grampy, who had been in and out of the hospital, died. Around the same time, Yayoi's uterine cancer returned, apparently triggered by stress from the bicycle accident. The young cyclist had sprinted

away, leaving her with a fractured femur that needed surgery. Once the cancer came back it spread right through
her, and within six months, in November of that same year,
she was gone too. Her death meant that the Shigemitsu
family, like the Saegusas before them, would soon face the
problem of land inheritance tax, but that wasn't all. A more
immediate problem was Masao, now a widower. He had always seemed to live on nothing but mist. Leaving him on
his own was impossible, and since he had no desire to leave
Seijo anyway, Yoko and her family ended up selling the Nogizaka condominium and moving to Seijo, along with Masayuki's architectural firm.

Looking back, that was never a very good idea. When
Grampy died, the Saegusa sisters had all the structures on
their property torn down and asked Masayuki to design
something new: a stylish three-story building for the clan,
one that would fit into that exclusive neighborhood and not
look like multiple-family housing. The project was com-
pleted in spring 1991, a few months after Yoko and her family
moved to Seijo. The Saegusas, who had been living in scattered rental apartments during the construction, all moved
into the new house, including Natsue, who had been in a
condominium near the station. Except for summers in Karuizawa, Yoko had always lived apart from the rest of them,
first in Chitose Funabashi, then Sapporo, then Nogizaka, but
from now on they were in awkward proximity. Moreover,
sadly enough, though she had moved to Seijo for her father-
in-law's sake, he soon developed pancreatic cancer and died
early in the winter of 1991. He was seventy-four. For a man,

that's close enough to a full lifespan, but his death coming so soon after Yayoi's made it seem as though he had willed it to happen. With him gone, I have no doubt that Yoko would have preferred to leave Seijo. For one thing, she was so used to living in her own world that social life was not easy for her. And then there was her involvement with Taro, which the Saegusa sisters looked on so unforgivingly. But Miki was thrilled to be living next door to her cousins. Yoko always felt guilty that her own fragile health had made Miki an only child, and seeing how happy her daughter was in Seijo must have made it difficult to suggest moving. Before long Miki fell in love with Mari's second son, whose nickname was Nimbo— a nice enough young man in both character and looks, but no scholar. With Miki in love, it became even harder to consider moving, since that might have been taken as a deliberate attempt to quash the romance.

IT WAS THE summer of 1992 when I found out that all was not well with Yoko, whom I had thought supremely happy. That turned out to be her last summer in Karuizawa. It was also when Taro took over the Karuizawa property.

"Aunt Harue always acts as if she owns the whole world," Yoko would say with a mocking smile. Sometimes the smile would have a tinge of sarcasm. "What if she knew this all belongs to Taro! I'd like to see her face then."

She was never small-minded, and I'm sure she was genuinely glad for their sakes that the three sisters were able to go on using their Karuizawa villa. But having been tormented by Harue for so long, deep down it must have given

her a kick to know that it was thanks to her—or rather
thanks to Taro, whom they had once treated as a servant
boy—that their holiday was possible. I felt the same secret
pleasure; she and I were partners in that.

That summer Yoko's sister, Yuko, came back to Japan for
the first time in a while, together with her daughter Naomi.
On her way to the United States to see Taro, Yoko had taken
to stopping off in San Francisco, and the two sisters were
much closer than they had ever been, though how Yoko explained those frequent trips abroad I have no idea. She had
Yuko and Naomi stay in the Shigemitsu villa, not the Saegusa one. The Saegusa attic rooms had been neglected for
so long they were no better than storerooms, but with her
parents-in-law now gone, the other house had plenty of unused rooms for guests. I worked in the Saegusa household,
and from the sound of Yoko next door singing to her sister's
piano accompaniment, I could tell how much she was enjoying not having her aunt around to say snide things like "Now
how about a little Callas to cleanse the palate?" During their
stay, Yoko was so busy entertaining them and doing things
with them that her underlying vexation barely showed.

The day after they went back to San Francisco, Yoko opened
the door to the Saegusa kitchen, darted her eyes around the
way she used to do as a child, and came in, having made sure
I was alone. She sat down at the big table, reached for a pillowcase I had just ironed, and folded it as she talked.

"I envy Yuko," she said.

In my eyes Yoko would always be a child, but glancing
down at her hands as she folded the pillowcase, I saw they

were the hands of a housewife, well accustomed to dish-water, with prominent blotches and veins. But she dressed much more carefully than ever before. Perhaps in that respect, being loved by two men made the difference. That day she was wearing a thin linen sweater with a gauzy scarf of gold silk. She somehow looked prettier than when she was young.

When I didn't react to her remark, she repeated it. "I envy Yuko."

"Do you?"

"She has more freedom."

She seemed envious that Yuko lived at such a great distance from the other Saegusas.

"*And* she's got a career." While her hands folded my ironing, she went on murmuring, half to herself: "I was lazy and never applied myself, so I've got nothing like that."

"You have your interior design work, don't you?"

"Nobody takes it seriously. And they're right not to."

So she knows, I thought, but I kept my head down and went on ironing.

"I wish I had some work that made me feel I was born to do it."

As times changed and more women entered the workforce, Yoko seemed to regret that she had reached her forties with no skills to speak of. Since she had not been given the same education as her sister, I thought this was not entirely her fault, but I didn't say so.

Yoko sighed. "Actually, I don't care so much about myself. It's Miki, really. If only she were more like Naomi!"

It seemed to embarrass her to run down her own daughter, but I too could see that among the grandchildren Naomi stood out. Unlike her brother Ken, who looked American, Naomi had more Japanese features and wanted to keep up her Japanese language skills. That's why she had come back that summer, which gave us a chance to get to know her better. Of course, she was a beauty, with a mother like Yuko and a father who looked "like Gérard Philipe." Even more striking was her figure, which was different from Japanese women's. If she had grown up in Japan, she would certainly have attracted more attention than she cared for. Eri's daughter, incidentally, was a tall girl who hoped to become a fashion model—an aspiration her grandmother disapproved of. "What is the child thinking? How vulgar! Why, she's no different from all those common girls!" But the girl in question couldn't have cared less what her grandmother said and went about wistfully comparing her measurements with Naomi's, sighing and saying, "Oh, you're so lucky!" As for Naomi herself, she wore baggy jeans and cinched her wavy brown hair in a simple ponytail. Usually she could be found in the shade of a tree with her glasses on, reading a book, or sitting at the porch table in front of her computer. She was still only twenty-one, but she had skipped a year of high school and graduated from college a year early, and in the fall she was to enter the medical school of Johns Hopkins University out east. Her goal was to become a medical researcher. Whether this had anything to do with her memory of the Utagawa grandfather whom she knew as a little girl, I don't know. She also liked collecting insects as much as any boy, and in Karuizawa she would often put on a straw hat and go roaming around the hills by herself, looking for them. Even though she was attached to Japan, the people her age streaming along the Karuizawa Ginza in droves seemed to baffle her. I suspect she felt as if they were from another planet. As a child she'd played happily enough with the Sae-gusa grandchildren, taking the part of a kindly elder sister, but I could see an emotional gap opening up between them as time went by. She seemed in fact to feel closest to my granddaughter Ami.

In stark contrast to Naomi, Miki fit in naturally with Harue's grandchildren.

"I wonder what mix of genes goes into the making of a child," Yoko said with a guilty little laugh that turned into a faintly bitter one. "I mean, what happened to Masayuki's genes? It's as if they disappeared."

Yoko took things seriously in her own way, and I think she tried to be a good mother. I saw her with Miki only while they were in Karuizawa, and as far as I could tell, she was making every effort to be neither too lenient nor overprotective. She was a far more conscientious mother than Natsue ever was. But as Miki got older, Yoko seemed at a loss how to deal with her. She had difficulty accepting that her own daughter blended in so easily with the Sae-gusa grandchildren. It would have been one thing if they felt strongly about each other, but aside from Nimbo, with whom Miki was romantically involved, her cousins didn't seem to mean much to her except as young people of her own generation; yet she was with them from morning to night, always doing things with them, talking about silly things like hairdos, eyebrow plucking, ways of wearing socks, and what kinds of little purses, datebooks, felt pens to get . . . it seemed absurd even to me. For a girl in middle school to obsess about this sort of silliness was understandable, but seeing a daughter about to enter college so preoccupied with it—especially with Naomi around by way of contrast—was bound to be disheartening for Yoko.

"I wonder if it's all my fault," she said.

"I don't know, I think it's the times." I never thought about such things; the words just popped out of my mouth.

"If that's true, it's sad . . ." Yoko paused in her folding, looking gloomy.

The Saegusa family that I first encountered with Uncle Genji was on the way out. Harue's daughters ended up becoming several times more ordinary than she was; as for her granddaughters, as Harue herself declared, they were indeed "no different" from the mobs of girls you see on the streets of Tokyo. When Miki was little, I thought she would probably outshine her mother, but as she entered adolescence, though she was still the most energetic of them, there was little to choose between her and Mari's and Eri's daughters. I think my granddaughter Ami showed more promise, perhaps because she was never spoiled. Harue's grandsons were pleasant enough, in the way of privileged young men brought up to be "cool" and carefree, but since many young men are brought up nowadays to be "cool" and carefree, it could hardly make them stand out.

The only person outspokenly critical of the third generation was Fuyue, who never married and had no children or grandchildren of her own.

"I don't know," she told me, "they just seem to get smaller and smaller. Only their bodies are big."

"How true." It was only around Fuyue that I could be so unguarded.

"They're Nietzsche's 'small people.'"

"What's that?" I asked.

"It's from *Thus Spake Zarathustra*, which I read when I was studying Wagnerian opera. 'Small people' are small to begin with and become even smaller and lazier, less capable of understanding greatness. People doomed to extinction." She went on with apparent enjoyment, "They're her grandchildren, so in the end Harue doesn't want to write them off. She'll stand up for them, say how decent and sweet they are, when they haven't got either brains or backbone. But nowadays even children with brains have no backbone anyway, so it's all the same in the end . . ."

Was she right? Are young people today of a lesser breed than before, or do they just seem that way to people like us, without children of our own? I suppose I'll never know the answer.

"Anyway, they're all shallow."

She said this with an odd kind of satisfaction.

CONSTRUCTION WORK ON the Long Island house ended in the autumn of that year. Yoko went to see the finished product in December. She stayed for around ten days and came back to Tokyo in the middle of the month—when the sound of "Jingle Bells" on every corner is at its most insistent—along with Taro, who had business in the city. Too excited to take a rest, she came rushing over to my apartment. Windrush was just wonderful, she said, beyond her wildest dreams. When you came through the front door, there was a high-ceilinged entrance hall, open all the way to the third floor. On the first floor, besides a drawing room, large dining room, small dining room, and so on, there was also a morning room where the eastern sun flooded in, a billiards room, and a library with floor-to-ceiling bookshelves covering the walls. A grand staircase led to the upper floors, with countless bedrooms. If you stepped outside and walked away from the sea, there in the middle of a Japanese garden was a teahouse, and going in the other direction, you came to the little chalk-stone building that Masayuki had designed. That was the best thing of all, she said. It had a wide balcony with round white pillars from which you could look far out across the winter sea. Just to set eyes on that stretch of water, with its leaden shine, made her heart take wing, she said. And from there you could go down the steps and walk along the shore where the waves roll in and recede. She was ecstatic, her words tumbling out, quite unlike the Yoko I had last seen in Karuizawa.

"Masayuki's design is terrific. The garden and everything." Then she added, looking straight at me, "We absolutely want you to come over to see it in the spring, Fumiko. That's what we said."

Though the age of foreign travel had arrived long ago, I had never once set foot outside Japan. I didn't have the courage to go by myself, and the idea of going with strangers on a group tour was unappealing. Yet, hearing her account, I felt a sudden urge to travel, to get out of Japan for once. It was ironic that soon afterward the whole thing came to an abrupt end.

YOKO'S DISAPPEARANCE CAME to light the day after Christmas, when Masayuki called me. He started to talk, then stopped, before mumbling, "It's about the time he'd be landing, isn't it?" He apparently had trouble saying the name "Taro" aloud. Taro had left for America the day before, Christmas Day.

"Yes, that sounds about right." I looked at my watch. It was nine in the morning on December 26, which meant that in New York it was seven at night on the previous day, his scheduled arrival time.

"I'm very sorry to bother you, but do you think you could telephone him for me?"

The voice didn't sound like the Masayuki I knew. Actually I had hardly ever spoken to him on the phone before, which may have added to the strange sense of disconnection I felt.

It seemed that he and Yoko had had some kind of row Christmas Eve. When he came home from the university the next day, she was gone. She had told the office people something about a sudden business trip, but Masayuki was convinced she had gone to New York, still angry with him. He wanted me to find out from Taro if he had heard from

Yoko the day before, if she had said she was going to New York or had perhaps actually flown there with him.

His voice was tightly controlled.

An image came into my mind of two figures standing on a balcony with white pillars, staring out at a lead-gray sea in a strong north wind. For a moment the image took on a firm reality. Yes. That's it. Yoko has finally left us and gone to New York. To be with Taro for good . . . I felt the air surrounding me become still. After hanging up, I called New York, only to find that Taro came on the line sounding like his usual self. He had just arrived. I sketched in the situation. He said he hadn't heard from her. Then he asked, "Do you think she would ever do that—leave home, and come here to New York?" I could picture him standing stock-still while he waited for my answer.

"Yes, of course."

He waited a moment longer before saying in a strangely distant tone, "I don't think so."

"Why not?"

He was silent.

I remembered Yoko's ecstatic face as she said, "The sea glowing dimly, seagulls flying, the gray sky hanging low. It was all incredibly lonely and sad but at the same time perfectly wonderful."

Without answering my question, Taro asked, "Did something happen between her and Masayuki?"

"Some kind of quarrel, I think."

He was silent again. I waited for a response, but as he said nothing I decided to hang up so I could report back to

Masayuki. "Anyway, if she gets there . . . if you hear from her at all, please phone here right away."

"What about Oiwake?" Taro asked suddenly, his voice rising. Before I could say anything, he groaned. "It's not spring now, Fumiko, it's winter—damn it. She could be snowbound."

I knew from the way he said this that he was remembering the "elopement," the time she caught pneumonia. That had been in early April. Annoyed by the degree of concern in his voice, I told him it wasn't snowing in the first place, and anyway Masayuki would surely have phoned Oiwake already. "The minute I find out something I'll call you, so you do the same, all right?"

He seemed to be thinking. There was no response so I hung up, putting the receiver down more roughly than necessary.

I called Masayuki back. When I reported that there had been no word from her yet in New York either, he said he was immediately setting off for Oiwake. He had been phoning the cottage steadily since the night before but thought she might be deliberately ignoring the telephone, and he had already decided to go there in case she hadn't been heard from. The scandals of the past—her "misconduct" and "elopement"—apparently made Oiwake spring to his mind too. Not knowing where the key to the cottage was, he asked if he could come to my place to pick one up. By then I had made up my mind to go with him. When I heard Taro's despairing groan, I had balked at his suggestion, but now that Masayuki was pinning his hopes

on Oiwake, the idea that she might be there seemed not
so unlikely.

"I'll go with you, if I may."

Masayuki sounded surprised. "Oh, no, no need for that."

He thought of me as being on Taro's side, so it never occurred to him to rely on me in a crisis. I insisted. She might
not just be ignoring the telephone, I pointed out. You never
knew, she might be ill, in which case my nursing experience
would be useful, and if more help were needed I could call
on my son and his wife. My words evidently had an effect,
as he changed his mind. "Well, all right," he said. "Thank
you, that would be a great help." Disturbed as he was, his
gratitude was clear.

"THIS IS ALL my fault."

As soon as I dived into the car waiting in front of Seijo
station, that was what he said.

I was less interested in knowing what had happened
than I was exasperated with Yoko for being so impulsive
and causing such a disturbance, a full quarter century after
that last stupid episode, especially considering that she now
had a young daughter to look out for. It was all I could do
to contain my vexation—not to mention my anxiety over
what it would mean if she wasn't in Oiwake after all. What
if she really had gone off to New York? If the situation was
only temporary until she calmed down, that was one thing,
but what if she had in fact left Masayuki? I naturally felt
concern for him and his daughter, but even more, selfish as
it may sound, I dreaded to think what I personally was going

to do with the rest of my life. My mind was in turmoil, full of uncertainties. Since the bursting of Japan's economic bubble, Taro's work in Japan had fallen off, and with Yoko in America, it was all too plain that he would feel no need to return to this country anymore.

Unaware of my selfish train of thought, Masayuki kept repeating as if to himself as he drove, "I should never have said what I did."

His handsome face, seen in profile, looked rigid.

We took Loop Road No. 8 north and then got on the Kan'etsu Expressway headed for Nagano. As the car sped along, Masayuki tried to explain what had happened. Now that I was involved, he must have felt he owed me an explanation. But this was the explanation of a reticent person holding his emotions painfully in check, and so I still had no idea what had happened, or in what order, until later when I put what he told me together with what I heard from Fuyue. Even then, there were gaps I had to fill in with my imagination.

It all started with an incident that took place the night before Taro left for New York, on Christmas Eve, when he accompanied Yoko as far as Seijo station and they were caught together yet again by the Saegusa sisters. Usually after dark Yoko took a taxi, but that day she needed to be back before six, in order not to be late for a Christmas Eve party at the Saegusa home, so she decided to take the Odakyu Line since it would be faster than traveling by car. Taro always wanted to prolong his time with her till the last possible moment, and since he was leaving the country the next day,

I'm sure he was more persistent than usual. According to Fuyue, Yoko sat down on the edge of a bench on the platform. Although she was already wearing a coat of her own, Taro put his overcoat around her shoulders and wound his scarf around her neck till her face was almost hidden, wanting to make sure she didn't catch cold. That alone was a strange enough sight, but then he crouched down in front of her and became engrossed in conversation, looking intently up at her. People hurried past them, and they were off in a corner, but the sight was so unexpected—a woman buried in a man's overcoat and scarf and, at her feet, someone like Taro wearing a black suit and gazing upward in an ardent way—once you did notice them, you couldn't help staring.

Then, who should come along but the three sisters. They had just emerged from the last car of the train on their way back from an expedition to Shinjuku. Their hands were full of packages—ready-made food and presents for the grandchildren—and Harue, with her rheumatism, was walking with a cane, so naturally they couldn't keep pace with the crowd and fell behind. Soon one of them noticed the little tableau and let out a cry of surprise that attracted the attention of the other two. They walked by without a word, holding their collective breath, but this time Yoko and Taro were too lost in their own world to even notice. Yoko had said she would be out all day and unable to help with the preparations, and she too had the same kind of plastic bags from the food section of a department store on the bench beside her, their very ordinariness serving to make the rest of the scene that much more distracting.

Natsue climbed the station stairs in a state of shock, scarcely believing what she'd set eyes on—even though it was her own daughter. At the top of the stairs she came to her senses. "Honestly, that girl," she muttered. Harue remained silent as they crossed the overpass and went through the turnstile.

This might be presumptuous of me, I know, but I think that for over fifty long years, ever since Noriyuki Shigemitsu died in the war on the threshold of his life, Harue had lived feeling vaguely aggrieved. Even if Noriyuki had returned safely from the front, whether he would have married her remains an open question, and even if he had, whether that would have made someone like her happy we will also never know. It was only his death that allowed her to go on thinking life had treated her unfairly. She had been born into such fortunate circumstances: she should have been happier. Yet somehow true happiness always slipped through her fingers. She never experienced the state of grace where one rejoices just to be alive. Seeing Noriyuki's nephew marry not one of her daughters but Yoko, of all people, and seeing that their marriage was clearly a happy one, must have deepened her bitterness. Still, that alone she might have borne. Then Taro reentered the picture, without dimming the couple's happiness in the least. Instead, the three of them had run off together into never-never land. Harue was a woman of keen perception, and she must have understood all this. And then came that scene on the station platform. The moment she saw it she had vivid proof of the way the two of them were wrapped up in each other, cocooned from the rest of the world—and *that* proved more than she could bear. I don't consider her a bad person, but unfortunately for her, she acted on a momentary impulse and lived to regret it.

When the three sisters left the station and came out onto the street, Harue finally spoke: "A good thing it was the three of us who saw that spectacle," she started off. "What if it had been Miki or her friends, or her friends' mothers?" She dragged Miki into it in order to find fault with Yoko. Miki probably wouldn't have appreciated it, but certainly that was where Yoko was most vulnerable, as the mother of an adolescent daughter. Taro and Yoko might have been together that day in the firm belief that Miki would go straight home from school and the Saegusa sisters would have long since returned home from shopping, but that didn't make Yoko's behavior any less outrageous. Natsue chimed in, "That's right, that's absolutely true." But Natsue was blind to other people's happiness, blind even to the fact that happiness like theirs had never come her way. She surely had no idea what lay behind her sister's outrage. Harue's mind seemed to be on something else while she went on complaining. Then she stopped and, tapping her cane, made her way home, preoccupied.

Perhaps she had already made up her mind then. Or did it happen later, when she saw Yoko at the party looking so carefree? Fuyue said she never dreamed that Harue would go so far as to haul Masayuki into it. It happened after dinner when the presents had been opened and people were scattered about the dining room and parlor having cake. All at once Fuyue noticed that Harue wasn't there. Feeling a sudden foreboding, she searched for Masayuki, but he too was missing. Usually she avoided confronting her sister Harue, but that day, she was ready to stop her if she intended to say something to Masayuki. But she was too late. When she opened the door and hurried out into the hallway, Masayuki was just coming back with a look on his face she had never seen before. He walked past her without registering her presence, took his coat from the closet, and disappeared.

"Harue, you said something completely inappropriate, didn't you?"

As she came along tapping her cane, Harue answered this accusation excitedly, her face flushed red. "I most certainly did not!"

"Oh, yes, you did. It is none of our business. We have no right to say anything."

"I have a responsibility to Yoko, as her aunt. She needs to pay attention to what people will think. Her behavior is way out of bounds. Masayuki is a fool to put up with it." Harue herself ordinarily scoffed at conventional notions of common sense or propriety, but that must have been the tack she took, keeping a close watch on Masayuki's expression as she described much too vividly the scene she had just witnessed at the station.

"Think of poor Miki," she added defensively to Fuyue.

"You had absolutely no right. Miki? This isn't about her."

What was done was done. There was no point in escalating the confrontation, so Fuyue showed her displeasure but held her tongue.

Sometimes the devil gets into people. That must be what happened to Masayuki then. The poison in what he'd heard must have spread inside him. Ten years had passed since that night he was so terrified that Yoko would leave him, and perhaps his guard was down. Just what he said to her, I don't know, but whatever words he may have used, when Yoko came back from the Saegusas that night, he confronted her. For all I know he just told her to act a little more like a normal mother for Miki's sake—the sort of thing that would seem only natural to an outsider.

"I never should have said it."

His eyes were fixed on the expressway ahead. The car windows showed a dark, wintry sky with not a speck of blue. I glanced at his profile. His eyes were looking far into the distance.

This much was evident: whatever he had said, his comment made it instantly and painfully clear to Yoko that he had stumbled—fatally.

He went on: "'How can you say something like that?' she said to me in shock. 'If you say things like that, it's all over.' That's what she said."

He wore a faint grimace, giving his face the same look of chilly loneliness that was in Noriyuki's memorial photograph. The contrast with his usual geniality, something he had inherited from both sides of the family, strengthened the impression of coldness.

I could picture Yoko retreating a step, her eyes wide open. How can you say that, Masayuki? How can you say something like that? If you say things like that, it's all over.

"I should have apologized right then." He closed his mouth, then opened it again. "But I didn't. I said, 'If it's over, then fine.' I said it without thinking."

"And then?"

"That was that. She ran upstairs to her bedroom."

I had heard before that the couple had separate bedrooms, his on the first floor and hers on the second. Yoko still had trouble sleeping, and Masayuki still read to her at bedtime, but she also had trouble staying asleep. When she woke up in the night she would read for a while before taking a sedative toward dawn and going back to sleep. And so she had the second-floor bedroom to herself.

He should have gone after her and apologized, but he didn't. For some reason, at the time he thought if it was over, then fine, let it be over. That might be the best thing for her, he'd even thought. Masayuki said all this in a detached tone.

"And the next day I went to work."

I heard him out in silence. I personally didn't think he had said anything wrong. "If it's over, then fine." If he said that, it was perfectly understandable. And yet deep down I understood the shock Yoko felt.

In any case, with Harue's poison still circulating inside him, the spell Yoko had cast on him for ten years seemed to wear off, and he saw himself as he appeared in other people's eyes. All the things he had willingly gone along with for her sake then revisited him in a new light, mocking his lenience. A change in perspective turns everything upside down. Where Taro's Windrush project on Long Island had seemed to offer him the chance of a lifetime as an architect, perhaps he, the odd man out, had only been given a toy with which to occupy himself. Perhaps there had been an element of pity for his firm, which was short of clients. And the gratitude he had felt toward Taro for buying the land in Karuizawa was just one more sign of what a fool he'd been. Others might have seen it as an unsubtle reminder of his, Masayuki's, own impotence. Inevitably his thoughts began to run along those lines. Once he started applying an ordinary yardstick to his predicament, nothing made sense anymore, so it was no wonder his mind began a downward spiral.

The next morning Yoko did not get up, but this wasn't unusual for her after a sleepless night. Masayuki made breakfast for their daughter, who went off to school suspecting nothing. He came to his senses in the middle of a faculty meeting at the university. Suddenly he felt queasy, his fingers and toes turned to ice, and he broke out in a cold sweat. "Are you okay, Shigemitsu?" his colleagues said, and he took the chance to excuse himself and go home. By then Yoko was gone. He felt sure she was on her way to Narita Airport. He couldn't quite bring himself to contact me and ask me to call New York in his stead, so he sat at home thinking she might call from the airport, and waited by the telephone until nightfall. Fortunately that had been Miki's last day of school before winter vacation, and after coming home she had gone off on a short skiing trip with her cousins and friends, still unaware that anything was amiss between her parents.

WE ARRIVED AT the Oiwake cottage just past noon. Being so small it took less than a minute to search. I went outside, rustling dry leaves as I walked, and checked the shed, which was of course empty. The bunk bed where Taro had slept long ago was surrounded by crisscrossing spiderwebs, making me feel all the more convinced that Yoko had gone to New York. Beside me, Masayuki seemed to feel the same way, staring tight-lipped at this empty place.

Just then we heard the faint sound of the telephone ringing in the cottage. It was uncanny; we had arrived only minutes before. It was as if someone were watching us from a distance. Masayuki was pulled back into the moment; he frowned and cocked his head uneasily toward the sound. I raced back to the cottage, kicking up fallen leaves as I ran, and picked up the receiver to hear a familiar voice.

"Fumiko, is that you?"

It was Taro. He must have expected we would go there and at some point had started calling every five minutes.

"Yes, it's me." Careful to keep my irritation under control in front of Masayuki, I said, "Did you hear from Yoko?"

Impatiently he asked, "She's not there?"

"No, she's not."

On the heels of this, he said, "I think she might be in Karuizawa."

I said nothing. We intended to have a look there too, but as both of the earlier adventures had taken place in

Oiwake, the likelihood of finding her anywhere else seemed slim.

"What about it?" Taro asked. "Did you try there?"

"Not yet, but we will."

"I have a hunch that's where you'll find her," he said gravely. "It occurred to me when I hung up before."

Why didn't he tell me a little more of what was in his mind? Why didn't he explain that by "Karuizawa" he meant the Saegusa house, not the other one? When I heard the word "Karuizawa," I had the fleeting thought that, given the freezing temperature, there really was some possibility that she might have gone there. Several years back, the Saegusa sisters had complained about the trials of getting old, the cold settling in their bones even before the end of summer, and had had kerosene heaters installed in each of their bedrooms. The Shigemitsu household did the same. Yoko's bedroom there was fully heated.

"Anyway," I said, "we'll go look. If we find her I'll call you, but if we don't, I won't." Aware of Masayuki's eyes on me from behind, I hung up without waiting for an answer.

"Go where, Karuizawa?"

"Yes."

He asked no more questions.

We stood there wordlessly in the deserted cottage for another moment, as if making sure that it was perfectly still. The chill that had settled in the small, old building as fall turned to winter seeped up through the floorboards, enveloping me. Amid the quiet and the cold, I got the distinct impression that Masayuki did not have much hope of finding her in Karuizawa. The flicker of hope that Taro's intensity had aroused in me quickly faded.

Outside, the dark gray winter sky hung lower and lower.

The two Western-style buildings stood together in lonely disuse, the very picture of winter, or of dying itself. Masayuki got out of the car with an absent look and plodded mechanically toward the Shigemitsu house to one side. I started off in the same direction but then decided there was little point in both of us searching the same building. "I'll look over here then," I called out to his back, and turned toward the Saegusa house.

I wanted Taro to be happy. Yet the thought that now at last he would be happy may have unnerved me. And my fear of his happiness may have convinced me that what I dreaded could only be true—that Yoko had in fact flown off to New York.

There's no point in trying to defend myself, but from the moment I set foot in the Saegusa house, my mind was made up that she was not there. It was nearly ten years since I had last seen her in the attic rooms. In the meantime, the attic had been turned into storage space, long unused as bedrooms. Besides, I was in my mid-fifties and my legs were not what they had been. After taking a quick look around the rambling house, beginning with the first floor, I finally started up the attic stairs but stopped halfway, checking only that all three doors along the corridor were shut before retracing my steps. If that was all, I wouldn't have blamed myself so much afterward. The moment I turned to leave, however, I felt something strange—at least, it seemed to me that I did. Perhaps it's a memory colored by what came later, yet the three closed doors seemed to be trying to tell me something. Or rather, in a way I still can't explain, I felt as if I heard the voice of a little girl, talking excitedly to herself. My surroundings were hushed, but for a moment I was hearing things. I remember that when I went down the stairs, I moved cautiously, not making a sound, trying to shake off the illusion. I remember that on the silent ride home with Masayuki, I fought off the urge to go back and check one more time.

THAT NIGHT, WHEN I got back to my apartment in Gotokuji, the red light on my answering machine was flashing. The first message was a request from Taro to call him as soon as I got home without worrying about the time difference. After that there were a dozen calls without any message.

I washed my face and hands thoroughly, changed my clothes, and took my time making a cup of hot green tea before I telephoned Taro.

"She's not there yet?" I asked.

"No," he answered shortly before asking, "Did you go on over to Karuizawa?"

"Of course we did."

"I called and called."

"Yes, I know."

"No, I mean I called Karuizawa."

"The Saegusa house?"

"Yes, over and over for about two hours."

Probably at five-minute intervals, as before, I thought. "They usually unplug the telephone before leaving, in case of lightning."

Taro paused before asking the question he already knew the answer to. "She wasn't there?"

"No, she wasn't."

"You looked in every room?"

I hesitated slightly before saying quietly, "I did."

He didn't press me anymore.

That night there was a light snowfall, and by the time I was about to turn out the lights I could see snow piled on the balcony railing.

In the morning, the snow had stopped and there was only a gray, overcast sky. The snow on the railing had gone. But when I switched on the television, the news reported heavy snow in Nagano that had started at dawn and was disrupting train schedules. I was standing in the kitchen making coffee, thinking about the snow, when the phone rang.

It was Masayuki.

"No word from New York yet?"

"No, not yet."

"I checked by telephone to see if her name was on the passenger list of any nonstop flight, but it's not on any flight that's landed so far."

"I see."

"I suppose she could have spent the night in Narita, or made a stopover somewhere . . ."

"True."

Not knowing what else to say, I was silent, and so was he. After the uncomfortable silence stretched on, I finally broke it.

"I'll call you as soon as I hear something."

"Yes, please do."

No sooner had I hung up and gone back to the kitchen than the phone rang again. I put down the kettle, rushed back to the living room, and picked up the receiver. This time it was Taro.

"I see they've had a snowstorm."

He must have been watching the NHK broadcast in New York. He seemed to be implying that Yoko was in Karuizawa. My own irritation and anxiety made me not reply.

"No word yet?"

"As soon as I hear anything, I'll call you." I think I said this fairly snappishly. Two grown men calling me in turns— what in heaven's name did they expect me to do?

Taro asked hesitantly, "Are you sure you checked every room in Karuizawa?"

He must have sensed something from my response the evening before.

Why did *I* have to run around searching for Yoko? Indignation welled up in me, and at the same time I was furious that my failure to check out the attic should come back to haunt me this way. I yelled into the telephone, "If you're that worried, why don't you just go look for her yourself!"

I heard a sharp intake of breath.

"All right."

That was all. The line went dead.

I sank down on the sofa and covered my face with my hands. I don't know how long I remained still. Even though the heat was on, I could feel the air in the room becoming steadily colder. When I raised my face, the dull Tokyo sky was dancing with snowflakes again.

FROM MIDDAY THAT day until the next morning, the Asama super-express train stopped running. It was around noon when I left Ueno station in bright winter sunshine. As the train emerged from each successive tunnel, the scenery turned whiter. In Karuizawa station a taxi driver opened his window to ask where I wanted to go, and only when I told him the house number and he was sure the place was accessible did he open the door. The car crawled through the snowy landscape, a landscape transformed since two days before. The sky that had then hung low and gray was now sparkling and clear. At intervals the breeze shook snow loose from branches, flinging it into the air, where it shone like crystal in the bright sunlight.

The roofs of the two villas were covered with snow.

As the taxi drew closer, I saw that the back door to the Saegusa house was standing wide open. The door was old, and no longer opened and shut smoothly; unless you locked it, the door's weight always swung it open. I looked from the taxi window at that gaping door without any surprise. It was pure coincidence that I arrived just after Taro, who drove directly from Narita by rental car, yet somehow I had known all along that it would turn out this way. The

SNOWY ROAD IN OLD KARUIZAWA

unchained gate, the curving tire tracks in the snow, the silver car reflecting the winter sunlight, the wide-open back door—nothing I saw surprised me.

Midway up the first flight of stairs I could already hear a shrill voice. As I climbed higher, the sound grew louder and louder. By the time I reached the open door to the room at the eastern end of the attic, it was almost ear-splitting. When I stepped inside, things were scattered about on the floor: an old electric heater, a blanket, plastic bottles, a boxed lunch, instant noodles. At the same time, a murky, freakish atmosphere hit me with full force. It felt as if I were being dragged feet first into a hole that gave a glimpse of the darkness below.

Yoko lay on her back, her hair bedraggled, shrieking something. It wasn't this that shocked me. On top of her lay Taro, still in his heavy overcoat; neither was this such a surprise. What did startle me—what shocked me to the core—was that overlapping with Yoko's screams I heard Taro crying in despair. It was so long since I had heard him cry like that . . . As I listened, it came back to me: the last time was after the "elopement," when he came to stay with me at Evergreen Apartments No. 2. He had cried that same way, utterly inconsolable, like a little child. The memory came back vividly, unconnected to the scene in front of me. Sadness filled the very air, a vast, all-encompassing sadness that enveloped me and made me feel that now, perhaps for the very first time, I truly understood these two.

Was the impossibly heavy burden of sadness they each bore something innate and inescapable? Or was it something they had acquired long ago by picking up on old Mrs. Uta-gawa's forebodings about their future, back when they were children too small to comprehend what the future might hold? A sadness that, once absorbed, had only grown over time, harbored deep in their hearts? Now I understood. On its own, the love they shared was hopeless and could only be illicit, and somewhere inside Taro knew it too . . . How long did he stay there like that? It might have been five minutes, or ten. However short or long it was, he couldn't drag Yoko up from her sorrow but was being dragged down with her, unable to do anything but dissolve in tears. Normally almost too capable, now he was foundering, pulled down by her despair at being deserted by Masayuki . . . I watched in utter helplessness as he went on sobbing.

Yoko had gone quiet and was staring at me with wide, bloodshot eyes. From beneath Taro's weight, she raised her head and said, "Fumiko . . ." She hadn't the presence of mind to see anything strange in my sudden appearance. "Masayuki said he wanted it to be over. Fine, he said, let it be over."

Then, overcome, she began wailing again. The sound grated on my nerves, as if her lungs had gone into spasm. With her eyes, nose, and lips swollen from so much weep-ing, her face looked awful: blotchy red, except for an area around her eyes, which was muddy and dark, an indication of high fever. I noticed the peculiar smell of a room whose occupant is feverish. Taro, whether or not he was aware of my presence, continued crying shamelessly.

"It's not true, though," I said.

Yoko, apparently unable to take in the meaning of this, raised her head again. Her bloodshot eyes stared up at me, wide open but unfocused. I continued, "The day before yesterday, Masayuki and I came here together to look for you. He looked next door and I looked in this house, but unfortunately I was too lazy to come all the way up here. That's what happened."

"Masayuki came?"

"Yes."

"To look for me?"

I nodded. Yoko seemed only slowly to take in what I'd said. Her raspy, convulsive sobs came at greater intervals, and eventually quieted down. The lessening of sound in the room only made Taro's crying stand out more. I kept my eyes on the long figure in the heavy overcoat lying facedown on top of her and simply added, "Taro knows it."

Yoko stared at his dark, shiny head, so close to her own. He was still weeping, though feebly now. After looking at him awhile longer, she raised her free hand and began gently stroking the black hair in front of her. "We need to call Masayuki right away," she whispered in his ear. It was the same tender voice she'd used with him before, her private voice. She went on stroking his hair, then repeated, "We need to call Masayuki right away," and tried to shift him off her, but he was too heavy, and she was too weak. Giving up, she let her head drop back on the bed and said again, looking vacantly up at the ceiling, "We need to call him." At this point Taro finally pulled himself together, as though regaining, for both of them, the will to live. Propping himself up, he swept back her matted hair and wiped the sweat off her forehead with a finger. "Let's get you to a hospital," he said huskily. A moment later he was on his feet beside the bed. Downstairs the telephone began to ring. "That must be him," said Yoko, turning her head toward the sound. But I thought it was unplugged. Confused, I ran down to the second floor and picked up the receiver. Just as Yoko had said, it was Masayuki. I learned afterward that toward dawn, her mind in a haze, she had gone downstairs and plugged in the telephone to call Taro, without knowing what exactly she wanted to say. He was by then flying over the Pacific. The phone had been working ever since. That Masayuki, driven to distraction with worry, should have called the Saegusa villa just then was another coincidence that in retrospect seemed almost eerie.

I myself was hardly able to think straight, and when he heard my voice come on the line I think Masayuki was thrown. After two or three halting exchanges, Yoko came down the stairs, supported by Taro. "Masayuki!" she shouted, grabbing the receiver and starting up the same strangled weeping as before. "You said let it be over. If it's over, fine, you said." Crying in bursts, she sank to the floor, where soon all we heard was that wordless, gasping, keening sound. There was nothing for it but to pick up the receiver and tell Masayuki in a few words how events had unfolded. My failure to search the attic was so hard to defend; I made excuses, but in the end all I could do was apologize. I could sense Taro behind me listening as I babbled into the receiver, explaining how after going back to Tokyo I had become increasingly concerned, and how I decided this morning as soon as the trains were running again to come back to Karuizawa to double-check—only to find that Taro had arrived just before me. The two of us were in the process of taking Yoko to Karuizawa Hospital. As I spoke, I saw that Yoko no longer had the strength to sit up. Still wrapped in Taro's coat, she lay on the floor like a rag doll. "Tell him to hurry," she said, her eyes rolling back till the whites showed.

"Yoko says you should hurry," I repeated into the phone.

The voice in my ear trembled with disbelief and joy. "Really?"

"Yes, really."

"I'm on my way," he said, unable to hide his emotion. "Tell her I'm on my way."

AT KARUIZAWA HOSPITAL, where Yoko was taken to the emergency room, she was diagnosed with nothing more than a bad cold. However high the fever, a cold was still a cold. And it was December 28, the end of the year, just the time when they were most understaffed. The hospital was unwilling to admit her, but we prevailed on the doctor and head nurse to let her stay until she had gained enough strength for the trip back to Tokyo. Taro's money might have had some effect, but it also helped that there were few other inpatients. When the arrangements were made, I took Taro's rented car back to the Shigemitsu villa, driving nervously along snowy roads, and picked up the things she would need: nightgown, slippers, teacup, chopsticks, toothbrush, mug, towel, and so on. By the time Masayuki arrived from

Tokyo, the evening was well advanced. Taro was holed up in the dark waiting room on the first floor, and I was alone in the sickroom with her. Masayuki knocked on the door but made no move to enter, probably thinking that Taro might be inside. When I went to the door and opened it, he stood there looking haggard. Remorse flooded through me. The words of apology I'd said in a daze over the telephone I now repeated in all earnest. Whether he heard me or not, I don't know. He took in the fact that I was the sole visitor in the room, but he was focused only on the bed. Yoko was asleep, having been given a sedative. He stole over to her side, careful not to wake her.

"She has a cold," I said in a low voice to Masayuki's back. "Her fever is high, but it's just a cold." Then I closed the door and went outside.

The Prince Hotel was full, even its suite, for the New Year holidays. Since it was too much trouble to look around for other hotels, Taro and I slept at the Oiwake cottage from that night on, lighting kerosene stoves for warmth. Luckily, we had wrapped the pipes in Nichrome several years ago, so there was running water in the house even in midwinter. I called my son in Miyota as soon as we arrived. This was the time of year when I was usually preparing to head there for the holidays, but I knew I was needed in the hospital, not only to take care of Yoko but to coordinate Taro's and Masayuki's visits. I told him that my plans had changed and I would be home later, after the first week of the new year. I didn't mention that I was in Oiwake, a stone's throw away.

I had not stayed in the cottage with Taro since the summer before old Mrs. Utagawa died. It felt strange. I decided to sleep in the maid's room behind Takero's study, the way I used to, and was lugging futon and quilts from the closet in the front room when Taro came out of the study looking annoyed. He practically ordered me to sleep in the front room, before quickly disappearing into the study again.

I had arranged my futon and was lying down with the musty, cold quilt drawn up to my nose, staring up at the yellow light dangling from the ceiling, when a wave of emotion spurred me into action. I threw my coat around my shoulders and marched to Taro's study, knocked on the door, and barged in.

He was sitting in the dark, looking out the window.

"It's all your fault!" I cried out.

I had meant to apologize when I knocked on the door, but completely different words came out. He looked at me, startled.

"It's all your fault for being so reckless and obsessed!"

He seemed annoyed, but said nothing.

"Masayuki is only human. He reached the point where he couldn't take it anymore, that's all."

"I've always, always, been patient. I hardly ever get to see her." His voice was low, as if he were holding himself in check.

"Well, you should be patient!" To cap this, I shouted, "After all, you're not the one she married!" And added, "Anyway, stop blaming me."

He opened his mouth to say something, but I went out, slamming the door behind me, so what he might have said I'll never know. I'd wanted to apologize for not having searched the attic properly, but I couldn't bring myself to say it. Even afterward—even after Yoko died—I've never been able to do so . . . to this very day. I was afraid I might fail to apologize as sincerely as I desperately wanted to.

Taro has never brought the matter up.

I gather that when Yoko arrived in Karuizawa, she went straight to the Saegusa villa and up to its eastern attic room, where, after crying her eyes out and staring at the ceiling all night, she was so exhausted that, as the sun came up, she took a sleeping pill and consequently never noticed that Masayuki and I had come. She did the same thing the next night, and got snowed in, and caught a cold. All this time, she kept the electric heater on, which made the air in the room so dry that she might have been better off without it.

But why that attic room? Was it because it was where long ago Masayuki had come to say he was sorry for making her fall down and hurt herself? Did she feel that if she stayed in that room he might appear unexpectedly, the way he did then, like a little messenger sent down from the night sky? Or was it because she somehow wanted to go back to those early years when she was so often neglected and had to nurse her own loneliness—to those years when not even Taro had entered her life? In any case, as her fever soared, she slipped into a delirium. What she had wanted to tell Taro on the third night by calling New York, I don't know. She may not have known herself—probably it came to her through the haze of fever that she didn't want to end up dying if she could help it.

AND SO SHE went into the hospital with what at first was just a bad cold. It was as if the three of them had been granted a final, blissful reprieve. On the first night, Masayuki telephoned Natsue and arranged that no one from Seijo should visit. The story he gave her was that Yoko had gone to an antique store in Komoro on business, decided on the spur of the moment to spend the night in Karuizawa, and then got snowed in, catching a cold and running a fever. Since I fortunately happened to be visiting my family in Miyota, I was on hand to help out, and so nobody from Seijo needed to come. She would be back in Tokyo in a few days, but until then he would be grateful if Natsue could look after Miki, who was due back from her skiing trip the next day. The people in Seijo may have had some dim suspicion that something had happened between the couple, but no one dared ask. Natsue pretended to take everything he said at face value. "If Fumiko is there, that's a big relief," she said, and as far as Miki was concerned, "Of course I'll look after her. You two take some time together for once and don't worry about a thing." She sounded good-natured. Had she known that Taro was there too, making a happy trio, she might not have been so accommodating.

Yoko had a private room on the northwest corner, with a view of Mount Asama. Masayuki and Taro came and went by turns. I worked out in advance the times they could come to see her, to prevent them running into each other. When it was Taro's turn, he and I would show up together. No one would ever have taken us for a married couple, but at least he was accompanied by a woman, which helped camouflage the strangeness of having two men pay constant sick calls alternately on the same woman. The time of year meant that the university was on vacation and the office was closed, so Masayuki had nothing better to do than come to see her. Some of the nurses looked star-struck at the alternating appearances of these two dashing men. I personally found it a bit ludicrous that two busy grown-ups should spend all their time taking turns coming to see her in the hospital, getting nothing else done—even granting it was New Year's vacation. I never thought that this would be the end.

THE AGITATION OF the three days and nights Yoko had spent scarcely eating or drinking, only crying wildly, took a long while to fade from her system. For the first couple of days she had a blank look, but from the third day on she started to come around. Her temperature went down almost to normal, and despite a nasty cough she gradually began regaining her physical and mental equilibrium. She took to calling Miki every night, being a responsible mother and asking, "Are you eating properly? Are you lonely?" But once the receiver was put down she herself looked childlike, so young and innocent that she might have been a double of herself sleeping at Okura Hospital after the "elopement" more than twenty-five years earlier. When a woman is seriously ill, she often retreats into a much younger self, a simpler and purer self. Yoko was the same. When she was asleep, there was even something almost unearthly about the way she looked.

With her temperature still hovering above normal, it was important that she not get excited, so both men tried to avoid getting her talking. Taro took his cue from Masayuki and sometimes sat at her bedside reading novels aloud. One day, she interrupted.

"You know, Masayuki is a better reader than you," she said. "There's something funny about your Japanese. You make too many mistakes."

Lying with her frizzy hair spread out on the pillow, her eyes on the wall opposite, she said this quite matter-of-factly. Taro laid the book he'd been reading in his lap and, despite this harsh verdict on his reading ability, just grinned.

"What's so funny?" she wanted to know, a little smile playing on her own lips.

"Nothing."

"But you're laughing."

Taro was reluctant to explain, but she kept pressing him, so he gave in. He'd known for a long time that Masayuki read to her at night to help her get to sleep, and he had always wanted to do the same thing. Now, here of all places, he'd been given his chance.

Yoko giggled, then burst out laughing too.

They both seemed to have put away the memory of lying entwined in the attic, crying together. To look at them you would never have guessed a scene like that had taken place.

YOKO'S COLDS ALWAYS took a long while to go away, so nobody was worried that as time went by she failed to get better. Her persistent cough didn't alarm any of us either. It was only after a week, when her fever shot up again and we were told that she'd developed pneumonia, that we grew concerned. But even then no one expected her to die. She was still so young. When the antibiotic had no effect and her temperature hovered up around the danger level for two days running, on the evening of the third day the doctor suggested that it would be a good idea to summon her close family. Given her youth there was probably nothing to worry about, but you never could tell with a second bout of pneumonia. It was better to be prepared, just in case. That was when the gravity of the situation hit us for the first time. From then on she deteriorated at a horrifying rate; she had little reserve strength, and her immunity was down. Before they could find an antibiotic that would work, she slipped past the point of no return.

From the time her pneumonia set in, Masayuki and Taro scarcely left the hospital. She was moved to a room near the nurses' station and Masayuki, the husband, stayed mainly in her room, while poor Taro sat on a bench in a far corner of the waiting room with his legs outstretched. I saw to all Yoko's needs, wiping beads of sweat off her forehead, giving her sips of juice, letting the nurse know when her IV had run dry. With her high fever she mostly slept, but occasionally she would open her hollow eyes wide and look at the chair next to the bed as if to make sure someone was there. And she would reach out a hand to comfort the person sitting by her, whether it was Masayuki or Taro.

"I'm going to get well, I know it," she would reassure them huskily.

But the night the doctor advised Masayuki to summon the rest of the family "just in case," Yoko cried out, despite her fever, in a voice that seemed wrung from deep inside her, "It's so sad!"

Knowing that her family had been sent for, she seemed to realize there was perhaps no hope. Her breath came in shallow gasps as she focused her eyes on the ceiling in fear. I thought she went to sleep, but apparently I was wrong; she was just waiting for the nurse to leave the room before she said anything. Masayuki got up and bent over the bed so that his face was in her line of vision.

"So sad," she repeated, and held out her near hand to him, the one without an IV needle in it. "You poor thing, poor, poor thing." She squeezed his hand as hard as she could and then closed her eyes. Soon her cheeks were wet, but she hadn't the strength to cry much. She looked up at him and said, "Miki still has her life ahead of her, but for you, my sweet silly man, it's over . . . over . . . when I die. You wouldn't marry again if I begged you to . . . Damn heaven and earth! I've been so stupid. Insane. And there's no going back, is there? It's all so sad . . ."

Masayuki bent down and pressed the back of her hand to his forehead. He stayed like that, as still as stone.

To give them some privacy, I stepped out and took the elevator down to the waiting room. Since it was after hours for the outpatients, the fluorescent lights were mostly turned off. Taro was sitting in the darkest part of the waiting room, hidden away on a bench far from both the elevator and the entrance. Two other pairs of people who seemed to be locals—an old woman with someone I guessed was her middle-aged daughter, and a young couple—had chosen the brightest places in the room to sit. Taro's appearance marked him as an outsider, and sitting alone in the darkness he looked sinister, like an escaped prisoner. I went over and stood in front of him, saying simply, "She's no better," then turned and went to sit on a bench near the elevator. I decided to distance myself from him, in case Masayuki came down in search of me.

About half an hour went by before Masayuki came down in the elevator, wearing his coat. When he saw my face under the fluorescent light, he told me that Yoko was asking for me and Taro. After delivering the message he went outside.

The room was ominously silent when I opened the door. Yoko lay facing the ceiling, motionless. After a moment I realized she was taking rapid, shallow breaths. Even though barely half an hour had passed since I'd left her, signs of her approaching death were cruelly apparent.

"Fumiko." She turned her head toward me, then paused for a moment to steady her breathing. "Taro and I were going to look after you in your old age . . . so I never did anything to thank you."

She was preparing to die, but I wouldn't have it and cut her off a bit tartly. "I'll look after myself in my old age, thank you. And if it comes to that," I added, "I've got Ami."

"Yes . . . dear Ami."

Yoko didn't seem to mind the way I'd spoken. Seeing her look up at the ceiling again with those sunken eyes and nod quietly in agreement, I felt contrite. More gently I said, "And you're young, so you'll get well."

"Perhaps," she answered. "Anyway, thank you. We owe everything to you," she said seriously. She turned her eyes back toward me, her gaze as pure as a ray of light.

For a while no one spoke.

"Taro . . ."

He was already there at her bedside, and when she called his name he leaned over the bed.

"Taro, you mustn't kill yourself." She reached up to touch his face, reaching out weakly with the arm that was free of IV equipment, so he bent down lower. She stroked his cheek with her fingertips and repeated, "You mustn't. If you do, I'll never forgive you as long as I—for all eternity, do you hear me?" Her voice was infinitely gentle.

"But why . . . ?" he murmured.

For the first time I realized what he had been thinking about in the waiting room below. Sick as she was, Yoko had known.

"Why?" he said again.

"Because if we both die first, how would poor Masayuki feel? . . . It would be as if we'd left him behind, alone."

Yoko shifted her gaze to me, where I stood behind Taro, and let her arm drop listlessly before addressing me in something like her usual tone, half demand and half plea.

"Fumiko, this is my last request. Watch over him and keep him from ever doing that." Then she looked back at Taro, deep purple shadows around her fever-moist eyes. "Swear it now, in front of Fumiko." Her lips were dry.

"Why should I?"

"Come on, now. Be a good boy."

She said this with great tenderness, as though comforting a child, and tried again to reach out to him. He pressed her hand gently and laid it on the bed.

"What if Masayuki dies?" he asked.

"He can't. He's got Miki to take care of."

Taro looked straight down at her hollow eyes and inhaled deeply, breathing them in. He let his breath out slowly. "But if he does?"

She thought for a moment, then looked away. Eyes on the ceiling, she gave a little nod. Her throat was even thinner than it had been when she was in the hospital after their "elopement."

"It would be all right then."

"It would?"

"Yes."

For the first time, he seemed almost happy as he took another deep breath.

"But . . ." She looked at him firmly. "You mustn't die in a strange way. I would be too miserable." She frowned, as if she were seeing things that frightened her. "Die in a way that would make me think you had a good life." A few tears rolled down her cheeks.

Taro groaned. "You call this a good life?"

"I do." She rocked his hand back and forth on the sheets as if to soothe him. That was all the strength she could summon. With the ghost of a smile on her dry lips, she told him, "It's been perfect. Couldn't have been better."

Taro jerked his hand away. "Couldn't have been better?" he protested, shoulders heaving. "The hell you say!" He fell silent. Then in a low, mournful voice he said abruptly, "You wouldn't marry me. You didn't want me. You said if you were with me, you'd be so ashamed you'd die."

After a brief pause, she said without a flicker of expression, "You still can't forgive me, can you?" She seemed to be looking somewhere far beyond the ceiling.

He too was expressionless. "No, I can't." He picked up her hand again. "I never could. You don't know how deeply someone like me can hold a grudge. You just don't know."

He wrapped his man's hand protectively around her small one.

"I don't care. I don't want to know."

"I wanted to kill you, the whole time."

She showed no surprise. Her hand still tucked in his, she continued to stare into space. "Starting when?" she asked. "After I said those terrible things?"

"No."

"Before that?"

"Long before."

She turned her head toward him. "You mean from when we were kids?"

"Yes." After a moment's hesitation, he went on, "From the very first time I saw you in the yard of the Chitose Funabashi house."

"Okay."

Still no surprise. She looked back up at the ceiling, out of breath, and that was all. When she regained her breath, she spoke, less in answer to Taro than to release her own emotions.

"I was always afraid. From the time I was a little girl, I always felt afraid . . . When I was with you, it was like the rest of the world was rushing away from us . . . as if we were getting farther and farther away from it . . . and it scared me."

Taro just went on with increasing vehemence. "I always wanted to kill you."

"I felt so lonely I was scared."

"I should have done it."

They each seemed lost in their thoughts. The silence grew, and then Yoko cried softly, "But we were happy, so happy." Clutching his arm, she raised herself slightly and looked up into his face. "Don't ever stop wanting to kill me—even if I die."

"I never will—even if I die." And he laid himself over her, as he'd done before.

"It's crazy how happy I am," I heard her say, then she whispered, "Take care of Masayuki . . ."

For a moment there was silence. She had slumped back on the bed. Then she gave a low, soulful cry: "But oh . . . I don't want to die yet . . . and let it all go to waste."

Clutching his arm again, she tried to lift herself a little, but she no longer had the strength. All this talking seemed to have exhausted her.

While I don't believe that without the disturbance she could have survived, I do think it shortened the little time she had left. As Taro and Masayuki switched places, her breathing became more labored and she drifted in and out of consciousness. It was nearly ten at night when the three Saegusa sisters and Miki arrived from Tokyo, driven by Nimbo, and by then she was in a coma. She stayed that way for an entire day. In the middle of the night she had greater trouble breathing, and her legs turned purplish from lack of circulation. Her dry lips became white.

Her poor daughter was stunned by the suddenness of it all. Harue looked angry and for once was close-lipped. Deep down, I think she too was stunned. Natsue shed tears continually from those large, round eyes of hers, but the sight of her daughter lying so near death seemed to make her queasy, and instead of moistening Yoko's lips herself, she asked me to do it. Fuyue alone looked calm; she behaved with even greater self-possession than she usually did.

Taro waited in his car in the hospital parking lot, out in the freezing cold. When everyone arrived from Tokyo he'd left the waiting room, not wishing to be seen as they came and went. He asked me to let him know if she regained consciousness, but she never did, so I had no occasion to go out to him. I only looked down at the parking lot from

the window at the end of the hospital corridor. It seemed
to me that Masayuki did the same every time he passed that
window. Taro didn't leave even to eat. On the evening of his
second day there, the car still hadn't moved.

She died just after two in the morning.

When the doctor pronounced her dead, his words were
mingled with Natsue's sobs. I slipped out of the room by
myself, pushed the elevator button, and went downstairs.
I headed for the emergency exit, the only one usable at
night. I felt no emotion. I was numb. I propelled myself
forward mechanically, thinking only one thing: Taro would
never forgive me. He would never forget how I failed to
look in the attic room that day. And I had spent decades—
no—virtually all my life thinking only about how I could
make him happy. Now at the end of it all he would resent
me, hate me. The thought went around and around in my
head. I did not feel in the least remorseful; only stunned by
life's cruelty, when all along I had been doing my best. I felt
almost more like laughing wildly than crying as misery and
derision roamed the emptiness inside me. If only Mount
Asama would erupt now in bright red bursts and bury us all
in ashes, the living and the dead.

I went out by the emergency exit. I saw the wintry sky
filled with stars, and from among them fell shards of moonlight, glittering on the asphalt parking lot. That's when it
sank in. Yoko was dead. The sheer, harsh fact of it struck me
with full force. The ground rocked, and the firmament with
its countless stars started to revolve around the moon, and

I had to cover my face with my hands and crouch on the ground from vertigo.

I heard the sound of a car door opening and closing, and footsteps coming toward me over the asphalt, but I didn't have the courage to raise my head and look.

10

# Drinks at the Mampei Hotel

FUMIKO STOPPED TALKING.
It had started to rain a little while before. What began as light drizzle turned within minutes into a torrential downpour. In the sudden absence of any talk, the noise made by the rain was even louder. Yusuke, seated directly across from the now silent Fumiko, listened absently to the sound of millions of raindrops landing on the roof. He remembered that half an hour earlier there had been a distant chime followed by the voice of a woman speaking over a loudspeaker, warning that a storm was on its way. When he'd asked about it, Fumiko had explained that someone from the town hall drove around making these announcements for the sake of local farmers working in the fields.

The hands of the pendulum clock on the wall pointed to six-thirty.

Pale yellow light shone through the milky glass shade above them, showing a fairly bare tabletop. Today he hadn't been sitting there listening to her talk from morning till late in the evening as he had the other day, and yet he felt that a vast amount of time had elapsed, as though there had been no interlude.

She was looking down at the table, still silent. She seemed so withdrawn that he wondered if she even registered the sound of the rain on the roof. It might have been the light, but her cheeks now looked hollow.

He let his eyes wander over the low wooden shelves on his right, behind her. On the top shelf, amid the jumble of cotton work gloves, a trowel, candles, coils of mosquito repellent, a disposable lighter, and other things, he noticed two bundles with rabbit-ear knots, the ones he'd seen the other day in Karuizawa, containing the urns. While he'd sat listening to Fumiko during the past few hours with his back to the porch, more than once those two small bundles had caught his attention. Now that she was silent, their presence asserted itself more insistently.

She picked up her story again after serving a fresh pot of tea.

AFTER JANUARY 1993 Taro stopped coming back to Japan, even when he had business in some other Asian country.

With Yoko gone, making money no longer meant what it had, and with the economy in the doldrums, there was no point in coming here in search of investors. I stayed in touch with him and his lawyers, and took care of unfinished business, but once I'd canceled the rental contract on his luxury apartment in Yoyogi Uehara, there was little or no

work for me to do anymore. Yoko's teasing me about being
a real *career woman* seemed a thing of the distant past. About
a year after she died, I floated the idea to Taro of my packing
up and leaving Tokyo to go home to Miyota. He answered
that he still had some ongoing projects involving Japanese
investors and would like me to remain in the city if there
was no particular reason why I had to leave. Of course there
wasn't, so I took advantage of his generosity and stayed
on. This was partly because after Yoko died I was at loose
ends, and partly for a more practical reason: I had taken my
granddaughter Ami under my wing in Tokyo.

From the time she was in middle school, Ami had wanted
to attend college in Tokyo someday. But in the fall of 1992,
about three months before Yoko disappeared, just as Ami
was preparing for the spring entrance examination, her parents told her to apply to a local prefectural university, for
financial reasons. The sudden decline in the economy had
taken quite a bite out of my son's salary at the local bank,
and with two boys to educate besides her, the plan made
sense. But when I heard about it, I felt I couldn't just sit
back and do nothing. I offered to take her in for as long as
my work as Taro's assistant continued—they may even have
been quietly hoping I would do exactly that. Since I was
quite willing to help the family, and Ami and I had always
been close, it only seemed natural. Then that January Yoko
died. I told Ami's parents that the situation had changed;
that if Taro's interest in Japanese investors dried up, my
work might end at any time. But they had their hearts set
on sending her to live with me in Tokyo. I said to myself, if

I lose my job, I'll worry about it when the time comes. So after Ami, a bright student, was admitted to Waseda, she started living with me when classes were in session. She was usually out of the house, either at school or at a part-time job, and when she was home she generally stayed in her room, the only tatami room in the apartment. As a little girl, she had been like a daughter to me, but now it felt more like having a lodger I could be comfortable around, which was fine. Knowing how I regretted, and would go on regretting to my dying day, not getting the education I wanted, I just hoped that I would continue to be subsidized by Taro so that she could go on living in the Gotokuji apartment and keep up her studies.

TARO STAYED ABROAD, and during the next six months, then a year, then two years that I lived in Tokyo, one by one the elder generation began to slip away.

In late 1993, Harue's husband died of diabetes. After rising to an executive position in the Mitsubishi Corporation, he had become president of a subsidiary, resigning that position a few years before the end. Fortunately, his eyesight didn't fail him, and with insulin injections, he went on playing golf to the last.

My mother died in the spring of 1994. She always blamed her poor health on the strain of the war period, but whatever the reason, she became prone to illness around the time I left for Tokyo. In middle age her heart weakened and she often had to take to her futon. She finally began to open up to me after my stepfather died some years before this, though no doubt she'd have said it was I who finally opened up to her. Her failing heart kept her from getting around, but even other people in the country no longer walked anywhere much, every family now owning two or three cars; so at New Year's, though my aunt O-Hatsu lived only a stone's throw away, we drove over to pay our respects. The talk turned to the past. In my mind's eye I saw my mother the way she was on those winter nights long ago when she sat by the hearth and pulled a cloth from her waistband, then covered her face and sobbed out her troubles. And again I saw the blank look on her face after she was told that my father had taken his own life.

As usual, O-Hatsu, now living in a house with an up-to-date kitchen, bustled around making green tea that she served with pickles—though, unlike in the old days, the pickles came factory-sealed in a plastic bag. My mother was a good fifteen years younger than her, but she seemed so frail I was afraid she might not last much longer. Sure enough, she died last spring after two heart attacks. Having rushed home after the first one, I was able to be at her side from then until the second one came and carried her off. Providing this final care helped remove a weight that I'd long felt pressing on my chest.

I should perhaps mention in passing that the husky-voiced woman who was my uncle Genji's companion for so long had the good fortune to be targeted by a land shark during the "bubble" era, which resulted in her selling the small property in Soto Kanda for enough money to let her live out her old age in comfort after the bubble burst. At the time of my mother's funeral she sent a telegram and a generous sum of condolence money, and when I went to call on her to thank her after I got back to Tokyo, I found her living in a cozy, brand-new apartment on the Marunouchi Line. She had given up her little restaurant, now pinned her hair up at the nape without any hairpiece, and was dressed in Western-style clothes, though she had the round shoulders you often see in women who are accustomed to wearing a kimono. She seemed glad to see me. They had never had any children and she lived alone, but she was continuing her lessons in Japanese dance, a hobby she'd taken up again back when she was living in Soto Kanda. This provided her with friends from that circle, and she wasn't lonely at all. In a sunny tatami room was a little Buddhist altar decorated with a picture of my uncle, one he'd chosen himself to be shown at his funeral, taken when he was "the Valentino of the Orient." She kept flowers and incense in front of it, along with offerings of water and white rice. I couldn't help feeling happy for him when I saw what care she took for the repose of his soul, with the old-time conscientiousness that's so typical of people in the entertainment trade.

It was around then that I learned of the death of Taro's guardian, Mr. Azuma. Taro had sometimes talked about sending the Azumas a substantial amount of money, mumbling about it in such a way that I was never sure if he was talking to himself or consulting me. I'm sure it wasn't gratitude that motivated him, but rather the desire to pay off a debt. Still, there's no denying that amid all the hardships of leaving Manchuria, they did share their meager food supply with him and bring him up. I suspect that the older Taro became, the more that weighed on him. But because of O-Tsune, he was hesitant about doing anything that would mean reviving his connection with her. Then, about a year after Yoko's death, he called me from New York and asked me to track them down. I took it as a sign that he was preparing to cut his ties with Japan, so I felt uneasy—even alarmed—but all I said was "I'll get right on it," and hung up.

They might still have been living in Kamata, so I checked the telephone book, but there was no listing for either Mr. Azuma or his eldest son. Just to be sure, I took the train out there, curious to have a look around and see for myself how much the area had changed in all the years since I'd seen it. The street I once walked along trying to escape the din of machinery and the sparks from acetylene torches had been completely revamped. The old backstreet factories were no doubt still there if you sought them out, but the main street was lined with the sort of low buildings you found anywhere in Tokyo. The wooden house where the Azuma family had lived was gone, as was the coffee shop where Yoko and Taro sat and glared at each other. I'd never heard of any relatives on the Azuma side, and I had no idea where old Roku might be buried. In the end I called Taro back and got the old address he had for O-Tsune's family down south. That's how I was able to track them down at their current location, which was surprisingly close to Kamata. It turned out that twenty years earlier, their eldest boy was in a car accident and changed his name on the advice of a fortune-teller. That explained why I couldn't find him in the telephone book. His father had been dead for three years, I was told.

My staying out of it would mean fewer complications down the road. All the arrangements were done in the name of Nakada Associates, and one of the firm's lawyers met directly with O-Tsune and her son. After Taro took off, the Azumas, I learned, were eventually able to hire another two or three workers and then move to Shimomaruko, where they had their own factory instead of a rented one, with a little more space. They survived the steep rise in the yen exchange rate, and for a while were doing quite well. However, to remain competitive, they'd bought a large and very expensive computer-controlled milling machine, only to have the economy collapse and business dry up, leaving them drowning in debt. The little boy O-Tsune was holding in her arms that time I visited them left the family business and became a truck driver; fortunately he was earning enough for them to live on, but with no hope of paying back their debts, they were on the point of selling their costly machine for next to nothing. Coming at such a time, Taro's gift of cash—which I suspect was in the tens of millions of yen—was more than welcome. The lawyer apparently explained to them in words of one syllable that Taro's assets were all overseas; that he had specified this was a one-time gift to his family; and that, on his death, none of the rest of his estate would go to them. I think he succeeded in getting the point across that the Azumas should not look for any future windfalls.

The lawyer told me O-Tsune was a "timid-looking, tiny old woman." The "tiny" part I could understand, since she had always been short and had probably shrunk further in old age, but hearing her described as "timid-looking" was rather a surprise. Her eldest boy was apparently dressed in a dark blue suit, without a trace of his old wildness, and looked as if he had gone through some pretty hard times. The subject of the second son never came up, so what became of him I don't know.

FROM THE MOMENT Taro asked me to track down the Azumas, I knew he was getting ready to sever his connection with Japan. At the same time, I couldn't quite bring myself to believe that he would actually do it. But I was forced to do so a month ago, when Masayuki died of liver cancer.

Now that I think of it, his parents weren't the only members of the Shigemitsu family to succumb to cancer. Yayoi's mother lived a long life, but she died of cancer too, and it could well be that Masayuki inherited a predisposition to the disease. He also inherited his father's tendency—call it devotion, or perversity—to relate to the world through a single woman only, so that once that woman died he lost the will to live.

After my work as Taro's assistant dropped off, I went back to helping out in Karuizawa for a full month during the summers of 1993 and '94, and Masayuki's manner was so strangely subdued that I used to check up on him quite often, out of concern. He seemed to feel committed to go on living for his daughter's sake, and in front of others he behaved normally enough, but when he retreated to the study in his villa, there was such an air of bleak loneliness about him one might have thought his spirit had already left him. I suspect it wasn't solely Miki's desire to be with Nimbo that made her go to the Saegusas', but that she couldn't bear the sight of her father like that. She was used to spending most of her time over at their house anyway, and soon she was eating her meals there too, going home only to sleep. It would have been peculiar if Masayuki had cooked for himself and eaten alone at home, so, except for breakfast, he started joining the others around the Saegusa table. But not always. As often as not, just before they rang the gong for a meal, he would call to say he was sorry but he was in the middle of something and couldn't leave and would just eat on his own. Then either Miki or I would carry a tray across to the other house.

Harue never said a word about it, but when Masayuki did not join them for a meal, her relief was obvious. He too, not surprisingly, seemed to find her presence a strain after what had happened. Still, once he was with the others he behaved as naturally as he could, presumably for his daughter's sake. Even in her seventies, Harue was the head of the Saegusa family, and there was a good chance that Miki would marry her grandson Nimbo one day. I believe Masayuki was determined to endure Harue's presence with that possibility in mind.

The only time he allowed his discomfort to show openly was when Harue and Natsue went on and on enthusiastically about the Dutchman Peter Jansen, speculating that it was he who had bought the property.

One day when I took Masayuki his lunch tray, he looked up from his desk in the study and turned toward me.

"Fumiko . . . ," he said. His computer screen glowed blue, with a scattering of drawings and papers around it, yet there was no sign that he had been doing any work at all. I knew he'd just been sitting staring out the window.

In full bloom just outside it were some white lilies that Yoko, the little flower thief, had once stolen from the woods.

"I've been meaning to say this for some time . . ." He looked at me, pale. "With Yoko gone, it's not right for us to go on using the property here like this. So tell him he can sell it anytime, would you, please?"

As usual, he avoided saying Taro's name.

"Certainly," I said. Then, to make him feel easier I added, "But land prices are falling, you know. He would only lose money if he sold now, so I doubt if he has any immediate plans to sell."

"I see. In that case, it's all right."

He looked out the window. Something in his eyes was more than I could bear.

"I am so sorry." Before I knew it, the words had slipped out of my mouth. Words that I could never bring myself to say to Taro.

Masayuki looked at me in surprise, but seemed to realize instantly that I still could not forgive myself. He hesitated, as if unsure how to respond, before telling me quietly that it wasn't my fault. "It was *my* fault," he said.

Soon after that, we learned he had liver cancer. It was as though his loss of the will to live manifested itself in the disease. After the diagnosis he had less than a year to live.

He died entrusting Miki's future to the three Saegusa sisters and Nimbo, but by then Miki was twenty: he'd managed to hang on until she became legally an adult. Perhaps he knew he wouldn't live long. As it turned out, he had a substantial insurance plan, and the money from the sale of the Nogizaka condominium (luckily sold just when the economy was at its most inflated) was still sitting safely in the bank, since he and Yoko hadn't bothered to do anything with it. With inheritance taxes for Seijo less than half what they once were, Miki was well provided for, and in due course she could rent out the house or sell it, so there were no financial problems. Everyone said it was that reassuring knowledge that must have allowed Masayuki to let go of his life in peace.

YOKO'S SUDDEN DEATH had come as a terrible shock to her sister, Yuko, in San Francisco. Since then she'd felt responsible for her niece, Miki, and kept in frequent touch with her. She even invited her to San Francisco for summer vacation, but as Miki didn't want to go on her own, that never happened. Yuko of course had come back for Masayuki's funeral a month earlier, and, watching from the sidelines, I could see how swamped she was with not only her niece but her own mother to watch over.

Miki flew off to the beach resort of Phuket in Thailand before her father's forty-ninth-day service because her cousin Naomi was having a wedding there that had been planned months in advance. It would have been even harder on her if she'd been left behind, so she was allowed to leave with the other young people. Naomi's fiancé was a fourth-generation Chinese-American she met in medical school. The Saegusa sisters may have wondered why a half-white girl like Naomi would want to marry a "Chinaman," but times had changed, her life was overseas, and whatever they might have thought in private, they never said a word openly.

Around the time the younger ones went to Phuket, I had a telephone call from Taro saying he was coming to Japan. He was going to dispose of the Karuizawa and Oiwake properties, he said. It seemed mean of him to take the step with Masayuki barely in his grave, but after I hung up, I told myself he wasn't a coldhearted person; perhaps he had decided that if he let this chance slip, doing it later would only be that much harder. Also, though this could be my own sentimentality, I felt as if he chose this particular week because he wanted to stay in Oiwake for the Bon holiday one more time, the way he used to when he was a boy.

And now he's back. He was away for two years and seven months.

FUMIKO'S STORY WAS well and truly finished. Something in the way she pursed her lips told Yusuke she was done talking. She was staring down at the table. After a short silence, he asked, "What will you do now, Mrs. Tsuchiya?"

She didn't answer. She lifted her head to reply, let her eyes stray to the window, and gave a sharp little cry.

"What is it?"

"Your shoes—they must be soaked!"

She jumped up and, going around behind him, opened the sliding doors to the porch, bent down to pick up his muddy sneakers, and put them on a mat inside the house.

"Thanks." Yusuke, who had turned his head to watch, got up.

"Using the porch to go in and out is handy," she said, "but when there's a storm and the rain blows sideways like this, shoes have to be put inside. In the old days there used to be a shoe cupboard outside." She disappeared into the kitchen and came straight back with a roll of white paper towels in one hand. Seeing Yusuke standing there she told him to sit down, then knelt by the doormat and began tearing off paper towels, crumpling them, and stuffing them into his sneakers. He watched the slight movement of muscles in her back.

"Thank you." He went on standing, embarrassed. When he saw that it would take some time, he sat down at an angle facing her back. Raindrops pelted the bottom of the glass doors and raced down in straight lines. His bicycle parked under the porch stairs would be getting soaked too, he thought. The rain was still coming down hard. The cottage, on the edge of collapse anyway, seemed to soak up the moisture, hastening the process.

For a while Yusuke went on watching her from behind. Then he asked again, "Mrs. Tsuchiya, what will you do now?"

"Good question." Standing up, she murmured, "What to do?" as if it concerned someone else. "I thought I'd put off thinking about the future till Taro came this summer, but now that he's here, it can't wait."

She went back into the kitchen apparently to wash her hands, as he heard her running the tap before she came back. She added fresh tea leaves and refilled the pot with hot water, then poured some green tea into both their cups. Yusuke had already had more than enough and left his untouched.

"Ami graduates from college in another year and a half." Fumiko didn't drink her tea right away either. She wrapped her hands around the cup on the table and spoke slowly, as if driving the point home to herself. "So I'm thinking of asking Taro if he'll let us stay in the apartment until her graduation."

"And after that?"

"I'll have no choice but to go and live with my son in Miyota, I suppose." Before Yusuke could comment, she glanced up at him and went on. "He and his wife are both good people, so I don't mind. It's just that I'm sure they'll feel a bit cramped and constrained, and I feel bad about that." She laughed forlornly. It was as if what was left of her prime were a burden to her.

"Couldn't you ask Mr. Azuma to leave this place as it is, so you could use it?"

Her reply came swiftly. "No, I couldn't." She let out a long sigh and looked down at her teacup. "Not just when he's come back to get rid of his properties here, how could I?" She said this as if she had gone over it in her head many times and always reached the same conclusion. She kept staring at the cup as she went on. "I'm all right. I never expected anything, and look at the life I've had."

She sounded as though she was trying to convince herself.

After a pause, he asked another question. "Will Mr. Azuma be going straight back to America?"

She looked at him and smiled wanly. "He might hang around here for a while waiting for Yoko's ghost . . . You know he sleeps out in the shed every night." She tilted her head in amusement: "Why on earth did she come to you, of all people?"

Yusuke laughed and asked, "What if she never comes to him? What will he do?"

"He's so stubborn, he might not go back to America till she does."

"What about after he goes back?"

"Mmm." She sipped her tea before replying. "He's got such a strong constitution, he'll have a tough time drinking himself to death, no matter how hard he tries. That might not be much fun." She smiled sardonically, then turned abruptly serious. "In any case, he won't be coming back to Japan."

"He won't?"

"No, not that I can see."

A tremor in her voice made him speak without thinking. "Then why don't you go see him in America from time to time?"

The answer came promptly. "He wouldn't like it."

Once again, he imagined she must have gone over this many times in her head.

"I've no intention of going where I know I'm not wanted."

Her expression was so disconsolate it was frightening. Yusuke found himself unable to speak. A chill, gloomy silence hung over them for a while, before she roused herself and said on a different note, "You must be starving!" There was a touch of gaiety in her wide-eyed look, perhaps something that had rubbed off on her from the Saegusa sisters over the years.

"Now that you mention it," he replied.

"Would you object to a bowl of iced *somen* noodles on a rainy night?"

"Not at all."

"It was so hot in the daytime today, I was sure it would be the same tonight, so I'm afraid I've prepared the ingredients already."

"Somen's good." Looking into her bright, wide eyes, Yusuke found himself responding with matching enthusiasm.

"All right, then, I'll boil some water."

"Can I help?"

"First the water has to boil."

THE TELEPHONE RANG just after she'd gone back into the kitchen and turned on the tap. He jumped, just as he had the other day, and somehow knew that it was Fuyue again. He got up to call Fumiko, but she had apparently heard it too. The sound of running water in the tin-plated sink stopped, and she came out, wiping her hands on her apron.

The call lasted less than a minute.

"That was Fuyue." Fumiko frowned as she put the receiver back in its cradle. "Once she heard that Taro's not here, she said she'd be right over, now, in all this rain."

The glass doors showed only a reflection of the room's interior lit by one dim bulb; the rain outside was now invisible. But the sounds—heavy drops pelting the roof, and wind sweeping through the trees and shaking the eaves—were so strong that he felt the presence of nature in a way he never did in Tokyo.

"It's just not fair," Fumiko muttered to herself as she turned on the porch light and drew the thin, faded curtains. Then, with a weary shake of her head, she began to clear the table. "Taro taking off to a hotel till tomorrow noon and leaving me here to deal with three hysterical grannies, all by my lonesome." Her tone was joking, but the underlying dismay was evident in her frown.

She kept up a running commentary while she stacked the dishes. "They should just be grateful they got to use the place for a while longer—that's how they ought to look at it, but they won't. Once they realize it's Taro's doing, they're bound to make a fuss."

Yusuke looked at his watch. "Well, I'd better be going." He needed to clear out before Fuyue arrived, and since he couldn't just sit back and wait for the rain to stop, he'd have to ask Fumiko to call a taxi.

"Oh dear." Her eyes widened in surprise. "Now, don't say that. Please stay, won't you? Your presence would be a buffer, so I'd really rather you were here."

She seemed to mean it. Anyway, she would go and boil the *somen,* she told him, and disappeared into the kitchen with the stack of dirty dishes. After a moment's hesitation he followed her to help out.

Later on, while they were having the thin noodles, served with chipped ice in glass dishes, Fumiko tried her best to act as if nothing were wrong, but she seemed unable to contain her apprehension. Yusuke could feel what she was going through and, without any desire to witness the approaching scene, sympathized.

THE SOUND OF rapping on the glass doors came just after Yusuke had laid down his chopsticks. Seated across from each other, he and Fumiko simultaneously held their breath and straightened up in their chairs. The rain had masked the sound of the approaching car. Yusuke, whose back was to the glass doors, got up and pulled the curtain aside, revealing a pale face—a face that stared back at him in astonishment. He slid the glass panel to one side.

"Take your shoes off inside the house," instructed Fumiko, now standing beside him, "or they'll get soaked."

"Yes, okay." Leaving only her umbrella propped up outside, Fuyue crossed the threshold unhesitatingly, her raincoat dripping. "I ran all the way from the car, and look at me!"

With that preamble, she turned straight to Fumiko and asked bluntly, "Did you know?" The look she gave her was probing.

"You mean about the land in Karuizawa?"

"Yes."

"Yes, I knew." She returned her gaze levelly. "At first I didn't," she said, and hurried on to keep Fuyue from cutting in. "But Yoko and Masayuki knew about it from the beginning."

She said this as if their being in on the secret justified her having kept quiet about it. After one more searching look, Fuyue turned her head away, pressing her thin, well-shaped lips together—the shape was the same in all three sisters—and slowly began undoing the buttons on her raincoat. She handed the garment to Fumiko, who hung it on a wall hook by the glass doors before turning back to face her.

"When I heard it was a Dutch company," said Fumiko, "the thought did cross my mind that Taro might be involved, since I knew he owned a company in the Netherlands. When he came back to Japan, I asked him, and he said yes, which is how I learned." She broke off briefly before going on. Her tone was challenging, as if to fend off an attack. "But he told me not to tell any of you." With that, she urged Fuyue to sit down and then disappeared into the kitchen, giving the other woman no opportunity to respond.

Fuyue sat primly on the edge of her chair. She apparently meant to take her leave quickly. Yusuke had sat down at the same time, but she seemed unaware of his presence. Looking withdrawn, she opened her purse, took out a handkerchief, and absentmindedly began wiping the rain from her hair. She wiped drops off her glasses too. Just as Yusuke was wondering whether he should get up and clear away the noodles, Fumiko came back carrying a cup of tea for her on a small tray. Fuyue slowly looked up into her face.

"That isn't the whole story," she said.

Something in her voice made Fumiko frown inquisitively as she set the teacup on the table.

"You really don't know?" said Fuyue.

"Know what?"

Fuyue only looked at her steadily without answering.

"What are you talking about?" Fumiko asked again.

"What do you think happened to the land?"

"I don't know."

"He gave it away."

"Really? To Miki?"

"No."

That was enough for Yusuke to guess what was coming, but Fumiko seemed not to understand, a puzzled look on her face.

Fuyue said, "He gave it to you."

For a second Fumiko's expression remained puzzled.

"Along with the land here in Oiwake, he gave you the entire Karuizawa property."

Fumiko said nothing. Her eyes all but bored holes in Fuyue's face.

"The lawyer said there's no reason to think you didn't know about it all along. Then Harue and Natsue started saying that after all, you are not exactly what you make yourself out to be, which would explain it."

Fumiko remained speechless. Finally she murmured, "I never had any idea."

She sat down heavily, setting the tray on the table, and stared into space for a few moments before slowly burying her face in her hands. Her elbows were on the table and she was taking shallow breaths, her shoulders faintly rising and falling. Yusuke thought she might start crying, but she just went on breathing quickly.

For a while Fuyue studied her, off to one side. Her eyes revealed nothing. After a minute or so, still with her face in her hands, Fumiko said again, brokenly, "I never . . . had . . . any idea."

"I couldn't imagine you not saying a word to us about it if you did know. But I couldn't very well ask you over the phone, which is why I had to come over to make sure."

"I never dreamed of such a thing." The words were for herself rather than Fuyue.

Fuyue went on watching the rise and fall of her shoulders before saying gently, "Taro has taken care of everything. The apartment in Tokyo is in your name, and he's provided you with enough cash to pay the gift tax too. It's none of our affair, so the lawyer hasn't told us this in so many words, but apparently that's how it is."

Fumiko was making a valiant effort not to break down and cry. Looking at her, Fuyue opened her mouth to say something but seemed to think better of it. The three of them were plunged into silence. In the lamplight, only Fumiko's shoulders seemed to be moving.

Fuyue glanced at Yusuke. Apparently she had not forgotten he was there after all. "Mr. Kato, how did you get here?" she asked. "Car? Taxi?"

"Bicycle."

"Then I'll give you a ride home. It's raining so hard, you should leave your bicycle here and come and get it tomorrow."

Her tone of voice, though not as commanding as that of the eldest sister, left no room for argument. She promptly stood up, purse in hand, and headed for her raincoat hanging on the wall.

"What about your tea?" Fumiko removed her hands from her face, letting them flop onto the tabletop, and looked at Fuyue. Her face was deathly pale.

"No, thank you. My sisters are waiting for me to get back, so I'd better be going."

"I see."

"Will you be all right by yourself?" Fuyue asked, buttoning her raincoat.

"I'll be fine."

The lawyer would be in touch in the morning, Fuyue told her, then added in a different tone of voice, "Anyway, congratulations. Harue and Natsue are still in shock, but in time they'll see what a good thing it is that the land is in your hands. So much better than having it go to complete strangers."

Still in a daze, Fumiko was gazing ahead at nothing. Yusuke wasn't sure if he should leave her like that or not. At Fuyue's urging, he half rose, then turned toward Fumiko and asked in a lowered voice, "Would you like me to stay?"

Her eyes finally found their focus. "It's all right," she said, looking at him. "Since you have a ride, you should go on home." She gave him the barest trace of a smile before adding, as if wrapping something up in her own mind, "Thank you for everything." Her gaze was fixed on his young face.

"No, thank *you*. Can't I at least clear the table before I go?"

His glass noodle dish now held only water from melted ice, but in the one on Fumiko's side, some noodles lay uneaten on the bottom.

"It's all right. I'll take my time cleaning up." Using the table as support, she pushed herself to her feet.

Fuyue slipped on her shoes, opened the door, and stuck her head outside. "It's letting up," she murmured, and stepped out onto the porch. She turned to look at Fumiko and said from under her open umbrella, "I'll call you tomorrow," then went down the steps and was gone.

Yusuke wasn't sure what to say. Since he was leaving someone else's bicycle there—"a piece of junk," admittedly, but it still didn't belong to him—he would have to come back before returning to Tokyo. But knowing that Fumiko had opened up to him precisely because she expected never to see him again made it difficult for him to say, like Fuyue, that he would call her tomorrow. He took the shoehorn she handed him and squeezed his feet into his wet sneakers. "I'll be going, then," he said, purposefully vague. After a polite nod of his head, he plunged out into the rain. Fumiko's face as she stood in the open doorway and saw him off remained unreadable. After descending the steps and going a few more paces, he turned to look back at the figure standing there, so thin and alone. He had a feeling this was going to be their farewell.

When the car drove off he turned around again. The little cottage was not only screened from view by the rain, but hidden as well by the trees and bushes, so that only a glimmer of yellow light showed. The next time he looked back, even that was gone.

For a time Fuyue said nothing. Probably she was focused on her driving. In the dark and the rain she had to navigate a narrow, twisting road that was unlit and unpaved, with only her headlights to rely on. After they came out on the main road, she broke the silence.

"You must have heard quite an earful," she said abruptly.

"Yes, I did, actually."

"Stories about the past."

"That's right."

"And about Yoko."

"Yes."

Looking straight ahead, Fuyue gave a slight nod. With a glance at the clock on the dashboard, she tilted her head in Yusuke's direction. "Do you have a little time this evening?"

"Uh . . . Well, yes." Then, in case this sounded impolite, he added quickly, "Yes, I do."

"Would you mind joining me in a nightcap?"

Unsure how to interpret this, he again murmured a yes. She might be planning to drag him back to the Karuizawa villa to make him listen while she and her sisters poured out their woes, but in that case the wording of her invitation was strange. He couldn't make out what she had in mind.

She added, "I'd feel more comfortable going somewhere I'm familiar with, so would it be all right if we went to the Mampei? I'll see that you get home safely afterward."

"Oh, yes, fine."

Yusuke felt himself growing tense. Apparently he and this woman—"old lady" seemed unkind, but she was well past middle age—were to go out drinking together. He remembered the night he'd stumbled into the Oiwake cottage and first heard her voice on the telephone, an affected voice of indeterminate age inquiring, "Is that Taro?" He never imagined at that time that things would develop to the point where he would be sharing a late-night drink with the owner of that voice. It seemed the bizarre sequence of summer nights that had started then was to go on, whether he wanted it or not.

Fuyue said nothing more as she drove, facing straight ahead. After a little while she reduced the speed of the windshield wipers and commented, "It's not stormy anymore."

The bar in the Mampei Hotel was off the lobby to the left, and around a corner to the right. It was marked with a hanging sign that read simply BAR in English. On entering, they saw a wooden counter lined with bottles of wines and spirits, and standing behind it a bartender dressed in black. The room was small and dimly lit. It was also rather old-fashioned. Against one wall was an upright piano, apparently well used. The place was surprisingly empty for a holiday weekend. Fuyue's eyes picked out some seats at the back of the room, and she murmured a suggestion that they take those. Holding herself erect and walking with a spring in her step, she signaled her wishes to the bartender with eyes and chin.

At the back was a little recessed space, apparently a remodeled terrace or sunroom, with a low, slanting ceiling.

Perhaps to appeal to foreign guests, the bar's decor had a flavor of traditional Japan, with wooden wainscoting and, instead of wallpaper, a sort of wickerwork similar to that found in tea ceremony rooms. The window blinds too were suggestive of *sudare* reed screens, but the floor had a tacky crimson carpet, and hanging from the ceiling was a crystal chandelier. Unless you knew this was the bar of a famous old hotel, it might have seemed a forgotten place at the edge of town. Yusuke looked around curiously, wondering whether it had existed back when Fumiko's uncle had first worked there as a busboy and what sort of clientele patronized the place back then.

Fuyue briskly seated herself in a black armchair. "You sit there, facing the door, will you? I'm more comfortable with my back to it."

Yusuke sat on the sofa she indicated, inquiring as he did so whether she came there often.

"I did until twenty years or so ago. These days, hardly ever."

A young waiter with an oval face came over and handed Fuyue a heavy leather-bound menu, which she passed on to Yusuke without a glance. "Whiskey for me," she told the waiter. "Straight. Make it a double."

"What label would you prefer, madam?"

"Ballantine's."

"We have everything from seven-year-old to thirty-year-old."

"Right. Well, I'll be extravagant and have the seventeen-year-old. There is such a thing as Ballantine's seventeen-year-old, isn't there?"

"Yes, madam."

Very well, she would have that, she said, and looked at Yusuke. "Have whatever you like. Wine, cognac, a cocktail." She flung her head back and leaned back in the armchair. Maintaining this reckless-looking pose, she fixed her gaze on Yusuke. Flustered, he turned the pages of the heavy menu, finally ordering the hotel's own original cocktail, named after what Westerners once called the surrounding area, *Happy Valley*. The words printed on the beige paper in bold type were "*Happy Vally*," which Yusuke, dredging up his high school English, decided must be a misspelling. He closed the menu, wondering if there were so few foreign customers nowadays that such errors went unremarked.

"How old are you, dear?" asked Fuyue, still with her head against the back of the armchair, after the waiter left.

"Twenty-six."

She gave a small laugh—a laugh so coquettish that Yusuke was startled.

"A fine, full-grown young man." The eyes behind her glasses were teasing.

"I don't know about fine, but I am full-grown, yes." Yusuke himself was surprised by his own words. They seemed to catch Fuyue off guard too; he saw a trace of surprise in her eyes. She leaned forward, close to the table, and took her glasses off with her long fingers.

"You probably haven't heard that Taro and Fumiko had a . . . sexual relationship. It happened a long time ago, before he left for America."

She folded her glasses in a leisurely way and laid them on the table as she spoke, all without raising her eyes; she seemed purposely to be avoiding the look of astonishment on his face. Only after playfully lining up the shiny silver-framed glasses alongside the ashtray did she look up at him. She let out a quick burst of laughter.

"Imagine telling a perfect stranger a thing like this—you really must forgive me." She laughed again.

But the next moment, just as she opened her mouth to go on with the story, she gave a little cry as she seemed to remember something. Reverting instantly to her usual brisk self, she reached for the glasses beside the ashtray and put them back on, then laid a hand on her purse and stood up.

"I forgot all about my sisters. I need to go and call them. I'll be right back."

As he watched her impressively erect figure pass through the room, Yusuke let out a long breath. What she said had taken him by surprise, but having once heard it, he had no doubt it was true. What an idiot he was for never having suspected that they had once been, if not lovers, physically intimate. Was he too naive a listener or was Fumiko too discreet a narrator? He couldn't be sure.

Through the window blind he could see into the adjacent room, a lively dining room where white-jacketed waiters glided to and fro, candles flickered on tabletops, and couples and families, their faces lit up with an air of mild intoxication, chatted with apparent pleasure.

Yusuke recalled Fumiko's matter-of-fact way of telling her story. She had even gone to the trouble of including words that seemed to cancel out the possibility of such a relationship. But as he thought further about it, he found her intention shifting. He began to suspect that at heart she hadn't been so discreet after all; that rather, while misdirecting him on the surface, she might secretly have been hoping he would figure it out. With hindsight, he began to catch hints in what she'd said that pointed at the true nature of her and Taro's relationship. He let out another long breath.

A dark figure materialized at the side of the table and laid a surprisingly stylish cocktail in front of him. The stem was green and the liquid in the transparent, conical glass was reddish violet, so that the drink looked like an exotic flower resting on a green stalk. On the table across from him, a tumbler, clear above, cut glass below, was set briskly down. It was faintly embarrassing to realize that of the two of them he, not she, had chosen the more feminine drink.

Some five minutes later Fuyue was back with apologies. "I didn't wait," said Yusuke, holding up his flowerlike cocktail. "No, no, of course not!" she said, sitting down. She took off her glasses again and laid them on the table. "My sisters just wouldn't let me hang up . . ." She raised the tumbler to her lips and drained half its amber contents. She had evidently stopped off at the ladies' room, for her lipstick shone more brightly against her freshly powdered skin. Beyond that, it seemed as if being away from her sisters had almost changed her physically. Altogether her appearance had an unexpected charm, something Yusuke found vaguely unsettling. This was a different Fuyue from the one who, as the youngest of the trio, was always at the others' command. Maybe her rather mannish look in their company was a form of resistance, he thought, or a means of self-protection, to ward off their constant bossing.

Without looking him in the eye, Fuyue let her long fingers play with the glass on the table in front of her as she asked, "Were you already aware of what I told you just now?"

"No, I wasn't."

"I didn't think she would tell you that part." She looked up. "Actually, she doesn't know that I know." Her eyes were now on the tumbler. "Thank goodness." She murmured this last almost to herself. "My sisters don't know that I know either. But they grew suspicious long ago, and today, after the lawyer left, they brought it up again, saying there must have been something like that going on after all. I didn't tell them anything, because I thought it wouldn't be right, for Fumiko's sake." She raised her eyes again.

"But when I went to Oiwake and saw your face through the glass door—remember?—I felt immediately I could talk about it with you, that no harm could come of it. To go my whole life and never mention it to anyone would just be too hard."

She downed the remainder of the amber fluid, turned toward the counter and held up her empty glass for the bartender to see, then turned around again. "A subject as improper . . . or as adult as this, I should say . . . is nothing to talk about sober."

Fuyue had learned about their relationship more than twenty-five years earlier, she said, when, after the "elopement," Yoko was released from the hospital and taken home to Sapporo by her mother. Though no longer in the

Utagawas' service, Fumiko had involved her own family in the search for Yoko and generally been such an enormous help that Fuyue had wanted to show her appreciation. That was how it started.

An ordinary thank-you gift of cash had seemed a bit too impersonal, and so one Sunday when she was out shopping at Mitsukoshi department store in the Ginza, she'd splurged on a black pearl brooch as a present for her. Wanting to see the look on Fumiko's face when she opened the box, and curious besides to see where she lived alone in the city, Fuyue had gone straight from the Ginza to Sangenjaya to deliver the gift, stopping to ask directions to Evergreen Apartments No. 2 at a police box by the station. This was a time when some apartment buildings still didn't have even a telephone in the hall, and if Fumiko was not at home she was prepared to mail the package later. After finally tracking down the address, she was surprised to find a squalid-looking building—somewhere she would never have connected with anyone as well turned out as Fumiko. Still, it can't have been easy for a single woman to support herself as an office worker in Tokyo, she'd thought, half persuaded and half hesitating as she made her way up a steep, narrow staircase where the smell of urine hung in the air. She located the room number and knocked softly on a door marked TSUCHIYA. No answer. She knocked a little louder. Again, no answer. She knocked still louder and called out Fumiko's name, to no avail.

Just then the neighboring door opened, and an anemic-looking woman of around thirty stuck her head out. Her hair was in curlers and she had a pink nylon scarf wound around her head like a turban. "Looking for Miss Tsuchiya?" she asked. Fuyue said yes.

"She's not here. She went out shopping for supper with her kid brother a while ago."

"Her kid brother?" Fuyue repeated, puzzled.

The woman, with her head sticking out at an angle through the half-open door, let out a dirty laugh. The indecency of the sound was startling. She opened the door wider, and Fuyue saw that she was wearing tight mambo pants, her bare feet stuck in high-heeled plastic sandals.

"Some kid brother!" the woman sniggered. She sized up Fuyue, who was dressed in a summery linen suit and carrying a shopping bag from an exclusive department store. "She acts all la-di-da, then brings home that sexy piece of work. Dark and kind of different, but a real hunk, all right."

Fuyue was speechless.

"I live right next door here, you see," the woman said, leering.

There was no escape.

"Every night they do it. Two months, and they're still doin' it every night! Hot and heavy, night after night, hours at a time. Today too. Like all Sunday mornings, they're at it first thing. Her voice carries right through the walls, know what I mean?"

To get away from that clinging gaze, Fuyue turned on her heel and headed down the corridor toward the staircase, hearing the woman's shrill laughter behind her.

"So that's how I know." She was still swiveling the whiskey glass in her fingers. After the "elopement," she'd been so worried about Yoko's condition that she hadn't had time to think about Taro, but she had assumed he went back to the Azumas. Everyone had been at such pains to keep the young pair from exchanging secret messages, the idea that Taro might be staying with Fumiko never crossed her mind. Once it became clear that he was in her apartment, however, it all fitted together: Fumiko's more than usual reticence when she came to help at the hospital; her occasional guilty looks; the alacrity with which she left for home as soon as she was done with what she came for. That summer, Fumiko had stayed away from Karuizawa, using work as an excuse. To Harue and Natsue it hadn't made sense, but to Fuyue it had. Then there was Fumiko's phone call months later reporting Taro's departure for the United States. After Taro had informed her about it, she thought she ought to let them know as well, she'd said, as if talking about a distant relative.

Fuyue had known Fumiko since she was seventeen, and over the years their relationship had developed more or less into a friendship. Besides being uncommonly bright, Fumiko was absolutely reliable. More than that, she was a woman of such moral integrity that Fuyue, with those two elder sisters of hers around, often felt embarrassed. The fact that for six months she had lived with Taro—slept with him—could mean only one thing.

"She fell for him. As he grew up, somewhere along the way she became deeply attached to him." Fuyue paused, then added, "Which was hardly unnatural."

And then he had gone off and left her.

The following spring, when Fumiko came to pay her respects in Seijo after Harue got back from New York, it was Fuyue's first encounter with her in a year, Harue's first in four years. As soon as Fumiko left, Harue had started. "Did you see? *That* is a woman who has taken a lover, no mistake about it. And the look on her face has changed too. There is something positively degraded in the way she looks now—not like the Fumi I remember. You know, it would not surprise me one bit to find out she has a secret private life, the sort she can't let on about to anyone."

Fuyue understood then for the first time why the sight of Fumiko had made her so uncomfortable. "How long has she been this way?" asked Harue. "Hmm, I wonder," Fuyue had said, pretending to have no interest, but deep down she was disturbed. When the "elopement" scandal first broke, Fumiko had still been her old self. In the period after Taro left, however, maybe loneliness had made her misbehave. Maybe, in the words of that woman in Evergreen Apartments No. 2, she had taken to bringing other "hunks" home. Suspicion grew in Fuyue's mind. Again that summer Fumiko had stayed away from Karuizawa, adding to the impression that she was leading the sort of life that would make her want to keep her distance from them. Natsue, who came down from Sapporo for the summer, hadn't seen Fumiko since the "elopement" and so didn't believe it at first when Harue insisted that she was definitely "leading a strange life"—but after having it drummed into her, she began to change her tune. What could have come over her, a serious girl like that? It was, after all, a bad idea, letting a single girl

live on her own in Tokyo. When she divorced, we should
have taken her up to Sapporo with us. Heaven knows, we
could have done with her help. Natsue started saying things
like this, frowning as she did so.

So when Fumiko sent out a wedding announcement the
following spring, and especially when they learned something about her new husband, the three sisters had rejoiced
for her and for themselves as well. If she had agreed to
marry a man who had spent decades working at the Miyota
town hall, in other words someone as solid and far from any
nonsense as a man can possibly get, she must have every intention of finally settling down. Moreover, since she would
be living nearby, she might be able to come and help out in
summer at Karuizawa again. And, as it turned out, when
Fumiko responded to everyone's pleas and returned to Karuizawa for the first time in three years, she had seemed
refreshed, free of whatever had made her different from the
young woman they had always known.

Harue's dim suspicion that she might have had a relationship with Taro took shape more than ten years later,
after his return to Japan. Her instincts in such matters
were weirdly sharp. She based her theory on the observa-
tion that Fumiko had a subtle way of avoiding all discussion of Taro. Yet for years it was impossible to say whether
she avoided the topic because of his involvement with Yoko
or for some less mentionable reason, and probing into it
was out of the question. Then today the lawyer had revealed that Taro had given the villas and land in Karuizawa
to Fumiko, someone who wasn't a close or even a distant

relation. Such generosity was completely unwarranted, however you looked at it. Harue's old suspicions had re-surfaced, darker than ever.

"After the lawyer left, that proud sister of mine broke down. 'So there must have been something going on be-tween Fumi and that boy Taro after all,' she sobbed. Since this wasn't really anything to cry about, it just shows what a shock it all was to her." Fuyue's tone was sympathetic, surprisingly full of sisterly affection. "But it wasn't only that . . ." She faltered for a moment.

"My sister may have her faults, but you know something, Mr. Kato? As we age, we all become much sadder, no mat-ter what. You're obviously too young to know, but it simply happens. When my sister heard that Fumiko was the new owner of the property, I suspect that all this sadness came welling up at once. She just couldn't stop crying."

Watching, Fuyue had been swept by the urge to tell them what she'd discovered that day twenty-plus years before when she visited Fumiko's apartment.

"But I couldn't bring myself to do it. I knew Fumiko would not have wanted anyone to know—especially us—so I held my tongue. I too didn't want my family to know about that side of her, either. But I was bursting to do it . . . which is another reason why I left the house tonight."

At that point the oval-faced waiter came back and with a gesture toward Yusuke's empty glass offered to bring him another cocktail.

Yusuke shook his head. Although he could hold his liquor fairly well, he wasn't a heavy drinker, by choice.

"No more for me, either." Fuyue, after downing the first whiskey in a quick series of gulps, had become so engrossed in her story that she had forgotten her second drink. The glass was still half full.

It was as if the waiter in passing had stirred the air around the table. Brought back to present reality, Fuyue looked at Yusuke again, and he returned her gaze. The dim light gave him the illusion that he was sitting across from a youngish woman. As he studied her face, pale and luminous against the black leather armchair, he thought he had been hasty in deciding that her two sisters were better looking.

She may have sensed something in his eyes, for a touch of bashfulness showed in her face. She changed her position, leaning back in the armchair so as to regain her adult poise before speaking.

"The one I feel sorry for is Taro." She was looking at, or rather through, Yusuke, perhaps seeing in him the young Taro Azuma. "After all, when it happened, he would have been . . . what, nineteen. Only nineteen! Fumiko was nearly thirty and had experienced married life, so I would imagine it was she who seduced him. He, of course, would not have been able to resist. He then got in deeper and deeper until he was in over his head . . . But being who he is, he probably doesn't see it that way. He probably blames himself, and Fumiko's being in love with him only makes it worse." She paused for breath, then murmured, "Poor kid." A moment later she added, "Poor Fumiko too."

Her thoughts then touched on the events surrounding Yoko's death. "She could easily have resented Yoko—wished her dead—but instead she was so good to her, she put me to shame. And when she realized Yoko wasn't going to pull through, she looked deathly pale herself."

He found this painful to listen to.

"Not being loved is agony."

Fuyue seemed to be engaged in an internal debate, still leaning back and staring into space. Yusuke waited for what might come next, but nothing did. He watched as a middle-aged couple, probably married, came in and sat down on the sofa by the piano, facing the counter. After placing their orders they sat without talking. But it wasn't a companionable silence. There was nothing the least bit cheerful in their mood. Each was looking in a different direction. The age-old question asked by the young passed through his mind: Why do people bother to get married?

"But it's fine." Fuyue's voice broke in on his thoughts. She was looking straight at him. "The way things turned out, I mean. Coming into all that property might not make Fumiko happier. It might make her sadder in a way, but in another way it's fine." Her lips curved in a lovely smile. "After all, making a man like Taro feel guilty for the rest of his life over the way he treated her ages ago is quite an achievement for any woman, wouldn't you say?"

Yusuke smiled despite himself.

Fuyue leaned forward and picked up her glass, gently sloshing the whiskey around. "The more I think about Fumiko," she confessed, "the more confused I get. On the one hand, I feel wretched for her, but, then, you know what? I often envy her."

As Yusuke looked at the pale face opposite him, he wondered just what sort of life this woman had led. Back when Noriyuki Shigemitsu died in the war, she was barely twenty. She must have made an attractive sight as she sat playing the piano for hours on end. Over the next fifty years, hers had surely been an enviable life, in ways her nosy sisters knew nothing about—far better than that of most Japanese women—and yet she often felt envious of Fumiko, she said.

Fuyue's second glass of whiskey remained half full. She ordered a glass of water and then needed another to help clear her mind. She said with a laugh, "Isn't this ridiculous!" then excused herself to go to the powder room, settling the bill on her way back.

"Do you drive?" she asked him.

"Not much. But I do have a license."

"Then you drive yourself home first, will you? Better to lessen the risk."

She had reverted to the businesslike manner she maintained when her sisters were around. She rummaged in her purse and handed Yusuke the car keys. They were on a silver holder the shape of a tiny harp.

BACK AT THE summer house in Mitsui Woods he found a note from Kubo on the kitchen counter. He was "zonked" from an afternoon of tennis, it said, and was turning in early. Looking at the slip of paper in the bright fluorescent light, Yusuke felt relieved that he wouldn't have to attempt conversation with Kubo that evening. Relief was quickly followed by a pang of guilt. Some friend he was, taking advantage of Kubo's hospitality while spending almost no time with him. True, Kubo was rapidly getting involved with the younger sister of his brother's wife and probably didn't care, but Yusuke still couldn't help feeling bad about being so unsociable, his mind elsewhere even when he was with him. Tomorrow he would go back to Oiwake just to pick up the bicycle, and spend the rest of the day with Kubo. Making this promise to himself, he switched off the light. In any case, Fumiko's story was now finished—and to top it off he'd even been made to listen to a story *about* Fumiko too. More tired than he'd ever felt before in his life, he clung to the railing like an old man as he quietly mounted the stairs in the semidarkness.

He got into bed, turned off the lamp, and lay staring up at the ceiling, feeling the nocturnal quiet of the mountain weigh on him, body and soul. Finally, unable to bear it any longer, he got up, threw open a window, and let the cool air pour in against his face. Outside, the quiet deepened. Yet as he listened hard, after a while, as if by magic, a faint sound came to him through the dark. It was the sound of misty rain on leaves.

That night he slept even more lightly than he had the past few days. His senses were tormented by dreams of two naked, sweating bodies intertwined. Sleek, pale flesh and glistening, brown, sinewy flesh vigorously pulled and pushed, opened and closed, pressed and was pressed in return. Hot breath seemed to brush against his ear. When he awoke in the night to an airless room, the back of his neck was coated with sweat.

IN THE MORNING Yusuke went downstairs before Kubo. Inspecting the contents of the still half-full refrigerator, he decided to cook something rather than let things go to waste, starting with the more expensive stuff, and took out some frozen beef fillets. The previous night he'd had nothing to eat but cold *somen* noodles, so a hearty meal in the morning posed no problem. He didn't know Kubo's plans but felt sure his friend would at least be eating breakfast at home.

By the time Kubo came down stairs, yawning, the salad and side dish of hot vegetables were ready, the bread was neatly sliced, and all there was left to do was pan-fry the meat he'd already defrosted in the microwave.

"Pretty fancy for breakfast." After surveying the table, Kubo headed for the bathroom.

Yusuke called after him, "How do you like your steak?"

"Medium rare." Kubo looked back and asked over his shoulder, "You?"

"Rare."

"Really rare?"

"Yup."

"Figures."

What that might mean Yusuke had no idea. Kubo yawned again and disappeared into the bathroom.

Over the meal they discussed plans for the day. Apparently in the evening there was going to be a barbecue, using all the refrigerator leftovers, with Kubo's brother and sister-in-law at her parents' cottage.

"I guess in that case there was no point in cooking up all this stuff for breakfast." Yusuke held up a piece of blood-red meat, impaled on a fork.

Kubo pointed out that they wouldn't get a plate of good beef like this at a crowded barbecue and have time to enjoy it, so it was just as well. Then, concentrating on cutting up his own meat, he said, "You're invited, by the way—want to come?"

"You bet."

Prompted by his resolution of the evening before, his response was almost too enthusiastic. Kubo looked up briefly in surprise, then gave a toothy grin. "A bunch of neighbors are coming too."

"Great. I just wonder, though—can you even have a barbecue in this weather?"

Ever since he got up, the sky had looked ominous. A fine rain was already falling.

"This'll clear up in no time," said Kubo reassuringly, adding that even if it didn't, there were large eaves over the deck, so there was no need to worry. For a while they chatted about this and that: each other's work, friends from high school and what they were up to, movies they'd seen recently. Finally Kubo bragged at length about what an easy conquest the little sister had been, and then the meal was over. He must have noticed that Yusuke had been distracted all week, but he seemed unwilling to probe. Perhaps he was being discreet. His not asking where Yusuke had been till all

hours the night before suggested that he sensed something
out of the ordinary was going on.

The rain stopped after noon. The sky outside the window suddenly brightened, and raindrops glistened on the
trees like glass beads. As if waiting for this moment, the
telephone rang. Kubo's voice was even more animated than
it had been the other day when his sister-in-law called. Must
be the younger sister, Yusuke thought.

"Right, okay, be over as soon as I can. Sure thing. See you."

Her father was out golfing again with Kubo's brother.
Her mother, sister, and she would be making all the preparations for the barbecue, but if Kubo was free she wanted
him to come over and help out.

"So what do you want to do?"

"You think I should go too?" Yusuke wasn't sure. Since the
weather had cleared, he wanted to go back for the bicycle.
Having failed to say anything about staying up late listening
to the woman in Oiwake the night before, naturally he had
failed to say anything about leaving the bicycle there either.

"Doesn't matter. There won't be all that much to do,
really."

"In that case, maybe I'll hang around here for a bit and go
over later in the afternoon."

He felt guilty, as if he were sneaking off to a secret
rendezvous. How he had become so preoccupied with his
visits to Oiwake he couldn't explain even to himself.

TAKING THE BUS and train would waste too much time—
there was only one bus an hour—so he went by taxi. Before

he got out of the cab, he saw Taro Azuma sitting in a garden chair on the porch. His pulse quickened. After all he'd
heard from Fumiko, he felt as agitated . . . as if he'd come
to see his own lover. He'd meant to say goodbye to her before riding off on his bicycle, but now it occurred to him
that what had actually brought him here might have been an
urge to see Taro again.

As the taxi turned around and sped off, Yusuke nodded
and said hello. He felt himself turning red. Embarrassed and
annoyed by this, he explained in a consciously casual way,
"Came for my bike." He looked toward the bicycle parked
by the porch. "I rode over yesterday, and it rained so hard I
left it here and went home by car."

The man remained seated and looked at Yusuke with
slight surprise, eyes narrowed. Now that he came to think
of it, they had met only once before, that time he'd stumbled into this place late at night. The last glimpse he'd had
of him was the back of his white shirt as he ran up the hill,
trying to chase after the little ghost in a *yukata*. Day after
day since that time, Yusuke had spent hours enthralled by
the story of his life, but it was entirely possible that the man
barely remembered his face.

On the porch table was an old-fashioned tin bucket that
held a dark bottle of wine. The man was holding a glass by
its stem, its shallow bowl filled with a clear pink liquid. He
must have had more than a few glasses already, but he didn't
look at all the worse for wear; he merely seemed to be
quietly enjoying the summer breeze. Yusuke found himself
staring at him just as he'd done on the first night. The man's

eyes, which had seemed at odds with the world back then, now seemed more at peace.

He worked up the courage to ask, "Is Mrs. Tsuchiya here?"

"Mrs. Tsuchiya . . ." With a slight, inexplicable smile, the man echoed her name before explaining that she had left for the Prince Hotel around noon to see his lawyer and then must have been trapped by her acquaintances in Karuizawa.

Although Yusuke had come expressly to see her, learning that he couldn't do so came as a relief. After what he had heard in the Mampei Hotel the night before, Fumiko was no longer the same woman to him. Nor was he the same person who had sat listening to her talk. But he was the only one who knew. To behave in front of her as though nothing had changed while she remained unaware of any difference struck him as somehow wrong—almost a crime.

The man was studying him with interest, unlike on that first night. Was it because he was wondering how much Fumiko might have told him? Or was it because he, Yusuke, had had that encounter with Yoko's ghost? He stared back, remembering that Taro had been sleeping out in the shed ever since.

Taro proceeded to talk without shifting in his seat. Apparently a youngster like Yusuke wasn't worth getting up for.

"As a matter of fact I just got here myself. I haven't seen her yet today."

"I see."

Yusuke realized that Taro hadn't stayed in the Prince Hotel the night before to escape the three sisters' fury; it was to avoid the full impact of Fumiko's reaction to what she would hear from them. Looking up at him from the bottom of the steps, he repeated for no reason, "I see."

He felt reluctant to leave. But he had no idea what to say. The man just looked down in his direction. After an awkward silence, he had no choice but to say goodbye.

"I'll be going back to Tokyo tomorrow, so please tell her I said hello. This is my address in Tokyo. Would you mind telling her to get in touch if she feels like it?"

It happened as he mounted the steps to hand over his card. The man looked at him and suddenly smiled. Gesturing with his glass at the ice bucket, he said, "Since you're here, why not join me in a glass of champagne?"

Apparently a little while ago he had bought a case of champagne at the local liquor store, and since they were selling old-fashioned saucerlike champagne glasses there he had bought two, meaning to share a drink with Fumiko when she returned, but she was taking so long getting back that he had finally started by himself. Indeed, another glass of the same shape was sitting on the table. Hearing the word "champagne," Yusuke was reminded of that other rich man, the one in Minamihara who had thrown an extravagant party, but this dark bottle in the tin bucket, with the summer green garden around them, was the picture of cool serenity.

"Pink champagne." The man poured pale bubbling liquid into Yusuke's glass, one side of his mouth twisting in a smile. "It's for special celebrations, so I bought some for the hell of it."

Yusuke spent the better part of an hour with him. Filled with an intoxication that had little to do with champagne, he felt as if he were afloat on a cloud. Assuming that Fumiko would already have talked about it, without any preamble the man began speaking haphazardly about life in the United States. Not about his own life, but about the country itself. He stared straight ahead as he spoke, looking at the trees instead of at Yusuke, while the latter secretly studied his face. He listened as if under a spell. The man's words didn't register on him in the usual way but seemed to pass along a different route into an unexplored part of his mind.

In the end Taro switched topics and started talking about Japan.

"Maybe because I don't expect to come back here anymore, I often think about this country." He stared with dark eyes at the garden, beyond which was a thicket with a dingy, abandoned cottage almost hidden by trees. Above it was a glimpse of sky, clear a little while ago but now once again heavy with low-lying clouds. "I never thought Japan would turn into the country it is now." His voice was emotionless. "For one thing, I never thought it would be so rich." His lips pursed for a second, then relaxed. "But somehow I thought it would turn out to be a better place, a more decent place than this." His eyes remained fixed on the yard.

"I had a grudge against Japan when I was growing up, so I never hoped it would turn out better, but over the past fifty years I assumed as a matter of course that it would. Maybe it was the times. Without even knowing it, I believed in the future, I guess."

Cocking his head in Yusuke's direction, Taro told him that one of his own parents came from a Chinese ethnic minority. He continued, "When I was little, I was told once I was lucky not to be Japanese."

He looked straight at him.

At the time, he had just felt happy that someone should have made this comment when everyone else picked on him for not being Japanese, and he'd thought no more about it, but lately he had started to think about the unintended meaning of the words.

"These days, I've begun to thank my stars that I'm not Japanese. Or not altogether Japanese, not in my DNA. That's the way I feel now." He laughed as if half joking.

Rather than taking offense, Yusuke asked an honest question. "Why? What's wrong with Japanese people?"

The man took in Yusuke's earnest face and seemed to hesitate.

Impulsively, Yusuke followed it up with another question. A word Fuyue was said to have used had stuck in his mind, and he asked, "Would you say they're . . . a little shallow?" This was probably his own conclusion as well, after only twenty-six years of life.

"Shallow . . . ," the man echoed, before saying simply, "They're beyond shallow. They're hollow—nothing inside." He brought the champagne glass level with his eyes and studied the bubbles in it. "Like these bubbles . . . barely there at all."

Then, as if remembering something, he looked at Yusuke and said, "So, you've met the Three Witches, have you?"

When Yusuke nodded, he explained that it was their house in Karuizawa that Fumiko had gone and got trapped in. "But there's nothing hollow about those three, I have to say."

He said this with a wry smile. Yusuke felt he was wrapping things up, so he got quickly to his feet and said he should be going. He had known he might be outstaying his welcome, but until then he'd been unable to move, as though chained in place. The man did not detain him but put his champagne glass down on the table and got up too. That was his way of saying goodbye.

Yusuke got on his bicycle and pedaled off. The seat was still moist from the previous day's rain.

THE BARBECUE PARTY at Kubo's sister-in-law's villa started at dusk and went on till midnight, attended by an assortment of guests. The rich neighbor from Minamihara showed up too, though fairly late; he had come on from another party and his face was already bright red from drinking. Fortunately, it didn't rain, so they trundled two enormous American barbecue grills out onto the lawn, and Kubo and Yusuke went to work flipping corn on the cob, char, and sweetfish on them. Kubo's sister-in-law seemed a bit miffed that her little sister had stolen Kubo, but she was a good sport, and even while Kubo and the sister were flirting, she was all smiles, a conscientious hostess. It was past midnight when Kubo and Yusuke started for home, laden with foil-wrapped bundles of leftover goodies and a pair of flashlights provided again to light their way.

The sky, which had continually threatened rain yet produced no drops, still remained overcast, the moon barely visible through haze.

"Whatcha gonna do tomorrow?" asked Kubo tipsily, spinning his flashlight in circles.

"Do?"

"How you goin' back to Tokyo, I mean."

Yusuke, who had been planning to take the train back with Kubo, couldn't make sense of the question.

"See, we could go by car."

Two cars would be heading to Tokyo the next day—one with his brother, his wife, and their two children, the other with the wife's parents and the little sister. Packed with things to bring back, neither car would have room for the two of them to ride together, but if they went separately, both could get back to Tokyo without taking the train. Kubo apparently wanted to accompany the little sister but couldn't come right out and say so.

"I'll take the train." Yusuke didn't feel like riding in either car.

"You sure?"

"Yeah."

Whichever car he was in, he knew he would feel ill at ease, so he would rather travel back by train even if it meant standing all the way.

Kubo, knowing his antisocial tendencies, didn't push the point.

"It's only August, and listen to the racket those crickets make. You'd think it was already fall, eh?" Instead of describing circles with his flashlight, he was now training it on neighbors' gardens along the way, as though hunting for chirping insects in the clumps of grass.

THE NEXT DAY when the two young men got up it was raining again. Fortunately, like the day before, from around half past ten the sun came out and blue patches in the sky quickly began to spread. Since the families intended to have supper in a service area along the highway, they would be leaving late in the day. With hours to kill, Yusuke and his friend took their time over brunch, then threw the sheets in the washer and ran the vacuum cleaner, only for the sky to darken again. The two German cars pulled in just as they finished closing the rain shutters. They said goodbye to each other, and Kubo got into the driver's seat in his chosen vehicle. Yusuke accepted a lift to the station in the other, already cramped with Kubo's brother, his wife, and the children.

At the station the wife got out to move into the front seat and said, "You don't have a reservation, do you?"

"No, I don't."

"Might not get a seat then."

"It's all right; it's a short ride."

"Not that short—more than two hours, isn't it?"

"I'll be okay."

Afraid she would insist on his riding with them, Yusuke edged away, backpack in hand, as he spoke. When he judged there was enough distance between them, he shouted out his thanks again and turned to go.

"Take care now," she called. "See you again sometime."

When he looked back, she was waving both hands like a young girl.

HE DIDN'T TAKE the Asama super-express back to Tokyo. Instead he bought a ticket heading in the opposite direction, on the local bound for Komoro. The train took a long time to arrive, and it was forty minutes later when he got off at rustic Oiwake station. There was a lone telephone booth with the number of Matsuba Taxis posted on it, but he didn't want to arrive at the cottage in any obvious way. He had no excuse for going there. In fact, he hadn't originally planned to go at all. Tucked in his backpack was his borrowed flashlight from the night before, which Kubo's sister-in-law had said he needn't bother to return, but even when he put it there he hadn't exactly made up his mind. He just wanted one more glimpse of the cottage—one more glimpse of its residents. This desire had made him hesitate—he couldn't just take off for Tokyo—and when he arrived at Karuizawa station, he'd just followed his instincts. Once in Oiwake, he set off with only a simple map and those same instincts to guide him, and after nearly an hour he reached Taro's summer cottage.

HE CAUGHT THE sound as he drew near the gateposts—a dull, pounding sound. In the hovering dusk, the figure of Taro was dimly spotlit crouching on the porch. Yusuke did not go through the gateposts but stole past the cottage, weaving his way through the heavy growth of weeds and vines and finally stopping in the shadow of a row of yew

OIWAKE STATION

trees that marked the former boundary of the adjoining lot. Some of the trees were thickly covered with hard-edged green leaves while others had lost most of their branches, so, depending on where he stood, he had a fairly unobstructed view. He craned his neck, held his breath, and looked in the direction the sound came from.

Some kind of large cloth was spread near the edge of the porch, and Taro was in front of it on one knee, swinging a hammer and making that dull sound. The railing prevented Yusuke from seeing what lay under the hammer. On the table behind Taro, he could see the tin bucket from yesterday together with the two champagne glasses and, alongside them, a pair of small white objects: the opened funerary urns. Only then did he realize that what lay under Taro's swinging hammer were human bones.

Unaware of the intruder, Taro continued pounding away, but as the ashes had been divided to begin with, the amount must have been quite small. In no time the job was done. He laid the hammer down and sat in the chair looking dazed, staring at the pile of crushed bones. The sky still held the last light, and through the branches Yusuke could see that a pale moon had risen.

Just then a pretty woman dressed in black stuck her face out of the cottage—it was Fumiko. She had apparently been watching over his shoulder from inside and, seeing that the job was finished, disappeared for a moment and came out carrying a variety of items in both hands, all of which she set down on the table before moving toward where Taro had been hammering. There she knelt down and bowed her head, pressing her palms together.

For a time all was still.

From the moment the stillness broke, it was like watching a pantomime. When she had finished her prayers, Fumiko rose, looking solemn, and went back to the table where she put on a pair of white gloves she had laid there. Then she approached the edge of the porch and knelt down again. The first ashes that she scooped from the cloth were Yoko's, apparently, since Yusuke saw her go and carefully set down a little red dish near Taro like an offering. Judging from its shape, the dish seemed to be a child's plastic bowl. Next, Fumiko fetched a larger container, probably a glass vase, and set it too at the porch's edge. The idea seemed to be to combine the ashes of husband and wife in that container, but they were evidently difficult to scrape into it. Eventually she picked up the spread-out cloth—a large *furoshiki* wrapping cloth patterned in arabesques. Wordlessly she signaled to Taro, and he stood up, also in silence, took the other two corners of the cloth in his hands, and helped her pour the ashes of husband and wife into the vase.

Once the task was finished, Fumiko turned her face away and flapped the square cloth in the air.

"I never knew bones had such a distinct odor," she said.

For some reason Yusuke could hear every word with sharp clarity. Taro made no response. Yusuke could not make out his expression. He only saw him go and sit in the chair in the same way as before.

Fumiko went back into the house, holding the glass container in her arms. When she came out again she was carrying her purse and, in the other hand, a familiar-looking shopping bag. She went out onto the porch and continued down the steps, heading Yusuke's way. He hurriedly withdrew his head. When Fumiko got into the car with the shopping bag, he understood what was happening. In her black dress she was going to Karuizawa for the ceremony of scattering the ashes. He wondered if she was wearing the black pearl brooch that Fuyue had given her.

Her car went up the narrow road without exposing Yusuke's hiding figure in its bright headlights.

TARO SAT FACING the little red bowl.

He was dead still. The madder-red sun glowed in the western sky as though loath to yield its shortening life, while all around him, moment by moment, Yusuke could sense darkness rising as if from the ground. The mosquitoes in the shrubbery were more aggressive. Then all of a sudden Taro stood up. Carrying the red bowl in one hand, he strode down the porch steps and out to the middle of the garden. Yusuke, unable to escape, curled up behind a yew. Taro now stood there threateningly close to where he was—but his eyes weren't looking at this world. Looking up, he hurled the contents of the bowl at the pale moon with all his might.

The dust of powdered bones flew in a misty swirl and came drifting down. Taro stood still in the moonlight with his eyes closed. As the fine white dust covered him from the head down, he never stirred.

THE FOLLOWING SPRING, Yusuke was chosen as one of the winners in the lottery for a green card, the U.S. permanent residency visa. Uncertain whether he ought to quit his job at the publishing house and move to America, he continued commuting between the office and the cheap apartment he'd been renting since he had first started working. Before long the trees were covered with budding leaves, and the smell of fresh greenery was in the air. A longing to visit Nagano again made him restless. As the leaves turned a deeper green, the lure became irresistible.

He left for Nagano in June, just before the rainy season set in.

Ten months had passed since that week the previous summer. He had waited for word from Fumiko, but none came. Assuming she preferred not to get in touch, he made no attempt to track her down in Tokyo. He undertook his trip without any hope or expectation of seeing her up there either: it was not the time of year she went to Karuizawa. But in the course of his daily commute to work, the events of that week were beginning to feel almost as if they had never happened, and the stronger this feeling became, the more anxious he was that he might be letting something precious slip through his fingers—something one was granted perhaps once in a lifetime.

At Karuizawa station he rented a car. The weekend traffic was surprisingly heavy; he realized that tourism in

Karuizawa was not limited to the summer months. The two Western-style villas stood unchanged, no different from the way they'd been when he first set foot in their grounds. But whether the light was different or something in Yusuke's mind had changed, he felt none of the deep attraction that had so affected him ten months before, though he was looking at exactly the same scene.

If anything, the memory of that summer seemed to retreat even further.

He turned onto Route 18, headed for Mitsui Woods, and dropped by the summer house belonging to Kubo's parents. While he was at it, he visited Kubo's sister-in-law's place too. Summer arrives late in the mountains, and he had expected to see only the first green foliage, yet it all looked much the same as before—though, again, nothing moved him. He returned to the main road, headed west, and then took the narrow lane off to the left that led to the cottage in Oiwake. This was the track he had followed in his mind time and again since going back to Tokyo. Being pursued by the strains of the "Tokyo Ballad," falling deeper under the spell of a fox or the moon as he pedaled along—how could he forget that first night here? But though the trees on either side remained the same, he felt none of that night's mystery now.

Then he came to the place where the cottage had been.

There was emptiness. The dilapidated house was nowhere to be seen. The two gateposts still stood, just as the surrounding thicket did, but the ground where the cottage had been was now nothing but black, bare earth. Only

then—only then did the week come back to him with painful clarity. He stood by the posts for a long time staring at
the dark earth. At last, a dusting of fine ash blew up from
the ground into the air, where, lit by beams of invisible
moonlight, it danced in space.

Yusuke left for the United States three months later.

# Epilogue

IN SEPTEMBER 1998, I took the new high-speed train to Nagano that had been built in time for the Winter Olympic Games half a year earlier. As I'd expected, Kinokuniya supermarket was gone, but following Yusuke Kato's directions, I turned a corner on a street lined with fir trees and there they were, behind an imposing gate, the pair of Western villas. Locating them was easy. The first thing I noticed was the new nameplate on one of the moss-covered gateposts, marked TSUCHIYA. It was a small wooden plate, hanging modestly below a granite nameplate marked SHIGEMITSU that was inlaid in the volcanic rock from Mount Asama. It was probably at Fumiko Tsuchiya's insistence that the Shigemitsu nameplate was left there. On the other gatepost too, the nameplates SAEGUSA and UTAGAWA still remained. Finding the site of the Oiwake cottage proved to be difficult. I eventually stumbled on a place that I thought must be it—only because there was a pair of wooden posts marking the driveway. There was no other sign. Surrounded at a distance by a number of abandoned cottages, and amid tall pampas grass heavy with silver plumes, only in that one place was the grass lower in height. I saw no trace of the bare black earth that Yusuke had described. Along with vines and weeds left to grow unchecked, the ground was covered with autumn wildflowers. That a mere three years earlier a cottage had stood there seemed like a figment of the imagination. Time had worn it all away.

PAMPAS GRASS

# SAEGUSA FAMILY     SHIGEMITSU FAMILY

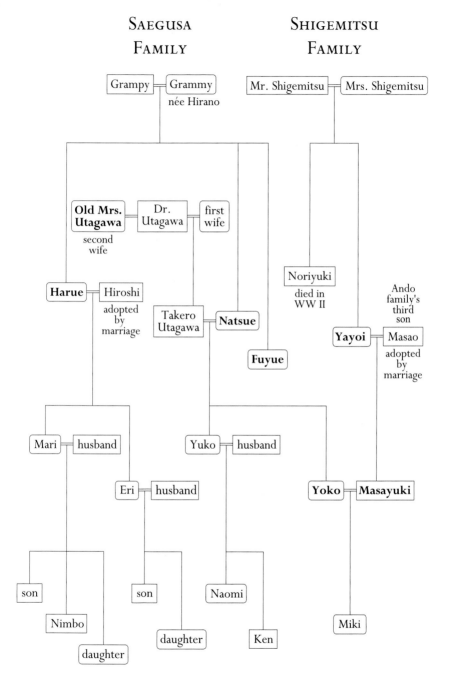

# THE FAMILIES

MINAE MIZUMURA is one of the most important novelists writing in Japan today. Born in Tokyo, she moved with her family to Long Island, New York, when she was twelve. She studied French literature at Yale College and Yale Graduate School. Her other novels include *Zoku meian* (Light and Dark Continued), a sequel to the unfinished classic *Light and Dark* by Soseki Natsume, and *Shishosetsu from left to right* (An I-Novel from Left to Right), an autobiographical work. She lives in Tokyo and is currently working on the English translation of her work about the fall of languages in the age of English.

JULIET WINTERS CARPENTER studied Japanese literature at the University of Michigan and the Inter-University Center for Japanese Language Studies in Tokyo. Carpenter's translation of Kobo Abe's novel *Secret Rendezvous* won the 1980 Japan–United States Friendship Commission Prize for the Translation of Japanese Literature.